"I only want to help him. If there's ever anything I can do . . ."

"Help him?" Big Mama seemed amused by Drusilla's innocence. "Honey, how you gonna help him do what he got to do?"

"Do? What is it he's got to do?"

"Well, it ain't hard to figure, isn't it? You think he gonna let them Klansmen get away with what they done?"

"Killing? There's going to be more killing?"

" 'Deed," Big Mama said with gloomy relish, "I 'spect the real killing ain't even begun yet. Huh-*uh*." She smiled, flashing two gold teeth, and, as if envisioning the wonders to come, shook her head. "Lawd, lawd, when that man gets well, look out. Them Ku Kluxers better give they souls to God, honey, 'cause they asses gonna belong to Gypsy Smith. . . ."

By Clancy Carlile:

HONKYTONK MAN
SPORE 7
AS I WAS YOUNG AND EASY
CHILDREN OF THE DUST*

*Published by Ivy Books

CHILDREN OF THE DUST

Clancy Carlile

IVY BOOKS • NEW YORK

Ivy Books
Published by Ballantine Books
Copyright © 1995 by Clancy Carlile

All rights reserved under International and Pan-American Copyright Conventions. Published in the United States by Ballantine Books, a division of Random House, Inc., New York, and simultaneously in Canada by Random House of Canada Limited, Toronto.

Library of Congress Catalog Card Number: 94-43918

ISBN 0-8041-1416-1

This edition published by arrangement with Random House, Inc.

Manufactured in the United States of America

First Ballantine Books Edition: November 1995

10 9 8 7 6 5 4 3 2 1

To Mariah Marvin

I get by with a little help from my friends.
Lennon and McCartney

CHAPTER ONE

SUPERINTENDENT JOHN MAXWELL STOOD AT HIS OFFICE WIN-
dow. Gazing across the schoolyard and agency grounds toward
the prairies beyond, he saw a wagon coming, pulled by two
bone-gaunt horses. He recognized the driver as John Black
Bear. Beside him was a boy.

The wagon stopped at the hitching rail in front of the school
building. John Black Bear got down, but the boy was reluctant
to follow. John Black Bear had to lift him from the wagon.

Superintendent Maxwell, slipping into his frock coat, went
out to the schoolyard, where the first-grade Indian students
were learning to play white children's games. As he approached the wagon, John Black Bear said, "Maxwell,"
friendly but unsmiling. Though nearly toothless and dressed in
tattered remnants of white man's clothing, John Black Bear
was a man of great solemnity, as became a leader of the Human Beings.

"Black Bear, *nimahaeaman*." Maxwell offered his hand.

Black Bear pumped it three times, mechanically, as if it
were the handle of a water pump, then dropped it. "I bring this
boy," he said in practiced English. "His mother say him go
white man's school, become white man."

Noting the boy's worn and dirty clothes and the look in his
darting eyes of a hungry wolf whelp, Maxwell assumed that he
had been brought to the agency boarding school not so much
for an education as for some new agency-issue clothes and
something to eat.

Black Bear switched to Cheyenne. "This boy is the son of
Chief Walks-the-clouds."

"Cloud Walker's son?" Maxwell asked in English.

Black Bear nodded, grunted.

1

"Does Cloud Walker know he's here?"

Black Bear switched back to English. "Him father gone long time white man's prison."

"Yes, but does he—"

"Boy's mother, Rainbow Woman, soon die of white man's coughing sickness. Rainbow Woman Christian now, want boy learn white man's medicine."

Speaking Cheyenne, Maxwell asked the boy his name.

"*Hokoxc*—Little Raven," Black Bear volunteered.

Maxwell offered to shake hands. The boy edged farther behind Black Bear's legs.

"Afraid white man. All time hear stories how white man kill the Human Beings." He used the old word for Cheyennes, *Tsistsistas*, which meant "the People," or "the Human Beings," as if there were no others.

"You will not be hurt here," Maxwell assured the boy in Cheyenne, then turned to a small group of first-grade girls who had been jumping rope nearby but had stopped to stare at the new boy. He beckoned to one of the girls and said in Cheyenne, "This is Martha Washington. Martha is also of the Hehyo band. Do you know her?"

Little Raven stared at the girl.

"Martha has been here for a year and has never been hurt. Ask her."

But Little Raven only stared at her as if her schoolgirl's uniform—plain blue jacket and skirt, white blouse, high-button shoes, and black stockings—disgusted him.

"Martha, run fetch Miss Tibbens," Maxwell said in English. "Tell her we have a new student."

Miss Kate Tibbens was the school's matron. An elderly woman with heavy hips and a pouter pigeon bosom, she dressed severely in ankle-length dark muslin, but often wore a gray red ribbon in her puffball gray hair. Her office and living quarters were on the school's top floor, the third floor, separating the girls' dormitory from the boys'. From her desk she took a piece of candy and went down to meet the new arrival.

"My my my," she clucked. "Isn't he a handsome little brave, though? Would you like some candy?"

The boy shrank away. Maxwell spoke to him again in Cheyenne, but it took Black Bear to persuade the boy to go into the school, and even then his moccasined steps were tentative and wary. Grasping his arm, Miss Tibbens said, "Come along, now. Don't be bashful. You'll like it here."

Little Raven looked over his shoulder at Black Bear as Miss Tibbens pulled him up the steps into the schoolhouse.

Miss Clarksdale, the school's seamstress, was in the sewing room conducting a crocheting class.

"Sorry to interrupt," Miss Tibbens said, "but we have a new boy. First we have a haircut," she informed him, raising her voice in an attempt to make him understand English, and mimed cutting off his shoulder-length hair. "I suspect there may be a few bugs in there."

A few of the girls tittered. Stung by being made a figure of fun, the boy tried to jerk away and run.

"Now, now, it won't hurt. If you would do the honors, Miss Clarksdale?" Miss Tibbens said. "I think I'll have to hold him."

Miss Clarksdale took from her sewing kit a pair of scissors and, examining the boy's hair, said, "Oh, yes," in a voice loud enough for the whole class to hear, "seem to be some cooties in there, all right."

The girls tittered again, and the boy, without so much as a sound, suddenly bit Miss Clarksdale's hand, then whirled and struck Miss Tibbens in the stomach. Miss Clarksdale screamed and fell backward, crashing into the students. Chairs were overturned. Girls shrieked. Miss Tibbens made a grab for the boy. Agile as a monkey, he jumped up on the desk and kicked her in the mouth. She staggered and fell to the floor on her hands and knees. The boy leaped onto her back as if onto a horse and pulled at her hair.

"Get help! Get help!" Miss Clarksdale cried. "Get help, before he kills us!"

Several girls bolted for the door. Two of the biggest girls rushed to help Miss Tibbens and managed to pull the boy off her back. Furiously he struggled against them and, breaking loose, scrambled to a tall yarn cabinet in one corner of the room, clambered up the face of it as easily as scaling a ladder, and, on top, out of everyone's reach, crouched there, facing the room, teeth bared, panting.

Maxwell dashed into the room. "What's going on?"

Miss Tibbens was licking her bloody and swollen lips. "We were just about to give him a haircut. He's a wildcat."

Maxwell took a few steps toward the crouching boy. *"Henova, naha?"* he said. John Black Bear shuffled into the room, and Maxwell spoke in English. "Tell him to come on down, nobody's going to hurt him."

Black Bear frowned disapprovingly, though there was pride and amusement in his eyes. "Shame on you, Little Raven. It is your mother's wish that you become a student here. Is this how you honor her wish?"

The ferocity in the boy's face dissolved, his eyes brimmed with tears, and he allowed Black Bear to coax him down from the cabinet.

Maxwell sent Miss Tibbens and Miss Clarksdale to Dr. Rooney to have their injuries tended. The girls he excused from class, and after they were gone and the door had been shut against the growing hubbub in the hallway, he again spoke to the boy in Cheyenne. "Little Raven, we are not your enemy. Would your mother send you to live with an enemy? We want to help you. Will you give us your trust?"

The boy stared at Black Bear for an answer. Black Bear nodded.

Aware that Cheyenne custom held hospitality and trust to be inseparable, Maxwell asked Little Raven to come and share the evening meal with him and his family. Although such an invitation to a student was unique, Maxwell saw that this boy would need special handling, not only because he was more than usually wild and mistrustful but also because he was the son of Chief Cloud Walker. If Maxwell could make a successful and contented student out of this boy, the other children on the reservation would be less reluctant to attend the white man's school.

The Maxwells' house, like the other houses on the square, had a front porch, a high foundation of limestone blocks, unpainted clapboard walls, and a picket fence around the yard to keep the animals and Indians out. There was a small corral and barn in the back where the Maxwells kept two horses, one Jersey milk cow, two pigs, and some chickens.

When Maxwell came home with the boy, his wife took him aside. "Is this the boy that attacked Miss Tibbens and Miss

Clarksdale today?" she whispered. "What if he attacks one of us?"

"Nora, the boy was just frightened out of his wits. He's never been around white people before."

"Then wouldn't he feel better eating with his own kind?"

"Not when he can't speak a word of English and the others are forbidden to speak anything else. At least I can talk to him, and I seem to be the only one he feels safe around. He wouldn't let them cut his hair unless I was right there with him."

"Never mind," she said, "I ought to've known," and turned from him. "Rachel!" she called. "Set a plate for the boy."

Maxwell and Nora sat at opposite ends of an oilcloth-covered table. Dexter, Nora's son by her first marriage, sat opposite Little Raven, whose hair had been cut so short it stood up all over his head like the quills of an alarmed porcupine. Instead of the soiled and worn corduroys and moccasins, he now wore his schoolboy's uniform: a starched linsey-woolsey blue suit, the jacket buttoned all the way up to his chin, and a pair of ironhard brogans. And his responses had changed, too, from fear and defiance to a sort of stoic acceptance of whatever fate might have in store.

Rachel, six years old, sat next to Little Raven. She had quick hazel eyes, a light sprinkling of freckles across her nose, and long, wavy auburn hair tied back with a pink ribbon. As her father was saying grace, Rachel turned her head just enough to see the boy from the corners of her eyes. He didn't bow his head or close his eyes like everyone else. He was, after all, a heathen. But Rachel was surprised that he was ignoring all her efforts to catch his eye. She tried a more direct approach as the food was being passed around.

"What's your name?"

"Hasn't got one yet," Maxwell said.

"Well, then, what's his Indian name?"

"Little Raven."

"I know! Let's name him Corby," she cried.

She had recently raised an injured raven chick. She had named it Corby, and tended it lovingly until it had healed enough to fly away.

"Corby? Too unusual," Maxwell said. "The Bureau wants

them to have simple, ordinary white names. George, for instance. Or Walter. How about Walter?"

"Oh, please, Daddy, let's do name him Corby." Rachel took
a swallow of buttermilk, leaving a white mustache on her upper lip, which she slurped off with the tip of her tongue.

"Stop that," Nora admonished. "Mind your manners, young
lady. You have to set a good example." She looked in disgust
toward the boy, who had lowered his head over his plate and
was picking the chicken out of the gravy with his fingers,
sucking the meat from the bones, then sucking the gravy from
his fingers.

"Please, Daddy?" Rachel said.

"Well, I don't know," Maxwell said, his code phrase for giving in. "What about a last name? Dexter? Got any ideas?"

Dexter's jaws stopped while he pondered; then, swallowing,
he said, "Why not name him White? We could sure use some
more whites around here."

Quick to neutralize Dexter's sarcasm by taking him seriously, Maxwell said, "Why not? That's a good name."

After supper Rachel followed her father and Corby out onto
the front porch. "Good night, Corby White," she said. "I hope
you like the dormitory."

The boy stared blankly.

She pointed to his chest. "Corby. You Corby." She pointed
to herself. "Rachel. I'm Rachel."

It was then the boy uttered his first word since arriving at
the agency. "Ray-chil," he said in a whisper. "Ray-chil."

"Yes, yes!" she cried. "I'm Rachel. You're Corby."

The boy made a quick gesture in the sign language of the
Plains Indians. *"Nahavesheeton,"* he said.

Rachel looked at her father.

"Means, 'We are friends,' " Maxwell said.

Rachel smiled, pleased as though she had been given a new
pet to replace the little raven that had flown away.

CHAPTER TWO

THE CHEYENNE-ARAPAHO RESERVATION WAS LOCATED IN THE western portion of Indian Territory. Not counting barns and outhouses, the agency consisted of twenty-five buildings and dwellings, most of them fronting on a large treeless square. A few of the first structures had been made of logs, but after 1873, when the agency's sawmill began operating, all buildings were constructed of unplaned pine and cedar and had windows and shingled roofs.

Among the clapboard buildings were the agent's office and dwelling, a post office, a boardinghouse, a council house, a Mennonite missionary church, an Indian police barracks, a warehouse, and two general stores. But by far the most impressive building at the agency was the school. Three stories high, with twenty-two rooms, six gables, a belfry, and four huge brick chimneys, it towered over the countryside and could be seen for many miles across the rolling prairies, a wilderness monument to the white man's education and ingenuity.

The school superintendent's office was in one corner of the building, its windows granting a view of the agency square and the school's playground. Maxwell, in the days that followed Corby White's arrival, often went to the windows at recess to watch the students at play. Rachel and a few other white children were among them, but it was the small figure of Corby White that Maxwell's eyes sought. Over a period of months he watched the boy slowly become integrated into the groups and games, and he was pleased to see that it was usually Rachel who served as his faithful friend and sponsor.

At first Corby wasn't prized as a teammate in the games because he didn't know the rules and didn't know enough English to understand them when they were explained, but he learned fast and eventually could hold a bat and wallop a ball as hard as any of the others in his own age-group.

He also did well in the classroom. Maxwell queried his teachers about his progress, and all reports were favorable. Corby had quickly picked up a few words of English and had not caused any more disturbances, and even Miss Tibbens, after her scratches had healed, was willing to admit that the boy might have some promise, and soon she even began to admire in him the same qualities that Maxwell had been quick to admire: his spunk, his quickness of mind, his stoic composure, his almost manly dignity. Indeed, Corby was exactly the kind of boy Maxwell would have wanted for a son, the kind of son he had once hoped Nora would give him.

He had first met Nora Bingham when he was a teacher at the St. Louis Normal School. Nora had been the wife of the school's chaplain, Clyde Bingham. Maxwell had never been on intimate terms with the Binghams, but when Mr. Bingham died of a sudden illness, leaving Nora a widow with a five-year-old son, Maxwell found himself spending more and more time in her company, and he always found her to be a good and respectable woman, a woman who believed in doing her duty toward her family, her church, her society. Moreover, even though she never wore cosmetics or fancy clothes, and was perhaps five or six years older than Maxwell, he found her an attractive woman, graceful and decorous. Frail, yes, and sometimes excessively self-righteous, perhaps, but a good person, one who would make a man a good and faithful wife. Also, when Maxwell was offered a job by the Bureau of Indian Affairs to teach Indian children, Nora hinted that she would welcome the opportunity to become the wife of a schoolteacher on an Indian reservation. It seemed to appeal to her sense of martyrdom.

So they were married and moved to the Cheyenne-Arapaho reservation in Indian Territory. Maxwell was soon promoted to superintendent of the agency school, and within a year Nora gave birth to Rachel. Although Maxwell couldn't have been more pleased with his daughter, he was very disappointed to learn from the doctor that Nora might not survive another pregnancy. He tried to reconcile himself to the idea that Dexter, Nora's son by Clyde Bingham, was the only son he would ever have. And that was too bad, because, however hard he tried to like Dexter, however earnestly he wanted to be a good stepfather and a friend to him, they just didn't get along. Among the things that he most disliked about the boy was his tendency to be a bully, and one of the things he most admired about Corby White was his refusal to be bullied.

At first Dexter only sneered at Corby, testing him. The story of Corby's attack on Miss Tibbens and Miss Clarksdale had brought with it a certain amount of respect and restraint on Dexter's part. However, when his first tentative bullying attempts brought no reaction from Corby, Dexter began to apply more abrasive tactics. He began to make contemptuous remarks when Corby was within hearing range, and because Corby continued to ignore him, Dexter's provocations finally became physical. He never missed a chance to jostle and shove the smaller boy when he passed him on the schoolgrounds, and once in the dining hall, as he passed the table where Corby was sitting with Rachel, he swung his elbow out and hit the back of Corby's head just as he was lifting a glass of milk. Milk splashed down Corby's shirt and over the table.

Corby didn't even look around. Rachel, however, who had also been splashed by the milk, jumped to her feet and sputtered, "Dexter! Look what you've done, you bully."

Dexter walked on, but his pal Riley Tanner stopped. "Oh, did the baby have an accident?" he said. "Hasn't learned to drink from a glass yet? Maybe he should still be sucking a titty."

Corby took his tray back to the kitchen and left the dining hall without saying a word.

Dexter smiled, wondering just how far he could push the little redskin before he would react.

It was months later, on a Saturday afternoon in late May, when Dexter found out. After the spring rains had passed and the rutted soil of the agency's square, with its sparse covering of stunted weeds and buffalo grass, had been trampled by boots and hooves and wagon wheels, the students—boys, mostly—gathered on the square for the first baseball game of the '85 school year. Everything went along fine until Corby came to bat. Dexter was the pitcher for the opposing team, and a good one—one of the best, in fact, that the school had ever had. And that was why it was hard to believe that his first pitch to Corby was so wild that Corby had to duck to keep from being hit in the head. Dexter shrugged apologetically, as if to say it was only an accident, then pushed up the sleeves of his jersey work shirt.

"Here comes a good one. Right over the plate," he yelled, and threw.

Corby ducked again, but this time the ball hit him on the shoulder and, glancing upward, smashed against his head just above his ear. He was knocked to the ground, blinded for a moment by pinpoints of bright lights and exploding colors. As if from a great distance he heard the noises of sympathy and anger coming from his teammates, and then someone asked if he was all right and began to help him to his feet. He waved the helping hand away and pushed himself up, bringing with him from the ground, tightly clutched in his right hand, a smooth stone about the size of a chicken's egg. He shook his head to clear his vision of the last exploding lights and then, without warning, hurled the stone at Dexter.

Dexter threw up his hands to protect his face. The stone hit him in the chest. Shock and disbelief twisted his face for a moment, and then he rushed at Corby. He assumed that Corby would run and that he would have to chase him down; instead of running, however, Corby brought the bat up and held it poised to strike, and even then Dexter believed he was only bluffing.

But as soon as he came within range, Corby swung the bat with all his strength. Dexter threw up his arms to protect his head, and the bat hit his left forearm. There was a loud crack, loud enough for everyone to hear. It sounded as if the bat itself had splintered, but the look on Dexter's face and his bewildered wail signaled that it was not the bat that had broken.

With his left arm dangling uselessly, Dexter grabbed for Corby with his right arm, crying, "I'll kill you! I'll kill you!"

Corby drew the bat back to strike again, but this time Riley Tanner, the catcher, wrested it from him. Defenseless, Corby started to run. Dexter caught him within a few strides, and with his good right hand he hit Corby between the shoulders, sending him sprawling into the dirt. Then he fell on Corby and pinned him to the ground with a knee on his back. Cursing and crying, he grabbed Corby's hair and slammed his face down into the dirt and gravel, twisting and turning and rubbing his face into the earth, shouting over and over, "You redskin bastard, I'll kill you, you bastard."

A few of the bigger Indian boys said, "Enough, that's enough," but no one interfered until Rachel pushed through the crowd and sprang on Dexter's back, pulling at him, punching him, crying, "Don't, Dexter! Let him be. You're gonna kill him!"

Dexter wrenched her off his shoulders and flung her sprawling into the dirt in a flurry of high-button shoes and bloomers and petticoats. But she sprang to her feet and was instantly on him again, pummeling his shoulders, pulling his hair, crying, "Let him alone! Let him alone!"

Dexter flung her away again, but now, emboldened by Rachel's example, a few of the bigger Indian boys placed restraining hands on Dexter and urged him away from Corby, saying, "Enough, Dexter. You hurt him too much. Come on, now, Dexter, enough."

Dexter appeared to allow the boys to mollify him, though it was really the increasing pain throbbing through his broken arm that caused him to stop. With tears flooding his eyes, he got up and clasped his right hand around the biceps of his left arm as if to squeeze off the pain. His forearm was swelling rapidly and turning purple.

Maxwell broke through the spectators.

Corby was sitting up now, glaring at Dexter with fierce hatred. Rachel was on her knees beside him, brushing away the pebbles and dirt that had been embedded in his face.

"Come on, let's get you over to Doc Rooney," Maxwell said to Dexter.

"I'm gonna kill him," Dexter said as Maxwell led him away. "I'm gonna kill that redskin bastard."

"Oh, be quiet. What you'd better learn to do is keep your hands to yourself," Maxwell said, and couldn't resist adding in a slightly sarcastic tone, "That, or learn to pick on somebody your own size."

Rachel sat on the ground beside Corby. "I'm glad you hurt him good," she said. "Now maybe he'll leave you alone."

But Corby knew better. Until today he had hoped that Dexter, unable to get a response from him, would eventually grow tired of bullying and leave him alone. Now he knew better.

Now he knew he and Dexter would be enemies always, until death.

CHAPTER THREE

THERE WERE TWELVE BANDS OF SOUTHERN CHEYENNES ON the reservation. Each band took turns coming into the agency once a month to collect its annuities and rations. The Hehyo band—about 320 in all—came to the agency in late June of that year, 1885, to collect its. Included in the monthly rations was a beef disbursement, which was a special event because it was conducted as a mock hunt. The band of Indians was split into family groups, and each group was given a longhorn steer as its meat ration. The wild Texas steers would be released from the corral through a gate leading out onto the open prairie, and a small group of mounted Indian men would wait at the gate, some armed with rifles, some with revolvers, a few with bows and arrows, and maybe one or two with lances. They would chase and shoot and lance the longhorns in an attempt to recapture some of the excitement of the buffalo hunts of years gone by.

The Hehyo band was named after its principal chief, an old man whose full name was *Ehohotohehyo*, He-follows-his-father's-ways; but that was too much for white people to pronounce, so they shortened it. As was his custom whenever he visited the agency, Chief Hehyo stopped first at the agent's office, where the agent, Elijah Tanner, a one-eyed man with a snuff-stained beard, met him on the gallery. Flanking Tanner was his brother, Brady P. Tanner, who was the chief of the Indian police, and a mixed-blood interpreter named Billy Blue Hand. Agent One-eye—as he was called by the Indians—greeted the chief ceremoniously and invited him into the agent's office, where the ritual called for the chief to complain and accuse, the agent to explain and excuse.

Toward the end of the meeting the chief tapped the dottle from his pipe into the palm of his gnarled hand and scattered the ashes on the wooden floor as he told Agent One-eye that he had a message for Little Raven, the boy of the Hehyo band who had now been a student at the reservation school for almost a year, a message that must be given in person. So a clerk was sent to fetch both the boy and Superintendent Maxwell, and when they arrived, the chief shook hands with Maxwell without getting up.

"*Namahaovo, Veho* Maxwell," he said in a gravelly voice.

"*Namahaovo, Veho* Hehyo," Maxwell responded. "How is my friend?"

"I grow old, as my friend Maxwell can see. Soon I will travel the Hanging Road to the Spirit Land. You must visit my lodge once more before I go."

"I will visit again soon, although I am confident you will be among us for many winters yet."

"*Pava.* Good." The chief grunted. "My wives will cook a fat dog for us." His muddy old eyes twinkled with humor, recalling the time years ago when Maxwell, having been invited to share food with the chief, forced himself out of politeness to eat the dog stew that the chief's wives had prepared as a ceremonial feast.

The chief then turned to the boy, who, shy and respectful, dressed in his school uniform, waited to be noticed.

"Is it really you, Little Raven? They have made you into a fine white boy. What is your white name?"

Corby glanced up at Maxwell for permission to speak his native tongue, and when Maxwell nodded, he said to his chief, "I am now called Corby White, grandfather," using the honorary form of address of a young Cheyenne to a respected elder of the tribe.

"A strange name. What does it mean in the white man's tongue, this Corby White?"

The boy was embarrassed. "I do not know, grandfather."

The chief grunted again, eternally bemused by the white man's customs, and then said, "Corby White, I must tell you that your mother has gone to the Spirit Land."

Corby seemed unable to respond.

"Two sleeps ago. Her dying wish was that I, Chief He-follows-his-father's-ways, tell her son, who was once Little Raven, that he must not mourn. She said to tell her son that she would be joyful in the Spirit Land with the white man's god called Jesus." Then, having performed his duty, Chief Hehyo nodded his dismissal.

Maxwell and Corby left the agent's office to thread their way back through the many Indian wagons and ponies and dogs on the square. Maxwell put an arm around the boy's small shoulders and said in English, "I'm sorry about your mother, Corby. But she's been sick for a long time, maybe she's better off. . . ."

As they were passing in front of Maxwell's house, on their way back to the school, Rachel darted out to meet them. Ignoring her mother's calls to come back, she slammed through the front gate and joined them.

"What's wrong?" she asked.

"My mother is dead," Corby announced in a voice of oddly mingled sorrow and excitement, as if he were somehow thrilled by the drama, by the importance that the closeness of death conferred upon him.

From her place behind the curtained windows, Nora watched, and when Maxwell and Rachel returned from the school, Nora sent Rachel out to the barn to help Dexter do the chores.

"Now, there's no use telling me they're not friends," Nora said to Maxwell. "I saw her holding his hand."

"For God's sake, Nora, the boy's mother just died. She was only expressing sympathy. And anyway, so what if they are friends? I've told you, I'm not going to forbid her being friends with him, just because he's Indian."

" 'Just because he's Indian'? My God, John, that little savage tried to kill Dexter, her own brother, and you don't seem to care."

"I've told you, it was just a schoolyard fight between two kids. What d'you want me to do, have him arrested?"

"I should think he would be arrested, yes—attacking Dexter with a baseball bat! But it seems to me the least you could do is forbid your daughter . . . tell her she mustn't be friends with that—that dirty little Indian."

"And that's it, isn't it? That's the real reason you hate him so much, because he's Indian. Well, I've told you before, and I'll tell you again, hating people because of their race is dangerous foolishness—stupidity—and I certainly am not going to stand by and allow a daughter of mine to be inculcated with such stupidity."

"Daughter of *yours*? She's *my* daughter, too!" But then a look of consternation crossed her face, and she added as if to herself, "Though, God help me, sometimes I wonder. . . ."

"What? You wonder what?"

Nora sat down on a straight-back chair and crossed her arms over her breasts. "Sometimes I don't think I know her at all. Like last Sunday. I got her all prettied up to go to church, and five minutes later I find her in the dirt playing marbles with some boys—Indian boys. And I looked at her and wondered, God help me, I found myself wondering if she was my child—*my* child. If she'd been born in a hospital, I'd have to wonder if they gave me the wrong baby."

"Nora," he gently admonished, "we've been over this a hundred times, and you know very well—"

"I know what I know, and I know you always take her side against me," she said, getting up and turning back to the hot kitchen stove. She used the hem of her apron to wipe the sweat from her brow, which left a streak of flour across her forehead. "Never mind. Go on. Wash up. Let me finish getting supper."

Outside on the porch he stopped to look around, disconcerted, absently noting the many new tepees being erected close to the agency buildings and all the way down the grassy and oak-studded slope to the main Loafers' encampment on the river bottom. Three of the tepees had been set up near his barn, and he guessed that some of the Indians would no doubt end up sleeping in his hayloft that night.

From the porch he could see Rachel and Dexter in the cow pen. Dexter was milking the cow with his one good hand, and Rachel was feeding the cow oats from her cupped hands. As Maxwell watched her, his heart was flooded with love, and he wondered once again at the puzzling antagonism between Nora and Rachel, an antagonism that had apparently begun before Rachel was even born, taken from her womb by cesarean section. Nora had hovered between life and death for days after the birth, unable to nurse the child. They had been forced to look for a wet nurse, and the only one available was an Arapaho squaw named Black Kettle who had a child of her own, a five-month-old daughter named Bonnie Blue Hand. Black Kettle came to the house three times a day, sat on the back porch, dangling her moccasined feet into the flower bed, and chewed tobacco while the two babies suckled greedily at her enormous black-nippled breasts.

Rachel's only bad times came at night, when she grew hungry and couldn't find that dark soft fount of milk. During these times Maxwell, who slept on a pallet on the floor in the front room beside Rachel's cradle, tried to appease her with a formula of goat's milk and syrup, but she would regurgitate the liquid within minutes and begin crying. Finally Maxwell began to let Black Kettle take the child with her at night to the Indian camp. She would bring Rachel back every morning, fed and content, and return twice more during the day to feed her.

Though Nora had survived the critical hours and days following the cesarean, her recovery was slow and fitful. Dr. Rooney kept telling her that she would be back on her feet in no time, but she was bedridden for almost two months, and she knew nothing of Rachel's nursing arrangement until the day she decided she was strong enough to get up and go to the privy rather than use her chamber pot. That was the day she stepped out onto the back porch and saw Rachel being nursed by Black Kettle. Horrified, she retrieved the baby and accused both Maxwell and Dr. Rooney of deceiving her. Maxwell tried to explain that the baby wouldn't take the formula and required a wet nurse, and there were no white women available, and what difference could it possibly make if the wet nurse was Indian?

"What difference can it make?" Nora asked. "My God, if you have to ask that, you'll never understand. I'll nurse her myself from now on."

Dr. Rooney implored her to be sensible. He told her that she had ceased lactating and therefore couldn't nurse the baby, but Nora believed that she would begin lactating again as soon as the baby began suckling. Two days later, after Rachel had begun to cry almost constantly, she held the child out to Maxwell.

"Take her," she said. "I have nothing to give her. Take her back to that savage."

And from that day forward, until the time came when she

could subsist on solid foods, Rachel spent not only her nights but most of her days, too, with Black Kettle in the Loafers' camp. Maxwell usually walked down to the camp two or three times a day to see how she was getting along, and often he brought her back to the house to bathe her in warm, sudsy water and dress her in the starched and ruffled pink clothes of a white baby. Rachel liked the baths well enough, but by the time she was eight months old she had begun to squirm and fret against the confinement of the baby clothes, and she wasn't really happy again until she was back in the Indian camp where, chubby and brash as a bear cub, she could crawl naked through the ashes and dirt in front of Black Kettle's tepee.

She was just over a year old when Nora reclaimed her and began the task of trying to make the child over into her own image. And as time went on, Rachel more and more readily submitted to being dressed up like a doll, and she especially loved the attention and praise that her well-behaved and well-scrubbed prettiness brought her, but it was never more than a game to her. A bauble could distract her, a pretty dress charm her, a birthday party fascinate her, but when she'd had enough, she was likely to be found toddling off toward the Loafers' camp or playing with some Indian kids behind the barn.

By the time Rachel was five and six years old, it had begun to be clear that the gulf between mother and daughter would never be bridged. Both tried at times to reach across that gulf but never at a time when the other was reaching out for the same purpose. Nora made her pretty clothes and put ribbons in her hair. She made her cookies and cakes. She took her to church and read to her from the Bible. She taught her how to be gracious and polite. But all her efforts seemed to have little effect, and sometimes, in exasperation, she believed that the milk from that savage's breasts had put Rachel forever beyond her reach.

Rachel tried. Sometimes—especially after having been disobedient—she would come to Nora for a hug, only to find that her mother would not allow her to gain forgiveness and approval so easily. Nora demanded contrition. But Rachel didn't want to be loved for being a good girl; she wanted to be loved in spite of being a naughty one. And Nora's rebuffs, rather than make her contrite and pliable, had the opposite effect: she became more defiant, more willful, more unreachable. And when she wanted love and approval, it wasn't her mother, it was her father, she went to. *He* never begrudged her a hug and a kiss and a pat on the head.

"You're not strict enough with her," Nora warned him any number of times, and once, when Maxwell reminded her that Rachel was, after all, only a child, Nora tapped the open pages of her Bible. "As the twig is bent . . ."

To placate Nora, he would sometimes scold Rachel and admonish her to mind her mother, but he refused to become an adversary and disciplinarian to her and was damned if he would support Nora when she was in the wrong, as when she demanded that he forbid the friendship between Rachel and Corby.

Indeed, now, as he stood on the back porch and watched Rachel feed oats to the cow from her cupped hands, he wondered if he would ever be able to forbid her anything. She was the source of his happiness, so how could he, within reason, refuse to be the source of hers?

Jarred from his ruminations by the sound of Nora dropping a pan in the kitchen, he sighed and turned to the washstand, on which was an enamel basin and bucket of water. A white towel hung from a peg on the wall, and above the washbasin was a small round mirror. Putting his silver-rimmed eyeglasses down on the stand, Maxwell rolled up his sleeves and washed his face and hands in the basin.

After rubbing his face with the towel, he stared at himself in the mirror as he might have stared at an old acquaintance whom he hadn't seen in a long time. Was he getting old? He was only forty-one, but were his jaws, once strong and square, becoming a little jowly? The youthful freckles that had once dotted his face seemed to be fading, as was the blue of his eyes, and his hairline—was it receding?

"Daddy," Rachel said. She had come up from the barn with a basket of eggs and a bucket of milk, barefooted again, in defiance of her mother's admonition that young ladies wore shoes. "Mother says I can't go watch the dancing tonight. Can I, please?"

"If she says you can't . . ."

"But she might change her mind if you talked to her. Please? You said next time I could go. Remember?"

"I'll see what I can do." After splashing the basin of water onto the puny young spinach and turnip plants in Nora's small fenced-off garden, he followed Rachel into the kitchen.

"Put those down and go wash yourself," Nora said to Rachel. "Just look at your feet! My goodness, you didn't even wipe them off after you came out of the cow pen. Go wash yourself and put on some shoes. How many times do I have to tell you?"

Rachel went back outside to wash, and as Maxwell began to strain the milk through a cheesecloth into a crock, "She wants to go out to see the dancing tonight," he said.

"I told her she couldn't."

"She was hoping you'd change your mind."

"Now, John, you know how I feel about her watching them do their devil dances. She's enough of a wild Indian as it is."

He didn't want to argue with her, though he saw nothing shocking or offensive in the buffalo dance. It was a hunting dance the Cheyennes performed in the days when they still hunted buffalo, a ritual that was intended to assure a good kill. Now it was only a relic, a travesty, since the only thing the Indians would kill tomorrow were a few of the white man's castrated cattle. Still, the dance would be performed with a frenzy exceeding any dance performed by white people, and for that reason Maxwell loved to watch it. There had even been times in the past when he had felt an urge to join in. He resisted such urges because he didn't want to shock Nora, who claimed that the dances were the devil's way of luring people into the dark path of hell-bound heathens. The Indians themselves might have ascribed his attraction to the dance as *Maheo Mashanghestoz*, the Indian equivalent of "divine madness," and he agreed that it was indeed a sort of divine madness he always felt during the dances, as if he had been transported back into history to a time when white men, too, had their rituals of exultant savagery.

Near the end of the meal Nora saw something in the window that caused her suddenly to cover her eyes and cry out in terror, startling everyone at the table. Maxwell turned to see three Indians with painted faces staring in at them, their noses against the panes.

"No need to panic," he said, and got up to go outside. He knew they meant no harm. They didn't even mean to be rude.

It was just that most Indians couldn't seem to get it through their heads that windows in a white man's dwelling were put there for purposes other than allowing passersby to peer in.

The three Indians nodded and grunted when Maxwell came out, and one of them greeted him as a friend. Prepared for the buffalo dance that would soon begin on the square, the Indians wore bands of jingling sleigh bells strapped to their wrists and ankles, while their bodies, naked except for beaded breech-clouts and moccasins, were completely smeared in wild designs with many-colored paints. It took Maxwell a moment to recognize the one who had called him friend. It was *Otatavoha*—Blue Horse—who asked, "Does Maxwell's lodge have coffee for his friends?"

"I regret that I do not," Maxwell said uncomfortably. Not only was he lying, but he was also going against the Indian code of good manners, for this was not shameless begging on their part. They were simply giving him a chance to be friendly and hospitable. Had he been a visitor to their village, he would have been invited to share *their* food and coffee. "But I will bring tobacco to the dance, and we will share a pipe."

"*Pava,*" the Indian grunted, "good," and then went on to join the other Indians gathering on the square.

When he went back into the house, Maxwell found Nora slumped forward in her chair, her face hidden in her hands. He touched her shoulder. "You all right?"

She slowly lifted her head. "I'm going to lie down," she murmured, pushing herself up, and then tottered toward the front bedroom, a wisp of a woman nearing the limits of her endurance. At such moments her only recourse was to lie down and put a cool wet cloth over her eyes and pray for the blessed release of sleep.

But there would be no sleep for her that night. The buffalo dance had begun.

CHAPTER FOUR

JOHN MAXWELL AND BOTH TANNERS—ELIJAH, THE AGENT, and Brady P., the chief of the Indian police—stood on the gallery of the agency's headquarters building. With them were many other agency officials and employees, including Billy Blue Hand, the agency's official interpreter. They were there to meet Chief Cloud Walker and three other high-ranking Cheyenne chiefs, all of whom had been held for four years as military prisoners and were now being returned to the reservation.

The prisoners had been the leaders in what became known as the breakout of '82, in which more than three hundred Cheyennes and Arapahos had left the reservation and made a desperate dash for their old homelands on the Great Plains. Having left in one of the coldest winters ever known in the region, they suffered terribly from cold and hunger, and when the army finally caught up with them—what was left of them—near Ogallala, Nebraska, a battle ensued in which thirteen soldiers were killed. The Indians suffered more than a hundred casualties, both men and women, but refused to surrender until they were completely out of food and ammunition.

Chief Cloud Walker and the other leaders of the breakout had been brought back to the reservation and tried by a military tribunal and sentenced to life imprisonment. But in 1887, after they had served four years in the military stockade at Fort Marion, Florida, the Great White Father in Washington commuted their sentences as a peace gesture toward his red children. They were escorted back to the reservation by a squad of 5th Cavalry troopers from Fort Reno. The squad was under the command of a lieutenant but was actually led by Gypsy Smith, a mixed-blood Negro-Cherokee, Fort Reno's chief of scouts.

In addition to the agency officials who waited on the gallery of the headquarters building, many Indians, some of whom wore the ceremonial war regalia of old times, came to the agency to meet Cloud Walker and the other prisoners.

Corby watched his father's return from a window in the boys' third-floor dormitory. He had wanted to go out to welcome him, but the school's rules did not permit any meetings between the students and their parents. Bureau of Indian Affairs policy required that young Indian students be totally severed from their families and backgrounds for the duration of their education. Otherwise too many students would take the opportunity to escape and go back to the blanket. But there was no rule that said Corby couldn't watch from his third-floor window.

At first he wasn't sure which of the prisoners was his father. Corby and his mother, Rainbow Woman, had been taken along on the big breakout of '82, but Corby remembered nothing of that, and since he had been only four years old when Cloud Walker was taken away to prison, he had only a vague memory of what his father looked like. He focused on the prisoner who seemed to be the center of attention, the one who received the greetings of the welcoming party with slight regal nods of recognition. Corby guessed that this was his father, the legendary Chief Walks-the-clouds, though it was true that he didn't look very imposing at the moment, with his hair short and uneven, giving the appearance of its having been hacked off with a hatchet, and his dusty gray prison uniform hanging on him like rags on a scarecrow.

Bringing the troopers to a halt in front of the administration building, the lieutenant presented some papers to Agent Tanner. The prisoners climbed out of the wagon and into a swarm of welcoming Indians. In the forefront was Black Buffalo Woman, Cloud Walker's wife number one, who presented him with the reins to a dappled gray stallion and then gave him a bundle she was cradling in her arms.

Cloud Walker broke the string and took from the bundle an elaborately decorated Ghost Dance shirt. He didn't bother to unbutton the prison shirt he wore but simply ripped it off and flung it away, to the accompanying cheers and shouts of the Indians. When he pulled the Ghost Dance shirt on over his head, a look of pride and defiance came over his face, and then he vaulted onto the back of the dappled gray stallion without using the stirrup.

Agent Tanner borrowed his brother's .44 Colt and fired it into the air. When the Indians gave him their attention, he handed the revolver back to his brother. "Cloud Walker!" he shouted, and to his interpreter, in a voice loud enough for everyone to hear: "Tell Cloud Walker that he and the other prisoners have been released into my custody, and if they break the law in any way, if they try to stir up the Indians and make trouble for the government, they will be returned to prison for the rest of their lives. Is that understood?"

Cloud Walker's only acknowledgment was a sullen stare.

"And there's one more thing," Tanner said loudly. "The Great White Father in Washington knows that many of you have been practicing a new religion called the Ghost Dance, and he knows that Cloud Walker has become a leader of this cult. So the Great White Father sent a message over the talking wire to all the Indian agencies in America. He says there is to be no more Ghost Dancing."

After this was translated, a roar of outrage and protest arose from the Indians. Agent Tanner waved them into silence.

"That is an *order*. From this day forward there will be no more Ghost Dancing. Here is the directive sent to me from the Indian Bureau." He waved a piece of paper at the Indians as though it were a magic weapon. "I read: 'Since the so-called Ghost Dance has been determined to be a subterfuge to cover degrading acts and to disguise immoral purposes, Indian agents are directed to suppress these evils forthwith.' "

Agent Tanner waited for a translation before continuing, but the outcry that arose was so charged with menace that he hesitated to go on. It was Cloud Walker who restored order by holding up his hand for silence; then he spoke, and a hush fell over the crowd.

"I understand your words, and I am not surprised by them. This order was to be expected." Like the legendary Indian orators of the old days, he gave a songlike cadence to his words, as if they were being spoken to the accelerating beat of a drum. "Everything that we have ever cherished has been taken from the Human Beings by the white man"—using the Indian word for Cheyennes, *Tsistsistas*. "First the white man killed all our buffalo."

There was a murmuring chorus of agreement from the Indians.

"Then the white man took our land and our freedom."

A dramatic pause, another chorus of agreement, and then Cloud Walker pointed toward the school building. "The white man has even taken our children and our language. And now . . ." A longer pause this time, giving his last charge the air of an ultimate outrage. "And now the white man would take away our religion, our dreams."

A few warriors had pushed their ponies in close to Cloud Walker, and when he finished speaking, they raised their rifles over their heads, shaking them at the sky in a gesture of challenge and defiance, and began chanting the old war cry, *"Hoka hey! Hoka hey!"*

Alarmed, the young lieutenant ordered his men to fall into a phalanx in front of the gallery to protect Agent Tanner and the other whites, but Gypsy Smith, the mixed-blood chief of scouts, quickly assumed authority.

"No guns!" he shouted. "They got women and children with 'em, they didn't come here to fight."

Then Cloud Walker spoke again. "Is it possible that the white man thinks there will be a day when he will see no more Ghost Dancers among the Human Beings? As long as I live, that day will never be, because from this day forward my name will be Ghost Dancer. And if the white man would put all the Ghost Dancers in jail, let him start with me. *Namatoan*—I have finished speaking," he added, and spun his horse around and rode out of the agency. The Indians parted in waves to make way for him and then closed in behind him and followed in his wake.

"Come back here!" Agent Tanner shouted, waving the piece of paper. "I haven't dismissed you yet."

But Cloud Walker—Ghost Dancer now—kept going and was quickly swallowed up by the dust of his followers.

"Well, by damn," said Police Chief Brady P. Tanner, "that sumbitch troublemaker didn't learn a thing in prison, did he?"

As Maxwell was crossing the square, he saw from the corner of his eye Gypsy Smith approaching at an angle.

" 'Scuse me, Mr. Maxwell," the scout said as he drew near, "I was wondering if I could ask you something."

Maxwell stopped and looked up at him. Gypsy Smith was in his late thirties, a tall, gangling man wearing a worn and soiled army coat, fringed buckskin pants, and star-roweled spurs that jangled when he walked. On his right hip he wore a low-holstered .44 Colt, on his left side he carried a huge hunting knife in a fringed and beaded buckskin sheath, and in his left hand he carried a Winchester rifle. He wore a faded brown wide-brimmed hat with a low crown, a planter's hat, from under which sprang a mass of hair that was neither kinky like a Negro's nor straight like an Indian's, but was instead a pile of woolly black curls, like astrakhan. And his face was such an even blend of Indian and Negro features that people were often unsure if he was one or the other, or both, or neither. At some time during his early days in the Territory a buffalo skinner had mistaken him for a Gypsy and tagged him with the name. His real name was Wannicha Smith, but very few people knew that.

"Name's Gypsy Smith," he said.

"I know. Something I can do for you?"

To avoid wasting the school superintendent's valuable time, Gypsy suggested with a gesture that they resume walking. "Well, it's like this. I got to wondering awhile back, you think a man old as me can still learn to read and write?"

The question was so unexpected Maxwell turned and stared at him. This man, who seemed so mild-mannered, was a former bounty hunter, a killer—not a murderer but at least a man who, for reasons presumed to have been lawful, was known to have killed many men.

"You?" he said. "You want to learn to read and write?"

Gypsy said with a crooked grin, "I guess I'd be too old, huh?"

"No, no, it's not that. Sure, you could learn to read and write, if you wanted to, but ... well, it'd mean going to school, sitting in a classroom. ..."

"Yeah, I reckon I'd look pretty silly, a grown man, sitting in a schoolroom with them kids?"

"No, no, I didn't mean that. I mean, how could you? An army scout, stationed a good four-hour ride from here?"

"Oh, I ain't gonna be a scout much longer. I been hearing 'bout how this Dawes Act's gonna do away with the reservations and the Indians are gonna be forced to settle down on farms. So the army ain't gonna need no more scouts like me. I figure I can make a living by going up to No Man's Land now and again, catching some wild horses. Well, that'd leave me some time to go to school. See what I mean?"

They stopped again at the bottom of the steps leading to the school's main entrance.

"Yes, I see." Maxwell was touched in his teacher's soul to find someone who really wanted to learn, especially since that someone was a bona fide killer. "Well, all right. Anytime you're ready to begin, just come to my office, and we'll get you enrolled."

"You don't think the kids'll laugh at me?"

"At *you*?" Maxwell chuckled. "No, Mr. Smith, I don't think anybody's going to laugh at *you*."

CHAPTER FIVE

CORBY WAS SURPRISED WHEN HE CAME TO HIS HOMEROOM reading class one morning to find that Gypsy Smith was his new bench mate. He remembered seeing Gypsy in the Hehyo village a few times. Known among the Human Beings as *Moxthaveho*, Black White Man, he was a highly respected warrior and tamer of horses.

They proved to be good bench mates, Corby and Gypsy Smith, and a real friendship between them began one day when their teacher, Miss Sutgood, asked the students to take turns reading. When Gypsy's turn came, he stood up, as awkward and embarrassed as any schoolboy, and began a stumbling reading from his soiled and worn textbook. As Maxwell had said, the other students would never have dared laugh at *him*, no matter how inept his reading was, but Gypsy was afraid they would and was embarrassed almost to fury when he reached an impasse in his attempts to decipher a word.

" 'Jack . . . went . . . to . . . fe . . . fe . . . ,' " he read.

" 'Fetch,' " Corby whispered behind his hand.

" '. . . *fetch* Jane. They went to the . . . me . . . me . . .' "

" 'Meeting,' " Corby supplied.

" '. . . *meeting,* ' " Gypsy said in triumph.

This happened a few more times during the reading, and when Gypsy finished and sat down again, he glanced at Corby and whispered from the side of his mouth, "Thanks, *navestax*. That's one I owe you."

Corby blushed. *Navestax* was a word the Human Beings used to address a brother in a warrior band, and to be called that by *Moxthaveho* was enough to make him almost giddy with a sense of importance.

After that they sometimes met in the school's dining hall to help each other with their homework, and one day Gypsy, to show how grateful he was for Corby's help, offered to take him along sometime on a wild horse hunt.

The prospect excited Corby for a moment, and then, crestfallen, he said, "But I cannot leave the school. It is not permitted."

"I reckon that's best," Gypsy said, realizing how thoughtlessly he had put temptation in the boy's way. "You stay in school, learn all you can as long as you can."

Corby stammered, "My—my father . . ."

"I know. Your father don't put much store in white man's learning. But I've known Ghost Dancer for a long time now and always respected him, even when I thought he was wrong, so I hope you don't take no offense when I say he's wrong about this schooling business."

"They say the Ghost Dance will . . ." He ran his finger over the cover of a McGuffey Reader on the table in front of him.

"I tell you, *navestax*, there ain't no dance, no matter how long you do it, that's gonna bring back the buffalo and the Indian dead. The Indian wars are over, the Indians lost, and the sooner we face that, the better off we're gonna be. What we got to do now is get educated. Learn to read and write. That's where the white man gets his power from, them books. And we gotta learn how to do it, too, or we ain't got a chance."

Gypsy's enthusiasm for learning had a beneficent effect on the other students. In whatever class he was in, the performance rates rose. Maxwell was sorry that Gypsy wasn't a full-time student, but he knew Gypsy had to make a living, as he did by catching mustangs. Three or four times a year he would get together with a few old cowhands and make a trip up to the Cimarron breaks in the Cherokee Outlet or into No Man's Land, where they would catch the wild horses.

Being away from school interfered with Gypsy's lessons and allowed the other students to get ahead of him, but he took his McGuffey Reader with him, and on those stretches of prairie where the horses could walk for hours with hardly a break in rhythm, Gypsy would drop the reins over the saddlehorn, take the Reader from his saddlebag, and read as he rode along. It wasn't long before he could read popular pulp-paper fiction and newspapers, though he had a particularly difficult time following the newspaper stories about the General Allotment Act of 1887, the so-called Dawes Act, which held for him such a pained interest that he even risked embarrassment by asking others what certain of the bigger words meant.

He learned that a Senator Dawes from Massachusetts introduced the bill in Congress that cleared the way for much of Indian Territory to be settled by homesteaders. The bill would force the Indians to give up the tribal lands they held in common in exchange for individual ownership of 160-acre allotments. So once more the politicians were going to move the Indians off the land promised to them "in perpetuity."

"The lying sonsabitches," Gypsy said of them. It was his general opinion of all politicians.

But they—the politicians—didn't plan for all the reservations to be thrown open at the same time. It would be done piecemeal, one reservation at a time, and indeed, the first land to be opened for settlement would be the tract called the Unassigned Land—land on which no Indians had yet been sent to live. Also known as the Oklahoma District, it was a large tract that had been left over after the rest of Indian Territory had been divided up into eighteen reservations that served as the relocated homelands for thirty-two different Indian tribes. The Oklahoma District—more than two million acres of prime ranching and farming land—lay smack in the middle of Indian Territory, bordered on the north by the Cherokee Outlet, on the south by the Chickasaw Nation, on the west by the Cheyenne-Arapaho reservation, and on the east by a number of smaller reservations of the Shawnee, Kickapoo, and Iowa tribes. This land had originally been set aside as a future reservation for still more Indian tribes, but the politicians had changed their minds and decided to give it to homesteaders instead.

Gypsy learned all this by doggedly deciphering the newspapers, and by the time the actual opening of the Oklahoma District was drawing near, he was able to read the letter he received from a man in Topeka, Kansas. The letter asked him if he would consider going to Tennessee to bring back a wagon train of colored settlers to make the run into the Oklahoma District. Gypsy read the letter a number of times and thought he understood the gist of it, but he finally took it to Maxwell.

"Can't figure out them big words yet." He pointed to the embossed letterhead. "What's that say, for instance?"

Maxwell adjusted the glasses on the bridge of his nose and leaned forward in his swivel chair, his forearms on his desk. "Oklahoma Immigration Association." His eyes went to the signature at the bottom of the page. "Well, well, would you look at that! Jolson Mossburger!"

"I read 'bout him in the newspapers once or twice. Some high muckamuck colored man up in Kansas, ain't he?"

"One of the best-known colored men in the country, in fact. Was once United States ambassador to Liberia, or something like that, and now he's some kind of elected official in Kansas. State auditor, I think. First Negro to hold an elective office outside the Reconstruction South. Read something a couple of weeks ago, about his trying to get hundreds of thousands of Negroes in the South to make the run for homesteads when the Oklahoma District opens to settlers in April. Seems he wants to make it an all-colored territory, Negroes and Indians, with him as the first governor when it becomes a state." After a pause to appreciate the scope of such grand ambitions, he asked, "You going to take the job?"

Gypsy scratched the nape of his neck. "Don't rightly know. Tell the truth, I don't hold much with sodbusters. Ranchers is bad enough, putting up barbed-wire fences across open range, but them farmers are a sight worse, all fences and plowed fields and towns. Fact is, I like this country the way it is, and I sure don't know that I want to help bring a bunch of sodbusters out here to ruin it."

"Well, they're coming, whether you help 'em or not."

"I 'spect so," Gypsy said, and figured that if they were com-

ing anyway, where was the harm in giving them a hand? It
wasn't a part of his easygoing nature to fret much about things
he couldn't change. Still, he'd have to know how much the job
paid, and how long it would last, and things like that, before
he could make up his mind, so he got Maxwell to help him
write a letter to Mr. Mossburger, saying he needed more information about the job before making a decision.

A few days later a telegram was delivered to him at Bixby's
Boardinghouse. It was from Topeka, Kansas, requesting him to
meet Mossburger five days hence at Guthrie Station in the
Oklahoma District. Mossburger was scheduled to stop over at
Guthrie Station for a day to meet with some prospective
wagon train guides, one of whom he hoped would be Gypsy.
Could Gypsy come?

Guthrie Station, a small collection of buildings alongside the
Santa Fe railroad tracks, had once been a stagecoach stop.
Most of the buildings were dusty and weather-beaten old clapboard and log structures, but the railroad station house itself,
and the station agent's house in the rear of it, were new. The
station's windmill was also new, a well-greased fantail that
filled the water tank alongside the railroad tracks where the lo-
comotives stopped to replenish their boilers.

Gypsy stopped to let his mare drink from the horse trough
beneath the windmill, then rode on past the station house to the
hotel, where four horses were tied to the hitching rail. The saloon was a smoke-darkened low-ceilinged room with a crude
plank bar on one side, plank tables and chairs on the other, and
a big stone fireplace at the far end, in which roared a fire of
fragrant blackjack. Behind the bar was Roy Lipscomb, the
owner, a paunchy man with tousled hair and unshaven jowls,
his baggy grease-stained pants held up by suspenders over the
top of his soiled long johns. His wife, a Tonkawa squaw, was
at that moment in the kitchen cooking a dinner of rattlesnake
stew for the hotel's guests.

There were three of them, all black. Gypsy knew one of
them, Chickasaw Charlie, who was about his own age and had
come from somewhere in Georgia to live with the Chickasaw
Indians and take himself a Chickasaw wife. And it turned out
that the other two were also squaw men, one living among the
Creeks, the other an adopted member of the Shawnee tribe.

They were Joe Peek and Nat Sayers, respectively, and, like Gypsy and Chickasaw Charlie, they were men of the plains who wore their guns on their hips and dressed in bits and pieces of agency-issue clothes and Indian geegaws.

"We all after the same job?" Gypsy asked after he had joined them at their table for a drink.

"Naw," said Chickasaw Charlie in his thick southern accent. "Way I hear it, they beating the bushes for every colored man they can find in the Territory. Say they wants us go down South and bring back as many of them po' ignorant dirt farmers as we can."

"You gonna do it?"

"I 'spect so. I got a squaw to feed, not to mention about umpteen in-laws." He pushed the bottle of whiskey across the table. "Have another."

"Not right now, thanks. Gotta get my horse taken care of first and grab myself a bunk."

He paid Lipscomb fifty cents for a bunk for himself and a stable for his mare. "How the bedbugs these days?" he asked.

"Real hongry," Lipscomb said in a gargling tone. It seemed he always talked through a throat that needed clearing. "They been looking forward to seeing you again, Gypsy."

As Gypsy was leading his mare around to the crumbling adobe stables behind the hotel, he noticed a blurred movement on the southern horizon. Out of habit and instinct, he stopped to watch until the blurred shapes began to be identifiable: horses and riders, moving in and out of the meandering line of green trees that marked the course of Cottonwood Creek. As best he could estimate from the distance, there were eight or nine of them—not Indians; cowboys, maybe, though there would be little reason for cowboys to be in the Oklahoma District now that the government had moved the ranchers out to make way for the homesteaders.

Their presence made him a little edgy, but he went on to the adobe stable and unsaddled his mare and gave her a burlap-sack rubdown while she munched oats from a nose bag. Then he took his saddlebags and bedroll and started for the back door of the saloon but stopped when he saw two riders coming. They were still about a half mile away, but he thought he recognized one of the horses—a piebald with unusual markings, easy to spot—as being one of the mounts in the gang of

cowboys he had seen a little while ago. Why had they split off
from the others? And where were the others? And what were
they up to?

These questions left him with a slight tingling sensation at
the base of his skull, like a doubtful dog whose hackles are
stirred by an uncertain sense of danger.

CHAPTER SIX

AFTER SWEEPING THE HORIZON IN EVERY DIRECTION AND DE-
tecting no other signs of movement, Gypsy went back into the
saloon, had some of the rattlesnake stew being served by
Lipscomb's Tonkawa squaw, and when the train carrying
Jolson Mossburger arrived, he and the others went out to meet
it. The only other persons on the platform were five bedraggled Kickapoo Indians squatting against the building, their
blankets pulled up over their heads. Their mud-spattered ponies were tied to the hitching rail beside the station house.
Gypsy wondered what had happened to the two riders he had
seen approaching the station. They'd had plenty of time to arrive, yet there was no piebald among the horses.

The locomotive screeched to a steaming stop directly beneath the water tank, putting the two passenger cars directly
abreast of the platform. A few Kickapoo chiefs got off, followed by three Negroes, one of whom could only have been
Jolson Mossburger: a light-skinned man in a brown derby hat,
a high stiff collar, a black silk vest, spats, and pin-striped
pants. The pince-nez that sat slightly askew on the bridge of
his nose was secured by a ribbon that draped over his left ear
and down his neck to its attachment on his lapel. He was followed by two other light-skinned Negroes, one middle-aged,
the other young, both dressed in suits and ties but not nearly
so meticulous in their attire as their boss. The middle-aged

man was Mr. Mossburger's executive assistant, Amos Fulton; the younger one was his stenographer and clerk. A Negro porter brought their bags.

"Is this all of you?" Mossburger asked after introductions were made. He carried an ebony walking stick in one hand and a leather lawyer's satchel in the other.

"Fur's I knows," Chickasaw Charlie said in his Georgia cotton field accent, and glanced around the platform to see if he had missed someone. "How many was you 'specting?"

"Ah, well," Mossburger said, and led them back to a table in the saloon. He had his assistant light the lamp above the table, requested Roy Lipscomb's Tonkawa squaw to furnish them with a pot of hot black coffee, and then announced over the chugging sound of the train pulling away from the station, "Gentlemen, the Oklahoma Immigration Association needs you. Your colored brothers and sisters in the South need you. After twenty-five years of 'freedom,' the Negro race is as bad off as it was in slavery days. They're no longer called slaves, but they're still working the white man's lands with the white man's mules and the white man's tools. They're still being lynched—three lynchings last Friday in Memphis alone—*three* in one day! That makes one hundred and sixty-two lynchings in the South during the last year. Not to mention having a colored school or church or home burned down almost every day by the Ku Klux Klan.

"Well, that has to stop. Our people have to have a land of their own, and this is it—Oklahoma! Here," he said, taking from his lawyer's satchel a sheaf of printed flyers. "This is what we're doing to make a Negro homeland a reality." He started to pass the flyers around the table, but suddenly stopped as if he had thought of something. "Can any of you read?"

After a brief pause, to give modesty its due, Gypsy said with a grin, "Sure, I can."

"I'll read it to you," Mossburger said, and, as if auctioning off something, proceeded to read the flyer from the Oklahoma Immigration Association addressed to the Colored Citizens of the South, promising them a veritable paradise, where land and peoples were free. It ended with an exhortation for colored citizens to contact the Immigration Association's agents and join the wagon trains westward.

"That flyer has been sent to thousands of churches and colored organizations and newspapers in the South, and the response, praise God, has been tremendous. Gentlemen, a stream of black humanity has begun to flow toward Oklahoma." Reaching into his lawyer's satchel, he brought out a fistful of telegrams. "Telegrams from all over the South." He looked at the top one. "From Buford, a small town in Kentucky. A party of fifty left there a week ago, and by the time they reached the Tennessee border, their numbers had swollen to three hundred." He discarded that telegram and looked at the next. "And here! A hundred and fifty immigrants passed through Banner Ford, Arkansas, yesterday, walking to join the hundreds pouring out of Missouri, pilgrim homesteaders on their way to the Promised Land. And here—"

"Walking?" Gypsy interrupted. "You say they're *walking*?"

"Some of them, yes. Some have horses or mules, some even have wagons, but I'm sure they'll all get here, even if they have to crawl."

"Well, mister, that's all well and good, but what're they gonna do when they get here? The District's gonna be opened by a run. The one who gets there first gets the homestead. How's any folks on foot going to beat them that's got horses?"

"That's where you guides come in. You all know this country. At least that's what my reports say. That's why we need you men as guides. Most of the people who make the run on horseback, they're likely to be strangers here. Many of them'll get lost, or won't know where to go, or won't be able to locate the section markers." He paused a moment, then went on in a slyly triumphant voice. "While you men, you'll lead our people into those areas where they'll have the best chance of finding a claim. And you yourselves will be staking claims for homesteads or town lots, whichever you prefer. Of course, we'll give you the maps of where our townships will be platted. . . . Well, then? What'd you say? Are you with us?"

"But why," Gypsy wanted to know, "would you be wanting to send us all the way back South? Why not let 'em get out here on their own, and then we'll lead 'em in when the run starts?"

"Think, men! Think. Those people are babes in the woods. I wouldn't be surprised if any of them have ever been more than a hundred miles from home. They're being harassed by white mobs. They're getting lost, breaking down. They don't know how to deal with frontier situations. And what'll happen to them when they get into Indian Territory? You men know how to deal with Cherokees and Creeks, but they don't. And what about the bands of white outlaws roaming around the Territory? They'd be easy pickings for such men, wouldn't they? They need leaders. They need you."

"Yeah?" Chickasaw Charlie said. "What's the pay?"

"A dollar a day."

Charlie hooted. "Hell, I can make more'n that punching cows."

"I realize it's not much, but remember it's the immigrants themselves, through the OIA, who'll be paying your wages, and you can imagine how poor *they* are. Actually, I was hoping I could appeal to you on the basis of race. You are Negroes, after all, and—"

"Half," Gypsy said. Ordinarily he wouldn't have mentioned it, but since it seemed to be an important issue with Mossburger, he thought he had better let him know.

"*Half!*" Mossburger sneered, and got to his feet, as if Gypsy's remark had made him so agitated he couldn't sit still. "Don't you know there's no such thing in this country as a *half* Negro? If you've got one drop of Negro blood, you're a nigger, and that's that. You can be half Irish, you can be half Spanish, you can even be half Indian, but you can't be half Negro. Look at *me*. What percent Negro blood would you say I have? Two percent! I could pass for white, and I have, when it suited my purposes. But when it becomes known that I'm only ninety-eight percent white, why, then, I become a nigger. I'm still the same color. I haven't changed the way I talk or dress. I'm still the same man. But suddenly I'm not white anymore, I'm colored. Well, all right, then, I'm colored, by God, and I'm proud of it. And I was hoping I could appeal to you men on that basis. These are your people, and they need your help. Will you help them?"

Three of them nodded grudgingly and said yes, they would take the job. Gypsy was the only holdout. Mossburger was a good man, Gypsy could see that, and he admired him, but noble sentiments had never played a big part in his decision making. And it wasn't mercenary motives, either, that made him shake his head. Well, what was it then? Mossburger wanted to know. Speak up!

Gypsy told him that he saw a disaster in the making. Of all those hordes of dirt-poor immigrants coming in, damned few would actually get a homestead—and those who didn't? What would happen to them? Would they be expected to turn around and walk all the way back to where they came from? And even if a few did manage, against all the odds, to get a homestead, how would they work it? Did they have plows? And mules to pull them? Did they have enough money to build cabins and fences and buy seeds? It would be a whole year before they could make a crop; what would they live on till then?

"I tell you, mister, this time next year, you might have thousands of those poor bastards wandering around out here, without any land or shelter or anything to eat, 'less they want to fight with the Indians for grasshoppers and tadpoles."

Mossburger thought he saw where the difficulty lay. He sat down again, dropped his derby on the green felt table, and asked, "Have you ever been to the South?"

"Can't say I have," Gypsy admitted. "But I hear it's good farming country, so I 'spect they get enough to eat down there anyway."

"Man does not live by bread alone."

"No, but if he ain't got it, he don't live at all."

"They couldn't be any worse off," Mossburger asserted.

"They're alive, ain't they? If they come out here, they may not be very long, and when you're dead," he added as a clincher, "you got no more reason to live."

As Mossburger was trying to figure out how to answer that, Gypsy turned his attention to two men who entered the saloon. On second glance he saw that one of them was dressed as a man, and carried a gun like a man, but the hip on which the .44 rested had an unmistakable feminine rotundity to it. And a still closer look revealed that it was a woman, all right, and not just any woman, either, but Rose Maddox herself, the Rose of Cimarron. With the possible exception of Belle Starr, Rose was the most famous woman outlaw in the Territory. Gypsy had first met her about eighteen years ago, over in No Man's Land, when she'd had a price on her head. As far as he knew, she had gone straight for a number of years now, but here she was, packing a .44 with a man who might have passed for a pig farmer except for the two revolvers he carried, one in a holster on his hip, the other in the front pocket of his bib overalls. Gypsy guessed from pictures he had seen on WANTED posters that the man was Ole Yantis, a back-shooting killer known to be a member of the Boss Beeson gang. Gypsy wondered which one of the two had been riding the piebald pony; wondered, too, what they were doing here at Guthrie Station. And where were the seven or eight others they had been riding with earlier in the day?

Rose pretended not to know Gypsy. As she came into the saloon, her eyes swept across every face in the room, and Gypsy was sure there was a flicker of recognition and surprise in her eyes when she saw him, though she pretended otherwise. She and Ole Yantis stepped up to the bar and ordered whiskey. Lipscomb's attempts to make conversation indicated that they were strangers to him.

"So what do you say, Mr. Smith?" Amos Fulton asked, trying to draw him back into the discussion. "Will you do it?"

Still glancing at Rose of Cimarron from the corners of his eyes, Gypsy said, "Naw, I reckon not. If they can make it this far and need somebody to lead 'em during the run, why, sure, I might show 'em where things are. Till then, though, you best count me out."

"Won't you please reconsider, Mr. Smith?" Mr. Mossburger urged. "It's very important that the immigrants be protected, and with your reputation as a gunman . . ."

"I'm sure my 'reputation as a gunman,' as you call it, don't reach all the way back to Tennessee, Mr. Mossburger, so I don't see what good I could do till they get here." He reached for his saddlebags and bedroll on the floor beside his chair. Glancing once more at Rose of Cimarron, he said loudly enough for her to hear, "Now, if you'll excuse me, gentlemen, I'll go on out and take care my horse."

CHAPTER SEVEN

HE WAS IN THE STABLES BEHIND THE HOTEL CURRYCOMBING his horse when Rose emerged from the back door of the saloon. She gave him a follow-me look and headed for the two-hole privy behind the hotel. When she disappeared into the door of the first privy, he followed and went into the second. The plank partition between the holes was thin enough to allow for conversation in normal tones.

"Well, if I'm not badly mistaken, it's the Rose of Cimarron herself," he said through the partition. He could hear her peeing.

"That you, Gypsy Smith?"

"What's left of me, Rose, after all these years. How you?"

"Not so good, tell the truth. Ain't like the old days, is it? You see that skunk I'm riding with?"

"Ole Yantis, ain't it? Last I heard, he was with the Beeson gang. You riding with the likes of that bunch these days, Rose?"

"Just for this job," she said defensively. "And looks like I'm gonna have to mess it up a little. You done me a favor once. I reckon I can finally return it."

"Well, I do recollect the last thing you said to me." Gypsy peeked through the quarter moon aperture in the door, keeping an eye on the hotel and saloon, and caught sight of three riders coming in from the south. They were about a quarter mile away, riding alongside the railroad tracks. "You said you always paid your debts."

"I do if I can, but I got to have your word on something. Promise you won't let 'em know it was me told you?"

"You got my word on whatever you want it on, Rose."

There was a long silence in the other compartment, and then

Rose took a deep breath and said, "Beeson and his bunch is coming here to kill them coloreds you're with."

"That so? Now, why'd anybody want to do a thing like that?"

"They been hired to do it: to kill that nigger that don't look like a nigger, anyway—what's his name? Mossburger? One that wants to make the Territory a nigger state. I don't know who hired 'em—some land company up in Kansas, I hear. Idea is to keep colored homesteaders from coming in here and taking the land."

"How they plan to do it?"

"Gonna string Mossburger and the others up on the water tank before the next train comes in. Be a man with a camera on the train to take pictures for the newspapers in the South. Anyway, I'm telling you so's you can save y'self."

"And I'm not supposed to tell the others, is that it?"

"If you do, if Beeson or any of his bunch finds out, my life won't be worth a fart in a whirlwind."

"Don't worry, I won't give you away." He kept glancing at the three riders approaching from the south. "Tell me, though, how'd you get mixed up in something like this? I heard you'd gone straight."

"Well," she said sheepishly, "times're hard, and . . . well, I sort of teamed up with Kid Bannister. You heard of him?"

Gypsy sifted around in his memory and came up with the name and face of a kid on a WANTED poster, but the reward was so low that only a few post office bulletin boards even bothered to put it up.

"Me and him's sort of a team now, see," Rose said, wadding up some newspaper. "He wants to get in good with Beeson, maybe get to be a member of the gang. Personally I think Beeson and his boys are a bunch of no-good, egg-sucking sonsabitches, but the kid . . . well, I sort of tagged along to look out for him, if I could."

"Three men riding in from the south," Gypsy said. "Who're they?"

"That'd be the kid, with Bill Ballenger and that crazy bastard they call Nez. Boss and Bill Harney'll be coming in from the north in a little while. Coming in scattered, so's not to alarm nobody."

"Dynamite Bill Ballenger? He must have a pretty good reward on his head, and Boss Beeson must be worth at least a thousand."

"Well, in case you're thinking about trying to collect it, just remember, there's been lots of bounty hunters tried it, and most of 'em are dead, and Beeson's still alive and kicking." The sounds she was making indicated she was preparing to leave. "Well, it wouldn't break my heart to see Beeson and his bastards get what's coming to 'em. But leave me and Kid Bannister out of it, y'hear? I want your word on that."

"You don't have to worry none, Rose," he said as he heard her lift the latch. "And thanks, Rose. I won't forget this."

"I owed you. Now we're even. Good luck."

Gypsy watched through the quarter moon in the door as Rose walked on back to the saloon. She was still a fine-looking woman, but time and hardships had taken their toll on the wild outlaw girl he had known so many years ago. At that time she was a member of an outlaw gang that hid out in No Man's Land and pillaged the towns and ranches in neighboring Texas, New Mexico, Kansas, and Colorado, maybe holding up a stagecoach one day, rustling some cattle the next, stealing some horses the next. The big Texas ranchers had finally hired Gypsy Smith to track the outlaw gang in their hideout on the Cimarron River. During the days and weeks that Gypsy had stalked the gang, he had learned a little about the Rose of Cimarron: that she was good with a gun, that she could ride a horse as well as any man he knew and was braver than most.

By the time he and the ranchers had closed in on the gang, Gypsy had come to admire her. So when she had had her horse shot from under her as she was trying to break out of the ambush in Piedras Negras Canyon, Gypsy had spurred his own horse to intercept her and had come face-to-face with her in the bushes, he on horseback, she on foot, he with a .44 revolver trained on her, she with an empty rifle.

"All right, sonofabitch, shoot!" she had said. "I'm not gonna surrender and be lynched, or have my baby born in no prison, so go ahead—shoot!"

It was then he had noticed that she was maybe four or five months pregnant. He had holstered his gun and had reached out to swing her up on his horse. "Come on, I'll make sure your baby don't get born in prison." She had climbed up behind him, and off they had gone. The ranchers had pursued them, but finally Gypsy had got another horse, put Rose on it, and wished her good luck.

"I'm much obliged to you, Gypsy Smith, and I always pay my debts. If there's ever anything I can do for you, just let me know," she had said, and had ridden away for parts unknown.

"Thanks, Rose," he said eighteen years later, and watched as she walked back toward the saloon.

He once again carried his saddlebags and bedroll with him when he went into the saloon. Rather than rejoin Mossburger and the others at the table, he took a place at the front end of the bar, where it curved around to meet the wall, so that he had his back to the wall and a clear view of the whole saloon, including its front and back doors. He placed the saddlebags and bedroll on the bar. He would have ordered a whiskey, but Lipscomb's attention was devoted exclusively to the three men who had entered the saloon just before Gypsy. Dynamite Bill Ballenger, having ordered a drink, was cursing and saying, "Call this swill whiskey? I've drunk panther piss that's better. Be all right for niggers and women, maybe"—giving Rose and the blacks at the table a contemptuous glance—"but a white man won't drink this swill. Where's your good stuff?"

"Yeah," said the one Gypsy guessed to be Nez, he of the buckteeth and adenoidal voice. "Give us the good stuff, or we'll—we'll . . ." He looked at Bill Ballenger. "What'll we do, Bill, if he don't? How 'bout if I blow his goddamned head off?" He put his hand on the double-barreled shotgun he had placed on the bar.

Ballenger gave Nez a look of long-suffering disgust. Ballenger had heavy jowls covered with a shaggy growth of coppery beard, small jaundiced eyes, a big nose reddened with ruptured capillaries, and a mass of matted copper-colored hair that sprang from beneath his shapeless, sweat-stained hat.

Kid Bannister stood a little apart from them and made faces as he sipped his whiskey, as if he weren't used to the rawness of both the whiskey and his companions. He had a small, delicate, beardless, slightly feminine face, with an expression of total concentration, like someone trying to keep his courage up.

Lipscomb tried to placate them with another kind of whiskey, but though Ballenger drank it and poured himself another, he complained that it, too, was worthless as panther piss, suitable only for women and niggers. He took the bottle to the ta-

ble where Mossburger and the others sat and slammed it down
on the table.

"This the kind of panther piss you niggers drink, ain't it?"

Although trying not to be goaded, the men stared at
Ballenger malevolently and Mossburger said, "If you'll excuse
us, we're trying to conduct some business."

Ballenger snatched up one of the flyers. "Yeah, I know what
kind of 'business' you're trying to 'conduct.' You that nigger
from Kansas, ain't you, that's trying to make the Territory into
a nigger state? Sit down, you!" he barked at Nat Sayers.

"Yeah, sit down," said Nez. He followed Ballenger to the
table and aimed the shotgun at Nat's face. "Or I blow your
goddamn head off."

Ballenger pulled his .44, and the others in the gang followed
suit, all except Rose. She turned to face the tables, leaning
back against the bar, resting her elbows on it, and gazed on the
scene with a look of mingled disgust and shame, but her hand
never went near her revolver.

"Now, all you niggers get your hands up," Ballenger said,
"and stand up real slow and unbuckle your gun belts, let 'em
drop."

"I'm unarmed," Mossburger said, holding his coat open to
show he had no weapons.

."Me, too," Amos Fulton said.

"Me, too," said young Horace, the secretary.

"What's the meaning of this outrage?" Mossburger demanded.

"Shut up," Ballenger said.

"Yeah, shut up," Nez said, waving the shotgun under
Mossburger's nose, "or I blow your goddamned head off."

"You shut up, too, Nez," Ballenger said. "You gonna scare
these poor darkies to death. The knives, too," he said to Nat
Sayers and Chickasaw Charlie, both of whom carried bowie
knives on their belts. They dropped them into the pile of gun
belts on the floor. "Now, step back. Go on. Get back against
the wall, all of you. You, Rose!" he barked, and wiggled his
gun at the weapons on the floor. "Make y'self useful. Take
these out and put 'em on the packhorse."

"What the hell're you doing?" Rose said. "You're supposed
to wait till Boss gets here."

"Never mind what I'm doing. Just do what you're told."

"To hell with you." She turned around to face the bar. "I take orders from Beeson, not from you."

Perhaps to avert a clash between Rose and Ballenger, Kid Bannister tried to divert their attention by pointing his gun at Gypsy and saying, "What about him?"

Gypsy was primed to go into action on the merest fraction of a second. But like a turning kaleidoscope, every second held innumerable possibilities, all of which had to be weighed for advantages and disadvantages in a search for the optimal moment for action. He had not thought to act until Boss Beeson and the other gang members showed up, but now that Chickasaw Charlie and the others had been disarmed, he had to be ready for the next best moment for action.

"You," Ballenger said to Gypsy. "What're you, anyway, injun or nigger?"

"Me Cherokee," Gypsy said in the voice of an Indian who could barely manage one word of English.

Ballenger seemed skeptical, and Gypsy's fingers moved imperceptibly a little farther up into the bedroll, but a noise from outside the saloon—the sound of men's boots clumping across the station platform—turned the kaleidoscope into yet one more pattern of possibilities, and Gypsy hesitated.

Boss Beeson and another member of the gang—Bill Harney—came into the saloon, pushing Station Agent Benbrow in front of them. Beeson had a .44 revolver in his hand. Harney carried a Winchester rifle. Beeson was a tall lean man in his mid-fifties, clean-shaven, wearing a black beaver hat and a long dirty duster. He had the baleful eyes and beaked nose of a bird of prey. Harney was a small squint-eyed man with a gray beard streaked by snuff stains at the corners of his mouth.

"Get over there," Beeson said, using the muzzle of his .44 to nudge the station agent toward the bar.

"We got 'em, Boss," Ballenger said proudly. "It's that nigger from Kansas, all right. Look."

Beeson glanced at a few words in the flyer, then looked at Mossburger. "Yeah, you're the one."

"You know who we are?" Ballenger asked Mossburger. "This here's Boss Beeson, and I'm Bill Ballenger, famously known as Dynamite Bill. You never heard of us? We—me and the boss here—back in the War, we used to ride with

Quantrill's Raiders, and when we used to make raids up into Kansas, you know what we'd do when we'd catch us an uppity Kansas nigger like you? We'd cut his balls off and string him up to the nearest tree. And by God, that's what we gonna do with you and your friends here, for trying to bring all them nigger homesteaders into the Territory. Now, what d'you think of that?"

"You can't be serious," Mossburger protested. "My God, man, this is not the South."

"Yantis," Beeson said as he holstered his gun and stepped to the back of the room to warm his hands at the fireplace, "you and the kid go get things ready."

Ole Yantis and Kid Bannister hurried out of the saloon.

Bill Harney had begun to stare at Gypsy. Gypsy didn't return the stare, hoping the puzzled, searching look on Harney's face would come to nothing, but recognition finally broke through. "Hey! You're that nigger bounty hunter, ain't you? Gypsy Smith? Yeah! I know you." Having leveled his rifle at Gypsy, he said over his shoulder to Beeson, who was standing with his back to the fireplace, "Hey, Boss! You know who this is? This's that nigger bounty hunter that got Bob Abernathy up in No Man's Land that time."

"That right, boy?" Beeson asked without moving from the fireplace. "You that sumbitch bounty hunter they call Gypsy Smith?"

Gypsy remained silent.

"Bob Abernathy was a good old friend of mine," Beeson said, apparently without rancor or even vindictiveness. "How much reward you get for taking him in?"

"More'n he was worth," Gypsy said.

"And you know what happened to him?"

"Sure. Hung him."

"That's right. And you know what's going to happen to you?"

Gypsy waited to hear. Nez had turned around and leveled the shotgun at his head.

"I'll tell you what's going to happen to you, boy," Beeson said in a businesslike way. "I'm going to hang you, just like they hung Bob. I might even let Bill cut your balls off first." Pause. "What d'you think a that?"

"Cut 'em off?" Ballenger said. "Naw. What I'd like to do is

blow 'em off." He reached into his shirt and brought out a stick of dynamite. What had appeared to be a lumpy paunch turned out to be a few sticks of dynamite that he carried inside his shirt. "I'll stick this up your ass, nigger boy, and blow you all to hell. Now, unbuckle that gun belt—left hand!"

With a pistol, a rifle, and a shotgun pointed straight at him, Gypsy figured he didn't have much choice, but he obeyed with an almost provocative slowness and let the gun belt drop to the floor at his feet.

"Now get over there with the rest of the niggers," Ballenger said, returning the stick of dynamite to his shirt.

Reaching for his saddlebags and bedroll on the counter as if he were going to take them with him, his hand went inside the bedroll, gripped the sawed-off shotgun, and pointed the bedroll at Nez's face. He pulled the trigger and ducked at the same time, expecting the contraction of Nez's nerves to discharge the shotgun, but that didn't happen. Nez's face disappeared. His body hurtled backward, but the shotgun he held didn't fire. And within a split second—before anybody could realize what had happened—Gypsy had fired the second barrel, this time at Harney, who caught the load of buckshot in the chest. Harney's rifle did discharge when he was hit, but by then Gypsy had dropped to the floor behind the corner of the bar, where he snatched his pistol from its holster and—all in one continuous movement, a movement that had a dancelike fluidity, a movement that was without hesitation, doubt, or fear—rolled from behind the counter, already firing at Ballenger and Beeson.

Ballenger fired two hurried shots from his .44, one of which nicked Gypsy's cheek, before Gypsy's first pistol shot hit him in the shoulder, spinning him around, sending him crashing over a table, and Beeson's .44 had barely cleared its holster before the second bullet from Gypsy's pistol hit him in the stomach, slamming him back into the fire in the fireplace.

Then Gypsy was on his feet, still moving like a dancer, ready to fire again, but finding himself momentarily without a target. Rose had thrown up her hands, Beeson was thrashing and screaming in the fireplace, his duster on fire, and Ballenger was on the floor, weaponless, groaning and clutching the bloody wound in his shoulder, and Nez and Harney were dead.

Chickasaw Charlie, Nat Sayers, and Joe Peek scrambled for

their guns. Alerted by the sound of running footsteps, Gypsy swung his .44 around to bear on Ole Yantis as Ole appeared in the saloon's doorway. Kid Bannister was about three steps behind him.

Rose yelled, "Stay out of it, Kid! Don't—"

But her voice was cut off by a shot. Gypsy's instinct didn't allow him to hesitate for the merest fraction of a second to see if Ole Yantis was going to drop his gun or fire. The bullet struck Yantis between the eyes, and the back of his head blew apart as his body was propelled backward and pitched off the station platform into the mud near the railroad tracks. This left Gypsy aiming at Kid Bannister, who, though he had pulled his gun from its holster, was so startled or frightened that he hesitated to shoot.

Gypsy saw that hesitation and shouted, "Drop it, Kid!"

But he neither dropped it nor aimed it. Instead he began backing up, confused, panicked, his eyes darting everywhere, as if he were looking for a place to take cover, to hide.

"I don't wanna have to kill you," Gypsy warned.

Though he didn't drop it, the kid let the gun dangle limply at his side, and probably would have dropped it, but at the most critical moment of decision, Rose cried from inside the saloon, "Jimmy! For God's sake, do what he tells you! Drop it!"

For some reason—defiance, spite, contrariness—Rose's plea caused the kid to change his mind and raise the pistol. Before he could pull the trigger, three almost simultaneous shots, fired from the pistols of Chickasaw Charlie, Nat Sayers, and Joe Peek, hit the kid in the chest, slamming him down on the platform with the force of a battering ram.

Rose cried out, but her cry was lost amid the cries and screams from Beeson, who, having thrashed his way out of the fireplace, now dashed headlong for the front door, his clothes and his hair on fire. He raced out the front door and across the platform toward the horse trough beneath the water tank, on whose lowest crossbeam hung three noosed ropes that Yantis and the kid had placed there. Beeson was visibly losing strength with each staggering step and was on his knees by the time he reached the water tank and threw himself into the horse trough.

While the eyes of the gunmen were on either Kid Bannister

or Beeson, Ballenger struggled to his feet. Clutching the wound in his shoulder, he staggered toward the back door but had barely stepped through the door and out onto the steps when the four men with the guns opened fire at him at almost the same instant, hitting him four times so rapidly that the sound of the shots made an almost continuous explosion. One of the bullets struck a stick of the dynamite inside his shirt, detonating it and the other sticks. The horrendous explosion shook the whole building, ripped a gigantic hole in the back wall where the door had been, sent a wave of concussion through the saloon that overturned tables and chairs and knocked everybody down, blew out all the windows in the front of the saloon, and scattered live coals from the fireplace all over the room.

After the few seconds that it took for the shock to wear off, people—coughing, groaning, cursing—began extricating themselves from the debris. They struggled to their feet, shook their heads, tried to get their bearings. Gypsy—hatless, but still clutching the .44—was one of the first to get to his feet and take stock of himself. Except for a ringing in his ears and a feeling of being stunned, he was all right.

"Anybody need help?" he asked, squinting into the shambles of the smoke- and dust-filled room.

Nobody seemed to be seriously hurt. Mossburger and his men were pushing aside the overturned tables and chairs and struggling to their feet, while Rose, on her hands and knees, was crawling toward the front door, and Lipscomb poked his disheveled head above the bar.

Gypsy stepped outside the saloon. He looked around for a moment, getting his bearings, then crunched over the shards of broken glass on the platform, past Kid Bannister's body. Intending to splash his face with water from the horse trough, he was brought up short by the sight of Boss Beeson's burned body floating facedown in the trough, his blood turning the water pink. Gypsy shoved the revolver down into the front of his pants and went to the spigot on the pipe leading down from the overhead tank, turned it on, and put his head beneath the flow of water.

Roy Lipscomb and his Tonkawa squaw, carrying buckets, ran out of the saloon and to the horse trough. The sight of Beeson's body caused them to recoil, but then they simply shoved the body aside, filled the buckets with the pink water, and ran back toward the saloon. Benbrow, the station agent, also carrying a bucket, came to the trough but set the bucket down and said to Gypsy, "I'd like to be able to tell my grandchildren I shook the hand of the man who wiped out the Beeson gang. By God, this is a historic occasion!"

After shaking the water from his hair, Gypsy had taken a bandanna from his hip pocket and was drying his hands when Benbrow extended his own, which Gypsy shook without pride or enthusiasm. It was always like this after a gunfight: the slight nervousness, the hollow feeling in the pit of the stomach, the dry mouth, the constricted throat. He had felt none of these things during the gunfight. Indeed, as long as the fight lasted, he had felt as impersonal as an avalanche. It was only when the fight was over and the danger past that he began to feel a sort of queasy nervousness and embarrassment, as if he couldn't quite believe what had happened, as if some impersonal and unfearing force had occupied his body for a while and then gone away, leaving him——a mild-mannered and easygoing man—to ponder the results and face the consequences.

"By God, I can't wait to see Marshal Renfro's face when he gets here," said Station Agent Benbrow. "You accomplished in about ten seconds what he hasn't been able to do in ten years."

"Marshal Renfro? What d'you mean? Is he coming here?" Gypsy held the bandanna to the slight bullet abrasion on his cheek.

"On the next train from Kansas," Benbrow said as he dipped his bucket into the pink water of the horse trough. "Be here in a little over an hour." He chortled. "I sure want to see his face. . . ."

Lipscomb and his squaw had emptied their buckets and were coming after more water. Others were straggling out of the saloon. Rose had crawled out and stopped at the body of Kid Bannister and pulled his head onto her lap. The explosion had knocked her hat off, and now her long thick chestnut hair fell freely about her shoulders and breasts, and she used some of her hair to brush away bits of glass from the kid's face. She was weeping.

Gypsy left the water tank and approached her. "I'm sorry. I tried to get him to . . ." He faltered, shrugged. "I'm sorry."

Rose said, "I didn't want him to be born in jail 'cause I

didn't want him to be marked for—for *this*." She brushed a lock of his hair off his forehead. "But what chance did he have? With me for a mother and Curly Bill Bannister for a father, what chance did the poor kid have? Being an outlaw was in his blood, I reckon. But he was . . . just no good at it. I tried to tell him . . . he wouldn't listen. Wanted to be like his daddy. Now they're dead. Both dead. All dead."

Gypsy said, "Rose, Marshal Renfro's gonna be on the next train. You shouldn't be here when he comes."

She nodded. "Can I take him with me? I don't want him to be buried with this bunch."

"Sure," Gypsy said. "Which are your horses?"

"The piebald and the gray."

Gypsy went around to the side of the station house and brought the two horses. He and Nat Sayers picked up the kid's body and tied it facedown on the gray. Rose mounted the piebald. Gypsy handed her her hat and said, "Rose, you've more than paid any debt you ever owed me, but I'd take it as a big favor if you could tell me something."

She waited.

"Was Renfro in on this?"

"I don't know. Honest to God. They never did trust me enough to let me in on anything. I don't know."

He pressed her hand. "Thanks, Rose. Take care y'self, y'hear?"

She rode away, leading the gray, without saying good-bye. Gypsy stood and watched her go. Mossburger, recovering at last from the shock of the explosion, stumbled about the platform like a man in a mad dance, gesturing wildly toward the ropes that hung over the crossbeam of the water tank, and said, *"This! This!"* Then he gestured toward the wrecked saloon and said, *"This! This!"* Hatless, with his pince-nez askew on his nose, his high stiff collar opened like wings, his hair disheveled, his clothes dirty and in disarray, he gestured toward the body of Ole Yantis and said to Gypsy, *"This* is why!"

"Why what?"

"Why you should go. Think, man! Think what'd happen if those poor ignorant colored immigrants met up with a gang like this!" With another wild gesture toward the ropes, he said, "Don't you see? *This* is why you should go!"

Gypsy shifted his weight to one leg, looked up and down

the railroad tracks like a man trying to choose a direction, and said, "Maybe so."

Surprised, Mossburger asked, "You'll do it then? You'll go?"

"I reckon so," Gypsy said.

CHAPTER EIGHT

WHEN GYPSY FIRST SET EYES ON THE IMMIGRANTS IN A CAMPground on the banks of the Mississippi River just below Memphis, there were about a thousand of them. He had to cut out all those who were too sick to make the trip or too poor to provision themselves along the way. He said: "If any of you are gonna make it, you got to get rid of those who can't."

This reduced the band to about five hundred, though even most of those didn't look as if they could arrive at the Oklahoma District in time for the run. To do so, they would have to travel at least twenty miles a day, every day, for twenty-two days. How could they possibly do it? Especially the ones who had no means of transportation other than their feet, some of whom didn't even have shoes? One of the walkers had a wooden leg.

Gypsy didn't have much confidence in some of the conveyances either. One man had a kiddie cart pulled by a big billy goat. Another had a sled dog harnessed to a child's little red wagon. An old woman rode a saddled milk cow. One family had a covered wagon hitched to a team of a Jersey cow and a walleyed mule. There were bicycles, burros, and pushcarts.

But all was not hopeless. Of those that followed Gypsy out of Memphis, about a hundred seemed well equipped for the trip. Some had well-matched teams of sleek Missouri mules and horses to pull good wagons that were loaded down with

farm tools and household belongings. Some rode Indian ponies, some rode plow horses, a few rode thoroughbreds.

From among those who had good riding horses Gypsy chose
ten section leaders and two scouts. It was their job to ride herd
on the immigrants, to keep them moving, "come hell or high
water."

There were two things for which he would allow the caravan to stop: a burial or a birth. It was a harsh rule, and Gypsy
hated to apply it, but what choice did he have? Some of the
immigrants complained that he was too ruthless, but he didn't
argue with them, didn't defend himself. He just shrugged and
asked if they intended to get to the Oklahoma District in time
for the run.

"If so, let's go. If not, drop out."

"But my wagon wheel is busted," one man said. "How I
gonna take it off and get it to a blacksmith shop if nobody
heps me?"

"I'm sorry," Gypsy said, and whirled his mare to face the
people who had stopped to gawk at the broken wagon wheel.
"Keep it moving! Only two hundred more miles to go."

Cantering his mare back toward the head of the caravan, he
kept an eye out for a mule-drawn wagon that had become very
special to him. It belonged to a young woman named Drusilla
Pointer.

Drusilla Pointer was a handsome young woman. She had
glossy black hair that bobbled on her head in long pigtail ringlets. She had teeth so white they gleamed. She had a tall muscular body with small high hips and small high breasts, and
smooth skin the color of roasted coffee beans. And you could
tell from the way she handled her team of spavined mules that
she was a strong and independent young woman, a woman
who greased her own wagon wheels, who cooked a good supper every night for herself and six children, and who was—to
top it all off—a schoolteacher.

A schoolteacher! Gypsy found that very impressive. The
children were her pupils, or at least they had come to her as
pupils. Over the years, however, these six—four girls and two
boys, ranging in age from six to twelve, all waifs, strays, orphans, or abandoned—had more or less adopted her as a foster
mother or big sister, and she had more or less adopted them as
her own.

She had taught in a one-room Tennessee schoolhouse that had been burned down one night by the Ku Klux Klan. Shortly afterward she had bought herself a span of mules and an old wagon, heaped the wagon with household goods and books and the six children who had nowhere else to go, and joined the caravan headed for the Promised Land. And though it was a brutal and demanding trip, she didn't neglect the education of those six children. Every night after the caravan went into camp, and after supper and the chores were done, the children gathered around the campfire and took turns reading from their textbooks or, if they were too exhausted to read, Drusilla might read to them from the Bible.

It was these nightly reading lessons that first brought Gypsy Smith into her camp. For the first few days out of Memphis she had noticed Gypsy looking at her in what she construed to be a lascivious way as he rode back and forth along the length of the caravan, and so she was skeptical when he came into her camp one night and said that he, too, was learning to read, and could he come and sit with the other students when they had their lessons? She suspected he was more interested in her than in reading, but she let him attend their lessons and was, over the period of the next few nights, surprised and puzzled to see that he really was trying to learn how to read—puzzled, because it seemed a humble thing for a proud man to do.

And he was proud. That had been the first thing she noticed about him on that day he rode into the Memphis campground on his black mare: the way he carried himself, with the quiet pride of a man who had never had to lick another man's boots. This manifested itself in the aura of authority that he carried about him, an authority so self-assured that he had no need to be arrogant or abusive, no need to prove himself. She had never heard him argue with any of the immigrants who had opposed his ruthless requirement of twenty miles per day, had never heard him raise his voice. She admired that in a man.

And yet, for all his aura of authority, he wasn't at all aloof. He could still plunk himself down among the children around the campfire at night and take his turn reading. What was she to make of him, this man who could be a man among men and a child among children?

One morning he came galloping up from the rear of the car-

avan and pulled the mare down to a leisurely walk beside her
mule-drawn wagon. As usual he touched the brim of his hat
and said, "Morning, Miss Drusilla." Shifting sideways on the
saddle, he put his left hand on the mare's haunches and leaned
back on his arm, rocking gently with the mare's walking
movements, facing her as if preparing for a rocking chair chat.
"Fine morning, ain't it?"

"*Isn't* it," she said, and gave him a quick look to see if he
resented the correction. "Looky here, maybe you'd better tell
me something, Gypsy Smith. If you're going to be a student of
mine, you want me to correct you anytime you make a mistake
or only when we're in a study class?"

"Why, Miss Drusilla, you just correct me any old time. My
old mama, she used to say there wasn't no shame in being ignorant, the only shame was staying ignorant."

To hear him mention his mother, even if in a tone of levity,
prompted her to try to draw him out by saying, "Smart
woman, your mama." But that didn't work, so she began to
pry, even though it was against her upbringing. "Was she a
slave?"

"Most of her life, yeah." But then he fell silent, as if embarrassed to be caught talking about himself. But with a little
more prodding and prying, Drusilla learned that his mother had
been owned by one of the chiefs of the Cherokees, a big plantation owner, whose Indian name was Otollotubbe, though he
had adopted the white name Smith. Gypsy was his son.

"He acknowledged you?" Drusilla asked. "Gave you his
name?"

"Yeah, I was a sort of half son, half slave. The Cherokees,
see, didn't treat their slaves the same way white folks did.
They was slaves, sure, but they was still human beings, and
when they was set free in '65, they was adopted into the tribe
as Cherokees."

Drusilla's body shifted lithely to and fro on the springless
seat as the wagon bumped and jolted over the rutted road. With
her shoes off and her feet planted on the floor of the wagon,
she leaned forward, her elbows on her knees, the reins held
slackly in her long-fingered hands. The long gingham dress she
wore was pulled up almost to her knees and fell in deep folds
between her legs. On the seat next to her was one of the
children—Ruby, it was, a girl of about eight, who was crack-

ing sunflower seeds and spitting out the hulls. The other children were about somewhere. Sometimes some of them could be seen in the piles of tied-down belongings on the wagon, their heads poking up here or there between boxes or rolled-up bedding. At other times some of them sat on the tailgate and dangled their bare feet as the wagon labored along. Or sometimes they walked beside the wagon, or ran to visit children at other wagons, or searched the roadside ditches for lamb's-quarters and wild mustard. The oldest one—Clarence, a boy of about twelve, who owned a small .22 rifle—sometimes ran into unfenced woods in search of rabbits and squirrels.

"Looky here, Gypsy Smith," said Drusilla when the conversation seemed to be faltering. She hesitated for a moment, summoning up her determination, and then blurted out, "Are you a married man?"

"Can't say as I am," he answered with a chuckle, as if the idea of his having a wife was somehow slightly ludicrous. But then he shifted back into the saddle, facing forward, and added in an absent, ruminative way, "Was once, I guess. I mean, she was my wife, though we was never married in a church or anything like that. Commanche, she was. That was, oh, a long time ago, when I was no older than you are right now, I 'spect—what's that? Twenty-one?"

"Twenty-two. So where's she now?"

"Dead." Reaching forward, he absently brushed a horsefly off the mare's withers and gave her neck a few rough pats. "Typhoid. I was out on a trail drive to Kansas at the time. Came back and half the camp was dead. The boy, too."

"The boy? You had a son?"

"Two years old when he died. She was nineteen."

"I'm sorry," Drusilla said.

His shrug was one of resignation, not indifference. "Oh, well, that was . . . a long time ago."

"You never wanted to get married again?" Drusilla was downright ashamed of herself for being so bold and forward, but there were certain things she just had to know before she started making plans for him.

"Lordy, no, Miss Drusilla. Wouldn't be fair to a woman being married to me. Ain't likely I'll ever stay in one place too long." He took the reins up as if getting ready to ride on. "I reckon I'm the kind of man that mamas warn their daughters about. Your mama ever warn you about rambling men, Miss Drusilla?" There was a slight tone of raillery in his voice now, betokening a growing familiarity, and it sounded as if he had almost added an endearment to the remark, like "Miss Drusilla, honey."

"Warn me!" she scoffed, and the little pigtail ringlets of glossy black hair bobbled around on her head. "She didn't have to. She let one get her with child before he ran off. She never saw hide or hair of him again."

A rider suddenly appeared, coming along the caravan from the front, at full gallop, with people scattering out of the horse's path. When he got within hailing distance of Gypsy, he jerked his horse to a spinning turn, calling, "Gypsy! Up front!"

Gypsy had already touched his spurs to his mare's flanks and sent her leaping forward into a run. He had almost caught up with the other rider before they reached the head of the column, which had gone around a bend in the road and stopped. Riders from the caravan were gathering in front of the column, staring at a burning cross that had been planted in the middle of the muddy road. The cross was about eight feet high with a three-foot cross member, wrapped thickly in kerosene-soaked rags.

Gypsy rode close enough to feel the heat and smell the kerosene. He didn't know quite what to make of it. He knew that it was something that struck terror into the hearts of superstitious southern Negroes, but to him, who had had no experience with the Ku Klux Klan, it was just silly. He put the sole of his boot against the flaming end of the cross member and shoved it over.

"Keep 'em moving," he called to the caravan leaders.

The burning cross lay sputtering in the mud as the horses and wagons and buggies and barefoot immigrants filed past.

A little farther down the road they found a crudely lettered sign on a board nailed to a roadside tree: NIGGER DON'T LET THE SUN SET ON YOU IN THIS COUNTY. And another one a little farther on: WE HANG STRANGE NIGGERS IN BAYLOR COUNTY.

"Be careful," Gypsy warned the immigrants that night in the campground. "Nobody is to leave the campground tonight." He posted twenty guards around the perimeter of the campsite and admonished them not to shoot unless their lives were in danger. "If you see any suspicious movement, just fire a warning shot in the air, and we'll all come running."

Later, after he had fed his mare a nose bag of oats and rubbed her down and staked her out to graze by a creek bank, he made his way through the many cooking fires in the campground and arrived at Drusilla's camp long before the nightly reading lesson was to begin. In fact, Drusilla was just cooking supper, frying two squirrels that Clarence had killed in a pecan grove that morning. Clarence was now getting the mules settled for the night, and the other five children were helping Drusilla with the camping chores: fetching wood, carrying water, unloading the bedrolls, and setting out the tin plates and eating utensils.

"Will you join us for supper?" Drusilla asked. "We've got plenty. Fried squirrel, beans, and hot biscuits."

Having very little capacity for polite lies, he said, "Well, if you're sure you got plenty. It's been a long time since I've had fried squirrel and hot biscuits, and I'm sure sick of my own cooking."

"Mingo," she said to the oldest girl, "get another plate." She was leaning over the fire and frying pan, turning the pieces of squirrel in the sizzling grease. Buried in the coals of the campfire was a Dutch oven, in which the biscuits baked.

"Actually, what I come to see you about—" Gypsy began, but she said, "Came," and he said, "Huh? Oh, yeah. Right. The reason I *came* to see you was that burning cross and them signs—*those* signs. What d'you think the Klan's up to? I mean, before they burned your school that time, did they do anything like burn crosses or something?"

"Yes. Especially 'or something.' The first night they came, they burned a cross. The second time they tied me to a post and whipped me. The third time was when they burned the school."

Gypsy haunched down and held out his hands to the cooking fire. "I didn't know about the whipping."

"It's not something I like to talk about."

"Yeah," he said. "So if this burning cross on the road was just a warning, you don't think they'll be trying anything tonight?"

"Not likely. They're cowards, they don't attack somebody unless they outnumber their victim. That's the one thing you can be sure of about Ku Kluxers, they're all sneaking cowards. That's why they wear those silly bed sheets in the first place, afraid they'll be recognized. Makes them look spooky, too. The ghosts of the Confederate dead—that's what they want colored folks to believe.

"Ruby, honey, hand me the platter," she said to one of the girls, and as she forked the pieces of crisp brown squirrel onto the platter, she continued, "So if you ask me, I'd say, no, they're not likely to try anything with us tonight—not as long as we've got plenty of men with guns who're willing to use 'em, they're not. DeLacy," she said to the other eight-year-old girl, "take the biscuits out of the oven, honey, and watch out, don't burn yourself again."

Gypsy was served the first plate of food, and though ravenous, he waited politely until all the others had their plates of food in front of them before he picked up a piece of squirrel. But he suddenly stopped with the squirrel leg already in his mouth when he noticed that the others—none of whom had as yet touched his or her food—were looking at him in a puzzled and perhaps even mildly reproachful way.

"Maybe we could get Mr. Smith to say grace," Drusilla suggested to the others.

Gypsy dropped the squirrel leg back onto the plate as if it were too hot to hold. "Oh. Oh, well, you see, I'm afraid I don't know any."

"Well, then, Clarence," Drusilla said, "I think it's your turn."

Gypsy sheepishly followed their lead as they bowed their heads over their plates and Clarence gave thanks to the Lord for providing them with the food they were about to eat, after which they all ate heartily enough, though the children didn't seem to be in their usual high spirits.

"It's because of the Klan," Drusilla said. "We all have some pretty bad memories. . . . Well, then, children, maybe we'll just skip our lesson tonight, and I'll read you something from the Bible."

And so, after the dishes and pans were cleaned and put away, they all gathered around the dying campfire, and Drusilla, by the light of a coal oil lantern hanging from the limb of a tree, read to them.

Watching her, Gypsy saw in her face and heard in her voice

a goodness and a gentleness that touched him in a way that he had seldom been touched before. At the same time, however, he felt so alien to it all. It was as if he were a stranger standing in darkness and peering through a window at a fire-lit scene that he could never share, as if he were a creature who lacked the capacity for such experiences.

He pushed himself to his feet. "I best be making my rounds, see the section leaders, and all."

"You kids go ahead, say your prayers and go to sleep," she said. "I'm going to walk a ways with Mr. Smith."

"You not going far, is you?" Sassy asked.

"No, honey, I'll be right back. And don't you worry, the Klan's not going to be coming around here tonight—not with Mr. Smith close by to protect us." With a look she asked Gypsy for confirmation.

"That's right," Gypsy responded. "Don't you be afraid now. We ain't gonna—we won't let them Klansmen get you."

Drusilla accompanied him across the crowded campground only far enough to be out of the hearing of the children, then stopped and said, "You're not a Christian man, are you, Gypsy Smith?"

"No, Miss Drusilla, can't say as I am."

"Were you ever?" she asked, as if there might be hope in history.

"Oh, when I was a kid, I reckon."

"What happened?"

He shrugged. "I grew up."

"You think it's just for children then?" she asked in a tone that held no trace of challenge or argument.

"Oh, I don't know," he said, slightly abashed. He hadn't meant to make such a flippant answer, but it had been a long time since anyone had tried to engage him in a personal conversation on such a serious level, and flippancy was his instinctive way of avoiding being drawn in. It was his way of remaining on the outside looking in. "I reckon it's for anybody that it helps." He shrugged again. "Whatever gets you through the night."

She nodded. "Well, good night then," she said, and reached out to give his arm a light brief touch before she turned and walked back toward her camp.

CHAPTER NINE

AFTER THEY HAD CROSSED THE BORDER INTO THE CHEROKEE Nation, immigrant trails from other parts of the country began to converge, so that a Conestoga wagon from, say, Stonetown, Ohio, might suddenly find itself in tandem with a mule-drawn cotton wagon from Needmore, Georgia, or a sleek teamed surrey from South Carolina—all on their way to Indian Territory.

Most of the converging immigrants were white, and they went their own way, singly or in small groups, but occasionally a band of Negroes would come out of a side road, and many of them, having been harassed along the way by the Ku Klux Klan, joined the caravan for protection, so that by the time the caravan reached Tahlequah in the Cherokee Nation it numbered nearly a thousand persons—all Negroes except for one, a woman whose white skin was not her only notable difference. She also had a harelip. Her name was Eula Rasmussen. She was from Minnesota and had walked all the way to the Cherokee Nation leading an old mule loaded with tarpaulin bundles containing household goods, clothes, and food—everything that she owned in the world. She was dressed in a threadbare coat, a patched ankle-length dress with a mud-caked hem, and a sunbonnet, one of those field hand bonnets with an oval projecting brim designed to protect the wearer's face from the sun. It also gave protection from curious and pitying eyes.

As a baby, born to some unknown mother who didn't want a harelipped child, Eula had been abandoned on the steps of an orphanage in Minnesota, and her deformity left her little or no chance of being adopted, so she lived in the orphanage for fourteen years and then was sent out to live and work on a farm.

It was a hard and lonely life. But Eula didn't waste time

feeling sorry for herself. She was a sensible girl. She recognized that she would never have a normal life, with a husband and a family, and she must make the best of it, and the best she could hope for would be to have a farm of her own someday, a home in which she would not have to hide her deformity by eating in dark corners. So that became her prayer, her hope, her obsession. From her meager wages as servant and field hand, she saved every nickel and dime she could, counting the coins, counting the days, the months, the years. Her best guess was that she would have enough money to buy herself a farm by the time she was forty or fifty years old.

Then she heard about the free land that could be had down in Indian Territory by any settler who could win out in a land rush, so she used her nickel and dime savings to buy herself a mule, packed all her worldly belongings on its back, and headed down the road.

She first came into contact with the all-Negro caravan when she found herself sharing a campground with it on the outskirts of Tahlequah. It had rained a little that day, causing her matches to get wet. She went to Drusilla Pointer's camp to ask for some live coals from her fire.

Drusilla was very suspicious of the white woman at first because of the way she kept her face hidden beneath the sunbonnet and the way she put her hand over her mouth when she spoke. But when she caught a glimpse of the ugly split in Eula's upper lip that exposed her teeth and gums, Drusilla's suspicions melted to sympathy and pity and shame.

Leaving Tahlequah the next morning, Eula Rasmussen, leading her mule, walked along the road with the caravan, not as part of it but as if she and the caravan were merely traveling in the same direction at the same speed. But she usually stayed within talking distance of Drusilla Pointer's wagon, so that the two of them could exchange idle snatches of conversation to help pass the time of day.

That night in the campground when Eula once again came to Drusilla's campfire to ask for some hot coals, Drusilla asked her to stay and share their supper of hush puppies and turnip greens, and so grateful was Eula for the invitation that she ran back to her own fireless camp and took from her pack a jar of cherries that she had brought all the way from Minnesota. She took it back to Drusilla's camp and used the Dutch oven to make a cherry cobbler for their dessert.

Thereafter Eula joined Drusilla and her small band every night for supper. She never came empty-handed or went away without doing some chores around the camp: washing dishes, fetching wood, carrying water, helping cook. And when two of the children—Sassy and DeLacy—drank some ditchwater and came down with stomach cramps and diarrhea, it was Eula who scoured the roadside woods for herbs that, when made into a strong tea, soon had them healthy again.

But the final bond of their partnership was forged when they were halfway across the Creek Nation, only three days away from the Oklahoma District. It was then that Drusilla woke up to find that one of her mules was dying. The mules had been staked out to graze, and the dying one had either eaten something poisonous during the night or just got tired of living. But the mule's death, for whatever reason, left Drusilla in a predicament. Now she would have to either drop out of the caravan or abandon her wagon and most of her belongings, including the books and other classroom paraphernalia with which she had planned to start a new school in the new land.

Well, she certainly wasn't going to drop out. She had come too far to quit now. She figured she could pack the cooking utensils and food stores on the back of the remaining mule, and by carrying a bundle of clothes and personal belongings on her own back, and with the children carrying their own bedrolls, they would just have to walk the rest of the way to the Oklahoma District.

But when she started to unharness the remaining mule, Eula said, "Wait," and went back to her camp. She brought her own mule to Drusilla's wagon, harnessed it to the wagon with Drusilla's remaining mule, tossed her belongings onto the wagon, and said behind her hand, "Let's go to Oklahoma."

They reached Fort Reno on April 18, four days before the run. By this time the caravan was back down to about five hundred immigrants, the others having left the caravan to make the run from other entry points along the District's borders. And of those who had made it all the way, even the complainers were now glad that Gypsy Smith had driven the caravan so relentlessly. Without the four days to rest themselves and their exhausted animals, they wouldn't have had a chance in the run.

The rest did wonders for their spirits, too. As they recovered from the ordeal of the exodus, they began to share the yeasty feeling of excitement that was growing more intense every day among the thousands of land seekers who were gathering along the borders of the Oklahoma District. And it was more than just circus excitement they felt. There was something else in the air, something that few, if any, of them had ever felt before or would likely ever feel again, a feeling that they were part of something bigger and more important than themselves, a feeling of belonging to a primal horde, poised to obey the edict of their God to go forth and subdue the land, and make it fruitful, and multiply.

Gypsy felt it—a rare feeling. For most of his life he had been a loner and never expected to be anything else. But that last night before the run, as he sat with Drusilla and the children around their campfire (Eula was somewhere in the background shadows, her head lowered so that the sunbonnet hid her harelip) and listened to the sounds of celebrations coming from the other campfires along the starting line, he actually enjoyed the giddy feeling of belonging to something bigger and more important than himself: a place, a people, a tribe, a family.

Drusilla must have sensed what was going through his mind, for when he got up to leave, she walked a little way with him. A three-quarter moon and millions of stars lit the landscape, so they didn't need a lantern. They skirted the neighboring campfires and found a place of some privacy beneath a big cottonwood tree in a dry wash, where they stopped.

"And what about you?" she asked. "What'll you be doing tomorrow night? Your job'll be finished."

"Yeah, but I 'spect I'll stick around for a little while, see what happens. Oughta be real entertaining, seeing people start a town from scratch."

"We all wish you'd be part of it."

"Well, I tell you something, Miss Drusilla—"

"Oh, I do wish you'd stop that!" she snapped.

Genuinely puzzled and apologetic, he said, "What? Stop what?"

"That *Miss Drusilla* stuff! It sounds so—so patronizing."

"What's 'patronizing'?"

"It means you sometimes treat me—you treat me as if I

were a child and you were an old man. I'm not a child, Gypsy Smith, and you're not an old man."

"No, no, you sure ain't no child, Miss Drusilla, honey, but, well, the fact is, I got a lot of years on you. Hell, I'm nearly old enough to be your—"

"Never mind." She turned to face him in the shadows again, moving within arm's reach in case he wanted to reach for her. "That's not important. Not to me. Is it to you?"

She was wearing a shawl against the chill of the April night, and as an excuse to touch her, he reached out and adjusted the shawl on her shoulder. Then he let his fingers stray up her long smooth young muscular neck to her cheek.

"Right now, Miss Drusilla, honey, it don't seem important at all."

He pulled her to him and kissed her mouth. She put her arms around his neck with the eagerness of someone greeting a long-lost lover. Pleasantly surprised by her eagerness, he bent down and picked her up with his arms around her slim waist and held her so that their mouths were on the same level. Then he lowered her back to earth so he would have his hands free to press and caress her small high buttocks beneath the gingham dress. She was breathing fast now and covering his mouth and face with many kisses, but when he made a motion to lay her down on the green grass beneath the cottonwood tree, she, as if suddenly waking up, said, "No," and pushed away from him. Taking a moment to catch her breath, she added, "I'm sorry, Gypsy," leaving off the "Smith" for the first time. "I want you to know that, but I won't be having any bastards, thank you. There're too many of 'em in the world, as it is."

"I know, and I kind of hate to hear you talking about 'em like that 'cause I happen to be one."

"I am, too. That's why I'm not having any."

Gypsy took a moment to let his erection subside before he tried to think straight, then said, "I figured as much." He sighed. "Drusilla, honey, you wouldn't want me to lie to you."

"Course not."

"And I wouldn't want to do it neither. I got too much respect for you to do that. So I think maybe I ought to tell you something. Hardly a night's passed on this trip that I didn't think about you in my bed. But I didn't do nothing, you see, 'cause I figured you was the marrying kind. I ain't."

" 'I'm *not*,' " she corrected.

"You're not?"—astonished that he could be so wrong about her.

"Yes," she said. "No," she said. "I mean, you're right. I am, you're not."

"That's what I—"

"Never mind." She pulled the shawl around her shoulders. "I'd better be getting on back." She hesitated for a moment to give him a chance to stop her, and when he didn't she said, "Well. Good night."

He watched her walk away through the moonlight and shadows. He heard crickets singing in the woods behind him, and from the myriad campfires strung out along the starting line the sounds of celebrations continued. He waited, listening, trying to sort out his feelings the way he could sort out the sounds, but that seemed impossible, so he walked on up the dry wash toward the grove of mesquite trees where he had pitched his bedroll in the camp of the caravan's section leaders. But he was too restless to stay in camp, so he got his bridle and went to a pasture behind the campground where he had left his hobbled mare to graze. He slipped the bridle over her head, took the hobble off her legs and hung it on the limb of a nearby tree, then grabbed the mare's thick mane and swung himself up onto her bare back.

He needed to do some thinking, and for this he rode to a treeless knoll about a quarter of a mile behind the campfires, where he stopped and looked across the vast moonlit prairies. The mare shook her bridle, snorted, stamped, and shivered as if she, too, took delight in what she saw. Gypsy patted her neck.

"Take a good look, Girl. Tonight it's still God's country, just like it was when He first made it. By this time tomorrow night every last piece of it'll be claimed by homesteaders. And by this time next month you won't be able to recognize it for the plowed fields and sod shanties."

He wondered once again if he had done the right thing in helping to bring the settlers here. This was a country he had loved since he had first seen it so long ago—twenty-four years ago, to be exact, when he was fifteen years old and had just been set free from slavery. His father and owner, Chief Smith, had told him that he and his mother would always have a home on the huge Smith cotton plantation near Vinita in the Cherokee Nation. But Gypsy (Wannicha in those days) decided he wanted to go adventuring into the West where the buffalo and wild Indians lived. His mother, who had no desire to leave the plantation, had asked him why he was going, and he had said, "I'm gonna get me some of that freedom people been talking about." And it was freedom that he had found on the pristine prairies of the West. He remembered that he could ride forever across these vast lands without coming to a single fence, a plowed field, or a farmhouse. He came to love the country and the Indians he found there. They were the freest human beings he could imagine. And he developed a special kinship with the Comanches. They were the greatest horsemen he had ever seen. They took him in and taught him about horses and gave him one of their women as a wife. They had called him *Ts'noxtaha*—Black Panther, or Black Big Cat, because of his uncanny ability to stalk game. Later they had called him Black Buffalo Killer because of his uncanny ability to kill buffalo, and this was a name of which he had finally become ashamed. When he had first become a buffalo hunter, he had thought that the buffalo were as numberless as the blades of grass on the prairies, but within a period of ten years he had seen them reduced from countless millions to a pitiful few, and he repented the part he had played in the monumental slaughter.

And now, by bringing in settlers, was he helping to kill the land as surely as he had helped kill the buffalo?

From where he sat astride his bareback mare on the knoll, he could see the endless line of campfires that traced the western border of the Oklahoma District. It was an impressive sight, but when seen from a distance the innumerable fires no longer evoked feelings of belonging, no longer made Gypsy feel himself to be a part of a primal horde. Now he felt himself to be only a spectator, more an Indian than an immigrant, and so he no longer was impressed with the comparison of the immigrants to a biblical horde about to go forth and subdue a land promised to them by their God. He knew that what he would see tomorrow at noon when the line broke would not be a spectacle of biblical grandeur. What he would see would be a truly historic spectacle of human greed.

CHAPTER TEN

THE MORNING OF APRIL 22, 1889, THE DAY OF THE FIRST RUN into Indian Territory by homesteaders, broke clear and fair. The immigrants arose early to stoke their campfires and cook breakfast. Some also cooked a noonday meal that would have to be eaten on the run. They examined their various conveyances for the last time to make sure that the iron tires were tight on the wheels and that axles were well greased. Those who had someone to stay behind and guard their belongings stripped their wagons to the bed boards. Others left the wagons themselves and prepared their dray horses and mules for riding.

Troops of cavalry from Fort Sill, Fort Reno, and Fort Supply had been sent to patrol the line and prevent the runners from stampeding into the District before the starting gun sounded. As the noon hour drew near, the patrols disbanded and the cavalrymen took up individual positions within seeing and shouting distance of one another all the way along the line.

Leading his black mare, Gypsy wandered for most of the morning among the black immigrants, discussing problems, advising, exhorting, encouraging, but by midmorning he was putting his own mount through warm-up gallops. Amos Fulton, the representative of the Oklahoma Immigration Association, had persuaded him to make the run himself in order to try to secure one of the three claims on which were located the springs that formed the headwaters of Cottonwood Creek. These would be the three most valuable claims in the vicinity of the new townsite, and it was imperative that they not fall into unfriendly hands, for the new town would need the water from the springs to survive until wells could be dug. Five other horsemen—all Negroes, all with good mounts—had also been persuaded to make a run for the three allotments, in hopes that at least one or two of them might succeed.

Gypsy thought he had as good a chance as any. Among the horses making the run were Kentucky thoroughbreds that could outrun his black mare over a distance of three or four miles but couldn't outlast her over a course of seven or eight. And the Indian ponies had more endurance than Girl but couldn't match her long-distance speed. Gypsy figured there weren't many horses in the run that could beat Girl over the ten-mile distance to the headwaters of Cottonwood Creek. Besides, he probably knew the country better than any of the other riders, and that would be his edge.

He had ridden by Drusilla's camp early that morning for a cup of coffee and a flapjack and returned a few hours later to see how things were going. They had stripped the wagon of everything except a canteen, and all the children except Clarence were being left behind with the belongings.

"Clarence'll be back to get you as soon as we stake a claim," Drusilla promised as she and Eula climbed up on the wagon seat. "Oh, Sassy, do stop that crying, will you, child? Clarence'll be back for you before dark, honey, I promise."

Sassy was afraid of being abandoned again.

Gypsy escorted Drusilla's wagon up to the starting line. In some places—the best starting places—the line was already two or three deep with horses and wagons and buggies and buckboards and bicycles and foot runners, but Drusilla, with Gypsy's help, managed to jockey the wagon into a good place in the front of the line. From there she could see horses and equipages and people of every kind and description strung out all along the starting line from horizon to horizon, with the animals and the people growing more tense and excited as the morning slowly ticked away toward high noon.

When the troopers took up their individual positions along the line, each had a carbine or pistol in one hand and a synchronized watch in the other. And as the minutes ticked down, they kept their eyes on the watches and their fingers on the triggers.

When it became quiet enough to talk without having to raise his voice, Gypsy touched the brim of his hat to Drusilla. "Well, then, here we go. Best of luck to you, Miss Drusilla."

"You, too, Gypsy Smith."

He touched his hat to Eula, too, but she didn't see him because of the sunbonnet. "And good luck to you, Miss Eula."

She had her hand over her mouth when she glanced up at him, so he couldn't see if she was smiling, but there was excitement in her voice when she said, "Thankee kindly. You, too."

A dead silence settled over the line. The troopers raised their carbines and pistols, pointing them into the air, and waited for the last few seconds to tick away.

At high noon the troopers fired their weapons, and at that moment a great roar of release was heard all the way up and down the line, from horizon to horizon, as the runners, in a dam burst of tension, echoed the signal shots with shots of their own, with accompanying yells, shouts, whoops, and screams as the mighty horde plunged forward in a convulsive movement, as if impelled from behind by some tremendous force. What the settlers had come to call the Damnedest Race in History was under way.

The riders on the fastest horses leaped into the forefront of the convulsive mass. Some of them raced only to the nearest section markers, which were no more than a few hundred yards from the starting line, and leaped from their running horses to stake their claims and then drew weapons to defend them, while all around them other riders and vehicles careered onward in a stampede that would not—could not—stop. Buckboards and buggies and wagons knocked into one another, some locked wheels, some overturned. One rider's horse stumbled within a few yards of the starting line and pitched headlong onto the ground, and the thrown rider didn't even have time to regain his senses before the moving wall of hooves and wheels hit him. A woman in a buggy just behind him tried to swerve, but her buggy slammed into a buckboard, the wheels of the two vehicles locked, sending both flying end over end, to smash to pieces on the rocky ground, the crashing sound accompanied by the broken-bone screams of humans and horses thrashing around on the ground as the oncoming riders and vehicles bore down on them.

The dangers of collision and getting trampled lessened as the mass pulled away from the starting line and began to fan out and break into fragments, but vehicles continued to be lost all along the way. Some smashed their wheels on boulders.

Others flipped over. Others, pulled by panicked, runaway horses, plunged into ravines and gullies at full speed and smashed.

The foot runners hardly had a chance to stake a claim, but they ran for all they were worth, bringing up the rear, where every allotment already seemed to have two or three claimants, and some of the claimants, with knives and guns drawn, were in fights to the death to settle their claims.

Gypsy saw only a little of this. He had left the starting line with the lead horses, though he himself didn't try for the lead, not at first. He knew how far he had to go and what pace would put him there first. So he put Girl into a steady lope, and after a mile the front-runners had begun to winnow out. Gypsy counted only eight riders in front of him, all mounted on good horses, most of them probably headed for the valuable allotments at Cottonwood Springs. One of them was a black man named Leroy King, who had been one of the caravan's section leaders, riding a Kentucky thoroughbred. Two or three of the others were also Negroes, but probably half of them were white men mounted on racehorses, some of whom were already a half mile ahead.

At about two miles Girl began to blow, getting her second wind, and at three miles her neck and chest were becoming lathered and her nostrils were flaring as she sucked in huge amounts of air, accompanied by groaning sounds, but Gypsy could tell from the steady rocking rhythm that she was nowhere near faltering. That was more than could be said for some of the horses ahead of him. Three of the front-runners had begun to falter badly, allowing the black mare to gain ground on them rapidly enough to overtake them within another mile or two. And while the thoroughbreds in the lead were no longer gaining ground, they were still holding their half-mile lead, and Gypsy began to realize that the black mare was going to have to be tested as she had never been tested before.

He saw one of the front-runners go down. All the riders had been checking the pace of their mounts when ravines had to be crossed, but finally one of the front-runners, desperate to take the lead, tried to cross a ravine without checking his pace, and the horse went down and didn't come up. Neither did the rider. And when Gypsy crossed the ravine, he saw that the horse had

cartwheeled, throwing its rider against the opposite bank of the
ravine about twenty feet away. The horse was thrashing around
on the rocky bed of the ravine, probably with a broken leg, and
the rider was lying where he fell, either unconscious or dead.

That left only four: Leroy King, on his Kentucky thoroughbred, and three white men, one riding a buckskin, another riding a sorrel, and the other one—the one in the lead—riding a
big beautiful chestnut stallion. All were racehorses, and all had
obviously been trained for a long-distance run.

The next front-runner to go down was the sorrel. It had been
losing ground rapidly, and then its legs went wobbly, though it
staggered for maybe a hundred yards more. The rider managed
to slip off the horse and then stood looking on with scorn and
despair as the horse, blood pouring from its nostrils, collapsed.

That left three in front, and it wasn't long before Leroy
King's thoroughbred began to falter. Leroy had to slow the
horse's pace to avoid running the animal to death, with the result that Gypsy had almost overtaken him by the time they
were approaching the low rolling tree-covered sandhills that
lay between the racers and the Cottonwood Springs allotments.

Gypsy knew these sandhills, and it was here that he made a
move that could prove decisive for him. He and all the other
front-runners had been following an old freight road that
swerved to avoid a barrier of deep-sand gullies and ravines
where a freight wagon could sink up to its axles; but a man on
a horse who knew the country could detour through the sandhills and cut at least a mile off the distance of the wagon route,
and that was what Gypsy did. He veered off the old freight
road and across the prairie, heading directly for the sandhills.
He quickly found the narrow old trail he was looking for and
pulled the mare down to a fast trot as he rode into the scrub
oak thickets and broken ground. The slower pace through the
difficult ground gave Girl a breather, which was also according
to plan.

When Gypsy came out of the sandhills and back onto the
old freight road, he was at least a quarter mile ahead of the
chestnut and the buckskin. Now *he* was the front-runner.

The other riders, astonished when they saw him come out of
the sandhills onto the road ahead of them, laid their quirts to
their horses in an attempt to catch up, but the buckskin simply
had no more to give, no matter how viciously its rider laid on

the quirt. The chestnut stallion, on the other hand, did have more, and he gave it all in a burst of speed that finally brought him up even with Gypsy.

Now it was between the two of them, though Gypsy thought that Girl still had the advantage. From now on it was mainly a matter of making the right moves at the right time.

As the chestnut pulled alongside him, the two horses running neck and neck, Gypsy glanced at the rider—a well-dressed young white man in a black Stetson hat and a Prince Albert coat, the tail of which flapped in the wind—and nodded in respectful recognition. The white rider returned the salute by touching the tip of his quirt to the brim of his hat. The two horses were lathered and blowing hard through distended nostrils. Slobbers of foam dropped from their mouths, and the sounds of their hoofbeats mingled in a continuous roar.

They were within a quarter mile of the old cow camp and about three quarters of a mile from the Cottonwood Springs when Gypsy made his move. He leaned forward and shouted, "All right, Girl! You ready? Here we go!" He took off his hat and slapped it against Girl's haunch and touched his spurs to her belly, and within three strides she was in full, flat-out run. Gypsy leaned forward to reduce the wind drag and used his hat to fan Girl's haunches as she mustered the last reserves of energy from her blood and bones to move the muscles that rippled with wondrous precision throughout her black shiny sweat-drenched body as she thundered across the land.

"Lay it on, Girl! Lay it on!"

The big chestnut, lashed by the rider's quirt, made one last desperate, lunging burst of speed that brought him once more alongside Girl, and the two horses ran neck and neck for about half a mile.

"He-yah!" shouted the white rider as he quirted the chestnut stallion. "He-yah! Go! Go!"

With manes and tails flying in the wind, flaming red nostrils distended, sides heaving with every groaning intake of air, foam flicking from the bits in their mouths, eyes wide and bulging, and hooves hitting the ground as rhythmically as drums, the two animals ran without heed of bursting lungs and breaking hearts.

With Gypsy and the white rider leaning forward in their saddles, casting sideways glances at each other now and then, with shouts of "He-yah! He-yah!" and "Lay it on, Girl! Lay it on!" they thundered through the old cow camp neck and neck.

Both horses began to fade before they reached the parcel that contained the springs, but the chestnut faded faster than the black mare, and soon, realizing that he had lost the race for that allotment, the chestnut's rider broke off. He gave Gypsy another salute with his quirt, then turned his breaking and stumbling stallion toward another, less valuable parcel.

"You did it, Girl!" Gypsy shouted. "Bless your heart, you beautiful thing, you did it."

He pulled her down to an easy lope as he neared the 160-acre allotment that was now his for the staking. It was a pretty piece of land, with plenty of post oaks and maples, with meadows of April green bluestem grass sloping gently down toward the cottonwoods and black gum trees that marked the spring and outlined the gently winding course of Cottonwood Creek.

CHAPTER ELEVEN

WITHIN TWO HOURS AFTER THE RUN STARTED, EVERY LOT IN the old cow camp townsite had been claimed. Some lots even had as many as three and four claimants. By two o'clock tents were going up everywhere—hundreds of them, of all shapes and sizes, from pup tents to the big round top that would open that night as a café, hotel, and saloon. And by three o'clock two lawyers had already opened their offices for business, their offices being nothing more than upended wooden crates that served as desks.

By three o'clock those who had made the run on foot began to straggle in, as did those who had failed to find any unclaimed quarter sections. By nightfall perhaps as many as a thousand people had converged on the townsite, all of them

Negro (the white homesteaders who were drawn to the encampment took one look around and kept going), most of them
losers in the race, and many were broke and hungry and de-
jected, not knowing where to go or what to do now.

Those who had been successful in getting town lots gathered
before dark on the lot reserved for the town hall to celebrate
and congratulate and listen to a speech by Amos Fulton of the
Oklahoma Immigration Association, who, addressing the
crowd from the bed of a wagon, suggested that the town be
named Freedom. Other all-Negro towns—six in all—were
planned and platted by the Oklahoma Immigration Association,
but Freedom was the first to have a name, a town council, and
a town marshal and on that basis laid claim to being the first
all-Negro town in Oklahoma Territory—or, for that matter, in
the United States.

But since some of the disputes over town lots were becoming gun and knife fights, and many of the runners who had lost
out were in an ugly mood, and squatters on public lots would
have to be removed, the immediate need for a law officer was
obvious, and Fulton, who had been at Guthrie Station the day
of the shoot-out between Gypsy Smith and the Beeson gang,
suggested Gypsy be given the job. The crowd concurred by acclamation.

Fulton sent a boy called Fast Talking Charlie out to Gypsy's
claim to tell him the news, but Gypsy wasn't on his claim. He
had hired an old man, one of the many losers in the run, to
stay on his claim and guard it against claim jumpers while he
went looking for Drusilla.

She had staked a claim about three miles southeast of the
townsite on a quarter section that had very few trees and no
water. Her mule and Eula's had pulled the old worn-out wagon
as fast as they could during the run, but that hadn't been fast
enough to get to the townsite before all the best surrounding
homesteads had been taken. So they had jolted in the wagon
across the broken land southeast of town for hours and finally
stumbled across two unstaked quarter sections side by side,
about three miles from the townsite.

"They're ours!" Drusilla cried as she and Eula leaped from
the wagon and ran to drive their stakes into the rocky soil on
opposite sides of the surveyor's mound.

Drusilla and Eula stood guard on their claims while Clarence took the wagon and went back to pick up the other children and their belongings. He returned about an hour before sundown, and Eula took her mule and belongings and went to make camp on her own claim.

Gypsy found Drusilla's camp shortly before sundown. She and the children were unpacking the wagon. They were all excited by the novelty of having land that they could call their own, but Drusilla was worried, too, because by now somebody else had also staked the claim. While looking for the best place to make camp, she had found a family of claim jumpers—a man and wife and three children—behind a small hill on the southeast corner of her quarter section. With their flagged stake in the ground, the family was in the process of unloading their own wagon and building a campfire when Drusilla, seeing their smoke, went to investigate. The man—a farmer in faded and patched bib overalls—claimed that he had been there first, but Drusilla was sure that she had seen the man's wagon moving through the area *after* she had already driven her own stake.

"What can I do about them?" she asked Gypsy.

"They're not sooners?" Gypsy asked, referring to those people who had ridden into the District a day or two before the run, hidden out in gullies or thickets, and then, as the legal claimants drew near, dashed out of hiding to claim choice allotments as their own.

"No. I saw their wagon in the run, but I know I was here first. I'm sure they just couldn't find another claim, so they put their stake on mine. What can I do?"

Growing ever more dismayed and disgusted by the chaos that the run had created, Gypsy said, "Fight it out, I reckon."

"Oh, for heaven's sake, Gypsy Smith, you're surely not suggesting I go over there and have a shoot-out with them."

"That's what a lot of folks seem to be doing."

As if to illustrate his point, a crackling of rifle fire could be heard coming from some distant claim to the northeast.

"Well, there's no piece of land in this world I want bad enough to kill anybody for," Drusilla said.

"Look," Gypsy said, "the only thing I know for you to do is, you get over to Guthrie Station soon as you can, to the Land Office there, and file your claim. If them others don't do the same thing, the place is yours. If they do, the way I understand it, you both have to get lawyers and witnesses and all that sort of thing, then go before something called the Land Commission, and they'll decide who gets the claim."

He smothered a curse, wondering who in hell—or in Washington, as the case might be—could think up such a crazy way to give away land. Instead of a lottery, say, or a simple drawing of names from a hat, some people in Washington had come up with a method that would bring out the very worst in people, that would incite them to the limits of their rapacity and greed. As a consequence, there were dead people and animals and pieces of broken vehicles lying scattered all across the whole District, and the worst was probably yet to come. Yesterday the runners had been celebrating their kinship in the primal horde; today many of them were bitterly disappointed losers who were forming into marauding gangs, and many of the people who had managed to stake legitimate claims would lose them in front of a gun before the night was over.

"Look, I best get on back to my own claim while I still got one," Gypsy told her, "but I'll drop by later, see how you're doing."

On his way back to his own claim he saw many people on foot and horseback and in conveyances still scrambling here and there across the land, desperately searching for a claim that had been overlooked. But there was one rider—Fast Talking Charlie, mounted bareback on a big Clydesdale draft horse—who wasn't looking for a claim. He was looking for Gypsy. He had a message for him that he delivered in such a rush of words that it was almost incoherent.

"Wait a minute, slow down," Gypsy said, but even after Charlie had slowed down enough to be coherent, Gypsy still couldn't believe what he was hearing. "I been what?" he asked.

"Yeah that's right Mr. Fulton he talk to the folks and they all 'gree the new town be named Freedom and you be the town marshal."

"Oh, hell," Gypsy groaned.

CHAPTER TWELVE

ON THE FIRST DAY OF THE NEW CITY OF GUTHRIE, ITS CITIZENS formed an assembly of forty, one from each state in the Union, for the purpose of nominating candidates for a city council, and with the help of a few volunteers from among the settlers who had had previous experience in politics or government, the forty-man assembly became a reality before the sun went down. And before the night was over, the assembly, working by lantern light in a Baptist tabernacle tent, hammered out a city charter that called for Guthrie to be governed by an elected city council of five men and a mayor, with elections to be held by voice vote on the following day.

The forty-member assembly chose the nominees for the five city councilmen from among themselves, and the next day the city council, having been duly elected by acclamation from a crowd of thousands gathered in Government Square, held its first meeting in the tabernacle tent and began to pass laws.

One of these councilmen in the new city of Guthrie was Shelby Marcellus Hornbeck, a man to be remembered, an anomaly: a seemingly unassertive man who loved power. He was barely twenty-eight years old, but he was already a leader—had always been a leader. As a boy growing up in South Carolina, Shelby Hornbeck had been the one among his peers who quietly took charge. He somehow always seemed to end up ruling whatever roost he found himself on. And that was exactly what he intended to do in Oklahoma: get rich and rule the roost. As a humble beginning, he got himself appointed to the assembly that wrote Guthrie's city charter, and then got himself elected one of the five members of the city council, and then almost got himself elected mayor. It was only his youth and lack of experience that lost him the mayoral election. The mayoral candidate who got the loudest chorus of yeas from the settlers gathered in Government Square was a middle-aged man who had once been the mayor of Springfield, Ohio.

This loss in no way daunted Shelby Hornbeck. For the time being, he would be satisfied to be the leader of the five-member city council and establish for himself the reputation of a man who was reasonable, generous, and just. In this, too, he was successful, though it soon became apparent to the other councilmen that Shelby Hornbeck was not perfect. He had one blind spot: he was a man with a quiet but profound contempt for the dark-skinned races.

This racial bias wasn't any liability to a political career in Oklahoma Territory, for the vast majority of his constituents shared it, but Shelby's preoccupation with racial matters did sometimes get in the way of the council's more important business. Shelby proposed a poll tax law, for instance, and the other councilmen thought it was a good idea, not only because it would bring revenues into the city treasury but also because it would effectively keep any riffraff and vagabonds— black *or* white—from voting in city elections. However, they thought Shelby was just wasting their time by proposing a law that would make interracial marriage a criminal offense, as well as a law that would make it illegal for colored and white children to attend the same school, not to mention a law that would prohibit colored and whites from eating in the same restaurants or even being buried in the same cemetery.

What was the point? There weren't more than two or three hundred Negroes in all of Guthrie. Why take the council's time dealing with something that didn't require immediate attention? There were more important things to do at the moment, such as establishing a fire department, creating judgeships, getting the squatters off public land, licensing businesses—things that were essential to the operation of a city that had sprung up in a wilderness overnight.

So Shelby Hornbeck's proposals for racial laws were put aside. Even so, it was his attempt to introduce the laws in the first place that brought him to the attention of the one man in the Oklahoma District who had the power to help him realize his greatest political ambition of becoming the first elected governor of the future state of Oklahoma.

That man was Milton Ford. When Milton Ford, ensconced in the opulent elegance of his private railroad car, heard of Shelby Hornbeck's good works on the city council, he sent his private secretary to fetch the young councilman for an interview. The secretary, Leonard Gerke by name, found Councilman Hornbeck emerging from the council tent for the noontime recess on April 28, a date that Shelby Hornbeck was not likely ever to forget. Gerke introduced himself and informed Shelby that Mr. Ford would like a word with him in his private railroad car.

"You've heard of Mr. Ford, I expect?" Leonard Gerke asked.

"Of course." Shelby found the question slightly insulting. Though perhaps not quite as well known as Vanderbilt, Rockefeller, or Carnegie, Milton Ford was nevertheless a man of renowned riches and far-reaching powers, and even to ask Shelby Hornbeck if he'd heard of him was to question his intelligence. "What's he want with me?" He shouted to be heard above the sounds everywhere of rasping saws, banging hammers, horses neighing, the squeaking of ungreased wagon wheels, the jangle of trace chains and harnesses.

Gerke couldn't say. "But there's no reason to be apprehensive," he said, an answer that Shelby also found slightly offensive. Who was this effete Yankee secretary to suggest that Shelby Marcellus Hornbeck might be apprehensive about meeting *any*body?

Shelby followed him through an area where tents were packed so closely that it was difficult to walk between them without stumbling over tent ropes or stepping over cooking fires, then out onto the wagon road that led past the Land Office building, around which, in a long and sinuous queue, thousands of homesteaders awaited their turn to enter and register their claims. Shelby had heard that it would take four or five days for the average homesteader to file his claim at the rate the queue was moving. Seeing the weary and tortured faces of the homesteaders who had already been waiting in the queue for two or three days, Shelby once again appreciated the perquisites of power. He and the other city officials had been allowed to enter the back door of the building and register their claims ahead of everybody else.

Two guards, armed with sawed-off shotguns, patrolled the

area around Mr. Ford's private railroad car, and a U.S. deputy marshal on the observation platform acted as doorman when Shelby followed Gerke up the steps and into the car's interior. Paneled with polished walnut, hung with tapestries, lit by crystal chandeliers, upholstered in plush red velvet, with walnut parquet floors and gilded cuspidors, tasseled window shades, and Chippendale chairs, the parlor of the car had the look of a Faustian fantasy. A partition of elaborately carved and polished walnut separated the front section, the parlor, from the room in the rear section of the car. The connecting door, kept closed, might have come from some ransacked palace.

"Excuse me, I'll tell Mr. Ford you're here," Gerke said, and disappeared through the door to the inner sanctum.

There were five other men in the room. One of them—the only one Shelby knew—was Silas Renfro, the United States marshal for the Oklahoma District, a big-boned Kentuckian with a weather-worn face and ice gray eyes. He was standing in front of a map propped on an easel, a plat that showed all the lots in the Guthrie townsite, with many of the lots marked with a red X. He was reading off lot identification numbers and symbols from a piece of soiled and wrinkled notepaper. One of Mr. Ford's executives was standing beside him, locating and marking an X on each identified lot with red crayon. Between the two men were frequent references to arcane matters of relinquishments, powers of attorney, kickbacks, and mortgages. Shelby quickly surmised that the red X's on the plat identified townsite lots that had been claimed by agents and employees of the Oklahoma Land Company, of which Milton Ford was the president.

On the other side of the room was yet another map on an easel, this one a plat of the entire Oklahoma District. Three men worked in front of this map, and Shelby sensed a mood of slight giddiness among them, the giddiness that comes with a mixture of red-eyed exhaustion and prolonged excitement. With sheafs of telegrams and field notes clutched in their hands, they were busy sticking red pins into the map. At one point one of them penciled quick calculations on the back of a telegram, clutched at his red beard, and said with awe, "By God . . ."

"What?" one of his partners prompted.

"By God, if we can hold them all, the Company'll be the biggest landowner in the District."

The door to the inner sanctum opened and Gerke beckoned Shelby into the gloomy interior. Shelby took his hat off as he entered, hearing the sound of Mr. Ford's phlegmy voice rebuking someone.

". . . out! Get it out of here! You expect me to eat this muck?"

Tapestries covered each window in the room, shutting out all sunlight. The only light came from the crystal chandelier, giving the place the gloomy look of a dungeon. In one corner of the room, propped up on pillows on a huge and richly scrolled bed, was Mr. Ford himself, the man who owned railroads and gold mines, newspapers and factories—not to mention congressmen, a governor or two, and lackeys beyond number.

It was one of those lackeys that he was now speaking to, gesturing toward a bed tray in front of him. "Go on, take this swill away. Where'd you get it, out of some pig trough?"

The lackey was an old black man, gray-headed, stoop-shouldered, wearing the rumpled livery and white gloves of a valet, who was nearly as fretful as his master as he said, "I does the bes' I can, suh. I can't hep it if dey ain't got no resrunt here where—"

"Never mind all the excuses, damn your black hide to hell. Just get it out of here, and bring me and this young man each a glass of brandy and a cigar."

"A brandy? A cigah? Fo' *you*? Now, Mr. Fo'd, suh, you knows de doctah he say—"

"I don't give a damn what that quack says." Mr. Ford spoke to the old black valet in the same tone of weary exasperation that a man might use toward a nagging wife. "And I give less of a damn what *you* say. Just do what you're told."

As the valet, grudging and irritated, was carrying out the order, Gerke introduced Shelby Hornbeck. Mr. Ford had no handshake or word of greeting but merely waved Gerke away and said, "Sit down, young man. Sit. Here, Thomas! Where's the brandy and cigars?"

"I's getting 'em, suh, fas' as I can. Ain't got but two hands."

Gerke quietly left the room. Shelby, hat in hand, made some needless adjustment of a Chippendale chair, sat down, crossed his legs, and hung his hat over his knee. All the while Mr.

Ford was saying, "So you're the young man I've been hearing about! They say you're trying to get some laws passed to keep the niggers in their place. Maybe you could get a law passed to send them all back to Africa? How'd you like that, Thomas? How'd you like to get sent back to Africa?"

"Ain't studying no Africa, suh," the old servant said indifferently, as if he were completely immune to his master's gibes and insults. From an ornate side table he brought two glasses of brandy and two cigars on a tray. He served Mr. Ford first, then Shelby, who took the brandy and the cigar even though he didn't drink or smoke. The valet held the match to the cigars. Shelby lit his but let it go out.

"Of course, he wouldn't want to. He's afraid he'd get eaten by some of his cannibal relatives. Right, Thomas? That right?"

"Naw, suh, I ain't skeered a getting et by no cannybull," Thomas answered as he picked up the tray of rejected food and started for the door. "I done worked all de meat off my bones. What a cannybull want with a poor old skin-and-bones darky like me?"

"Work! Why, you thieving rascal, you've never worked a day in your life. You call this work? Hell, if we still had slavery, I'd sell your black ass down the river to a cotton plantation, then you'd see what it is to work."

"Yes, suh," Thomas agreed. He turned at the door. "You want me to go back to dat resrunt, see can I—"

"No. Just get your black ass out of here."

"Yes, suh," Thomas said, and closed the door quietly.

"Huh!" Mr. Ford snorted. "If we'd left them over there in the first place, they'd still be living in mud huts and eating one another." He dipped the unlit end of the cigar into the brandy as he might have dunked a cookie, then sucked the smoke through the brandy-soaked end. Occasionally he took a sip of the brandy, holding the glass in a slightly palsied hand, on which grew fingernails that were discolored and misshapen and were probably half an inch long. He abruptly fixed his eyes on Shelby and said, "Young man, you know who I am?"

Shelby hesitated for a long moment before answering, wondering what answer the old man expected. Of course, he knew who he was, and Mr. Ford knew he knew who he was, so what was he really asking? Shelby searched the old man's wizened face for clues, but the pale prismatic light from the chandeliers and the fog of cigar smoke in the closed room made it difficult for him to read Mr. Ford's face. What he could see was the twiglike body sitting up in bed against the ornate headboard, dressed in rumpled pajamas, hair thin and gray and lank, complexion the fish belly white of an old man who had seldom been touched by the sun.

"Yes, sir," Shelby said finally, and that was all.

"I," Mr. Ford went on to say, as if the question had only been rhetorical, "am, as of today, the biggest landowner in the Oklahoma District. Through one of my holding companies, I now control over a hundred and fifty thousand acres of the best land in the Territory." He puffed the cigar in a self-congratulatory way. "And as soon as we get rid of those red niggers on the reservations, I'll own ten times that much—twenty times maybe. Who knows?" He coughed, cleared his throat, and went on. "And when Oklahoma's made a state, I'll be the biggest landowner in the state." After another brief cigar-puffing pause, another cough and throat-clearing rattle, he said, "Well, I'm sure you'll agree that that makes the political future of the Territory of vital interest to me. Right? Right?"

"I can see how it would, yes, sir," Shelby said, still waiting for the point.

Mr. Ford prided himself on being a very quick and shrewd judge of character, and thus far he had been favorably impressed with Shelby Hornbeck. Thus far Shelby had shown himself to be polite, cagey, and self-composed—all character traits that ranked high in Mr. Ford's esteem. Besides, he was a strikingly handsome young man—not in a pretty-boy way that would make him the target of masculine scorn, but handsome in a rugged, square-jawed, blond-haired way that would win the approbation of both sexes. But most important of all, Hornbeck could be agreeable without being obsequious. Mr. Ford hated obsequious men. They brought out the worst in him. Whenever he met a man who acted like a worm, he felt an irresistible urge to step on him.

"Young man, I assume you're a Democrat? Silly question, I suppose," he went on without waiting for an answer, "since all men in the South are Democrats these days, aren't they? Of course. All white men, that is. Aren't they? Niggers don't count, since you folks down there made it so they can't vote. Stupid idea, wasn't it, giving niggers the vote? It's men like me and you, young man, we're the ones who made this country what it is, but when it comes to voting, why, my vote has no more power than that of some penniless black baboon who can't even sign his own name, his own damned name. I'm a Yankee, of course, but I'll tell you right now, young man, I wasn't in favor of the War. No, sir! Stupid waste of lives and money! And for what? To free the slaves! It's like saying you're going to 'free' a man from his own inferiority, inferiority. Hah! Don't you agree? Don't you?"

Shelby started to say something, but Mr. Ford waved his words away with his cigar. "But that's neither here nor there. I didn't ask you here to talk about a dead issue like slavery, a dead issue. The question is, what're we going to do with the niggers now? What now? They're flooding into Oklahoma by the thousands, with thousands more to come, with a plan to make this an all-nigger state. Can you imagine such a state of affairs? Can you?"

"Yes, sir, I'm very well aware of what blacks do when they get into positions of power. In the South, as I'm sure you know, sir, black legislators were forced upon us during Reconstruction. Anybody from the South can tell you what chaos followed."

Mr. Ford dipped the end of his cigar into the brandy, puffed on it. "Well? What are we going to do about it? Eh? What?"

"Well, sir, as you know, I've been trying to get the city council to pass some laws regulating—"

Mr. Ford waved him to silence. "Yes, I know, I know. And we'll get those laws passed yet, don't you worry, and not just city laws either. No, sir! When this place gets to be Oklahoma Territory, and then a state, well, you can bet your bottom dollar there'll be laws passed to keep the niggers in their place. But laws ..." He shook his head sadly. "Laws aren't going to be enough now, I'm afraid. Not now. You can't make a law against 'em coming out here in the first place, can you? No. And once they're here, you can't make a law against 'em staying, can you? No. I'm afraid we're going to have to have something stronger than laws now, something stronger. Laws won't keep them from pouring in here like droves of cattle, like sheep, trying to make this a nigger state. So what's the answer? What?"

Shelby already knew Mr. Ford well enough to know that the

question was purely rhetorical. Mr. Ford had the answer, and all Shelby was expected to do was to listen.

Making a few dry cracking sounds in his throat that might have been a chuckle or the beginning of a cough, Mr. Ford cleared his throat and said, "I was just thinking, just thinking about that organization you folks in the South got, the Ku Klux Klan. Now, from what I understand, most of the niggers that come out here are running from the Klan. I was just thinking, wouldn't it be something if Oklahoma had its own Klan, to keep 'em running? Keep 'em on the move? Eh?"

So that was it. Up until now Shelby had been puzzled about the nature of this interview, but now everything came into focus. Now he could relax, knowing what was expected of him.

"Well, sir," he said, "I wouldn't be at all surprised if that actually happened."

"You think so? Hah? Think so?"

"I expect so, yes, sir. Most of the homesteaders here are from the South, you see, and it's reasonable to assume, I think, that there'll be Klansmen among them. I suppose it would be the most natural thing in the world for them to get together and form a Realm here in Oklahoma, with Dens in all the major towns."

"You think so, eh? Eh?"

"It wouldn't surprise me, sir," Shelby said slowly, with emphasis, pleased to see that he and Mr. Ford understood each other.

"But what about leadership? Surely there're no Klan leaders among those dirt farmers and drifters that're coming out here from the South. Not leaders."

"Not likely, no, sir, but I wouldn't worry about that. They're here. As a matter of fact, I personally know one of them—a Grand Cyclops from a South Carolina Den."

"Do you, indeed? Well, I'm glad to hear that. Glad to. And if you were to guess how long it might take them to get organized, what would you say? Just speculation, of course. What?"

"Oh, a month or two, maybe. That'd be my guess anyway. But from what I know about the Klan, I don't suppose they'd go into action until the federal government turns law enforcement over to the local jurisdictions. According to my understanding, the Klan tries to avoid any clash with federal troops."

"Sensible," Mr. Ford said with a nod. "Very sensible, indeed. Running niggers out of town is one thing, starting a civil war is another, something else entirely, eh? Eh? Well, then, I'll just have to see what I can do to make Congress give us territorial status as soon as possible. And incidentally," he went on, "speaking of territorial status . . . as soon as we get it, you know, the voters will elect a territorial legislature. Now, the fact is, I'm looking for someone from Guthrie who'd make a good candidate for territorial representative. Somebody I could back, and believe me, when I back a man, I can damn sure get him nominated, and I can usually get him elected. Know anybody who might make a good candidate, do you? Eh?"

"Yes, sir, as a matter of fact, I do."

"Who? Yourself, eh?" Mr. Ford said, as if he could divine Shelby's clever-devil thoughts.

"Yes, sir."

Mr. Ford appeared to give the idea some thought, as if it had never occurred to him before, and then, with a slight frown, said, "Tell me, young man, are you married?"

"No, sir."

"Ah. Too bad, too bad. Voters like their candidates to be married. However," waving that consideration away with his cigar wand, "there's plenty of time for that. Eh? Eh? Well, then, let me ask you this. If you were elected as representative to the territorial legislature, I suppose you'd push to get those Jim Crow laws enacted?"

"Absolutely. As soon as possible. I expect the first thing I'd do is introduce a voting rights bill with a grandfather clause, to keep the blacks from getting the vote."

"Ah. Good, good. And this grandfather clause, it's not unconstitutional? I know it's been in effect in many southern states for a number of years now, for years, but I'm told the Supreme Court might someday find it unconstitutional. What then? Eh? Unconstitutional. What?"

Shelby shrugged. "Then we'll make another law, and if that one is declared unconstitutional, we'll make another. And then, if everything else fails, there's always the distinct possibility that the Klan will become active."

Mr. Ford nodded his approval, took another puff from his cigar, then went into another coughing fit, a severe one this time. A long peal of retching, convulsive coughs ensued with sufficient force to shake the chandelier, and when it ended, Mr. Ford managed to say, "Well, then. Well, what about it then? Eh? As I say, I'm looking for a man to be the Guthrie representative in the territorial legislature—not just any man, mind you, not just anybody. Got to be smart and ambitious and have a real gut hunger for political power. I don't want to be caught betting on some milksop loser. Are you a winner, young man? Are you? A winner?"

"Yes, sir," Shelby answered with quiet but emphatic confidence.

Mr. Ford looked directly at Shelby, then gulped the dregs of his brandy and set the empty glass on the bedside table, leaving his right hand free, which he extended to the younger man.

Shelby rose from the chair and took the outstretched hand. The hand was old and bony, with slack white skin, clammy and cold, and the fingernails were so long they curved like claws.

"You're my man," Mr. Ford said. "My man." And coughed.

CHAPTER THIRTEEN

OVER TWO THOUSAND CHEYENNES AND ARAPAHOS WERE ENcamped around the agency on the night of July 23, 1890. They had been told to gather there to vote on accepting the provisions of the General Allotment Act. Some officials from the Bureau of Indian Affairs had come down from Washington to convince the Indians to accept the provisions of the Act, so that the government could appear to be in compliance with the Medicine Lodge Treaty, the historic treaty in which the Plains Indians had agreed to exchange their Great Plains ancestral homelands and hunting grounds for the land of the reservations, which would be theirs—the treaty promised—for "as long as the grass grows and the rivers flow." Contained within that treaty was a clause that stipulated that the white man's government could not in the future change the provisions of the treaty unless a majority of the adult Indian males voted for the change. So the government went through the motions of having the Cheyennes and Arapahos discuss the matter and vote on it, even though the conclusion was foregone: no matter what the vote, the Cheyennes and Arapahos were going to have to give up tribal ownership of the reservation's 5 million acres and accept individual land allotments of 160 acres each, and the 4 million acres left over would be opened to homesteaders, and that was that, and there was no use to argue about it.

But argue they did, and sometimes very heatedly. In the dusty warmth of the July evening they gathered in front of the agency's administration building, on the gallery of which sat the three representatives from the Bureau of Indian Affairs, a congressman from Indiana, Agent Tanner, a few clerks and stenographers, and two interpreters, one of whom was Maxwell. And though the Indians called the white men everything from betrayers and thieves to forked-tongued devils, the white officials remained unmoved. They had anticipated such objections and insults and, secure in their knowledge that the Indians had no choice but to submit, had steeled themselves against them.

Their only moment of real concern came when Ghost Dancer appeared as if out of nowhere. Most of them had heard of this man, the most feared war chief of the Cheyennes, who had taken on the trappings of a legend. They had heard that he never stayed in one place very long but kept moving here and there among the different bands of Cheyennes and Arapahos and was sometimes reported to have been seen in the Cherokee Outlet or down with the Comanches and Kiowas, either by himself or with a small band of Ghost Dancers. In the last year he had been riding a big beautiful white stallion that had been presented to him by a group of Apache Ghost Dancers, who had stolen the animal from a rich hidalgo's racing stable in Mexico. Though not an albino, the stallion was milk white, with silken mane and tail, all of which, from a distance, gave him a vague resemblance to a cloud, or a ghost, and soon the horse acquired the name Ghost.

And so, dressed in the skins and petroglyphed finery of an Indian warrior of the old days, repudiating everything of the white man's except his metal weapons, Ghost Dancer lived somewhere in the wilderness with a few devoted followers and was seen only rarely when he attended a Ghost Dance in some remote place, far from the prying eyes of white men.

Though the Ghost Dance had been outlawed, it was still spreading through all the reservations of the Plains Indians by the words of Wovoka, a Paiute who claimed to have died and gone to heaven and been told by the Great Spirit that if the Indians faithfully practiced the Ghost Dance, an Indian messiah would soon appear and bring an end to the white man's reign on earth. Wovoka then returned to earth to spread the news of the Ghost Dance gospel. He became the Prophet, and Ghost Dancer was his messenger, and wherever a Ghost Dance was held, Ghost Dancer was likely to be there. The Indian police and the white soldiers sometimes hunted for him, hoping to catch him in the act of Ghost Dancing, so that he could be sent back to prison, but they could never find him. It was said among Indians that he and his horse, like ghosts, could become invisible to the eyes of policemen and soldiers.

No wonder, then, that a hush fell on the crowd that evening in dusty July when Ghost Dancer, carrying a war lance with seven scalps attached—seven white scalps, it was said—and mounted on the sleek white stallion, rode out of the twilight shadows and stopped on the outer edge of the grumbling throng. There, without dismounting, he waited in silence as the news of his presence swept across the gathering like a wind over long grass, causing a diminution of noise that ended in a silence as profound as his own.

And even then he didn't speak. All eyes, including those of the white men on the gallery, had turned on him, but he remained impassively silent until Chief Hehyo, fearing the tension that was building during the long silence, stood up and said in a voice loud enough for all to hear, "We will now hear what Ghost Dancer has to say about this thing."

Gaunt and solemn, Ghost Dancer finally said, "It is useless to exchange words with the white man. His words have no truth or honor. He says one thing today, another tomorrow, and never means what he says." He paused for a moment while Maxwell translated this for the officials on the gallery, and then he added, "So I say this only to the Human Beings who are gathered here to listen once more to the white man's lies.

The day the white settlers come to take our land, that will be a good day to die."

Then he rode his white stallion out of the agency, followed by his retinue, and disappeared into the gathering twilight, leaving the Indians with feelings of both dread and wonder. They realized, as the white men did not, that Ghost Dancer had just made the Plains Indian pledge to sacrifice his life, to "throw himself away," as the Indians termed suicide.

The white men from Washington dismissed Ghost Dancer's words and saw no reason to continue the meeting. It was getting too dark to talk, anyway, and they wanted to get some supper and have a drink or two before going out to see the lunar eclipse that was due to take place just before midnight.

The Indians had heard the white man's prophecies that the moon would disappear for a while that night, but who could take such prophecies seriously? It was just another effort by the crazy white men, by boasting of their magical powers, to frighten the Indians into voting to relinquish their tribal lands. So they remained unconvinced even when, just before the eclipse was supposed to take place, all the white people at the agency began to gather in the square and gaze expectantly up at the full moon in the cloudless sky. Even the students from the school were allowed to leave their dormitories to view the expected event. Their teachers had given them a scientific explanation for the eclipse, lest the students ascribe some supernatural significance to it.

Maxwell stepped out of his house a few minutes before the eclipse was due to begin. Rachel and Dexter were already in the front yard, and Nora soon joined them. It was a measure of her curiosity that she would come out of the house when there were so many Indians about. She counted on Maxwell's presence to give her the necessary courage, but just a few seconds before the eclipse was due to begin, Maxwell deserted her. Seeing some horseplay developing among a few of the older boys gathered in front of the school, he left the yard and walked toward the school. Rachel dashed after him. She took her father's hand as they made their way through the thronged Indians.

"You should've stayed with your mother," he said.

"I wanted to be with you," Rachel said, which was all she needed to say to forestall any further rebuke from him.

Maxwell's presence had the intended effect: the students stopped their horseplay as soon as they saw him approaching. He took his place in front of them with Rachel beside him and pulled a gold watch from his waistcoat and sprung the lid. The hands on its moonlit face stood at 11:08.

"All right," he announced to the students, "any second now."

They turned their faces toward the moon. As they waited, Corby emerged from among them and edged forward, like a metal filing being pulled by a magnet, to stand beside Rachel.

Then a dark shadow began moving—so slowly at first that it was almost imperceptible—across the face of the moon.

The Indians reacted to the beginning of the eclipse with a great collective intake of breath and then for a few seconds were gripped by a profound silence, but soon moans of terror began to be heard. The first shouts were from the medicine men of the tribes, who began issuing frantic orders to the Indians, telling them what to do to frighten the Great Bad Spirit and make it turn loose the moon, so the Indians began yelling and screaming, banging on drums and pots and pans, firing their rifles and pistols at the shadow on the moon. This outburst set dogs to barking and howling, ponies to plunging and neighing, children to crying. And as the black shadow continued to creep across the face of the moon, the pandemonium became more and more desperate and frenzied.

Some Indians began to gash their faces and arms and breasts with knives until their bodies streamed with blood, believing some sort of sacrifice might help. Others hurriedly cut off their hair. Some threw their most precious possessions into their cooking fires as burnt offerings.

But the dark shadow continued to devour the moon, and the pandemonium continued: the shrieking, screaming, the banging of pots and pans, the ceaseless barrage of bullets fired from many hundreds of guns, the howling and yelping of dogs, the crying of children. And the panic proved contagious even to those who didn't believe that the eclipse was a supernatural event. Like buffalo or cattle in a stampede, like patrons in a burning theater, nearly all of them at the agency felt themselves being sucked down into the panic.

The students felt it, and many succumbed. Maxwell felt it, too, the dizzying pull of the vortex toward some primordial horror. But as soon as he realized what was happening, he ran to the teachers and shouted at the top of his voice, "Get the children back inside! Inside! Get them inside!" In the strange darkness of the total eclipse, he pushed Rachel and Corby and others up the school steps.

But before all the children could be herded back into the building, another great hush slowly descended upon the throng when they saw the edge of the moon gradually emerging from the dark shadow. Then, as they began to realize that their tactics had worked and that the Great Bad Spirit was disgorging the moon, the Indians' shrieks and yells of horror turned to shrieks and yells of triumph. They began to chant and dance to show their gratitude to the Great Good Spirit for saving them from the calamity of a moonless world.

Maxwell remained at the school until most of his charges were rounded up and sent to their dormitories. Then he and Rachel went back across the square, threading their way through the singing, dancing, celebrating Indians. When they arrived at the house, they found that Nora and Dexter were no longer in the front yard and that the front door was standing open. Maxwell hurried into the house and was met by Dexter rushing out of the front bedroom.

"It's Mother!" he cried. "Something's wrong with Mother!"

Maxwell found Nora cringing in a corner of the bedroom closet. She, too, had succumbed to the panic. The vortex had pulled her down into it and still held her. Her body shuddered as if with a chill, and her eyes were like those of a small animal caught in a trap.

"Nora?" He knelt and reached for her hand. "Nora, what is it? What's wrong?"

Dexter and Rachel stood behind Maxwell, staring over his shoulders at their mother's stricken face. Maxwell told Dexter to run and fetch Dr. Gresham, then coaxed and helped Nora out of the closet and held her trembling body in a comforting embrace.

"What is it, Nora? What's wrong?"

"I'm—I'm afraid . . . I'm—" She began to weep.

"Afraid? Of what? There's nothing to be afraid of now. The worst is over. They'll quiet down in a little while, and you'll be able to sleep. Come on, lie down now."

"I'm afraid I'm . . ." She faltered again, but then, as if

forcing herself to confess to a dark secret, she said in a small, weeping voice, "I'm afraid I'm losing my mind."

With soothing words and gentle handling, he got her to lie down on the bed and then gave her a spoonful of laudanum to quiet her nerves, for that's what it was, another "attack of nerves," as she called it.

"Nervous exhaustion" was what Dr. Gresham called it. "A condition with many causes and few cures," he told Maxwell, and then added, "You know, don't you, that she's going through the change of life?"

No, Maxwell hadn't known. She hadn't told him. "But she's only forty-six."

"This country ages some women faster than others" was the only explanation the doctor had.

"Will she get better? Afterward, I mean?" Maxwell asked as they conferred on the front porch that night. In the square the Indians were still drumming, dancing, and chanting, but the noise level by now had diminished enough to allow Maxwell and Dr. Gresham to talk without raising their voices.

Dr. Gresham, who had become the agency doctor after the death of Dr. Rooney, was a man in his early thirties who wore a homburg hat, steel-rimmed spectacles, and a brown, bushy beard. Though in a hurry to be gone, he lingered long enough to say, "I don't know, John. I just don't know. Her problems are more than just physical, as you well know, but I don't know what they are. I'm a medical doctor, and I've still got a lot of doctoring to do before the night's over, if you'll excuse me. Three Indians were wounded by stray bullets, one was crushed by a horse, and a squaw slashed herself so deeply she almost bled to death. God Amighty, have you ever seen anything like it in all your born days?" Shaking his head in total dismay, he said, "Well, good night," and stepped off the porch, but turned and added, "I'm sorry I couldn't do anything more, but I think she'll be all right. A few days in bed, she'll be her old self again."

That struck Maxwell as being an infelicitous phrase, and as things turned out, it also proved to be a very incorrect prognosis. Nora was never her old self again. She recovered enough to function around the house, it was true, but never more than in a marginal way. She seemed forever befuddled about something. She would come into a room in her jerky, purposeful steps, only to stop suddenly and look around and say, "Now, what did I come in here for?" And she seldom combed her hair anymore, or bathed, or changed her clothes.

The only thing that seemed to hold her interest was her garden. In a fenced-in area behind the house she had cultivated a plot of fertilized ground in which she tried to grow vegetables, melons, and herbs. In spite of her labors, however, the garden did not thrive, for she often planted things in the wrong place at the wrong time and watered too much or too little. But even though the earth was grudging with its produce and unforgiving of her ignorance, she could be found on just about any day weeding, chopping, watering, digging, working with a sort of dumb distraction, neglecting her house, her husband and children, her personal appearance.

Once Maxwell even found her working in the garden at night. He had thought she had got up to go to the privy, but when she didn't return, he went to look for her and found her on her knees in the moonlight, a trowel in her hands, stabbing and gouging at the rocky soil, thinning a row of turnips.

"What're you doing out here?" he asked gently as he knelt beside her.

"These turnips. I have to work them. They're not growing."

"Because you haven't thinned them?"

"Because this soil is so ungiving," she said. "This country . . . it doesn't like me. Nobody likes me. My own daughter doesn't like me. You don't like me."

"Oh, Nora, dear heart, that's not true." He reached out and gently stroked her graying hair. "Rachel loves you. I love you. We all love you."

She looked at him with surprise. "Do you? Do you, John?" She began to weep. "Do you love me a little?"

"Oh, Nora, of course I do. I love you. I'm sorry if I don't tell you often enough. Please, come back in now."

She let him lead her pliantly back into the house, and he hoped that if he could convince her that she was loved by her family, she might be less obsessed with her plants. But the next day she was in the garden again. Wearing a sunbonnet and a ragged, dirt-soiled old cotton shift, she was once more on her knees, troweling the soil with a sort of meek desperation, as if her body, barren now, had acquired an obsessive need to bring some form of new life into the world, to nourish it and watch it grow, before it was too late.

Too late for what? She didn't know. But she always seemed to be glancing over her shoulder as if she expected to see someone or something—an Indian, time, the end—creeping up on her. Then one day in September it finally happened: she glanced over her shoulder, and this time she saw it, something that struck terror in her heart. It had the appearance of a cloud, but a very peculiar cloud, a sort of huge gray-green mass against a backdrop of burnt-blue summer sky, with the sun sparkling off the top side of it in places as if reflecting off something wet. Scum was what it most resembled, an enormous tide of scum moving massively toward the agency, thick and dark in its center, thin and frayed on its edges, blotting out the sun and casting the earth in a pale crepuscular light.

Then she noticed that others at the agency were becoming alarmed by it, whatever *it* was. She could see people dashing about, shouting to one another, as if they were about to be attacked, and the mounting terror she felt caused her to run whimpering into the house.

From the side window in the front room she could see the mysterious cloud coming. She could also see Maxwell and Rachel leave the school building and, holding hands, race across the square toward the house. She saw students begin streaming out of the school, carrying blankets and sheets and odd pieces of clothes, running toward the school's garden.

"Grasshoppers!" Maxwell said as he burst into the room, puffing from the short run across the square; then to Rachel: "Go get Dexter. Hurry! Now, look, Nora, we don't have much time. We've got to cover as many of your plants as we can before they get here. Grab quilts, blankets, tablecloths, everything—winter coats, gunnysacks—anything we can use to cover the plants in the garden."

He dashed into the front bedroom and jerked the quilts and sheets off the bed, pulled the oilcloth cover from the table as he hurried through the kitchen, and then slammed out the back door, headed for the garden.

Nora still couldn't quite comprehend what was going on, but being told that her plants were in some sort of danger stirred within her a fierce protectiveness. She hurriedly stripped the beds in Dexter's and Rachel's rooms, then dashed into the garden.

The cloud was descending upon them, darkening the sky, a great mass of millions of grasshoppers, countless millions on murmuring wings. A few in the vanguard had begun to drop to earth here and there, striking the ground with a *plop* sound that was almost like hail, and within a few seconds after they had hit, they hopped onto the nearest green leaves and began to eat.

As Nora bent to spread the covers, a few grasshoppers landed on her shoulders and head, *plop plop plop*, and began to tug at her dress and sunbonnet with their jaws, eating the cotton cloth. She uttered small cries and tried to brush them off, but then the main body of the cloud descended. It was as if a blizzard had suddenly struck. Grasshoppers poured out of the sky like enormous snowflakes, in swirls, in torrents, a deluge of flying, crawling, hopping, ravenous insects. So numerous were they that within a few seconds the earth was covered with them to a depth of two or three inches, a squirming mass of bodies that crunched under boots like compacting snow, covering every inch of ground, every building, every plant and shrub and blade of grass. Cornstalks bent to the ground under their weight, bean vines were mashed flat, branches snapped.

Nora shrieked. With grasshoppers completely covering her body, eating at her clothes and sunbonnet, crawling up her legs under her skirt, crawling on her face, in her eyes, in her hair, she shrieked and stumbled around, trying frantically to brush the insects off. Feeling the grasshoppers entangled in her hair, she ripped off her sunbonnet to rake them out, but immediately her hair filled with them so that, Medusa-like, it seemed to come alive in a squirming mass.

Maxwell tried to restrain her, but she tore away from him, shrieking, trying to rip off her clothes, clawing at the grasshoppers on her face so frantically that her fingernails raked bloody scratches in her skin. She stumbled and fell thrashing among the grasshoppers on the ground, squashing so many beneath her that her dress became covered with a brown slime, all the while shrieking, wail upon wail, broken only when she gasped for breath or spit out the grasshoppers that got into her open mouth.

Maxwell picked her up and carried her through the unrelenting blizzard of grasshoppers to the house, and it was only by an act of will that he himself didn't panic as the insects crawled all over him, up his legs on the inside of his pants, down his collar and into his shirt, in his hair, everywhere, gnawing at his clothes. He carried her into the front bedroom and dropped her on the bed. To his horror, he saw that some of the insects had managed to get inside the house, but a far greater horror for him was Nora's continued thrashing and clawing and shrieking as he held her down on the bed. Her panic seemed to have gone into the realm of madness. In trying to claw the insects out of her hair, she had crushed many of them, matting her hair with the brown slime, and now, rather than try to get them out of her hair, she was trying to pull her hair out.

He pulled Nora's hands together behind her back, and then, holding both her hands in one of his, jerked one of the flimsy curtains off the window. He used it to tie her hands and then used another curtain to tie her feet. By now her body was exhausted enough to become still, but the sounds themselves were unceasing, the wails, moans, and sobs of a mindless horror.

CHAPTER FOURTEEN

"SOMETHING NEEDS TO BE DONE, JOHN," DR. GRESHAM SAID one day in December. They were in Maxwell's office. "I know of a pretty good asylum up in Ohio. Rather expensive, I'm afraid, but they do look after their patients. I could write and see if they'd take her."

"Would she like that, do you think?"

"I doubt she'd know the difference, to tell the truth." He scratched at his bushy beard. "Well, it was just a suggestion. The fact is, John, she's not getting the attention she needs. She needs to have someone with her all the time. The fact is, it may be dangerous for her to be alone."

But where was Maxwell to find a woman who would take care of Nora? He could have hired one of the older Indian girls from the school, but given Nora's hatred and fear of Indians, there was no telling what she would do if one tried to feed and bathe her. The wives of the agency's employees had been helpful in the beginning, but they had families of their own to take care of. A classified advertisement in the *El Reno Dispatch* had brought only one applicant for the job, a slatternly, snuff-dipping hillbilly woman, who left after just one week, declaring that if she had to take care of that crazy woman one more day, *she* would go crazy. She stole some of Nora's things when she left.

After Dr. Gresham had gone, Maxwell stood at the window and gazed down at the schoolyard as the students poured out of the building for a fifteen-minute recess. The first snow of the year had fallen, covering the earth in a blanket three or four inches deep, and the children were eager to play in it, build snowmen. Of late Maxwell had often stood like this at the window during the afternoon recesses and watched Rachel and Corby. When everything around him seemed to be nothing but a jumble of dark confusion and failure, he had only to watch the two children at play for a few minutes to feel that he had, after all, done *some*thing worthwhile in life. At such moments he sometimes found himself wishing that Corby were his son. However, it was clear that he could never even consider adopting an Indian boy as long as Nora was alive, and especially not Corby.

"If only she . . ."

But he never finished the thought. He could rationalize and say that Nora, suffering as she was, would probably be better off dead, but the thought stopped in a flush of shame and guilt.

That evening at supper he told Dexter and Rachel what Dr. Gresham had suggested. Dexter was aghast.

"A crazy house? He wants to put Mother in a crazy house? No! Never! Never, by God, as long as I have a breath left in my body!"

These days Dexter seemed to look for pretexts to show that he was equal to any man, and the superior of most, and his job at the agency gave him ample opportunity to prove it. As one of the agency's census-and-allotment clerks, he never let the Indians forget how much power he had over their lives.

Maxwell was sorry now that he had used his influence with Agent Tanner to get Dexter the job. So few jobs were available to the Indians who graduated from the school every year, Maxwell thought the job should belong to one of them, but Dexter, having graduated from school and begun to shave, had let it be known that he would soon be going off to Guthrie or Oklahoma City to look for work, and Nora, before her breakdown, was desperate to keep him at home as long as possible, so Maxwell had interceded with the agent to get the job for him.

"Dexter, nobody *wants* to put your mother in an asylum. I'm just telling you what Dr. Gresham says. He says—"

"I don't care what he says. Being put in one of them crazy houses'd kill her, and you know it."

"I don't know any such thing. But I do know that she's not getting the kind of care around here she needs. Now, maybe you'll want to challenge that? Go ahead, and I'll tell you how the doctor came in here today and found her lying on the floor near a dead stove, half frozen, and why? Because you neglected to come home this morning, as you were supposed to, and put wood on the fire and make sure she was all right. Do you call that taking care of her?"

Dexter stared at his plate for a moment, chastised, but he was bristling again when he looked up. "I couldn't help it. I was swamped with work. We're supposed to process a hundred Indians a day, and we can't do half that many with the help we've got, and them red niggers arguing with us all the time about their allotments. I don't see why Rachel can't do more. Her going to school's not half as important as what I'm doing, and I can't just walk out anytime I want to."

"Red niggers?" Maxwell said. "Red niggers? Now, from which of your smart aleck friends did you pick up *that* term?"

"Mr. Tanner—that's what he calls 'em," Dexter shot back in a tone that implied that if it was good enough for Mr. Tanner, by God, it was good enough for *him*.

As Agent Tanner had grown older and more enfeebled, he had more and more left the running of the agency to his subordinates. As a result, the chief clerk and his underlings became powerful people, and as one of four census-and-allotment clerks hired especially for the complex task of assigning the Indians their individual allotments of land, Dexter was in a position to exercise a great deal of power over their lives. The pay wasn't bad either. With a salary of forty-five dollars a month, Dexter soon found that he could afford to buy himself a new suit, a pair of kid gloves, and a bowler hat. And in keeping with his new status, he allowed himself to take an occasional evening meal at Bixby's Hotel and Boardinghouse, where he could hobnob with men of his own kind, men whom he could envy and admire, ambitious men from big cities who, in response to the government's announcement that the Cheyenne-Arapaho lands would soon be opened for settlement, had begun converging on the reservation by the hundreds to make fortunes in land speculation and town development schemes. Dexter loved to sit at one of the big dining tables at Bixby's, rubbing elbows with these admirable men and listening to them talk of arcane schemes and hoodwinked fortunes. And whenever they learned that Dexter was one of the agency's allotment clerks, they flattered him by offering him cigars and pumping him for any information that could help them. What's more, they seemed to think his reference to Indians as red niggers was very witty.

That Maxwell didn't think so was no concern of his. He was a man now, doing important work, and no longer to be chastised like a child. So when Maxwell said, "I don't care what Tanner calls them, you know I don't like to hear racial slurs in this house," Dexter pushed his plate away and stood up.

"Then I'll go eat at the hotel. At least nobody there tells me what words I can and can't use." He made a contemptuous gesture toward the table. "And the food there don't taste like pig slop." He slammed the door as he left the house.

Maxwell stared down at his plate for a moment, then pushed it away. Dexter had at least been right about the food, it did taste a little like pig slop. He and Rachel had thrown together the meal with foods poured from tin cans—corned beef hash, spinach, hominy—and Rachel had made a batch of biscuits that tasted like hardtack.

"You're not hungry?" she asked. She had spots of flour on her face.

He shook his head.

Rachel pushed her own plate away. "I'm not either." She sighed, as if released from some unpleasant obligation.

"Maybe we should go to the hotel, too," Maxwell joked.

Rachel started to speak but was silenced by something she saw behind Maxwell's back. He turned to see Nora in the bedroom doorway. Leaning against the doorjamb, bracing herself with both arms, dressed in a rumpled nightgown, her gray hair uncombed, gaunt and frail, she stood in the lamplit shadows, staring at them with meek mad eyes.

CHAPTER FIFTEEN

FOR A WEEK OR SO AFTER THE RUN, FREEDOM HAD A POPULA-tion of about two thousand people—Negroes, all of them. Most of them were settlers who had lost out in the run, and they were glad to take jobs as carpenters, laborers, masons, well diggers, waiters, and washerwomen. This labor force, combined with substantial investment capital coming in from Negro businessmen in the North, resulted in the rapid construction of a town hall, a schoolhouse, and a cluster of falsefronted buildings on Main Street that would eventually accommodate all the stores and offices necessary to a small town.

"Boomtown fever," as it was called, was acute in Freedom, where the builders not only experienced the excitement of seeing a town taking shape before their eyes but enjoyed the additional novelty—most for the first time in their lives—of being able to vote for their town officials, of being able to elect men of their own race as their leaders.

But Gypsy Smith was not happy. He had nothing but goodwill and admiration for the people who were building Freedom, but he didn't want to be the town marshal. He didn't want the responsibility. And the salary was too small to be an inducement. Since he had insisted on sharing with Chickasaw Charlie, Nat Sayers, and Joe Peek the rewards for killing the Beeson gang, it had taken a couple of months for the monies to be doled out; but he finally received his share, and he figured he would spend most of it on a trip to Mexico, maybe even go to South America. He had sometimes wondered what Argentina would be like.

But he made the mistake of allowing Mayor Amos Fulton to talk him into being the marshal of Freedom. "At least for a little while," Mayor Fulton pleaded, "until we can find somebody else who can handle the job," though this was somewhat disingenuous on the mayor's part because he knew that he would never find anyone for the job as good as Gypsy. "With your reputation as the man who got the Beeson gang, why, there's not an outlaw or troublemaker in the whole Territory who wouldn't think twice before trying anything in Freedom. We need you, Gypsy."

Gypsy was flattered to be considered so valuable, but the only person whose opinion could affect his decision to go or to stay was Drusilla Pointer.

Drusilla had been hired as Freedom's new schoolteacher. The officials had decided to build a school as soon as possible on a site at the north end of town. The plans also called for a three-room cabin to be built behind the schoolhouse as a rent-free residence for the teacher. It was to be a subscription school, financed by parents of the students, and the teacher's salary was to be thirty-one dollars a month.

Drusilla couldn't have been more delighted. She figured, in fact, that the hand of the good Lord must have been in it somewhere for things to have worked out so well for her and her brood of tag-along foster children. Now she would be saved not only the time and expense of building her own cabin but also the time and expense of making a legal fight for her claim. So she and the children broke camp, loaded the wagon with their belongings, borrowed Eula Rasmussen's mule, and moved to Schoolhouse Hill, where they pitched their camp until the teacher's cabin could be built.

Gypsy knew that Drusilla hoped he would stay around. She had said so. But he reminded himself that she might not mean anything special by it. That was just the way she was. She had a particular caring spirit that made her different from all the other women he had ever known, and it was that capacity to care, that generosity of spirit, that Gypsy found so appealing.

And yet it was this difference that made him reluctant to

push his advantage with her. It was unfamiliar ground. And he
felt the same way about her being Negro. He had never before
been involved with a black woman. His wife had been a Comanche, and after she died, there had been a Kiowa girl who
took his fancy for a while, and a few years ago he had spent
some time with a Mexican girl over in Santa Fe, but she was
a whore, so she didn't count. As for Negro women, there had
never been any in his adult life, not one, and he didn't know
quite how to deal with them, what the signals were, what was
expected of him.

So it wasn't strange that he was having a hard time trying
to figure out what he really felt about her. He didn't have a
name for it, except that it was an entirely new kind of feeling,
a kind of protectiveness. But there was one thing he did know:
if he stayed in Freedom as the town marshal, it would be because of her and not because of Mayor Fulton's pleas.

Then something happened that profoundly affected his
growing intimacy with Drusilla: Lieutenant Beauregard Pierce
came to town. Lieutenant Pierce was a troop commander of the
Buffalo Soldiers, the all-Negro 10th Cavalry Regiment stationed at Fort Sill on the Comanche-Kiowa reservation. Although all the Buffalo Soldiers were Negro, Lieutenant Pierce
was the regiment's only Negro officer.

No doubt the best known of all the Buffalo Soldiers, Lieutenant Pierce's fame began when he was graduated from the
U.S. Military Academy at West Point. He was one of the first
three Negroes to do so and the first to be graduated with high
honors. In addition, he was one of the fourteen Buffalo Soldiers who had received Congressional Medals of Honor for
bravery above and beyond the call of duty, the enemy in this
case having been a band of Comanches who had left the reservation for a raid into Mexico. Three troops of Buffalo Soldiers pursued the Comanches, and in the ensuing battle on the
banks of the Rio Grande, Lieutenant Pierce had, at the risk of
his own life, saved the life of his white commanding officer,
for which he received the Medal of Honor and a promotion to
first lieutenant and the command of his own troop.

Like the cavalry units from all the other forts in the Territory, the Buffalo Soldiers had been brought in to help police
the run, and then Lieutenant Pierce took them around to the
all-Negro towns that had been established during the run. He

wanted to show the southern Negroes, who were in need of heroes, some bona fide black heroes.

Although Gypsy had never scouted for the 10th Cavalry, he had met Lieutenant Pierce a few times in the field and considered him a passing acquaintance. But when the lieutenant greeted Gypsy that day in Freedom in the town hall tent, Pierce almost made it seem that they were long-lost friends. With an outstretched hand, a curt military nod, and a small practiced smile, he said to Gypsy, "Well, here he is, the man who got the Beeson gang. Glad to see you again, Gypsy. It's been awhile."

"Yeah," Gypsy said.

"And congratulations on being named Freedom's town marshal. They obviously couldn't have picked a better man for the job."

"Thanks."

Lieutenant Pierce was a tall man with wide shoulders, narrow hips, and long legs, a body whose every movement reflected an at-ease military bearing. He habitually rested his left hand on the hilt of his saber and stood with one leg cocked slightly forward, a stance made famous by Napoleon in his official portraits. Every button on the lieutenant's well-tailored tunic was buttoned, his pants were creased, his boots highly polished. His clean-shaven face, cinnamon brown, seemed as smooth and flawless as silk. His hair was combed like a white man's, parted on the left side by the parting line's being shaved, and it was combed right and left, plastered to his head with pomade.

He included the other men when he said, "I'm going to be here for a couple of days, gentlemen, to give my troops and horses a chance to rest. Where can I find a good bivouac area for my outfit?"

Gypsy volunteered his own claim. "There's water there, and forage, and wood. Half mile northeast of town. I'll show you."

Lieutenant Pierce put his hat carefully and squarely on his head so as not to muss his hairdo. The right side of the hat's broad brim was turned up and fastened to the crown with a cavalry rosette. This turned-up brim was ostensibly for the purpose of allowing him to fire his rifle while at a full gallop, but it also—and perhaps mainly—gave him the look of a dashing cavalier.

"Until tonight, then, gentlemen," he said to the mayor and
the other men, confirming his acceptance of an invitation to
join the city fathers for a small celebration in honor of Freedom's beginning.

He and Gypsy stepped out into the busy and noisy street,
and the first sergeant ordered the soldiers—thirty-seven in all,
with two supply wagons at the rear of the column—to fall in.
An orderly was holding Lieutenant Pierce's big blaze-faced
chestnut gelding near the entrance to the town hall tent. The
first sergeant yelled, "Mount up!" and the column was soon
ready to move out in double file, but Lieutenant Pierce's attention was distracted. He had seen Drusilla Pointer, who had
brought her brood of waifs to see the Buffalo Soldiers. Gypsy
had stopped to speak to her when he emerged from the town
hall tent, and now Lieutenant Pierce, leading his horse, approached Drusilla, touched the brim of his hat to her, and said
to Gypsy, "May I have the honor of an introduction?"

Noting the look of admiration in her eyes, Gypsy introduced
him to Drusilla.

"Mrs. Pointer," the lieutenant called her.

"Miss," she corrected.

"Ah," he said, with obvious delight at the news. "I
should've known. You're not nearly old enough to be the
mother of this robust ménage. Your brothers and sisters, then?"

"We orphans," Sassy said, offering up the one bit of information about herself that was sure to get sympathetic attention
from adults.

Mayor Fulton, quick to see the lieutenant's interest in
Drusilla, stepped forward to say, "Miss Pointer is going to be
our schoolteacher." To her he said, "You'll be coming to the
celebration tonight?"

"I don't know, we've got lots of work to get done."

"Oh, please, 'Silla, can't we come?" Ruby begged, and the
others began with their own pleas.

"I join the children in urging you to come, Miss Pointer,"
Lieutenant Pierce said. "And if there's any dancing, I hope I
can look forward to a waltz."

"Well," she answered, doubtful but flattered, "we'll see."

Lieutenant Pierce once again touched the brim of his hat,
bowed slightly, then swung astride his blaze-faced chestnut
gelding and dashed smartly to the head of the column.

When the first sergeant barked the orders that moved the column out, Gypsy mounted and took his place beside Lieutenant Pierce at the head of the column. Lieutenant Pierce took a silver-handled swagger stick off his saddle horn and used it to salute the people who stopped whatever they were doing to watch and wave to the troops as they rode along Main Street.

"That Miss Pointer," the lieutenant said to Gypsy as they rode along, "what can you tell me about her?"

The keenness of his interest in Drusilla was unmistakable, and Gypsy didn't know quite how to respond. "Not much," he said, opting for a flat, disinterested tone, the better to draw the lieutenant out. "She was with the caravan when I joined it in Tennessee."

"Interesting young woman, don't you think? Very brave, to come all the way out here by herself—without a man, I mean." He gave Gypsy a significant glance. "She *is* alone, isn't she? Hasn't got a fiancé lurking about somewhere?"

The conceit of the man was remarkable. Gypsy could see that the lieutenant had never given any thought whatsoever to the possibility that *he* might have some interest in Drusilla. It wasn't that the lieutenant had thought of it and then dismissed the possibility but that it never occurred to him that a good-looking young schoolteacher could possibly have any interest in an unschooled frontiersman nearly twice her age. It made Gypsy realize that he must be getting on in life, that he had reached some over-the-hill point where younger men no longer saw him as a potential rival. Still, he knew that he had no rights in the matter, being neither father nor lover, so he finally cleared his throat and said, "I spect she's got her eye open for a man, but far's I been able to tell, there ain't nobody around who meets her qualifications."

Lieutenant Pierce smiled as if to say that here, at last, was a man not lacking in qualifications.

So Gypsy was the first to know that Lieutenant Pierce, the boy wonder of the Buffalo Soldiers, had developed more than a casual interest in Drusilla Pointer. Drusilla was perhaps the next to know, though just about anybody at the town celebration that evening could see that the lieutenant had more than a passing interest in her.

The celebration began shortly after sundown. The people congregated along Main Street. A makeshift speakers' platform

had been erected in front of the town hall tent for the benefit
of the town notables, who commenced the celebration with
some ringing oratory. The platform had no bunting, but a banner, made of a number of bed sheets sewn together, was
stretched from the scaffolding of one unfinished building to another across the street, proclaiming in crude letters, FREEDOM,
ESTB. 1889. A band had been put together from the musicians
among the settlers, a few of whom had been professionals in
New Orleans and Memphis, though most were just plantation
banjo pickers and gutbucket thumpers.

In addition to the lamps and lanterns used by the construction workers to light their nighttime labors, the celebrants
brought their own lanterns, and the speakers' platform was lit
with hanging lamps and footlight lanterns.

On the platform, with nail kegs being used for stools, sat
many of the town's dignitaries: Mayor Fulton, of course, and
Preacher Pangborn, as well as Ike Jones, and the town's special
guest, Lieutenant Beauregard Pierce. Gypsy was not among
them.

Preacher Pangborn led the settlers in an opening prayer, asking God's blessing on the new town of Freedom, and then
Mayor Fulton gave a rousing speech about the new Land of
the Negro, where colored folks would at last have power over
their own destinies. The crowd responded with shouts of "Hal-
lelujah!" and "Amen!"

"Up till now," he declared, "most of us've had to live on
white folks' land, or in white folks' towns, having to move every time a landlord come around, saying, 'Nigger, you git.'
Well, you won't be hearing that anymore! This is *your* land.
This is *your* town. And Lord help the white man who ever
comes around here saying, 'Nigger, you git.' "

Next came Ike Jones, the owner and editor of Freedom's
newspaper. He made a short speech that ended with a flag wa-
ver's flourish and the ringing declaration *"Ad astra per aspera!"* Then Lieutenant Pierce, the main attraction, was asked
by Mayor Fulton if he would please say a few words to the audience.

To a burst of applause and encouraging calls, Lieutenant
Pierce stepped to the front of the platform, rested his left hand
on the hilt of his saber, cocked his right leg a few inches
forward of his body, and apologized for not being a public

speaker. In a sardonic voice he said, "I've had some experience addressing troopers, of course, but I can assure you, you wouldn't want to hear what I say to *them*."

The field uniform Lieutenant Pierce had worn earlier in the day had been changed to a dress uniform, a uniform with yellow piping on the sleeves and legs, gold-braided epaulets, a fancy yellow-piped belt with a brass buckle, and a yellow cord with tassels that looped under the epaulets and across the polished brass buttons on the tunic, all of which made him by far the most resplendent man on the platform. And that didn't even take into consideration that not only was he the sole man present who was wearing gloves, they were white gloves.

"But I do want to welcome all of you brave and hardy people here to your new homeland. As you probably know, *Oklahoma* is a Choctaw word that means 'Land of the Red Man.' Now Mayor Fulton refers to it as the Land of the Negro. It is said that the land belongs to those who take it, tame it, and make it bountiful. Up till now that task has mainly been left to the white folks. But you've changed that. You've shown that colored folks can be pioneers, too, and I'm proud of you. You're a credit to your race. As my friend Professor Booker T. Washington said, 'Brains, property, and character for the Negro will settle, once and for all, the question of civil rights: excellence is the best antidote for racial bigotry.' In plain English, we'll show 'em!"

He waited for the cheers and applause to die down and then added in the same climactic tone, "As your distinguished councilman Ike Jones so eloquently said, '*Ad astra per aspera!*' " He paused for a second before he did what Ike Jones had not done: supplied a translation. "To the stars through difficulties!" And as the whoops and cheers rang out, he smiled at Ike Jones as if to say that the newspaper editor was not the only man around here who knew Latin. Then he ended by saying, "But enough of this speech making! I was told there'd be some music and dancing around here tonight. I've been promised a waltz."

He made his way from the platform through the parting crowd to where Drusilla Pointer stood, surrounded by her brood of foster children. Mayor Fulton hurriedly announced that the speakers would now turn the stage over to the musicians and that dancing would commence as soon as the crowd cleared an area in front of the platform. Taking the lieutenant's hint, he suggested to the musicians that their first tune be a waltz. Not many of them knew any tunes in three-four time—that was a white man's rhythm—but the fiddle player said he knew a three-four song called "Love's Old Sweet Song."

Lieutenant Pierce would have preferred a Strauss waltz played by a chamber orchestra, but he knew that "Love's Old Sweet Song" was probably as good a waltz as he was going to get, so he asked Drusilla if she would do him the honor.

She was wearing her Sunday dress, a plain but pretty thing, though wrinkled from having been packed away in a trunk for so long. Her hat was a little boater with white lace ruffles and wax daisies on the crown. Compared with the gold-braided splendor of Lieutenant Pierce's uniform, her attire was downright dowdy, but they did make a handsome couple as they danced.

At first Drusilla was uncertain of her ability to do a grand ballroom waltz, but Lieutenant Pierce led with such ease and grace that she soon caught on. Holding her skirt up with her left hand, as if it were a ballroom gown, she held on to the lieutenant with her right hand and let him whirl her around with the assurance of a man who had studied dance steps with the same fervor that he had studied military maneuvers. With Lieutenant Pierce, everything was by the book.

Soon other dancers joined them. None of them seemed to know how to do such a highfalutin dance, but a few, especially those in the crowd who had been drinking, wanted to give it a try, and their enthusiasm made up for their lack of expertise. Their antics brought hoots and cheers and a rising tide of merriment from the crowd.

When the dance ended, Drusilla was out of breath, not only from physical exertion but from excitement, too. The children, dressed in their Sunday clothes, were standing in the forefront of the crowd, watching Drusilla with wonderment, and when Lieutenant Pierce escorted her back to them, Mingo said, " 'Silla! We didn't know you could dance like that!"

"I didn't either." Drusilla smiled. To Lieutenant Pierce she said, "You're a very good dancer," and he answered in his courtly way, "A dancer's only as good as his partner," and then he added, "But I confess I'm very limited. I'd like to dance with you again, but I'm afraid I couldn't do this sort of thing."

The musicians had begun some syncopated music that was currently popular in the barrelhouses of Memphis and New Orleans, and the crowd whooped encouragement to the dancers who were beginning a cakewalk, a dance developed from walking steps in which the prize of a cake was given to the contestant who showed the most accomplishment in strutting, leaping, prancing, and cutting figures.

At first Drusilla joined the crowd in cheering the dancers, but when she realized that Lieutenant Pierce was viewing the spectacle with what was at best condescending curiosity, she toned down her own enthusiasm. But the children continued their own noisy reaction to the dance, and Link even took a turn out into the dancing area himself, imitating the steps of one of the more accomplished strutters, much to the delight of the other children. Drusilla tried to keep a straight face but couldn't.

"He's a little dickens, that one," she said, and then suffered a moment of confusion, wondering why she felt compelled to offer any mitigation for her delight in Link's antics. Why should she care so much for the lieutenant's good opinion? She wondered if she was smitten by the man.

She was in awe of him, that much was certain, and flattered by his attentions, as what female in the crowd wouldn't be? But what she couldn't understand was, what could a man who wore white kid gloves possibly see in *her*? And when he said, "You have a lovely smile," as they were applauding the end of the cakewalk, she didn't know quite what was expected of her. Had such compliments been flattery for the sake of seduction, she would have known well enough how to take them, but they seemed merely the requirements of a courtly manner, as if they might have been memorized from a book—a book of etiquette, say, with a section entitled "Compliments for Every Occasion."

In her confusion she found herself occasionally glancing around at the faces in the crowd, as if looking for someone who could rescue her.

Gypsy was elsewhere. He didn't want to make a speech, and he didn't know how to dance, so he had stayed away from the area lest he be expected to do either. He wouldn't have minded having a dance or two with Drusilla, as an excuse to hold her, but he didn't know how to do these Negro dances. He could do an Indian dance, but that would hardly have been appropriate, so he busied himself elsewhere in the settlement. His rounds carried him past the dancing area a few times, but it wasn't until about ten o'clock that he stepped up on a nail keg to get a look over the crowd's heads. His eyes swept the musicians, the dancers, and stopped when he located Drusilla. Actually it was Lieutenant Pierce that he located first, since the lieutenant's dress uniform and white gloves made him the most conspicuous person in the crowd. Drusilla was standing beside him, like a little brown hen standing beside a champion cock. The lieutenant smiled down at her and said something, and she smiled up at him and answered. They seemed to be getting on very well. Gypsy went on his way.

Drusilla hadn't seen him. She had been explaining to Lieutenant Pierce in an apologetic voice that she and the children would soon have to be going back to their camp on Schoolhouse Hill. They had been moving all day, she explained, and were very tired and had to get up early in the morning. Sassy, in fact, had sat down on the ground, leaned her head against Drusilla's leg, and begun nodding off. The other children, though still excited by the dancing and the music, were too tired to argue or complain.

"I'll walk you to your wagon," Lieutenant Pierce offered.

"Oh, we didn't bring the wagon. We walked. It's just outside town."

"Then I'll walk you to your camp."

"Oh, I couldn't put you to that trouble," Drusilla said, releasing him from any obligation he might feel to be gallant. "We'll be all right—if Sassy can walk at all, that is. Sassy? Get up, we're going now."

"Trouble?" Lieutenant Pierce said. "Why, it wouldn't be any trouble at all, Miss Pointer. It'd be a pleasure. Besides, some of my troops seem to be pretty liquored up by now, I'm afraid, and if they saw a pretty young woman like yourself walking down the street, unescorted by a man, why, they might just start a riot, and then I'd have to have the lot of them horsewhipped. So you see, real trouble might result if you *don't* allow me to escort you to your camp, and you wouldn't want that on your conscience, would you?" And without waiting for a response, he glanced down at Sassy as she struggled to her feet, sleepy and cross, and said, "Maybe I could carry her to my horse? It's just down the street. She could ride back to your camp."

The lieutenant's chestnut gelding was picketed with other cavalry horses on a rope stretched between two building construction sites. The lieutenant lifted Sassy into the saddle, then said to Link, "You must be tired, too, huh, fella? After all that dancing, you'd probably like to ride, too," and the lieutenant lifted him up behind Sassy and handed the reins to Clarence. "How about you, young fella? You look like a leader. Would you like to lead him?"

By such maneuvers did Lieutenant Pierce manage to get some time alone with Drusilla as they walked to her camp. The three oldest girls went on ahead with Clarence, giggling behind their hands with delight at the courtship, leaving Lieutenant Pierce and Drusilla to amble along by themselves through the settlement and out across the moonlit prairie toward Schoolhouse Hill.

"Don't worry about Trojan," he told Drusilla as Clarence led the horse away. "He's gentle with children."

"You are, too, it seems. You have some of your own?"

"Oh, no. I'm not married."

Drusilla was glad to hear that he assumed he would have to be married before he had children. He wasn't the kind to go around fathering bastards.

"Not much chance of marrying out here," he went on. "As you might expect, marriageable colored ladies out here on the frontier are about as rare as the proverbial hen's teeth. That's one of the reasons we're so glad to see Negro pioneers coming in. Why, it's been three or four years since some of my men have even spoken to a respectable colored woman."

He questioned her about herself, and their progress was so slow across the moonlit prairie that he knew quite a bit about her by the time they reached the hillock on which the angular outlines of the tent stood out in dark silhouette against the backdrop of the moonlit sky.

"Drusilla," he said. "Is it all right if I call you that?"

"Of course."

"My first name's Beauregard. I'd be pleased if you called me that. Beau, if you like. That's what my friends call me, Beau, and I'd like for you to be a friend. I have great admiration for your courage and spirit—a young woman like yourself, I mean, with six children to take care of, and no man to take care of her, coming out here to Indian Territory to be a homesteader. I've never known another woman with that kind of pluck."

"Oh, I don't know. I reckon it would've taken more courage to stay back there and fight the Klan," she said, pleased but discomfited by his praise. "Out here we have the Buffalo Soldiers to protect us," she added in a coquettish voice. She was very seldom coquettish and disliked herself when she was, but there was something about Lieutenant Pierce that seemed to bring it out in her.

At the campsite Clarence had left the lieutenant's horse tied to a wheel of the parked wagon and was now making a pallet on the ground behind the tent where he and Link would sleep. The girls had gone into the tent and lit a lamp and made their pallets on a tarpaulin inside the tent, all the while giggling and gabbing in suppressed voices about Drusilla's new suitor.

"Well, then," Drusilla said when she turned to face Lieutenant Pierce. "Good night. Thank you for seeing me home." And following his example, she clasped her hands behind her back.

"My pleasure, entirely. And I hope it won't be the last time. I'll be keeping the troops here for a couple of days. I'd like to visit with you again before we leave. Tomorrow, perhaps?"

"Tomorrow." She tried to keep from batting her eyes. "Tomorrow! Well, I'll be working all day, getting camp set up, but tomorrow night there'll be a prayer meeting at Preacher Pangborn's tent. I'm sure you'd be more'n welcome to come. You and your men."

"A prayer meeting . . ." He considered the idea and then, with a sudden, approving smile, said, "Just the thing! An old-time prayer meeting. I haven't been to one in years. Not since I was a boy. And would you allow me to escort you to this momentous meeting?"

"Well," she said, and smiled. "Why not?"

He moved closer. She sensed that he was getting ready to kiss her, and she hadn't decided yet if she would let him, though she thought she might allow a small, chaste kiss. Sensing her indecision, however, he turned, mounted his horse, and tipped his hat.

"Good night, then, Drusilla."

"G'night," she said. "Beauregard."

Riding away, he had the distinct feeling that she was watching him go. He didn't glance back to find out, but he swaggered a little in the saddle for her appraising eyes, inviting adulation. Adulation from whatever source was always a satisfaction to him, but to be adulated in Drusilla's eyes would be more than merely satisfying to his self-esteem; it would be propitious. It would crystallize all the vague feelings and plans that had begun to swirl through his heart and head since he first saw her earlier that day. He had liked what he saw, and since then he had learned to like everything about her. He congratulated himself for having found such a woman out here on the frontier, a woman who was not only good-looking, respectable, lovable, maternal, and marriageable but also a credit to her race. Perfect! What more could a man want in a wife?

CHAPTER SIXTEEN

BY SEPTEMBER THE TOWN OF FREEDOM HAD ASSUMED THE ESsential shape and size that it would have for all its days. Main Street was hardly more than a wide path churned and rutted by horses' hooves and wagon wheels, inches deep in powdered dust during the dry season, a quagmire of mud in the rain. Prairie grass and tumbleweeds grew under the protective edges of storefront sidewalks, and the planks in the sidewalks cracked and warped in the summer sun and thundered hollowly to the thuds of boots and high-button shoes. The false-fronted frame buildings that housed most of the town's businesses were clustered along Main Street, while the residents' houses and shacks were scattered helter-skelter across the treeless lots and along the grassy and rutted paths that served as the town's back streets.

The town had two public wells, each with a windmill and water tank, and boasted a telegraph line, a stagecoach stop, a small brick bank, an Abyssinian Baptist church on the south side of town that could seat a hundred worshipers, an African Pentecostal church on the west side that had a twenty-five-member choir, and a two-story town hall with a jail in the basement.

Gypsy lived in the jail. Two cells had been built for prisoners, but when it came time to install the steel bars, the town treasury found that it couldn't afford them, so Gypsy set up rudimentary housekeeping in one of the cells by moving in a cot, a cast-iron stove, and a few pieces of makeshift furniture. He took most of his meals at the hotel's dining room or at the Bluejay Café across the street from the jail and stabled his horse at Cooley's livery behind the feed and grain store.

He had kept his homestead quarter section. He had thought to sell it after the wells had been dug in Freedom and the spring on his claim was no longer essential to the town's water supply. Since there was no urgency to get rid of it, however, he went ahead and made the improvements that the Homestead Act required in order to claim ownership, but mostly he lived in his barless jail cell. Prisoners, when there were any, were kept in the cell next door, chained to the wall. They slept on cots, used chamber pots for a toilet, and their meals were delivered from the Bluejay Café.

Gypsy didn't like most of the duties of a town marshal and finally threatened to quit unless the town's tightwad treasurer agreed to hire a deputy marshal to take over some of the unpleasant chores, such as emptying the prisoners' chamber pots. Thus it was that Buck Tyson, a toothless old black cowboy from Texas, was hired as Gypsy's deputy, not because he was the best man for the job but because he was the only man remotely qualified who would take the job for twenty-five dollars a month and jailer's grub.

Gypsy was glad to get him, though he was sorry to be deprived of his reason to quit. Now he would have to find another, though the real reason he stayed on in Freedom was his unresolved feelings for Drusilla Pointer. It was true that he hadn't seen much of her during the summer because he hadn't wanted to get in the way of Lieutenant Pierce's courtship. But whenever he did see her—in town, at school, or even when she was with the lieutenant—he never failed to feel a confused mingling of emotions that included joy and sadness, a sort of sweet sorrow, protectiveness, goodwill, and an almost aching envy of the man who would make her his wife.

That would be Lieutenant Pierce, of course. The lieutenant and his troops had gone back to Fort Sill as soon as civilian law had been established in the Territory, but during the summer he had made periodic visits to Freedom to court Drusilla. Generally he would arrive on the stage from El Reno, take a room at the hotel, rent a buggy, and then go calling on her. Sometimes he took her and the children to church, sometimes he took them on picnics, and sometimes he and Drusilla went for a buggy ride in the country by themselves. These visits, combined with the frequent letters Drusilla received from Fort Sill, naturally led everyone to believe that the dashing young officer and the pretty young schoolteacher were headed for the altar.

But because Lieutenant Pierce was not the type of man to rush into anything except a battle, his courtship of Drusilla lasted throughout the summer and into the fall. People began to get curious about what was taking them so long, and none was more curious than Gypsy himself. He had decided that on the day Drusilla announced her engagement to Lieutenant Pierce, he would turn in his badge and ride out of town. On those occasions when he saw her, he was tempted to bring up the subject of Lieutenant Pierce, but whenever he did, she got grumpy and withdrawn, possibly her way of saying that it was none of his business. And by the time school started in September, he had virtually given up going to visit her and the children in their cabin behind the school, much to Drusilla's growing displeasure with him, a displeasure that finally erupted into outright anger one Saturday in late September, when she came face-to-face with him on the sidewalk in front of his office.

Hatless, rolling a cigarette, he had come out of the hot stuffy office and stopped on the shaded sidewalk. He leaned against a gallery post and lit the cigarette, then glanced up and down the street, just keeping his eyes on things, and what he saw first was Miss Drusilla Pointer emerging from Frank's General Store and Post Office a few doors down the street. In one hand she held a basket filled with groceries, in the other she held a letter to which she was giving her total attention, and she was smiling.

But when she glanced up and saw Gypsy, her smile vanished. She shoved the letter down into the groceries in the handbasket, saying, "Looky here, Gypsy Smith, why don't you ever come around and see us anymore? The kids miss you."

"The *kids* miss me?" he teased.

"Oh, all right, then, I miss you, too," she grudgingly confessed. "You've even stopped coming to our Thursday Literary Readings. Why?"

"Well, Miss Drusilla," he said, as if making a painful admission, "you know how it goes. Every time I get around you, I can hardly keep my hands to myself, and I got that lieutenant of yours figured to be a mighty jealous man."

"Damn you, Gypsy Smith!"

"Miss Drusilla! Such language! A nice churchgoing schoolmarm like yourself!"

"Well, you're enough to make a preacher cuss, Gypsy Smith." She had started on her way but suddenly turned back. "And don't call me a school*marm*. I'm a school*mistress*. A *marm* is married. I'm not."

"But from what I hear, you soon will be."

"I have hopes. I wasn't cut out to be an old maid, I can tell you that."

"No, Miss Drusilla, you sure wasn't. You're too good a cook for that. Why, someday somebody'll want to marry you just for the way you fry chicken." He nodded toward the two plucked chickens in her shopping basket. "That what you having tonight?"

She held the basket in front of her, both hands clasping the handle. "And giblet gravy, yes. Supper's at six, if you care to come."

"I'll be there, thank you kindly."

"I'll tell the kids you're coming."

Gypsy watched her as she walked away, wondering how long it would take her to resume reading the letter she had stuffed into the grocery basket. Pedestrians and horses obscured her from view now and then, but by the time she was passing Ledbetter's boardinghouse, the last commercial building on Main Street, she had the letter in her hand again, reading it as she walked, and he presumed she was smiling.

The fried chicken that night was fine, and the children enjoyed having Gypsy around again, but there was something bothering Drusilla all evening. She seemed distracted. Gypsy asked her what was wrong, but it wasn't until the next day that she told him. Returning from the barbershop, he found her waiting for him in his office, sitting on a bench with an empty shopping basket beside her. She looked very fetching, in her starched and ironed gingham dress, her high-button kid and cloth shoes, her lace-trimmed straw boater perched on the top of her ringleted hair.

When Gypsy said, "Good morning, Miss Drusilla," she managed a small smile but seemed reluctant to meet his eyes.

"What's the matter?" He hung his floppy-brimmed planter's hat on a peg, but she still seemed reluctant to talk. "Look, you can tell me, can't you? Whatever it is that's bothering you, you can tell your old Uncle Gypsy."

She stared at her hands folded in her lap. "It's just that I have to make a decision, and I wanted to talk to you about it." She took a deep breath. "I got a letter from Beau yesterday. He asked me to marry him."

Gypsy, bowing to the inevitable, tilted his head. "You gonna do it?"

"I'm not sure yet. I wanted to ask you what you thought."

"Why should it make any difference what *I* think?"

She gave him a quick look. "You know damned well it does, Gypsy Smith. Don't play the dunce with me."

After a moment Gypsy nodded again, as if resigning himself, and then walked to his desk and sat down in his chair, facing her. "Well, Lieutenant Pierce will make you a good husband, Drusilla. He's young. He's educated. A distinguished young officer. Like they say, a credit to his race. What more could a young woman want?"

She had resumed looking at her hands.

"You love him?"

"Sometimes I think I do," she murmured, "and sometimes . . ." But then, as if she had almost betrayed some shameless weakness, she threw her shoulders back. "Yes, I do."

"Well, then . . . ? Of course, it'd mean giving up your job as a schoolteacher, wouldn't it? You'd probably have to follow him around from one army post to another for the rest of your life. You willing to do that?"

She got up, grabbed her shopping basket, and stepped to the

door. "Well, I'll tell you one thing I'm not willing to do"—
turning to face him—"and that's end up an old maid. Like I
said, I'm not cut out for that. Good-bye, Gypsy Smith." She
walked out the door, leaving Gypsy to watch her as she walked
across the dusty street and out of sight.

Gypsy felt none of the satisfaction that was supposed to be
the reward of having done a noble deed. He hadn't done
enough of them in his life really to know what he was supposed to feel, but he was surprised that the noble deed of putting someone else's interests ahead of his own would make
him feel like a fool. But as he got used to the idea that he had
just given away a fortune, he began to feel a what-the-hell
sense of relief, a sort of sour comfort in having nothing left to
lose, nothing left to worry about. Good. Drusilla and Lieutenant Pierce were going to be married. Now he felt no further
obligation to stay around town.

Taking the building's central stairway two treads at a time,
he went upstairs and walked into Mayor Fulton's office unan-
nounced. The mayor was behind his desk, reading the *Guthrie
Gazette* through his steel-rimmed bifocals, a look of bilious
displeasure on his face.

At one end of the desk, facing the mayor, sat Ike Jones,
wearing a green celluloid eyeshade, red garters on his
shirtsleeves, red suspenders, and a sweat-stained red bandanna
around his neck—his usual costume while working on his
printing press. On his crossed legs rested a reporter's notebook
covered with penciled scribblings. He had been taking down
Mayor Fulton's reactions to Guthrie's new Jim Crow laws—
CITY ADOPTS NEW RACE LAWS, said the headline in the *Gazette*.

Gypsy took off his badge and tossed it onto the newspaper.
"I quit."

Mayor Fulton didn't seem especially surprised, but he did
need a moment to appraise this development.

"Buck can take care of things around here till you get a new
marshal." Gypsy turned to leave.

"Wait," Mayor Fulton said. "Where you going? What's the
matter? Let's talk about this, all right?"

"Nothing to talk about, Amos."

"But what'll I tell the council? They'll want to know the
reasons."

"And so will my readers," Ike Jones said.

With a small shrug Gypsy said, "Tell 'em personal reasons," and once more turned to go.

Mayor Fulton suddenly stood up, leaned across the desk as if inclined to lunge for Gypsy, and said in a pleading voice, "Can't I persuade you to put personal reasons aside for now? The truth is, Gypsy, we need you, dammit." He tapped the newspaper. "You know about this, don't you?"

"I read the paper."

"Well, these race laws won't stop in Guthrie, you know. Guthrie's already been picked to be the capital of the Oklahoma Territory, and it'll probably be the capital when we become a state, and the people running Guthrie now are gonna be running the state. If we don't stop 'em, they'll have us living under Jim Crow laws every bit as bad as those in Mississippi and Alabama. We've got to fight them."

Gypsy's thoughtfulness didn't indicate reconsideration, but merely an effort to find a way to make Mayor Fulton understand, and finally he said simply, "It ain't my fight, Amos."

This brought Mayor Fulton from behind his desk. He took a few lunging steps toward Gypsy. "You! With your black face? Where d'you think you can go to get away from it?"

"Back to the reservations, to live with the savages. What y'all call civilization's too complicated for this old cowboy."

Mayor Fulton spoke over his shoulder to Ike Jones. "Jones, can't you say something to him?"

Gypsy stopped at the door and turned to hear what Ike Jones had to say.

Jones thought for a moment. *"Quisque suos patimur manes."* He waited for a moment under their puzzled gaze, then supplied the translation: "Each must suffer his own destiny."

"You said it, Jones," Gypsy said, and walked out the door.

Fulton turned on Jones. "You're a big help, you and your damned Latin quotations. I suppose you got one to cover the situation we're in now?"

"Sure," Jones said, glad to oblige. *"Fata viam invenient."*

"And just what the hell does *that* mean?"

"Means we're up Shit Creek without a paddle."

CHAPTER SEVENTEEN

THE RACE INTO THE OKLAHOMA DISTRICT BECAME KNOWN AS the run of '89, to distinguish it from subsequent runs, such as the Run of '92, when the Cheyenne-Arapaho reservation was opened for settlement. And the government, by announcing that April 19, 1892, was the date that the reservation would be opened, effectively announced the date of Ghost Dancer's death. He had publicly proclaimed that the day the settlers took over the last homeland of the Human Beings would be a good day to die.

Three of his followers volunteered to join him in what was essentially a suicide pact—"throwing themselves away," as the Indians called it. They sent out the word that they, just the four of them, would meet the onslaught of settlers on the day of the Run of '92 and kill as many as they could before they themselves were killed. Ghost Dancer even sent a challenge to Colonel Caldwell, the commanding officer at Fort Reno, telling him that he—Ghost Dancer—and three warriors would attack the settlers in a place called Lame Cow Valley, and if the army wished to stop them, the colonel should bring all of his troops to the valley by midmorning on the day of the run and be prepared for a fight to the death.

Colonel Caldwell could hardly believe it. Four Indian warriors, challenging three hundred U.S. cavalrymen? Was the man crazy? If he wanted to kill white settlers, why didn't he use the usual Indian hit-and-run tactics and put the army to the task of chasing him down?

Major Phillips, Fort Reno's executive officer, guessed that Ghost Dancer was trying to draw the troops into an ambush, using himself as bait. And this guess gained credibility on the evening of April 18, when army scouts informed the colonel that Indians from all over the reservation were, as suspected, converging on Lame Cow Valley.

"I thought so," Major Phillips said. "They're trying to draw us into an ambush."

"But the scouts say the Indians don't have weapons and that there are as many women and children among them as there are warriors. So they aren't going there to fight," the colonel reasoned. "Hmm. Spectators, then? That must be it. They must be going to see Ghost Dancer and the other three warriors throw themselves away."

Colonel Caldwell had no choice but to oblige them. It could prove inconvenient, of course, since his troops would be expected to be on the starting line of the run, policing the settlers, but if Ghost Dancer and his cohorts showed up by midmorning, there would be time to kill them and get back to the starting line before the run began. In any event, he couldn't ignore the challenge, couldn't take the chance that some white settlers might be killed by four suicidal Indians. So, early on the day of the run, he marched three troops of cavalrymen, nearly three hundred soldiers, out to Lame Cow Valley, spread them out across the valley in a three-tier firing formation facing the western end of the valley, and waited.

The Indians, converging on the valley from all parts of the reservation, were gathering on the ridges on both sides of the valley.

Maxwell, Rachel, and Corby arrived in a surrey at Lame Cow Valley more than two hours before the run was to take place at high noon. They left the surrey in a draw at the foot of the valley's southern ridge, so that it and the team of horses would be safely out of the way of the settlers during the run. Then they climbed the ridge to where Chief Hehyo and his band had gathered at a vantage point that was almost within shouting distance of the eastern border of the reservation, the starting line for the run. From there they could easily see the settlers jockeying for positions along the line. They were also directly above the place where Colonel Caldwell had formed his cavalrymen into a skirmish line across the floor of the valley. In the center of the skirmish line was the colonel and his staff.

"What is my old friend Maxwell doing in this place?" Chief Hehyo asked after greetings had been exchanged. "Why are you not down there with the white people who have come to take our lands?"

Maxwell lit a pipe, took three puffs, then passed it on to Chief Hehyo as he said in Cheyenne, "I have no wish to take any land from the Human Beings, grandfather."

Chief Hehyo had no teeth at all now, and his mouth was like a slit in his prune-puckered face. He took three deep puffs on the pipe and passed it to the other chiefs. His hair, hanging in braids down his chest, was completely gray now, and his squinted old eyes watered in the bright sunlight, the water gathering at the corners of his eyes and spilling over to run down the deep crevices alongside his large nose, so that he appeared to be continually weeping. And except for a few Indian geegaws that he wore—a bear claw necklace, a beaded buckskin belt, and a few bright feathers stuck in the band of his battered top hat—his clothes were agency-issue, threadbare and shabby, grease-stained and dusty.

"Then you are the only white man who does not." He used the word *veho* as a pejorative. "Look at them. I think the white man must breed like grasshoppers. They come with the greed of grasshoppers and destroy everything in their path. That is what I think."

"I think you may be correct," Maxwell said. "But I have a worry now, and it is not about the loss of lands. It is about the loss of lives. I have been told that the Human Beings have come here only to watch Ghost Dancer and the others throw themselves away, but perhaps the soldier chief is not entirely certain that the Human Beings have not come here to fight, and this uncertainty makes the pony soldiers nervous and afraid. Remember Wounded Knee, where such soldiers killed many Sioux men, women, and children who were neither armed nor wearing war paint. I have a fear that the same thing could happen here."

"We told the pony soldier scouts that we come in peace."

"*Pava.* Good. But perhaps you, Chief He-follows-his-father's-ways, should go down to assure the soldier chief himself that the Human Beings have not come here to fight."

"I will do this thing if my old friend Maxwell will come with me and say the words in the white man's tongue."

Maxwell agreed. Chief Hehyo ordered one of his subchief sons to bring two horses, and after Maxwell instructed Rachel and Corby to stay with the Hehyo band until his return, he and Chief Hehyo rode down the ridge toward the center of the skirmish line. Maxwell waved his white handkerchief as they approached the troops.

Of the nearly three hundred troopers in the formation that stretched almost across the valley floor, about two thirds had dismounted, and horse handlers had taken their riderless horses back to the rear. Some of the dismounted men took kneeling positions in the front of the formation, others formed a standing firing line behind them, while others, still mounted, formed a third firing line, so that each tier of carbines could fire over the heads of the troopers in front and thereby produce a virtual wall of bullets.

Sitting astride a big sorrel in the center of the formation, Colonel Caldwell received Chief Hehyo and Maxwell cordially and said he appreciated the chief's reassurances that the Indians scattered along the ridges were there only as spectators.

"But where is Ghost Dancer?" he asked as he pulled out his watch to check the time. Then he glanced over his shoulder toward the settlers crowding the starting line about three hundred yards to their rear. "If he's coming here to get himself killed, I wish he'd come on and get it over with. Where is he?"

Chief Hehyo answered with a gesture toward the western end of the valley that meant "Out there somewhere."

"Who are the three men with him?" the colonel asked, though he knew who they were. He was simply testing the old chief's willingness to be forthcoming.

Maxwell translated the names: "As far as he knows, Hawk's Head from the Whirlwind band and Little Pipe and Howling Wolf from the Sand Hills band."

Satisfied with the chief's answers, Colonel Caldwell dismissed him with a warning: "If so much as one bullet is fired from either of those ridges, at either the pony soldiers or the white settlers, all the Indians will be considered hostiles—understood?"

Yes, Chief Hehyo understood, and once again he assured the colonel that the Indian spectators posed no danger to the army.

"And make sure they stay on the ridges and don't get in the way of the settlers when the run starts," the colonel warned.

Maxwell started to ride back to the ridge with Chief Hehyo,

but Colonel Caldwell asked him if he would stay with the military formation.

"Since you're the only interpreter the Indians seem to trust," the colonel said, "I'd be much obliged if you'd volunteer your services, just in case I get a chance to talk to Ghost Dancer."

"You surely don't think he's coming here to powwow?"

"No, but I'm not going to kill him unless he gives me no choice."

Maxwell agreed to stay. Chief Hehyo rode back to the ridge.

Major Phillips asked Maxwell if he thought Ghost Dancer would actually show up, and Maxwell said, "He'll show up."

It was a statement that reflected the colonel's own certainty. The colonel knew Ghost Dancer, had, in fact, felt a sort of fateful connection with him ever since the Battle of Little Bighorn, when the colonel had been a twenty-six-year-old captain on General Cook's staff, and Ghost Dancer—Cloud Walker in those days—had been one of the Cheyenne dog soldiers who rode at the side of the legendary Crazy Horse. He remembered that Ghost Dancer killed many 7th Cavalry soldiers during that battle and had even counted coup on General Custer himself.

Colonel Caldwell had not seen battle that day, but he had been one of the first to ride through the carnage of Custer's slaughtered command, and while he had to hate the Indians as savage enemies, he had to admire them as fierce and courageous warriors. During the years since, his and Ghost Dancer's paths had crossed many times, and the colonel had come to admire in Ghost Dancer those qualities that one warrior might admire in another, even in an enemy: bravery, loyalty, pride. So the colonel, unlike Major Phillips, had little doubt that Ghost Dancer would show up. He did, however, wish he would hurry. He was anxious to get his men back to the starting line before the settlers became hysterical with excitement and jumped the gun.

It was just past ten-forty when one of the colonel's uniformed scouts rode up on a lathered and blowing horse to report that he had spotted Ghost Dancer and three other warriors in a ravine at the other end of the valley.

"Making medicine," the scout said. "Putting on war paint."

"All right," Colonel Caldwell told the scout, "pass the word, make sure the troopers are ready. Won't be long now."

Major Phillips said, "If they find out their medicine's bad, maybe they won't come."

"They'll come," Maxwell said.

Major Phillips looked right and left at the bristling arsenal of carbines. "Well, they're crazy as hell if they do."

"No, they're not crazy," the colonel said.

"Then why would they do it?"

Colonel Caldwell gave Maxwell a challenging look. "You tell him."

Maxwell swept his eyes toward the spectators on the ridges. "They're doing it for them."

"For them?" Major Phillips asked.

Colonel Caldwell said, "They want the other Indians to see them make a stand and die."

"Showing them how to live proudly by showing them how to die proudly," Maxwell said.

The major snorted scornfully. "Sounds crazy to me."

"Well, in that case maybe I'm crazy too," the colonel said, "because if I were Ghost Dancer, I think this is the day and this is the way I'd choose to die."

Quite suddenly four Indian warriors in full battle regalia rode up out of a ravine at the far end of the valley, about four hundred yards in front of the troop formation. They stopped abreast on the rim of the ravine, and a great cheer went up from the multitude of Indians on the ridges. Ghost Dancer, astride his milk white stallion, flanked on one side by Hawk's Head and on the other by Howling Wolf and Little Pipe, raised his lance high into the air in response to the ululant cheers. It was the lance from which hung seven scalps.

"Well, by God, there they are." Major Phillips spoke to make more real what still seemed to him utterly fantastic: that four Indian warriors were actually preparing to attack a force of nearly three hundred cavalry troopers.

Murmurs of awe and admiration swept through the ranks of the waiting troopers. When a few along the line took aim and cocked their carbines, Major Phillips snapped, "Hold your fire! Wait for orders!"

All four of the warriors were dressed in Ghost Dancer shirts decorated with bright red sacred designs of suns and horses and flashes of lightning. Their faces were painted in black and red and yellow designs. Little Pipe and Howling Wolf each

wore two eagle feathers attached to their scalp locks, while
Ghost Dancer and Hawk's Head, both chiefs, wore magnificent
warbonnets made of eagle feathers tipped with downy red
plumes. All wore fringed and beaded buckskin leggings and
moccasins. Only Ghost Dancer carried a lance. The others
brandished rifles. Ghost Dancer's rifle was slung across his
back by a rawhide thong.

On their ornately decorated and nervously prancing horses,
the four warriors held their position for a moment, waiting for
the cheers to die down, and then they began to sing their death
songs. The Indian spectators along the ridges fell silent when
the first notes of the high-pitched chant were heard, echoing
between the ridges and down the length of the green valley.

> Man dies,
> The mighty buffalo dies,
> Only the earth and the mountains live forever.

The death songs continued for perhaps a minute, and when
the last notes had echoed down the valley and died in the still
air, Ghost Dancer raised his lance toward the waiting soldiers
and shouted at the top of his voice the traditional Plains Indian
battle cry "*Hoka hey! Hoka hey*, white man! It's a good day to
die!"

The other warriors raised their rifles over their heads, and
each in turn yelled the war cry "*Hoka hey! Hoka hey!* It's a
good day to die!"

Their horses, catching the excitement and tension of the
cries, shuffled and snorted and stamped, but the riders held
them in check until Ghost Dancer plunged his lance deep into
the earth and left it there like a planted flag. He then jerked the
Winchester off his back.

The horses started down the valley in a prancing walk. The
sound of drums began to be heard from the ridges, their
rhythms matching the rhythm of the horses' hoofbeats: slow at
first, and then faster as the horses broke into a trot, and faster
still when the riders slacked the reins and let their horses hit a
cantering stride. And now there was a new sound coming from
the ridges, a sound of hundreds of women trilling in rhythm to
the drums, a strange and unnerving ululant sound.

"Hold your fire," Colonel Caldwell cautioned, and the order

was passed down the line by the platoon sergeants: "Steady, now ... Hold your fire."

The warriors were within range of the cavalry's Springfield 45.70s now, but the colonel wanted to give the warriors every chance to change their minds. But they showed no indecisiveness and, when they had covered about half the distance to the waiting troops, they kicked their horses into a full gallop. The drums and the trilling from the ridges increased in tempo to match the sounds of the pounding hooves. They dropped their reins onto the necks of their horses so they would have both hands free to fire the repeating rifles, and by the time they fired the first shots they were yelling their war cries in full voice.

They were a little over a hundred yards from the troops when they began firing. Their first bullets were wild, but as they levered cartridges into the rifles, firing as fast as possible, the bullets began to fall into the troop formation. Running at a full gallop, they could not aim at anything other than the formation itself and hope for a lucky shot, and out of the first few shots the only thing they hit was a cavalry horse, which screamed and went down thrashing.

"All right, if that's the way they want it," Colonel Caldwell grimly said to Major Phillips, "cut 'em down."

"Fire!"

The first volley from the nearly three hundred Springfield carbines brought down the two outside riders. Little Pipe was knocked off his pony in a backward somersault and never moved after he hit the ground. His wounded pony turned aside and went staggering off across the valley, dragging its entrails. Howling Wolf and his screaming horse went down together, both of them to thrash around in the grass in their death agonies.

To the amazement of the cavalrymen, both Ghost Dancer and Hawk's Head got through the first volley. Both were hit and badly wounded, but both managed to stay on their mounts, and both kept firing. The troopers, in their awe and excitement, had apparently aimed most of their fire at the outriders, leaving it to others to bring down the magnificent warrior on the beautiful white stallion. But when two of the standing troopers were hit and felled by the incoming fire, they were quick to follow the major's orders: "Reload! Fire at will!"

Hawk's Head's pony turned a forward somersault, but Hawk's Head himself, though bleeding profusely from a number of wounds, leaped from the falling horse and hit the ground running. With his broken and bleeding left arm dangling uselessly by his side, he raised the rifle in his right hand and fired wildly one more time before a barrage of bullets tore his body apart.

Ghost Dancer, also bleeding from a number of wounds, got within about forty yards of the formation before the wounded white stallion screamed and reared up into the line of fire. The stallion's body took a hail of bullets meant for Ghost Dancer, who went down behind the stallion's convulsing body.

Shot in the right shoulder, Ghost Dancer dropped his rifle when he fell with the stallion, and a bullet grazed his head, knocking his warbonnet off. The cavalrymen, apparently assuming Ghost Dancer was done for, slacked off in their firing, and that was when he leaped to his feet, pulled a scalping knife from his belt, and started running in a zigzag course toward the cavalrymen, many of whom were so rattled and frightened by the man's ferocity that they could hardly get the cartridges into the single-shot carbines and take aim at him. Many of them, seeing that Ghost Dancer was armed only with a knife, looked to the colonel, wondering confusedly if they should keep firing.

But enough were still firing to knock his legs from under him. By then he was within less than twenty yards of the formation, and even then he didn't stop. One of his legs had been broken by a bullet, but he put the knife between his teeth, and began crawling toward the formation on his belly, his many wounds trailing long swaths of blood on the green grass.

The Indian drums had stopped. No longer threatened, the troopers stopped firing. They watched with horrified fascination as Ghost Dancer continued to pull his bullet-riddled and blood-covered body along the grass toward them with the knife clamped between his teeth.

When he was within ten yards of the line, one of the sergeants in the formation, perhaps thinking to end this grotesque display of savage unwillingness to die, fired one last shot. The bullet had been aimed at Ghost Dancer's head but missed by a few inches and tore away the lower part of his face.

"Hold your fire!" Colonel Caldwell shouted.

Ghost Dancer collapsed facedown in the grass. His body quivered violently for a moment in its death agony. But before he died, he raised his head one last time. With blood streaming from the massive wound to the lower part of his face, he slowly raised his head and stared with ferocious hatred across the few yards separating him from the soldiers. Then his eyes began to close, and his face slowly sank back to rest on the bloody earth. His body quivered once more, then lay still.

The troopers who had been kneeling in the front rank began to rise. From somewhere on the right came calls for a medic. A young lieutenant came riding through the formation to give the colonel a casualty report: "Three men wounded, sir. One might be serious."

"Tell the doctor I'll be along in a few minutes." Checking his pocket watch once again, the colonel glanced over his shoulder toward the settlers on the starting line and then nudged his horse forward. He rode to Ghost Dancer's body and looked down at it. Hearing the women on the ridges beginning to keen for their dead, he glanced up the valley to where the bodies of the other warriors lay scattered in the grass. To Major Phillips he said, "Bring the bugler up."

"Bugler! Front and center!" Major Phillips shouted, and then rode out to face Colonel Caldwell across Ghost Dancer's body. "What call, Colonel?"

"Taps," Colonel Caldwell said, and in response to the major's look of confusion, he added, "These were brave men, Major. I think we can honor them without dishonoring ourselves. We have time yet. Bring the troops to attention."

The bugler emerged from the formation and cantered his mount to front and center. The major called the troops to attention, ordered them to present arms, and told the bugler to blow taps.

Colonel Caldwell and the other officers drew their sabers and held them in salute position as the first bell-toned notes from the bugle silenced all other sounds in the valley. Even the keening and crying Indian women, hearing the white soldier play the bugle sounds over the bodies of the fallen warriors, fell into an astonished silence and then, like all living things in the valley, listened.

As the sounds resonated across the quiet valley, the only movement that could be seen was that of a young Indian leaving the fringe of blackjacks on the valley's southern ridge. He was on foot, dashing across the valley toward the place where Ghost Dancer had fallen.

It was Corby. In his schoolboy's uniform and brogan shoes, and unarmed, he offered no threat to anyone, so he was allowed to approach. He stopped a few feet away from Ghost Dancer's body, panting, and waited until the last sad sweet sound of taps had faded down the green valley, and waited until the officers had barked the order that terminated the ceremony, before he approached the bullet-torn body. Maxwell and the soldiers watched as Corby dropped to his knees in the grass beside the body and reached out to touch Ghost Dancer's blood-covered back.

"Good-bye, my father," he said in Cheyenne, and added the customary Cheyenne farewell to one who is leaving this life to travel to the Spirit Land, "*Nimeaseoxzheme*—May your journey be a good one."

CHAPTER EIGHTEEN

THE PEACE OF THE VALLEY WAS SUDDENLY SHATTERED BY A mighty, many-peopled roar. The Run of '92 was scheduled to begin at high noon, but something happened to make the line break ahead of time. Later some said that a drunken cowboy on the line more than two miles from Lame Cow Valley could no longer stand the suspense. Firing his revolver into the air and crying, "Whooooo-eeee!" he spurred his horse and made a dash onto the reservation, and because there were so few troops to stop them, some of the other settlers on horseback joined him in a dash to claim the best allotments. Other settlers along the line, determined not to be left out, immediately laid whips to their animals and bolted forward onto the reservation, yelling and firing their guns into the air. And when the other settlers along the line saw that those who had jumped the gun were not going to be turned back, they, too, joined the breakaway. Like a disintegrating dam, the breakaway rapidly gained momentum all the way along the line, from horizon to horizon.

The rumbling flash flood of settlers pulled apart and scattered as they left the line, but those at the entrance of Lame Cow Valley were funneled into the valley and formed an almost solid wall as they bore down on Colonel Caldwell and his men. The cavalrymen who were not mounted began a wild dash for their horses as Colonel Caldwell yelled, "Scatter! Scatter! Find cover!"

Maxwell rode out to Corby kneeling by his father's body and grabbed him by the arm. Corby swung up behind the saddle and held on tightly as Maxwell kicked the pony into a headlong dash for the ridge. They reached the safety of a ravine at the bottom of the slope just before the front-running horses of the settlers thundered past. But even after reaching safety, Maxwell kept slamming his heels into the pony's ribs, all the way up the ridge to where Rachel and Chief Hehyo and his band were watching the run with appalled fascination.

"The sonsabitches!" Maxwell cursed as he brought the blowing pony to a stop. After Corby dropped to the ground, Maxwell swung down from the saddle. "They couldn't even wait till twelve o'clock. They couldn't even wait *that* long."

Chief Hehyo shook his head. "Crazy white men. The Ghost Dance Prophet Wovoka was wrong. He said that a great flood would come and wash the white man from the face of the earth. But the white man himself is the flood. That is what I think. I think it is the red man who is being washed from the face of the earth."

The torrent of settlers rushed on down the valley, swirling around boulders and trees and prickly pear cacti. Most of them tried to ride around the bodies of the dead Indians scattered in the grass on the valley floor, but so closely packed were they that many of them didn't see the bodies until they were already upon them, and the bodies were trampled by many hooves and run over by many wheels before the first wave of settlers had passed.

When the front-runners began to disappear in a thin cloud of dust to the west, Maxwell, with a look of deep disgust, turned to Corby, who was staring at his hand, the hand that he had placed on his father's back. The palm was covered with his father's blood. He was trying to keep from crying.

Maxwell put his hands on the boy's shoulders. "I'm sorry, *naha*. I can only hope that your father's death doesn't make you hate the white man, though I could certainly understand if it does." Then to Chief Hehyo he said in Cheyenne, "We must go. I do not wish to see any more of this."

Chief Hehyo seemed almost in a state of shock. "It is the same with Chief He-follows-his-father's-ways. I have lived for a long time. I have seen many changes since the coming of the white man, and after this day these old eyes do not wish to see anymore. I have seen enough." He glanced around at the land and the sky, as if taking stock of the world, then added in a calm, resigned voice, "Ghost Dancer was right. This is a good day to die." And without further ceremony, he laid his old body down on the ground, grunting and wheezing, and faced the sky, crossed his arms over his chest, and said, "I will die now."

The women present—daughters and granddaughters, mostly—immediately increased their keening to a frenzy, while the men grunted their reactions, from protests to sympathetic understanding, and his youngest son, Long Shadow, knelt by his side and wished him a good journey to the Spirit Land. But Corby respectfully approached the old man's recumbent body, and said, "Please do not die, grandfather. Today I lost my father. I do not wish to lose my grandfather also. We need you."

Chief Hehyo had closed his eyes, but when Corby spoke, he opened them again, seemed to think about it for a moment, then said, "Very well, I will live for a while longer yet, to see that this son of Ghost Dancer becomes a man of the Human Beings."

Corby and Long Shadow helped the old man up, and the sounds of keening diminished.

"I am sorry for this day, grandfather, but I am glad you have decided to live," Maxwell said, embarrassed and ashamed. To Rachel and Corby he said, "Come on, let's go."

Corby balked. He turned once more to stare through a film of tears toward his father's body, where it lay trampled in the grass on the valley floor. Maxwell sensed that the boy was on the brink of some watershed rebellion, a rebellion that often occurred when Indian students had to make quick and fundamental choices between the worlds of the white man and the red. Corby seemed on the verge of saying, "No." It wouldn't have surprised Maxwell if he had ripped off his school uniform and gone to join the Indians.

"There's nothing you can do, *naha*," Maxwell said, and switched to Cheyenne as he added, "Chief He-follows-his-father's-ways will see that your father is buried with all the honors of a great warrior." He looked to the chief for confirmation, but at that moment their attention was diverted by a man, a white man mounted on a ribby old plow horse, dressed in faded farmers' overalls and a straw hat, who came riding up the ridge, waving a pistol and shouting through a snuff-stained beard, "Git offen my land! Git offen my land, y'hear?"

"Are you crazy, mister?" Maxwell snapped when the horse came to a panting stop a few feet from him. "Put that gun away, for God's sake. These are Cheyenne warriors."

"Don't give a damn who they be," the settler said. "This here's my land. I staked it fair and square. Now, y'all git!"

From the looks of him he was a man who, on a normal day, might say howdy to a stranger or do a kindness for a neighbor, but now he was as unreasoning and threatening as a bull moose in rutting time, as if, indeed, he were in the thrall of some overpowering lust.

For the most part the keening Indians in the area ignored the crazy white man, but a few of the younger men were readying old hunting rifles and bows and arrows, in case they had to kill him.

"Mister," Maxwell said, approaching the man, ostensibly to talk to him confidentially but actually to get within reach of him, "this may be your land now, but if you don't put that gun away, you won't live to work it." He recognized immediately that this was the wrong thing to say. The settler took what was meant to be a warning as a threat.

"Git!" he shouted, waving his pistol. "Git offen my land, all of you, or I'll shoot!"

Maxwell reached up and grabbed the man's arm and jerked

him out of the saddle. All eyes were on them, but Maxwell's actions were almost faster than anyone could see. Having tumbled the man headlong out of the saddle, he stamped on the hand that held the pistol. With the sounds of bones cracking and a cry of pain from the man, Maxwell picked up the fallen pistol and whacked the man over the head with the barrel, knocking him unconscious, then flung the pistol into the bushes.

"Now, by God, maybe you'll live long enough to file your claim," he said, and turned back to Rachel and Corby. "Let's go."

Corby was no longer inclined to balk. He and Rachel were staring at Maxwell. Neither of them had ever before seen him become violent, and even then it wasn't the violence itself that surprised them so much as the coolly efficient way in which he had knocked the settler senseless. As if to confirm what they thought their eyes had seen, they exchanged glances and then turned back to gaze at Maxwell with new respect and admiration.

CHAPTER NINETEEN

A FEW MONTHS LATER CHIEF HEHYO, WEARING HIS TOP HAT, rode into the agency, sitting in a dusty and ragged overstuffed parlor chair in the back of his creaky old wagon. A boy stood behind him and held a parasol over his head. The chief's son Long Shadow was on the wagon seat, driving the team of pinto ponies. The wagon was accompanied by two riders who were leading a fine-looking bay between them. Each of the riders had a slip-knotted rope around the bay's neck to choke the young stallion into submission when he got too frisky. And even with the ropes around his neck, the bay tossed his head and pranced alongside the chief's wagon as if taunting the other horses for their tameness.

Maxwell and Corby were behind the house, repairing the corral fence. When the Indians arrived, Maxwell reached up and shook hands with the old chief and asked in Cheyenne, "To what do we owe the honor of the chief's visit today?"

"My eyes grow weary and weak," the old chief said, squinting in his effort to see Corby. "Is this boy the son of Ghost Dancer?"

"Yes, grandfather," Maxwell said.

"I bring a gift for him."

Maxwell eyed the bay stallion uneasily. "What kind of gift?"

"A gift that will make a man of him," said the chief from the depths of his chair in the shade of the parasol. "It is good that he learns the white man's medicine, but when will he learn the ways of the Human Beings? He has no father now. Who is to teach him how to be a man?" And then, as if he had just thought of something more important, he added, "You have tobacco?"

Maxwell took his pipe and tobacco pouch from his shirt pocket. The chief was silent until the pipe was filled and lit, as if speech would be out of place while a pipe was being prepared. Then he said, "I have brought this pony as a gift for Ghost Dancer's son."

Maxwell almost choked on the first puff from the pipe. To refuse the gift of a Cheyenne chief was a serious discourtesy, so Maxwell had to search for a polite way to frame the refusal. In the meantime, the old chief, having taken the pipe from Maxwell and inhaled a puff of smoke and exhaled with a long slow sigh of satisfaction, added, "On the day Ghost Dancer threw himself away, I also was ready to die, but I told this boy I would live long enough to see that he became a man of the Human Beings. To tame this horse will make him such a man, and then I will be free to die."

Corby began edging toward the bay.

The pipe had been passed to the driver of the wagon and to the two riders before it came back to Maxwell, who puffed meditatively before he said in Cheyenne, "A splendid gift, yes, but I regret that I must refuse it for Corby. The rules—"

With beseeching eyes, Corby asked in English, "Please?"

"Now, dammit, Corby," he said in English, "you know I can't allow you to keep a horse at school. If I made an exception in your case, every boy in the school would want to keep one."

Rachel came out of the house with six glasses of iced tea on a tray. The ice, brought in wagons from the new ice plant in El Reno, was a novelty for everyone, but especially for the Indians. When they had first seen the blocks of ice made during the heat of summer, they had once more marveled at the white man's magic. And Rachel's sweet tea, with chunks of the ice in it, was greatly prized by the Indians, who each swallowed the tea in mighty gulps and managed a burp to show appreciation.

Rachel revealed that she had been eavesdropping when she said, "But, Daddy, why couldn't he keep the horse in our barn? No one has to know it's his."

"I'd work for free, cleaning the barn, taking care of him," Corby pleaded. "He wouldn't be any bother to you, I promise."

"But this is a *wild* horse," Maxwell said. "Look at him," he added with an attempt at disdain, though his voice betrayed a note of admiration. The bay was a very handsome piece of horseflesh, there was no denying that, but it would take a grown man, an experienced wrangler, to handle him. What chance would Corby have to break a horse like that? "Why don't you just wait till you graduate and then get yourself a horse that's already broken? One that's not likely to kill you?"

"Thank you, sir, but it's this one I want."

Maxwell sighed. The fact that the stallion was a gift from Chief Hehyo made it almost impossible to refuse, but the rules . . . Finally, after another meditative puff on the pipe, he sighed again. "Well, I don't know. . . ."

"Now we'll both have ponies," Rachel said to Corby. "Daddy promised me a pony for my birthday, so we'll both have ponies. And saddles! We'll have saddles, too, won't we, Daddy? I want a red one. I want a pretty pinto pony with a red saddle."

"I didn't say he could have it," Maxwell protested, and Rachel smiled at him and said, "But he can, can't he? Please? Then I'll have someone to ride with after I get my pony."

In a grudging way, so as not to seem too compliant, Maxwell at last said, "Well, I don't know. Maybe you can keep him here till you finish school. But," he added as a quick warning check to Corby's and Rachel's growing sense of triumph, "you have to take full responsibility for him, mind you. You'll have to feed him and take care of him, and all at your own expense."

Chief Hehyo, sucking on a chunk of ice, concluded that permission had been granted. "*Pava.* Good. It is done. I have done my duty to the boy. Now I can go to sleep and rest my weary eyes."

Corby could hardly wait to begin the process of taming the stallion, a process that Maxwell assumed would begin by gelding the animal. A few days later, when he came out to the corral to watch Corby working with the horse, he said, "I'll get some of the agency wranglers to do it tomorrow. The sooner, the better."

Though reluctant to oppose Maxwell, Corby, standing outside the corral with a bucket of oats in his hand, finally forced himself to say, "No, thank you, sir. I'd rather not do that to him."

"What? Not geld him? Why, look here, *naha*, this horse'll be mean enough as a gelding; as a stallion, he'd be downright dangerous."

"Maybe so, sir, but I want him to be my friend. Would you do that to a friend?"

"Friend, hell. What you've got to do is show him who's boss, right off. He wouldn't be here unless you forced him to be, would he? And he won't let you ride him unless you force him to, and a situation like that doesn't leave much room for friendship."

Corby showed the first signs of becoming sullen and withdrawn.

"I'm just trying to help," Maxwell said.

"Yes, sir, but this's something I have to do by myself. That's what Chief Hehyo said."

"All right. But I don't see how you're going to do it. You don't know anything about breaking horses. You'd better at least wait till Gypsy Smith gets back, so he can tell you what to do. Otherwise you're going to get yourself killed, messing around with a wild stallion like that."

"I'll be all right."

But Maxwell worried. He watched daily as Corby crawled into the corral with the stallion, ready to offer the stallion a lump of sugar or an apple. But no matter what kind of present Corby offered him, the stallion would make a dash at him with teeth bared and hooves slashing and kicking. Corby always gave himself plenty of time to scramble back through the fence before the horse came to a dust-billowing, snorting stop at the fence and whirled to flick his rear hooves clattering like gunshots against the railings.

Finally Corby decided he had to take stronger measures, so he cut off the horse's water supply. He shut off the flow at the windmill, then emptied the corral's horse trough of its mossy water, and said to the haughty and nervous animal, "All right, either you drink water that I give you, or you don't drink at all."

By the next morning the stallion was thirsty enough to approach the bucket with his neck outstretched, his nostrils flaring, stiff-legged, with little nervous tics of energy and pride rippling beneath his sleek red coat. It took him a long time and many uncompleted approaches before he finally got close enough to get his pendulous lips into the bucket of water, and even then—even after gulping the water with gurgles and snorts and groans—he showed his contempt and ingratitude by trying to bite Corby's hand.

But every approach became easier, and by the end of the first week of drinking from the bucket, the stallion allowed Corby to reach out and pet his head and scratch his ears. This first physical contact seemed to work a small miracle in the horse's behavior. Once he learned that Corby, unlike all the other human beings he had ever known, wasn't reaching out to hurt him, he began to tolerate Corby's pets and scratches with a certain amount of probational pleasure. And by the time spring was edging into summer, Big Red—as Corby had decided to call the stallion—even allowed Corby to enter the corral and currycomb his red coat and black mane, though he still kicked if Corby tried to get behind him to curry the cockleburs from his tail.

One day Corby brought Bess, Maxwell's gentle old mare, into the corral and tied the two horses together by means of a short rope from Bess's halter to Big Red's neck, and Bess's gentleness had a calming effect on the stallion.

Maxwell knew of no other wrangler, professional or amateur, who would have gone about breaking a wild horse the way Corby did. An ordinary wrangler, armed with spurs and lariat, a quirt, a snubbing post, a Spanish bit, and a saddle, would have entered the corral to break the horse, and it would have been a desperate fight from beginning to end, a fight in which the horse was the almost certain loser, the defeated, the broken-spirited. But Corby wasn't trying to break the bay stallion; he was trying to win the animal's cooperation. Where did he get such notions? Not from the Indians, surely, for their methods of breaking horses were just as brutal as the white man's.

Maxwell found himself taking as much pride in the boy as he would have taken in his own son. It was good to have Corby around as a balm for the disgrace that Dexter had recently caused by getting himself fired from his job as one of the agency's census-and-allotment clerks. It seemed that Dexter had been supplying land speculators with confidential information from the agency's files. He had denied it, of course, and vehemently challenged his accusers to prove it, knowing that he wouldn't be arrested, even if caught red-handed. It was the Indian Bureau's policy not to expose and publicize wrongdoing on the part of agency employees. Unless the crimes were of such a magnitude that they couldn't be hushed up, they were usually handled by quiet dismissal, lest the Indians get the idea that they were being exploited and robbed on every hand.

So Dexter hadn't been afraid of going to jail, and he didn't give a damn if they did dismiss him. He said he didn't want the job anyway. In fact, to hear him tell it, they were doing him a favor by firing him. He was meant for better things than being a pencil pusher in a dirty, backward Indian agency.

Dexter had left for Guthrie, and Rachel soon got a postcard from him, telling her that he had gone to work for none other than Shelby Hornbeck himself. He said he would soon be sending some money to help pay for a nursemaid for his mother so that Maxwell wouldn't have an excuse to send her to an asylum. The money never came.

So the pride Maxwell felt in Corby was a sort of antidote for Dexter's disgrace, and he never failed to take an interest in the progress Corby was making with his very unorthodox way of breaking the stallion.

"Why're you doing that?" he asked one day as he stood with Rachel at the corral. Corby stood near Big Red, doing nothing more than hold his hand firmly against the animal's chest.

Discomfited by having to put things into words, Corby hesitated a moment before he mumbled, "Just feeling the life moving through our bodies."

"Doing *what*?"

Feeling foolish for having offered the explanation in the first place, Corby shrugged and took it back. "Just letting him get used to me."

"Well," said Rachel, "he sure ought to be getting used to you by now, much time as you spend with him."

She was jealous. Since the day he had come into possession of the stallion, Corby hardly had a moment for anyone else. He had always been Rachel's best friend, and now a horse had come between them. But there were more things coming between them that summer than just a horse. She had been having experiences and sensations that she couldn't bring herself to share with Corby. Changes were taking place within her body that made her feel secretive and set apart. But many of the changes could hardly be kept secret for long, especially not from Corby. As her breasts budded and her gangly limbs began to show the first signs of womanhood, she sometimes found Corby glancing at her in a peculiar way, as if she were a stranger.

Maxwell bought her a pony for her fourteenth birthday. It was a pinto pony, as she had wanted, but it was a rather lazy animal. It needed a quirt to make it run, and that was very annoying to Rachel, who wanted to ride across the prairies like the wind. What's more, she had to ride sidesaddle. She had wanted a shiny new red leather cowboy's saddle, but Maxwell insisted she use her mother's shabby old sidesaddle. She said she would rather ride bareback, but Maxwell said, "No, you have to use the sidesaddle, and you have to wear a dress when you ride. Rachel, the time's come when you must learn to ride like a lady, you hear? You can't be a tomboy *all* your life."

She sighed, reconciling herself to the inevitable.

Even so, she sometimes disobeyed him, not out of defiance

so much as impish impulsiveness, such as the day she climbed
up behind Corby on the bare back of the old mare Bess, sitting
astride, her dusty bare feet dangling down, her skirt bunched
up around her thighs.

That was the day Corby took Big Red out of the corral for
the first time. He had the snorting stallion tied halter to halter
with the old mare by a piece of rope about four feet long.
Corby and Rachel rode the old mare bareback as she ambled
toward the river with Big Red in tow. It was late August by
then and the day was hot and Corby was without a shirt, and
when Rachel leaned against his sweating back, he could feel,
through the thin cotton blouse she wore, the small soft firm
mounds of her breasts pressing against him.

On the river about a half mile below the Loafers' camp was
a pool that the Indians used as a swimming hole. There were
a few naked Indian children swimming in the muddy water
when Corby and Rachel arrived, but they quickly vacated the
hole when they saw what Corby was going to do.

First he stopped the horses on the riverbank, where he took
off his boots and trousers; then, dressed only in his baggy
agency-issue shorts, he got back up on the mare and rode her
out into the pool, pulling the snorting and plunging stallion
along with her, leaving Rachel to sit in the shade of a cottonwood tree on the bank and watch.

When the horses were chest-deep in the water, Corby gave
the stallion a few soothing pats and words, then adroitly
slipped off the mare's bare back and onto the stallion's. The
stallion was startled into a momentary immobility, which gave
Corby the time he needed to get set and grab a handful of the
stallion's flowing black mane; then, with wild explosions of
water and a fireworks display of sabering hooves, tossing head,
thrusting body, flaring nostrils, and rolling eyes, with snorts
and grunts and whinnies of indignation, the battle was joined.

Big Red was at a distinct disadvantage. Anchored to the old
mare and constrained by the chest-deep water, he could hardly
buck at all. But he could still plunge and thrash and kick, and
he managed to buck the boy off a few times, but Corby was
cushioned by the water and the spills amounted to no more
than duckings, after which he pulled himself back up onto the
stallion, streaming water, and the contest was once again
joined. There were whoops and yells from Indian children on

the riverbank, and now and then he could hear Rachel's voice among them, repeating the calls used by the wranglers around the agency's corrals: "Whooo-eee! Ride 'im, Corby! Ride 'im!"

But on their third visit to the swimming hole the old mare got tired of having her head jerked and snapped by the lunging and plunging young stallion, so she decided to leave the water. Corby leaped off the stallion and grabbed her reins to keep her from gaining the riverbank, but it was Rachel who solved the problem by dashing fully clothed into the water and taking the mare's reins from Corby.

"I'll handle her." She pulled herself onto the mare's back and swung astride, her flimsy cotton dress streaming water and clinging to her skin.

"No." Corby was standing waist-deep in the muddy, hoof-churned water, catching his breath. The stallion had come to a momentary standstill, straining at the halter, trembling. "You might get hurt."

"Oh, come on, I'm not a kid. Stop treating me like one. Go ahead, I'll handle Bess."

That was one of those moments when Corby looked at her the way he might have looked at someone he didn't know at all. He let his eyes linger for a moment on the shape of her small breasts beneath the clinging dress, then lowered his gaze for a lingering look at her exposed thigh, then returned his gaze to her breasts. She blushed and pulled the dress away from her skin.

"All right," he said. "Get her into deeper water."

On their fourth visit to the spot Rachel brought a picnic basket and Corby brought his flute. They let the horses graze peacefully on the riverbank while they sat under the huge cottonwood tree and ate food prepared by Rachel's own hands: hard-boiled eggs and bacon-biscuit sandwiches, the bacon overdone and the biscuits underdone, but edible, and after they had eaten, Corby played his flute. It was made from the hollow wing bone of an eagle, and it could make only a few high-pitched notes, but Corby managed to coax a screechy sort of music from it. And while he played, Rachel borrowed his pocketknife to carve a heart into the soft bark of the huge old cottonwood. Within the heart she carved "RM + CW."

As a small child Corby had been impressed with the importance of signs, Indian signs that partook of magic, and so he was respectful of the sign carved by Rachel, though he didn't know what it meant. He reached up and placed his hand on the sign, as if attempting to divine its meaning by touch.

"Means we're ..." But she fell silent, unable to find the words to describe what it meant; then she blushed and blurted, "Well, that we're sort of sweethearts, I guess." She giggled. "Means we're betrothed."

CHAPTER TWENTY

THAT WAS THE DAY CORBY RODE THE EXHAUSTED AND BIT-terly frustrated stallion to a standstill in the water. Then he stroked the animal's neck and trembling shoulders, saying, "Good boy. Easy, now. We'll be friends. All right?"

But this new accommodation by Big Red lasted only until Corby tried to put a snaffle bit in the stallion's mouth, at which time he reverted to his unruly ways. It took Corby more than a month to get him to accept the bit, and by then it was wintertime, and still the contest went on. In the rain and in the snow, unrelenting, unwavering, Corby won by increments.

It was over a year from the time the contest first began that Corby finally climbed into the saddle one day and found the stallion willing to do his bidding without any show of contrariness, without any sign of rancor, spite, or mistrust. And on that day they celebrated their partnership with a wild ride across the prairie.

The stallion's gait was smooth and fluid, all his movements harmonious, and his hooves moved with a swiftness that made them nothing but a blur to the human eye. Corby had never before experienced such speed, and the joy of it caused him to let out a long Indian howl of triumph as Big Red plunged across the prairie, his black mane and tail streaming in the wind like banners, his throat emitting soft rhythmic grunting sounds, the sounds of a steady bass drum punctuating the cadence of his hooves.

He ran free. Corby let the reins fall slack, and Big Red took any direction he pleased. After they had gone for about half a mile, the horse came out of a long shallow valley and onto an alkali plateau, where they met a band of Cheyennes on their way to the agency—the Hehyo band, with old Chief Hehyo's wagon in the forefront of the column.

The Indians were in full ceremonial regalia. Those who still had beaded buckskins were wearing them, and there were some who wore warbonnets and feathered headdresses that hadn't been worn for years. Faces were painted like warriors of old, and the ponies were decorated with painted markings on their bodies and with feathers braided into their manes and tails.

For a moment it seemed to Corby that he might be seeing a column of bright and gaudy ghosts bearing lances and leather shields, materializing out of the blurring heat waves and enshrouding dust like specters from a more festive and barbaric age.

He guided Big Red through the column's outriders and rode directly to Chief Hehyo's wagon as it creaked across the prairie, pulled by two pinto ponies and driven by Long Shadow, the chief's youngest son. Inside the wagon, sunk into the shabby and dusty overstuffed parlor chair, was Chief Hehyo, with a boy standing behind his chair holding a parasol over his head. His shrunken body was dressed in the relics of a scalp-hunting warrior: a moth-eaten warbonnet, a bear claw necklace, a porcupine quill breastplate, a red flannel breechclout, and fringed buckskin leggings.

"*Vahe, namsem,*" Corby said, gentling Big Red to a prancing walk alongside the wheel-wobbling wagon. A few of the younger men were bringing their ponies in close to get a look at the bay stallion.

Without opening his eyes, the old chief turned toward Corby and asked, "Who speaks?" He swayed back and forth in the big chair as the wagon creaked along. His wrinkled face was covered with a layer of fine alkali dust.

"It is I, Little Raven, son of Ghost Dancer."

Chief Hehyo's toothless mouth stretched into a slash of a

grin. "Little Raven, yes. I remember I gave you a stallion to break. What happened to the stallion?"

"I am riding him, grandfather."

The old chief crowed. With the feathers of the moth-chewed warbonnet rising from his gray head like a battered cock's comb, he stretched his scrawny neck forward and made a sound that could have been the squawk of a bedraggled old rooster. Then he turned his face full toward Corby and opened his eyes, straining to see him, an effort more of habit than hope, for there was no hope that he would ever see Corby again. His eyes, clouded over with cataracts, sightless except for the ability to see vague shapes and movements, had the opalescent sheen and dead flat opaqueness of pearls. This blindness had come upon him during the last year, the result—or so his medicine man said—of the chief's own prophecy and divination. "I have seen enough," he had said on the day of the Run of '92. "These old eyes do not wish to see anymore." So the evil spirit of blindness had caused clouds to grow over his eyes. At first the clouds had been thin and hazy, but soon they gathered and became denser and denser still, and so the old chief began saying good-bye to all the beautiful things he would soon be unable to see.

"Good-bye, river," he said. "Good-bye, bird. Good-bye, snow. Good-bye, tree. Good-bye, flower."

And when he realized he had only a little sight left, he began to keep his eyes closed most of the time to keep from using it all up. He wanted to save what little seeing power he had for important things, such as the sight of Corby riding alongside the wagon on the bay stallion.

"You broke the stallion?"

"Yes, grandfather."

"How many winters have you, boy?"

"Sixteen, grandfather."

"A boy whose medicine is strong enough to break the wild stallion is ready to take his place among the men of the Human Beings. I think you should now drop your boyhood name and choose your manhood name. Has Little Raven considered this?"

"No, grandfather. At the school we were not allowed to have Indian names or to change our white names. The same will be true at the school called the Carlisle Institute in the place called Pennsylvania. They asked if I want to go to this school, now that I have completed my studies at the agency school. If I do go to this school, I must keep the white man's name I was given."

"So what will Little Raven do?"

"I am not sure, grandfather. I have considered returning to the Human Beings rather than go to the faraway white man's school. What does Chief He-follows-his-father's-ways think?"

The old chief had now closed his eyes to conserve his eyesight, but he still had his face turned toward Corby as he worked his toothless mouth for a moment, as if trying to produce some spittle or some wisdom. "I am torn by this question. I want to say, 'Return to our lodge fires, so that you will know what it is to be a Human Being, before it is too late.' But I know it is already too late. Go to the white man's school. Learn all you can of the white man's medicine. His medicine is stronger than ours. To live, you must learn it. The time of the white man has come. The time of the Human Beings has gone."

"Black White Man, whom the white men call Gypsy Smith, once spoke the same words."

"Black White Man spoke the truth." He gestured with both gnarled hands toward the others in the band. "These are ghosts you see, dressed in the garments of the dead."

"I see they are ceremonial garments, but I have not been able to guess why they are being worn. The chief and his band are going to a ceremony for the dead?"

"In a manner of speaking," Chief Hehyo said, growing weary, leaning back in his overstuffed chair. "We go to entertain the white man."

"To entertain?"

"Long Shadow will tell Little Raven," Chief Hehyo said to his son on the driver's seat. "I grow weary of words."

With his moccasined feet propped against the dashboard and his forearms resting on his knees, Long Shadow looked straight ahead, as if he were explaining something to the pinto ponies pulling the wagon: "Agent One-eye sent a message to our camp. He asked us to come to El Reno and help the white people celebrate the first anniversary of what they call the Run of '92, the day they took our reservation. He asked us to wear our warbonnets and war paint and march in the white man's parade. He promised us whiskey and extra rations if we do this."

The old chief roused himself. He turned his eyes on Corby again, straining to see through the dust and the cataracts. "Once I wore this warbonnet when I went on raids to kill the white man. Now I wear it to entertain him. Now I help him celebrate the day he took the last of our lands from us." Then, spent, he closed his eyes, withdrawing into darkness and silence.

Seeing that the powwow between Corby and the chief was over, a few of the young men challenged Corby to a race. Corby believed that Big Red could outrun the Indian ponies, but he had no idea how the stallion would behave while running in a bunch, and he had his worst fears confirmed when Big Red began making a display of himself in the starting line—nipping at the ponies next to him, rearing—and so wasn't set to run when the old man fired the starting shot. But he lunged after the other horses and caught up with them within a hundred yards. Rather than speed ahead of them, however, he came up behind one of the slower ones and gave it a bite on the rump to make it go faster. It was as if he were taking charge of his herd to make sure that even its slowest members escaped a pursuing predator.

The race was about half over before Big Red, perhaps because he decided it was time to switch from driving the herd to leading it, made a hard dash for the lead. He shot past ponies that were already being pushed to their limits with quirts and yells and kicks.

Three ponies were tied for the lead when Big Red came up behind them. By now the racecourse had narrowed down to the rutted road leading through the outlying log cabins and wickiups and tepees near the agency's main entrance. Children and dogs and chickens scattered with cries and squawks when the ponies came down the road, and the Indians camped alongside the road stopped what they were doing to watch.

The three leading ponies wouldn't give way until Big Red, with flashing teeth, nipped the middle pony on the hip. This sent the pony stumbling and slamming into the pony on the outside, sending that pony, in turn, careening off the road toward a wickiup. The rider managed to avoid a collision with the wickiup and the scattering people and animals, but he couldn't avoid running under a clothesline, from which hung an array of newly washed clothes and blankets. Though one end of the clothesline broke, the weight of the tangled wet clothes alone was enough to pull the rider off the pony and deposit him on his backside in a wild confusion of dust and flapping clothes and flying warbonnet feathers.

Gypsy Smith and Maxwell were standing in front of the telegraph office when they heard the pounding hooves of the racing ponies coming in under the log arch entrance to the agency, the race's finish line, with the red stallion in the lead.

"That's Corby?" Gypsy asked. He hadn't seen the boy in four years.

"You don't recognize him? He's grown a right smart since you saw him last."

"Sure as hell has. Well, I'll be damned." Gypsy watched Corby trying to bring the runaway stallion under control, plunging along the dusty street, past the agency headquarters, hotel, stores, and residences. "And that horse! Where'd he get him? I think I know that horse."

Concerned about the difficulty Corby seemed to be having bringing Big Red under control, Maxwell said with a preoccupied air, "Old Chief Hehyo gave it to him as a coming-to-manhood present. I'm sure he really didn't expect Corby to be able to break it, but by God, he's done it . . . maybe."

Leaving a path of pandemonium in his wake, Big Red plunged through the pedestrians and riders and wagons along the street, missing some only by inches, before Corby finally managed to bring him to a spinning stop.

"Corby broke him? All by himself? Well, I'll be damned. I traded that horse to Chief Hehyo, unbroke. Caught him in a bachelor herd over in the Blue Hills of Mendota a couple of years ago."

Corby was now bringing Big Red back toward the finish line in a prancing, sidestepping gait.

Gypsy snorted. "Where'd he learn to ride like that?"

Maxwell shrugged. "Beats me."

"Rides like a Comanche."

With his glossy black astrakhan hair, like black lamb's wool, springing from under a rolled red bandanna, Gypsy needed only an earring to look like a real Gypsy, though his costume was pure Comanche: a soiled and sweat-stained polka-dot shirt, a wide red sash around his waist, and black vaquero pants that were skintight at the thighs and bell-shaped at the ankles. Around his neck he wore a gaudy Navajo silver and turquoise necklace. Though clean-shaven still, his face had taken on the crinkled roughness of leather left too long in the sun and wind.

"Well, I'll be damned," he said again. "Now there's a boy after my own heart."

CHAPTER TWENTY-ONE

GYPSY SMITH HAD BROUGHT A HERD OF MUSTANGS DOWN from the Cherokee Outlet to sell to the settlers. He had stopped at Agency—the name of the town that was growing up around the Cheyenne-Arapaho agency—for some supplies and a quick visit with Maxwell. He was also looking around to see if he could find some other way to make a living. The Cherokee Outlet was soon to be thrown open to settlers in what was to be the last of the great land rushes, the Run of '93, after which there would be no more wild land, no more wild horses.

Gypsy figured he was getting too old for that anyway. He was forty-three now, and sometimes felt fifty, and his aching bones and stiffening joints had begun to prefer the comfort of a rocking chair to that of a rocking saddle. He had even begun to reflect fondly on the days when he had been a town marshal and could sometimes sit around all day in a nice warm office with his feet on his desk.

So he considered it almost providential when he checked at the Fort Sill post office one day and found a letter waiting for him from Amos Fulton in Freedom. Amos wanted to know if Gypsy would consider returning to Freedom and once again become its town marshal. Very dangerous troubles were developing between white men and the residents of the all-Negro

communities in the Territory, Fulton explained, and the present
marshal of Freedom didn't have the nerve to deal forcefully
with white men, especially if those white men were Klansmen.
The Klan, in cahoots with local white ranchers, had begun a
campaign to rid the country of established Negro communities
and to discourage new Negro settlers from coming in. And
there was no use asking the white authorities for protection,
Fulton wrote, since most of them were themselves involved in
the violence or were at least sympathetic to the Klan.

"I feel it only fair to warn you," the letter concluded, "that
the Klan has threatened to kill any colored man found wearing
a lawman's badge."

Gypsy left for Freedom the next morning. He was riding an
Appaloosa now. His clothes were a mixture of Mexican and
Comanche, the results of a recent trip to Mexico, where he had
bought the peon's straw sombrero and a vest made of rattlesnake skins, the skins sewn together in such a way that the rat-
tlers formed a fringe around the bottom of the vest and
sounded a castanet accompaniment to the jangling of his star-
roweled spurs.

He followed the stage road to El Reno. Riding at a leisurely
pace, he kept his eyes on the countryside, bemused by the grim
marvels of encroaching civilization. In spite of the barbed-wire
fences, however, and in spite of the windmills, corn cultivators,
and wheat-thrashing machines, in spite of the churches and
schools that were springing up at many crossroads, in spite of
all these nature-taming implements and institutions, the land
was not prospering. For the second time in as many years
drought had withered the crops. For eight weeks now no rain
had fallen on the Red Bed Plains of Oklahoma Territory, and
a hazy cloudless sky held no promise of any. The drought-
dead leaves of the stunted corn in the fields beside the road
rattled in the random gusts of hot August air. Now and then a
gust of wind would suddenly form into a funnel-shaped whirlwind of red dust, to eddy and undulate for a moment across a
field of wheat stubble or parched pasture and then stop, as if
in confusion, and slowly dissolve back into the heat-
shimmered air.

The drought was causing some of the farmers to desert their
homesteads. Thousands more were still pouring into the area,
however, to make the upcoming run into the Cherokee Outlet.

With more than ten million acres of virgin prairie up for grabs, and more than a hundred thousand settlers expected to grab for them, the Run of '93 into the Outlet promised to become the biggest and most famous of all the great land rushes, the one that would make an indisputable claim to the distinction of being, now and forever, the Damnedest Race in History.

Gypsy could have reached Freedom by late afternoon on the second day of the trip, but he decided he didn't want to ride into town looking like a saddle tramp. His clothes were dirty and smelly, he was covered with dust, and he hadn't shaved in a week or more. So he decided to make camp for the night, get himself spruced up a little, and then ride on into town in the morning, looking good.

He found a good camping place on Dead Indian Creek, only a short distance off the road, where he could bathe and wash his clothes and shave and scrub his teeth with sand. He refused to admit to himself that all this sprucing up was anything more than just pride in appearance. He wouldn't admit that he was sprucing up for Miss Drusilla Pointer. All he would admit to was a little curiosity about her. He hadn't seen her in nearly four years. He had assumed that she would be married by now. He knew that she hadn't married Lieutenant—now Captain— Beauregard Pierce, had known it ever since the day, only a month or so after he had left Freedom and gone back to live with the Comanches, when he visited Fort Sill and happened to meet Lieutenant Pierce. "How's the missus?" he had asked the lieutenant, and the lieutenant had replied in a voice as hard and cold and sharp as an icicle, "There is no missus."

Gypsy learned later that Drusilla had called off her engagement to Lieutenant Pierce shortly before their wedding. Nobody seemed to know why. Whenever Gypsy happened to meet someone he knew from Freedom, he always brought the talk around to that pretty young schoolteacher and thereby learned that she was still unmarried. Everybody, including Gypsy, agreed that was a crying shame, she being such a pretty young thing and all, and it wasn't because she didn't have plenty of suitors.

But it had been over a year now since Gypsy last had word of her, and he figured she was bound to be married by now. Surely by this time one of those young suitors had got her to the altar. As she herself had said, she wasn't cut out to be an old maid.

So it wasn't for her sake that he was sprucing up. He just wanted to look halfway decent when he rode into town tomorrow, and if it happened that he met Miss Drusilla on the street, why, so much the better if he was looking good.

From where he was camped under the trees on the bank of the creek, he could see about a quarter-mile stretch of the road. Though he hadn't expected any traffic on the road after dark, he was awakened that night by the sound of distant hoof-beats. Even while he was sleeping, something in his senses distinguished between the ordinary night sounds around him—the chorus of frogs in the creek, the chirruping crickets in the dry grass, the sounds made by his tethered horse gnawing the bark of a cottonwood tree—and those of the distant, dust-muffled hoofbeats, growing louder, like a drumroll. This sound sent an alarm through his sleeping body. He came awake and cocked an ear toward the sound. As yet the hoofbeats weren't even as loud as the nearby frogs and crickets, but already Gypsy could tell that there were maybe ten horses—shod horses—and they were coming in a steady gallop, headed northeast, toward Freedom.

He tumbled out of his bedroll, snatched up his sawed-off shotgun, and hurried to his horse. The Appaloosa had faced the direction of the sound, his ears twitching forward searchingly, and a small nicker had begun to form in his throat by the time Gypsy squeezed off most of his wind just above the nostrils. Then, naked except for his underwear, obscured by the shadows of the cottonwood trees, he trained his eyes on the road. The light from a dust-reddened quarter moon wasn't enough to let him distinguish the road from the surrounding landscape for a distance of more than two or three hundred feet, but the silhouettes of the telegraph poles running alongside the road allowed his eyes to follow the curve of the road for about six hundred feet, to a hazy mass of blackjack trees, from which the riders would appear. By using his ears to focus his eyes, he was looking directly at the horses as they came into sight around the curve of the road, running hard.

But his eyes could hardly believe what his ears were telling him. Rather than a posse or a formation of cavalry troopers, as he expected, what he saw was at first unrecognizable. The hoofbeats were produced by a sort of white cloud, a blurred, amorphous mass of cottony white cloud undulating along the road out of the dimness of the red moonlight like some sort of mystical many-hoofed beast. Then he began to distinguish individual riders and horses within the mass, and realized what he was seeing: Klansmen, about ten of them, dressed in their hooded white spook costumes. Even their horses were fitted out in flowing white costumes, cut to the patterns of those covering the mounts of medieval knights.

As they rode past his shadowed hiding place, Gypsy automatically swept his eyes over each of the horses and men, searching for some distinguishing mark, but the costumes seemed to cover all such identifiable markings. Only on the last horse did he see something that could be helpful: the horse had white stockings on one front leg and both rear legs.

As soon as they had galloped past his hiding place, Gypsy, scurrying and stumbling about in the darkness, got dressed, saddled his horse, and spurred the Appaloosa into a run as he gained the road. He figured the Klansmen were headed for Freedom, but by the time he had ridden to within four or five miles of the town, he sensed by the diminished amount of dust in the air that they had probably turned off onto a side road or a cross-country trail somewhere, in which case they hadn't been headed for Freedom, after all. But if not to Freedom, where?

He glanced eastward and saw something that caught his attention. It was so faint at first that he wasn't even sure he had seen it, but then he saw it again. At first he assumed it was a lantern flickering on some faraway homestead, but soon the light began to change from a flicker to a pale glow that emanated upward from behind a dark and distant rise of land. The glow was spreading, creeping northward behind the distant rise of land. A grass fire?

He spurred the Appaloosa into a run back down the road in the direction from which he had come. He kept his eyes on the fence to his left, looking for a farm road, and finally located one of the small rutted grid roads that marked the boundaries between homestead sections. He turned the Appaloosa onto the road and headed toward the fire. And even though he couldn't as yet see the active flames, he guessed from the brightening glow on the horizon that the fire was spreading very rapidly in a northerly direction. Because the wind was from the west, blowing at right angles to the thrust of the fire, he had to suppose that it wasn't the wind that was causing the fire to spread so rapidly. It would have to be men, riding at a gallop, dragging bundles of burning grass behind them on ropes, spreading fire crackling and roaring through the drought-dry grass and fields.

When he topped the crest of the rise, he saw the roaring flames for the first time. Somebody's house and fields were burning. He didn't know whose farm it was at first, but as he was riding toward the house and barn, almost at a parallel to the westernmost front of the grass fire, he began to see, in the vast flickering light of the flames, the dark shadows and silhouettes of people fighting the fire a couple of hundred yards away, and one of them, a woman, was running toward the house. Drawing nearer on a gradually converging course, Gypsy began to hear the woman, distant-faint above the crackling roar of the fire, screaming, "Not my house! Oh, please, God, not my *house!*" She was running, stumbling into the hot ashes, and scrambling to her feet again even before she had stopped falling. Flames swirled furnacelike from the house's windows and doors, roaring skyward in great eddies of sparks and smoke.

As Gypsy rode into the yard and dismounted, he recognized Eula Rasmussen. Running at full speed, she collided with the heat from the burning house as though the heat were a soft wall. She was engulfed in it for a moment and then was sent reeling backward, her arms raised to protect her face. But as soon as she recovered her breath and her balance, she once again dashed toward the flames, only to be sent reeling backward again.

Gypsy grabbed her shoulders from behind. She struggled to get free, but he pulled her away from the flames, saying, "There's nothing you can do, Miss Eula, take it easy, there's nothing you can do," until her hysteria subsided and she wilted to the ground. Her sunbonnet had fallen off, and now she made no attempt to cover her harelip as she sat lumplike on the ground and stared at the house while it burned and collapsed into a huge pile of sparks and glowing embers, moaning over and over between sobs in that voice of crazed despair and denial, "Not my house . . . oh, please, God, not my *house.*"

CHAPTER TWENTY-TWO

DRUSILLA WAS COMING DOWN THE DUSTY FARM ROAD IN A buckboard, bringing wicker baskets filled with sandwiches and jugs of hot coffee to the firefighters. Gypsy recognized her even from a distance. She wore a man's floppy felt hat over her curlicued hair, a yellow shawl around her shoulders, and the high-buttoned dress of a country schoolteacher. And she was just as attractive now, at twenty-seven, as she had been at twenty-three.

Pulling the team of mules to a dusty stop as Gypsy approached, she said, "Morning," as if to a stranger. "Is the fire out?" Perhaps because she was riding directly into the glaring red light of the rising sun, she didn't recognize Gypsy.

"All 'cept the mopping up. And a good morning to you, Miss Drusilla." He removed his hat with a flourish.

Drusilla brought her hand up to shield her eyes. "Gypsy?" she cried. "Gypsy Smith! Lordy mercy, is that *you*?"

"My own mammy might not recognize me, the way I look now, but it's me, all right, in the flesh." He gestured with mock despair at his clothes, which could have been the attire of a hobo who had been living in a coalyard, and his flimsy Mexican straw hat had burn holes in a dozen places where hot sparks had fallen on it. "Believe it or not, I got myself all spruced up last night, just on the chance of meeting you when I rode into town today, and now just look at me."

Excited at seeing him, Drusilla began a series of questions that almost left her stammering: Where had he been? What was he doing here? Would he be staying in Freedom for a while? How did it happen that he was out here fighting a fire? And when he told her that he had followed a gang of Klansmen to the fire, she said, "So it was the Klan. We heard it was. We heard they burned Eula's house."

"Right down to the ground—barn, outbuildings, everything."

"Poor Eula. Lord, how hard she worked on that house, and how she loved it! For years she scrimped and saved every nickel and dime to buy a board, a windowpane, a doorknob. I've never in my life seen anybody work harder, taking in washing, scrubbing people's floors—anything to make a few pennies she could put into that house. And now . . . Her own people!" She shook her head with the wonder of it. "How's she taking it?"

"She's there poking through the rubble, seeing what she can save, which ain't gonna be much—*isn't* going to be much," he added, falling into the old habit.

"They didn't whip her or anything like that?"

"Nothing like that."

"And weren't trying to kill her in the fire?"

"No, they suckered her out of the house by setting fire to the pasture. When she went out to fight it, they circled back and torched the house."

"Poor Eula! Her own people, doing that to her! Why?"

"She says they throwed a rock through her window, had a note tied to it, accusing her of being a nigger lover. And from what I hear, if there's anything them Klansmen hate worse'n a nigger, it's a nigger lover. Anyway, I 'spect she'll be needing some help now."

"I'll take her back with me. If she doesn't mind sleeping on a pallet, she can stay with us."

"Us? Does that 'us' include a husband these days, Miss Drusilla?"

Her smile was uncertain. "Not yet, but I still have hopes. Just me and the kids, as usual." Then she hurried on evasively. "And how about you, Gypsy Smith? Where'll you be staying? Your claim's been taken over, you know? A couple of months after you left, some lawyers from Guthrie got the Land Commission to declare it abandoned. It's part of the Olanco Ranch now."

"Yeah. Well, too bad it was the Olanco that got it, but what did I want with a hundred sixty acres of dust and dry grass? Me, I'm looking forward to clean sheets on a soft hotel bed and getting my meals served up in a nice café where the dust ain't blowing so thick it turns my coffee to mud 'fore I get it drunk."

"Getting soft at last?" She smiled, flashing her white teeth. "Well, I better be getting this stuff on down to the folks at the fire 'fore the coffee gets too cold."

Gypsy touched the brim of his sooty, fire-damaged straw hat to her and turned in the saddle to watch the buckboard go jolting down the road in the deep ruts, trailing a roiling plume of red dust in its wake.

He rode on to town and found that it hadn't changed much since he left. While it had never become the bustling farm town that the founders had hoped for, it had at least held its own against the withering forces of drought and the lack of a railroad, and now, with caravans of new Negro settlers using it as a staging area for the upcoming run into the Cherokee Outlet, it had even temporarily regained the look of a frontier boomtown.

Gypsy left the Appaloosa in the livery stable to be fed and groomed. He carried his parfleche pack to the hotel, where he rented a room, and then he went to the barbershop, where he got a haircut, a shave, and a hot bath. Because of the scarcity of water, a bath was now a dollar, but Gypsy didn't begrudge the price. Nor did he begrudge the twenty-five cents he had to pay for the bubble bath to soften the hard alkaline water.

It was in the tub, with only his head visible above the froth of pink bubbles, that Deputy Buck Tyson found him.

"Damn my hide, Gypsy Smith," he said, "I'd done give up on ever seeing you again." He clicked his teeth and leaned over the tub for a closer look. "That is you, down there under all them bubbles, ain't it, Gypsy?"

"Stand back, Buck, you might get ass-fixiated. I been letting farts under here. Stirs up the bubbles real good. So how you doing, Buck? Got some new teeth, I see."

"Damn things don't fit too good," Buck complained, and went on with a *click* every few words. "Listen, Fulton gave me orders to let him know the minute I found you. Wants to get Mayor Sawyer and the town council together right away. Wants to know when you can come."

"Evening'll be soon enough, won't it? I been out fighting

that fire all night, and I ain't doing nothing else till I get me some shut-eye."

Buck hurried away to report to Amos Fulton, and before the water had even turned cold in Gypsy's bath, a delegation of city officials burst into the bathroom to find Gypsy in his co-coon of pink bubbles. Besides Fulton, there was Freedom's current mayor, Philo P. Sawyer, and a new member of the city council, Dr. Homer Upchurch.

When greetings and introductions were over, Amos said, "Sorry to barge in on you like this, Gypsy, but with all this Klan activity going on, we figure we haven't got any time to lose. They may be back tonight to burn somebody else out, who knows?"

Dr. Upchurch and the mayor drew up stools. Amos sat on the edge of the tub.

"What d'you want me to do?" Gypsy asked.

"I'm now coordinator for an organization created by the Ok-lahoma Immigration Association called the Federation of Col-ored Communities of Oklahoma Territory," Amos said. "It's my job to coordinate public policies between the fourteen all-Negro towns in the Territory, and the implementation of one of those policies is what's brought me back to Freedom. We've decided to fight the Klan. That's why we need you. I'm pre-pared to offer you a job as troubleshooter for the Federation. That means you'll not only be marshal of Freedom but be boss over every marshal in every one of the all-Negro towns in the Territory. The marshal we got here in Freedom now, Rufus Margrave, he's a good man, and we're all obliged to him, but he'll tell you himself, what we need now is a . . . what we have to have is . . ."

"A killer," Gypsy supplied.

"Well, all right, if you want to put it that way. We got to put a stop to these Klan raids, Gypsy, even if it means killing a few of 'em."

"A few? You think you can stop with that? You kill a few, others'll come for revenge, and if you kill them, you'll likely be starting a race war. You ready for that?"

"If it comes to that," Amos Fulton argued, "the governor'll be forced to send in the territorial militia to keep order or bring in federal troops, one. Then, at least, we'd have some organized protection against the Klan. As it stands now, we don't have any."

"So who we got to turn to?" Mayor Sawyer chimed in. "Ourselves, that's who! Only ourselves."

"And we got to do *something*," Dr. Upchurch said in a peculiar accent—northeastern, Gypsy judged. He was a young man, light-skinned, with black horn-rimmed eyeglasses and a small goatee that gave him a scholarly look.

"And we've got to do it soon," said Amos. "You living out there with the Comanches, you maybe haven't heard, but Klan outfits are springing up in nearly every major city and town in Oklahoma Territory, with lots of men joining 'em. Pretty soon the Klan'll be as strong here as it is in Tennessee or South Carolina, and by then it'll be too late for us."

"Who are they? Got any names?"

"Nobody knows who they are," Fulton said. "The Klan's one of the most secret organizations imaginable. Only the members know who the other members are, and it's worth their life to betray that knowledge to an outsider."

"Might be best to start with the Olanco Ranch," Mayor Sawyer said. "They're in this up to their necks, burning people out so they can take over their claims and add them to their ranch. It's owned by the Oklahoma Land Company, one of the biggest corporations in the Territory. Shelby Hornbeck's the chairman of the board. You heard of him? He's Guthrie's representative in the territorial legislature. The Democrats are grooming him for governor when we become a state."

"A Klansman?"

Amos tilted his head doubtfully. "Nobody knows for sure."

"I'll need a posse. Thirty or forty men who'll do what they're told. No hotheads."

"What do you intend to do?" asked Dr. Upchurch, betraying the first twinge of apprehension.

"Nothing much we can do right now," Gypsy said. "I'll ride out to the Rasmussen place, try to pick up their trail. I 'spect, though, that the fire took care of that. And without names to go on, we'll just have to wait for them to make the next move. And when they do, we'll be ready." He lifted a handful of bubbles and puffed them off his palm. "If they want a war, we'll give 'em one."

CHAPTER TWENTY-THREE

AFTER THE RUN OF '92 THE CHEYENNE-ARAPAHO RESERVATION was broken up into counties, and a territorial school system was established to educate the children of the settlers. The Bureau of Indian Affairs proposed that the agency boarding schools be abandoned and the Indian students be integrated into the territorial schools, but this brought indignant protests from the settlers, most of whom were from the South. They didn't want their children going to school with coloreds, whether Negroes *or* Indians. So the politicians intervened, the proposal was dropped, and the boarding school system for educating Indian children was continued indefinitely.

Maxwell received this news with mixed emotions. He was glad that the Indian students wouldn't be turned over to the white schools because their language handicap would have doomed them to humiliation and hopelessness, but why keep educating them in Indian schools? Why prepare them for a white world that didn't want them?

It was for this reason that he was reluctant to pressure Corby into continuing his studies at the Carlisle Institute after he was graduated, with honors, from the agency school in June of '93. It wasn't that Corby objected to going to Carlisle or even argued against the idea; he just sort of dillydallied the days away, unable to come to grips with the issues involved, unable to make a commitment to live in the white man's world. At first he used as an excuse the training of Big Red, and then, when that was finally accomplished in July, he decided to stay around the agency at least for the summer and make some money racing Big Red against the local Indian ponies.

Rachel encouraged his procrastinations. She couldn't bear the thought of his going away and leaving her to spend a friendless and funless summer at the agency by herself. So she made it easier for him to stay by suggesting that he move into the barn after graduation, when he had to give up his living arrangement at the school. And Maxwell went along with the idea because the alternative was for Corby to go back to living with the Indians, and the influence of Indian life, Maxwell feared, might prove irresistible to the boy. So they all fixed up the tack and feed room in the barn as a place for Corby to stay until autumn, by which time, it was assumed, he would have become reconciled to the necessity of going to Carlisle.

It proved to be quite a nice little room. Maxwell helped put in two windows, Rachel swept and dusted and hung flour sack curtains, a cot and a small table were borrowed from the school, cushioned seats were made from sacks of oats, and a lantern provided a reading light. There was no stove, but Corby had no need for one during the summer, and food was provided by Rachel, who brought him a plate of whatever it was that she and Maxwell had for their meals.

Never before having had a room of his own, Corby was very pleased with the arrangement, especially since the room was next to Big Red's stall. If the stallion got restless during the night, Corby could soothe him by talking to him through the partition. He usually spoke to the horse in Cheyenne, but Big Red seemed to be soothed by English words as well, and he especially seemed to like it when Corby played his flute softly in the night. He seemed to find that very restful.

So the summer passed pleasantly enough, and the beginning of the autumn school year might have passed without any drastic changes had not a delegation of agency ladies—Mrs. Poggemeyer, Miss Clarksdale, and Miss Sutgood—come to Maxwell's house one day in late August, ostensibly to visit Nora but actually to have a little talk with Maxwell about his daughter.

"In the absence of Nora's mothering," Mrs. Poggemeyer said, "we feel we should do what we can to be a mother to her. Now, you're a good man, Mr. Maxwell, but you don't see what a mother would see."

Maxwell sighed. "What's she done now?"

"It's not what she's done, it's what she needs to do. She needs to be sent away from here to a young ladies' school somewhere where she can learn to be a proper young lady in white society. Otherwise I'm afraid—we're afraid—she's going to . . . well, you must realize that . . . well, that her and that boy should be separated."

Maxwell didn't know whether to reproach the ladies for their suspicions or thank them for their concern. He did neither, finally, and was inclined to dismiss their warnings as nothing more than the collective man-under-the-bed fears of two old maids and a preacher's wife. But while he told himself that the affection between Rachel and Corby was nothing more than childhood friendship, he began to watch them more closely when they were together. And perhaps because the ladies had put it in his mind, he did begin to see certain signs— touches, glances—that were more appropriate to childhood sweethearts than to mere friends.

Then one day he saw Rachel and Corby in the corral with Big Red, and a little while later Maxwell found himself gazing through the screen door toward the corral and not seeing them. Because he hadn't been consciously looking for them, it took a minute or two before he became aware that Big Red was prancing back and forth along the corral fence, making nickering sounds toward the two mares in the next pen, and Corby and Rachel were nowhere to be seen.

He stepped out on the back porch and started to call Rachel, but something caused him to keep silent. Instead he strolled down to the barn and waited until he was within a few steps of the plank door to Corby's room before he called, "Rachel?"

There was a sound of sudden scurrying in the room, and then Rachel, in a surprised and disconcerted voice, in what seemed both exclamation and question, cried from behind the door, "Daddy?"

Maxwell opened the door. Rachel had been approaching the door, hurriedly shoving the tail of her blouse back beneath her skirt. Surprised and disheveled, she stopped in the doorway and finished tucking her blouse into her skirt as she said, in that same voice that wavered uncertainly between statement and interrogation, "Daddy! You're looking for me? I was just . . . Corby and I were just . . ." Then she giggled, and that, in a way, was reassuring. It was a giggle characteristic of her when she had been caught doing something that was impish but not seriously naughty.

At the moment he had opened the door, Maxwell had seen

Corby spin away from where he had been standing in the center of the room and step to the nearest window, where he now stood, with his back toward Maxwell and his nose nearly against the windowpane, as if he had suddenly discovered something outside that demanded his full attention.

"What's going on here?" Maxwell asked, though it took him only a second to assess the situation. As near as he could guess, they had been embracing, probably kissing. But if that was all, it was enough.

Silence pervaded the room, broken only by the flies sluggishly buzzing against the windowpanes and the clucking sounds of the chickens in the barnyard, and then Maxwell said to Rachel, "Go in the house. I'll talk to you later."

"Oh, Daddy." Her voice was both placating and chiding, as if she thought he was taking the incident far too seriously. "We were just . . . practicing kissing."

"I assumed as much," Maxwell said with cutting asperity. "And that'll be the last time you ever do it, you understand? There'll be no more of that. Now, go on to the house."

Genuinely puzzled and a little alarmed by his gravity, Rachel stared at him for a moment, then dashed out of the room, slamming the door behind her.

Corby remained at the window, unable to turn and face Maxwell, fearful of finding accusations of shame and betrayal and maybe even condemnation in the eyes of the man whose good opinion he valued above all others.

Maxwell sighed and said, "Look at me, Corby," and Corby turned to face him. He blinked once and then focused his eyes on a spot on the wall just behind Maxwell's head. He showed no emotion. His attitude was that of a man determined to take his medicine with as much stoicism as he could muster.

Maxwell demanded in the voice of a stern schoolmaster, "How long's this been going on?" And when Corby gave him a questioning look, he prompted, "This . . . 'practicing kissing.' How many times has it happened?"

"Once or twice only."

"Well, which is it, once or twice? Surely it'd be something you wouldn't have any trouble remembering."

"Twice before this."

"Well, let this be the last time." Maxwell was slightly mollified, even a little sympathetic when he added, "Nothing can come of it, boy, except bad. You hear me?"

It was only after a slight hesitation that Corby said, "Because I'm Indian?"

"Yes!" Maxwell snapped, and then said, "No. I mean, sure, but not entirely. I mean, this hanky-panky would stop here and now no matter what color you are. The fact that you're not white only makes it worse for both of you. For you because the last thing in this world you'd be allowed to have is a white woman. And for you to aspire to it would only mean bringing down a terrible unhappiness on your head—on your head, and on the head of any white woman who was"—he searched for the right word—"imprudent enough to get involved in such a predicament. And I don't want that to be Rachel. You hear? Things've been tough enough for her already, with her not having a mother and all, and being raised out here, but it'd be a lot worse if she got the notion that she could with impunity"—again he took a moment to search for the right word—"be intimate with an Indian." He gave Corby a searching look. "You understand?"

Corby said in a sad but sensible voice, "Yes, sir, I understand."

Maxwell shrugged. "I'm sorry it's that way, but that's the way it is, and people who ignore it do so at their peril, and I don't want that peril to be Rachel's."

Corby nodded his grudging agreement. Maxwell placed a hand on his shoulder.

"You, neither," he said. "I want only what's best for you, too. For both of you. I hope you realize that."

Corby turned away slightly as a reason for moving his shoulder away from Maxwell's touch and said, *"Namatoan,"* the Cheyenne word for "I have finished speaking."

"Well, *I* haven't," Maxwell snapped, annoyed by Corby's impertinent use of Cheyenne, "and I want you to listen. I want you to go to Carlisle. It's time you found some direction. You've been doing nothing but drifting ever since you got out of school. Oh, I know, I know, going to school sometimes seems to cause more problems than it solves, but you're going to have to make your way in this world, and without an education, you don't have a chance."

"In the white man's world," Corby corrected him. "But I

don't know," he added after a brief pause. "What if I don't want to live in the white man's world?"

"You think you have a choice? Listen to me, *naha*. You know as well as I do, the only choice you have is, live with the white man or die with the Indians."

"I guess so. But I thought I might at least try . . . just for a while, to see if . . ."

When it became apparent that Corby wasn't going to finish the thought, Maxwell finished it for him: "To see if you can be an Indian again? Oh, for God's sake, boy, you're not thinking of going back to the blanket, are you?" But there was no need for Corby to answer; the truth was evident in his face. "Don't do it, Corby. You've had eight years of education, don't throw it away. Go to Carlisle." He cleared his throat as if asking for special attention. "I'll be sending Rachel away to school, too. Probably to St. Louis." His tone was almost incidental, but his message was clear: if Corby's reluctance to go to Carlisle was in any way based on his reluctance to be separated from Rachel, he had better know that the separation was going to take place, regardless of what he himself decided to do. "She'll be leaving as soon as things can be arranged."

He went back to the house. Rachel was in the kitchen, putting wood into the hot cookstove, on which boiled a pot of beans and ham hocks. Sweating and fretful, she went to the scullery board and began cutting up an onion, and Maxwell gave her more or less the same lecture he had given Corby. However, he began by saying that he had nothing against Indians, that he could hardly be fonder of Corby if he were his own son: "And you know that's true. But—"

By the time he finished, Rachel was shedding tears. "It's the onion," she said as she wiped her face. "I'm not crying. But what— What if— I mean, Corby's always been my best friend."

"And he can continue to be your friend. But that's *all* he can ever be. You understand? And I'm saying this to you in the same way I'd say 'Stop!' if you were a baby and I saw you crawling toward a cliff or about to put your hand in a fire." And then he said, "I think Mrs. Poggemeyer's right, it's high time you went away to school. And I know just the place: Miss Finwick's Young Female Academy in St. Louis. Miss Finwick's an old acquaintance and colleague of mine, from the days when I was a teacher in St. Louis, and I've no doubt she'd find a place for you for the fall term if I ask. I could take you to St. Louis on the train. Would you like that? It's a nice school. You'd like it, I'm sure."

Having put the diced onion into the steaming bean pot, Rachel wiped her hands on her apron and wiped away the tears. "School? St. Louis?" Soon her expression became one of her most appealing, a look of excitement that had an element of fear in it, the fear of the unknown, which was, to her, a necessary ingredient of excitement. And the possibility of going away to a girls' boarding school in St. Louis generated that kind of excitement. It would be a delightful adventure, a chance to travel and see new places, wear pretty clothes, meet new people, live in a great teeming city. And seeing her response, Maxwell prided himself on knowing her well enough to be able to turn her sadness into joy. Even as a child she could always be distracted from tears by a bauble, by a novelty dangled in front of her eyes.

But suddenly, without her having said a word or uttered a sound, her look of excitement collapsed into a frown of hopelessness.

"Oh, but Mother. Who would . . . ?"

"You're not to worry about that anymore, you hear? I'll manage to find somebody, don't you worry. I've just put a new ad in the *El Reno Dispatch* and—well, who knows? In the meantime, anyway, we'll see if we can get Miss Clarksdale started on a new wardrobe for you. Most of the girls at Miss Finwick's Academy are from St. Louis's professional class and pride themselves on being fashionable. We can't have them thinking you're a little backwoods waif, can we?"

Rachel was once again flushed with excitement, the same kind of giddy excitement she felt whenever she listened to ghost stories, a sort of delightful fright.

"Oh, I can't wait to tell Corby," she said, but was then struck by the realization that going away to school meant she would be parting from him, parting, in fact, from the only two people in the world she loved: Corby and her father.

"He already knows. I told him. And I told him I want him to go away to Carlisle."

Then, once again excited, she said, "Oh, wouldn't it be wonderful if he did! Tell me about it! The school in St. Louis, I mean. Does it have lots of students? Does it cost a lot? Will I be staying in a room with other girls? But what if they're all silly and I can't stand them? You won't make me stay if I don't like it, will you?"

Maxwell answered her questions until the beans and ham hocks were ready to be dished up, at which time he took a plate of the beans and a slab of corn bread out to Corby.

"Dinner," he said as he stepped into Corby's room.

Corby had been lying on his cot, his hands clasped behind his head, staring at the cobwebby ceiling. He sat up on the side of the cot and took the tray from Maxwell. "Thank you." He set the tray down on the wooden crate used as a bedside table.

Maxwell sat down on a stack of sacked oats that had been arranged as a chair. "Well?" he said. "You thought about it? Carlisle, I mean? Rachel thinks it's a good idea that you both go."

He seemed surprised. "She *wants* to go?"

"Oh, yes. Very excited about it, I'd say. I'm going to take her to St. Louis on the train. If you decide to go to Carlisle, we could all make the trip together. Make it a sort of holiday. And after we dropped Rachel off in St. Louis, you and I could go on to Pennsylvania together. It's about time I paid a visit to the institute, seeing as how I've sent them nearly three hundred students during the last sixteen years."

"And how many *vehos* have they sent you back?" Corby asked.

Maxwell was disturbed and hurt to hear the inflection Corby gave to the Cheyenne word for white man, an inflection that made it a venomous racial epithet.

CHAPTER TWENTY-FOUR

DRUSILLA AND EULA STOOD NEAR THE OPENED DOOR OF THE stagecoach. Eula wore a new dress and a new sunbonnet, but their newness was the only thing noticeable about them. Drab brown in color and plain in design, her clothes seemed calculated to turn away attention, not attract it. Drusilla's dress was also plain, made for durability rather than beauty, but there were always little touches—a lace choker, bright buttons, a cameo brooch pinned on her bosom—that invited attention. Now she wore over her head a bright yellow silk scarf that she drew around her face whenever a gust of hot September wind swirled a cloud of dust around her.

Gypsy approached just as the stagecoach driver and the shotgun guard came out of the depot, carrying a strongbox between them.

"Aw right, let's get loaded," the driver called out as he and the guard deposited the strongbox on the floor of the driver's box.

Drusilla and Eula hesitated for a moment, uncertain what form their good-byes should take, and then, reading each other's inclination, suddenly threw their arms around each other. They embraced for a long moment, with Eula saying from beneath her sunbonnet, "God bless you, Drusilla, and thankee for everything. You been a good friend to me, and I ain't gonna forget it."

With her hands on Eula's shoulders, Drusilla said, "I just want you to remember that I *am* your friend, and I'll want to know how you're getting on, so you be sure to write us once in a while, y'hear?"

Speaking from behind her hand, Eula said, "I'll do that, I surely will. God bless you. And God bless you, too, Marshal," she said to Gypsy. "And thankee for your help."

Gypsy touched the brim of his dusty new hat. "Bye, Miss Eula. And don't you worry about a thing now. You'll be all right. John Maxwell's a good man."

Eula climbed into the coach, and the driver was about to close the door, when he noticed the seating arrangement of the four passengers. "Naw, naw, naw," he said. "This ain't gonna do."

Three passengers—two men and a woman—were black. Two of the blacks—a man and his wife—were seated on the rear seat, facing forward. The lone black man had taken a place on the forward seat, looking backward. Eula had taken the seat beside him.

"White and colored passengers can't ride on the same seat," the driver reminded them. Nobody moved. "It's the law. Law says coloreds occupy one seat, whites t'other, and if they ain't enough seats to go 'round, coloreds have to give up their seats and ride the baggage rack on top."

Nobody moved or said anything. Her head lowered guiltily, Eula sat in a frozen attitude of distress. The black man on the seat beside her fidgeted with sullen defiance but didn't move.

"Marshal?" The driver turned to Gypsy. "You the lawman here, you tell 'em."

"Jim Crow law," Gypsy said. "We don't recognize no Jim Crow laws here in Freedom."

"Well, it's the territorial law, and I ain't gonna risk my job by disobeying it. Now, you people in there, you can either do what the law says, or we ain't going nowhere. We ain't moving from this spot till you coloreds are all sitting together. It's up to you." He pulled a sack of tobacco from his shirt pocket and began rolling a cigarette.

After a long moment of tense and embarrassed silence, the black man sitting beside Eula got up and squeezed onto the rear seat with the other two Negroes. The driver struck a match and held it in cupped hands to light his cigarette, then snapped the match away into the dust and hitched up his gun belt.

"Aw right then, let's get on the road." He slammed the coach door closed and climbed up into the driver's box. "Hey-yaw! Het up!" he shouted, slapping the reins across the horses' backs. The coach jerked into motion.

Drusilla waved. "Bye! Bye!" she called. "Be sure to write now." She pulled the end of her scarf across her face to shut out the dust spinning off the wheels of the coach.

Eula waved from the window of the coach until the rising dust hid her from view.

Although disturbed, Drusilla and Gypsy made no reference to the Jim Crow incident as they walked away.

"I left my grocery basket at the store," she said. "Walk with me? I'd like to talk to you about something. It's Clarence," she continued as they thudded along the warped-board sidewalks. "He's beginning to worry me. He's only sixteen now, but he's beginning to think of himself as a man. You understand? With girls, I mean. That's all he seems to think about anymore— girls, girls, girls. Doesn't even try to do his schoolwork. And there's no use me threatening to expel him from school. He'd like nothing better. Then he could hang around with that Fast Talking Charlie and the other hooligans in town."

"Want me to horsewhip him?"

Ignoring his bantering tone, Drusilla said, "I thought maybe you could give him a good talking-to, a man-to-man sort of talk."

"The birds and the bees?"

"Gypsy," she chided, "this is serious. I'm serious. He needs to be told by a man how a boy can get into trouble with girls."

"Well, I'm just the man who can tell him about *that*."

She stopped and turned to him, lowering her voice so the passersby and the sidewalk loiterers couldn't overhear her. "It's not funny, Gypsy. The other night he got caught, he and Charlie, peeking into—into a neighbor's window. They were caught watching a woman get undressed. Her husband caught 'em. He knew Clarence, always knew him to be a good boy, he said, so he brought him to me 'stead of to you." She pivoted and walked on. "He said if it ever happened again, though, he'd have Clarence arrested."

"All right. Sure. I'll have a talk with the boy, but I wouldn't take it so serious. Never knew a boy his age who didn't try, one time or other, to get a peek at a naked woman."

She had started to go into the grocery store but stopped and turned on him. She glared at him in silence, though her expression said as well as words could, "A fine father *you'd* make."

Gypsy followed her into the grocery store. Her shopping basket was ready to go, having been filled by the grocery clerk from a list she had left him, and it was heavy—too heavy for her to carry, Gypsy figured, so he offered to carry it home for her. She didn't refuse. On the contrary, she seemed rather to expect it, not because she couldn't carry the basket herself but because she needed to test his tolerance for domesticity, just as, for the same reason, she had asked him to have a talk with Clarence. She wanted to give him a good dose of domestic life, and see if he could handle it, before she would even consider taking him for a husband.

Not that he had actually proposed. There had been a few teasing hints and allusions between them concerning married life, but the subject wasn't openly faced until that evening. She invited him to stay for supper, and he accepted, not only for the pleasure of her company and a good home-cooked meal but because he thought he might find an opportunity to speak with Clarence. He assumed that such an opportunity would somehow present itself without any contrivance on his part, and when it didn't, he was just as glad to put it off for another day.

"Plenty of time for that," he said to Drusilla when, after supper, they were sitting alone on the porch swing in the dark.

"You mean you've decided to stay on here in Freedom this time?" she asked.

"Well, I'll tell you, that might partly depend on you."

"Me?" She fanned a little faster. "What's it got to do with *me*?"

Sitting in a porch swing—Gypsy learned that evening—was not the best place for courting a girl if the girl wasn't eager to be courted. Whenever he tried to turn sideways on the seat and face her and begin to maneuver for a kiss, Drusilla gave her end of the swing a shove, causing it to wobble, making a kiss difficult. She also had the fan, of course, which was a perfectly natural thing to have on a hot airless autumn evening, but it wasn't easy to kiss a girl while she was fanning herself, especially if she fanned herself faster and faster as the mood grew more intimate.

"Well, the fact is," he said, "I been thinking about settling down—you know, maybe getting married and all that."

"Don't tell me! The man who said he wasn't the marrying kind has changed his mind?"

From inside the house came the noise of Mingo and Sassy arguing about whose turn it was to wash the supper dishes. Clarence and Link had been sent to fetch water. Gypsy and Drusilla were alone for one of the few times since his return to Freedom. They sat in the porch swing, looking toward the town, where lamps and lanterns were being lit. The haze of red dust in the air gave the lights a reddish glow. From among the immigrant camps on the outskirts of town came the howl of a dog, and another dog somewhere across town took up the howl, giving a lonesome sound to the lonesome look of a small dusty settlement lighting its lamps against the engulfing prairie darkness.

"The country's changed," he said. "Maybe I've changed with it. A man can change, can't he?"

The fan went a little faster. "And you—you're telling me . . ." She faltered but finally blurted it out: "What're you saying? That you want to marry *me*?"

"Well," he drawled, "I 'spect I could be talked into it."

She sprang to her feet. "You 'could be talked into it'! You've got your nerve, Gypsy Smith! Why, a girl'd have to be crazy to marry you! You think you can just run off for four years, without so much as saying good-bye or writing me so much as a postcard in all that time, and then come back here and say I might be able to—to . . ." Sputtering into silence, she abruptly crossed to the porch railing and stood with her back to him, the fan going at full speed. "Why, a woman who married you, what'd she have to look forward to? Waking up some morning and finding you gone like some wild goose in the night. And you talk about 'could be talked into it.' Why, I wouldn't marry you if you got down on your knees and *begged* me."

He slowly got to his feet and moved to stand behind her. "Now, that's real disheartening, Drusilla darling." He put his hands softly on her shoulders, careful not to make any quick moves, as if approaching a skittish animal.

"Don't you 'darling' me." But her body wasn't as rejecting as her words. She allowed his hands to remain on her shoulders.

"Real disheartening, indeed." He slowly pulled down the high collar of her dress, exposing the side of her neck, which he leaned down to kiss.

The fan stopped. Contending forces within her held her immobile for a moment as Gypsy nuzzled her neck, but then, as if released by a spring, she spun around so forcefully that his hands were jerked from her shoulders.

"Looky here, Gypsy—"

He cut off her words with a kiss. Stifled in her throat, her words trailed off into an uncertain hum and then turned into a small moan of pleasure. She put her arms around him and returned the kiss.

The lamplight from inside the house filtered through the screen door and dusty windows and fell in fan-shaped patterns on the front porch. Gypsy and Drusilla stood in the darker shadows on the porch, silent except for the small sounds of kissing, so the man approaching the house didn't see or hear them. And because Gypsy and Drusilla were too involved in their own activity to hear the man's dust-muffled footfalls as he approached, they were taken by surprise the moment his foot touched the porch. Drusilla tore herself from Gypsy's embrace and whirled to face the man, who, catching sight of the suddenly separating bodies in the shadows, froze in the attitude of a peeping Tom caught in the act.

"Homer! Dr. Upchurch! I didn't—we didn't . . ." She was rapidly fanning herself again, and it would have been difficult to tell who was more embarrassed, she or the doctor.

"Oh," he murmured. " 'Scuse me. I didn't—I didn't see you there. I was just out for an evening stroll, you see, and thought I'd . . . I didn't know you had company."

"This is Gypsy. Marshal Smith. You know Marshal Smith, of course"—compounding her feeling of foolishness by speaking the obvious. "We were just going to have a glass of cool tea. Would you join us?"

"Tea? Uh, no thank you. I was just out for a stroll, thought I'd drop by for a minute, see how you were." And now that his own embarrassment had begun to abate, his voice took on a barely discernible edge of jealous resentment. "Mrs. Drew's expecting her baby sometime tonight. I'd better go look in on her."

Gypsy watched her face as she watched Dr. Upchurch disappear into the darkness. He was trying to discover what she felt for the young man. She was obviously fond of him and sorry that she had embarrassed and possibly hurt him, and there was something in the way she kept looking after him long after he had disappeared that made Gypsy wonder if she regretted his departure. In an effort to lighten the mood and, he hoped, to resume their passionate kissing, Gypsy touched her shoulder and said fondly, "Drusilla, darling—"

"No." She jerked away from his touch. And now the fan was going again. "You'd better go, too. I can't trust myself with you anymore tonight. Lordy mercy, you do bring out the devil in me. You best go on now. I'm not wrestling with the devil anymore tonight."

He said good night without trying to kiss her again, but he had stepped off the porch and gone only a few feet when she called his name. Turning, he saw the light from the doorway behind her, giving her the appearance of a dark depthless form surrounded by a soft nimbus of lamplight.

"Gypsy Smith," she said again. "Do you love me?"

The question was so straightforward that Gypsy was forced to examine his feelings once again, just to be sure, in the same way that he would have had to look up at the stars, just to be sure, had she asked him matter-of-factly if the stars were still there.

"It's a simple question," she said. "You can answer with a simple yes or no."

And as if she had actually asked him if the stars were still there, he answered, "Ain't it obvious?"

After a pause she said, "We'll see. G'night," and went back into the house.

As Gypsy walked down the long dark gentle incline into the lamplit town, he pondered the implication of that "We'll see" and came to the suspicion that his capacity for being a husband to a spirited young wife and a foster father to a bunch of waifs was going to be tested to the utmost. And he knew that the children, foster or not, would come first with her—as Lieutenant Beauregard Pierce had found out, to his sorrow. Drusilla had always been reluctant to reveal to anyone why her engagement to Lieutenant Pierce had not ended in marriage. She considered it nobody's business. But when the subject became germane to Gypsy's renewed interest in her, she informed him—cautioned him—that she had broken off her engagement to Lieutenant Pierce because of the lieutenant's attitude toward her brood of foster children. The lieutenant had been evasive on the point until only a few days before their marriage was to take place, and then he broke it to her gently that there would be no place for the children on the army post where they were going to live. He had suggested that they find other foster homes for the children. She broke off her engagement to him and vowed that any man in the future who might want her as a wife would have to prove himself to be a settled-down hearth and home man who had room in his heart for half a dozen waifs.

Well, Gypsy didn't mind being tested. He thought it was a good idea, in fact, and even enjoyed some of it. Carrying Drusilla's grocery basket home for her, for instance, the way a smitten schoolboy might carry his sweetheart's books home from school, had the piquancy of novelty, and he found that he rather enjoyed sitting around at night after supper, telling the children heroic stories of his adventures as a frontiersman, buffalo hunter, wild horse wrangler, and Indian scout.

But Drusilla's request that he have a man-to-man talk with Clarence left him feeling a little inadequate. Having come to maturity among Indians, he always found himself slightly disconcerted by Christian attitudes toward sex, and he wasn't at all certain what Drusilla expected him to tell the boy. So he procrastinated—a day passed, two days, a week—and then something happened that rendered any such talk irrelevant and made Gypsy sorry indeed that he had put off the talk even for a day.

CHAPTER TWENTY-FIVE

MAXWELL MET EULA WHEN SHE CAME IN ON THE AFTERNOON stage from El Reno. She was among six white passengers riding inside the coach. There were three Indians riding on top and two on the boot, segregated by color, though all the passengers were the same color now: the rusty red of the dust that covered all their faces and clothes.

Scanning the passengers as they stepped off the coach, Maxwell said to one, "Miss Rasmussen, is it?" and managed not to show any adverse reaction when she said, "Yes, sir," and dropped her hand for a second to let him see her harelip. Then she lowered her head once again to hide her face beneath the hood of the sunbonnet.

"Well!" Maxwell said, slightly rattled, not by Eula's deformity so much as by her own painful self-consciousness about it. "Welcome to Agency, Miss Rasmussen. Which bag is yours?"

"This here bundle's all I got. Fire burned up everything else."

"Oh, yes, the fire. I read about it in the newspaper. Terrible business. I'm sorry. Here, let me carry that for you."

"No, thankee, it ain't heavy."

"Well, then," he said, starting for the house.

Eula walked at his side but a little behind, hanging back to let him go first. He slowed down to allow her to catch up, but she also slowed down, always a little behind him, like a faithful dog who had been trained to heel.

"I'm sorry the house's in something of a mess at the moment," he said over his shoulder. "My daughter's leaving to go to school in St. Louis in a few days, so we've been doing lots of packing and planning, but very little housework, I'm afraid. That's why we were so glad to get Gypsy's telegram about you. Very fortuitous, that was. My daughter—Rachel's her name—she's been doing most of the work around the house since our last housekeeper left and helping to take care of her mother, who's an invalid— You know? Did Gypsy tell you?"

He stopped. She stopped. She glanced at him from beneath her dusty bonnet, and her hand came up to cover her mouth.

"Yes, sir, he told me."

He went on. She followed a little behind, both feeling awkward: he, because he didn't like to see anyone as subservient as Miss Rasmussen; she, because she had expected to be treated like a servant, not like a guest. Having worked most of her adult life as a servant in the homes of Minnesota farmers, none of whom had ever greeted her with a handshake and addressed her as Miss Rasmussen, she didn't know how to respond to such treatment. Also, he was an educated man, and Eula was in awe of education. To her, educated people were on a higher level of being. So the prospect of her going to work for one—a schoolmaster, in fact, a scholarly-looking man with inkstained fingers—was enough to make her more than usually self-conscious.

"Well, there'll be time to talk about all that—about the missus, I mean, and your salary, and what you'll be doing. I expect you'll want to wash up a bit first, after such a dusty trip."

"A pan of water'd be a blessing, thankee kindly."

He opened the front gate of the yard fence and stepped back

and waited. She waited, too, for a moment, glancing at him to
see what was expected of her.

"After you."

"Thankee." Flustered again, she passed through the gate but
fell behind again as they went up the walk.

Rachel was in the front room. She had been standing at the
window, watching through the dusty pane as Maxwell and
Eula came up the walk. She opened the front door for them
and gave Eula a thorough scrutinizing as she was introduced.
The few housekeeper-nursemaids who had come and gone
over the years of Nora's illness had been middle-aged women,
used-up women, who didn't have anything better to do, and as
soon as they found something better, they left. But Eula was
different. She didn't seem old and used up. True, there was the
puzzling way she hid her mouth when Maxwell introduced her
as Miss Rasmussen and she said, "First name's Eula, if you
want to call me that." She looked rather dowdy, too, in that
dusty old-maidish dress, but there was a sort of stolid good
cheer about her which, considering what she had recently been
through, bespoke a rock-bottom optimism, and Rachel liked
her for that.

But Rachel's eyes went to Maxwell for an explanation of
why Eula was so shy about showing her face, and Maxwell's
expression said in response, "Behave yourself, don't stare, I'll
explain later." And to divert her attention, he said, "What're
you doing here? I thought you were over with Miss Clarksdale, getting your new dresses fitted."

"I was, but I couldn't stand still, worrying about Corby. He
left a little while ago, said he didn't know when he'd be back."

"Well, we won't concern Miss Eula with that," Maxwell
said. "Come, the washstand's out on the back porch."

Rachel was tempted to follow and peep through the screen
door to see if Eula would take off the sunbonnet and reveal her
face when she washed, but she managed to resist the impulse.

"Now, what's this about Corby?" Maxwell asked when he
returned. "Where'd he go?"

"I don't know. He said he was going on a vision quest.
Whoever heard of an educated Indian going on a vision
quest? I thought only ignorant blanket Indians did that. Oh,
Daddy, does this mean he's going back to the blanket? Can't
you make him go to Carlisle? If you can't, I don't think I

should go away to school either. What's the use? I couldn't do my work, wondering what was happening to him."

"All the more reason you have to go. I'm damned if I'll see you throw your life away just because he does. Anyway, it'll be all right, I'm sure. I expect I'll have him in Carlisle before the year's out. But you go on back over to the school, now, see that Miss Clarksdale gets those dresses properly fitted. Go on now. I have to talk to Miss Rasmussen."

"Say, what's wrong with her?" Rachel asked in a whisper. "Why's she keep her face hidden?"

"Harelip," he whispered.

"Oh," Rachel said. "Oh, the poor woman."

CHAPTER TWENTY-SIX

FAST TALKING CHARLIE WAS BENT OVER AN OPERATING TABLE, naked, sweating, clenching his teeth to keep from crying out, while Dr. Upchurch picked buckshot from his buttocks with a pair of needle-nosed tweezers. Clarence, dressed only in trousers, sat on a chair nearby.

"How bad?" Gypsy asked as he and Buck Tyson entered the room.

Squinting through his horn-rimmed eyeglasses, Dr. Upchurch extracted another pellet and dropped it into a metal dish. "The pellets are just under the skin. Nothing to worry about medically. The worry is, who shot 'em? A white man, they say, but they're pretty closemouthed when it comes to why. Only three more to go," he told Charlie. "Hold still now."

Gypsy turned to Clarence. "All right, Clarence, let's hear it, all of it, and it better be the truth."

Clarence was leaning forward in the chair, his elbows on his knees, holding his head in his hands. He was big for his sixteen years, a boy whose wits hadn't kept pace with his body. On his upper back were four small beads of blood.

"Listen to me, Clarence," Gypsy said, "and listen good, boy. I want to know who shot you, and why, and I want to know *now*."

"Yes, sir," Clarence murmured, raising his head, his light-skinned face blanched with fear and pain. He stumbled evasively into the story of what happened, and between yelps of pain as the last of the buckshot pellets were extracted from Charlie's backside, Charlie threw in a few fast corrections or elaborations. Within a few minutes Gypsy knew the worst of it.

The two had been shot by a farmer named Tully, who had caught Charlie fornicating with his fourteen-year-old daughter as Clarence stood by. It seemed that Charlie had met her one day at a swimming hole on Cottonwood Creek about a mile from the Tully farm, and the girl confessed that she often came there to hide in the bushes and watch colored boys swim. "And she say it be all right if I diddles her," Charlie said, " 'cause she diddled with lots of white boys she say but she ain't never diddled with a colored boy. She crazy."

But crazy or not, Charlie had obliged her, and liked it so much he went back to do it again. When he bragged to Clarence about this crazy cracker girl who couldn't get enough, Clarence begged to go along next time and diddle her, too. Charlie took pity on poor Clarence, who had never diddled a girl in his life, and took him along that morning to meet the girl at the swimming hole.

"And I didn't even get to do it," Clarence complained.

Charlie had been on top of the girl and Clarence was standing by, waiting his turn, when they heard somebody on foot crashing through the bushes, then saw the man emerge—a white man, carrying a shotgun. The man's momentary paralysis of disbelief at what he was seeing gave the boys time to grab their clothes and start running before he recovered his senses and fired the shotgun. The man was too far away for the buckshot to do any serious damage, though the boys weren't so far away that they couldn't hear the girl screaming and crying when the man began beating her.

"All right," Gypsy said. "Buck, as soon as the doc gets 'em patched up, bring 'em down to the jail."

"Jail?" Charlie whined. "What's we done to get locked up?"

"For your own protection, you young scamp," Buck said, "and let's hope it's protection enough."

Gypsy hurried back to his office, where he found Deputy Rufus Margrave sitting behind a desk doing some paperwork. On taking over the job of town marshal from Rufus, Gypsy, at the urging of the town council, had kept Rufus on as a deputy, and he'd had no reason to regret the decision. Rufus was good at paperwork, a chore that Gypsy was more than happy to relegate to him.

Gypsy went to the maps on the back wall and scrutinized the Land Commission map that showed all the quarter section homestead claims in the county. Within each square was the name of the person who owned the claim.

"You know anything about a white farmer name Tully?" he asked Rufus. "Got a farm about five miles northeast of here, on Cottonwood Creek." He put his finger on the map. "Here it is. Lester Tully."

"I knows they's a white farmer living out there, but I don't know him. Passed him on the road a few times. White trash, by the looks of him. Why?"

"He ain't never come to Freedom for supplies?"

"Not that I know of."

"Lives about five miles from here and about fifteen from Guthrie, and yet he must go all that way to Guthrie for supplies 'stead of coming here. Why you reckon he'd do that?"

"Must be he don't want nothing to do with colored folks."

"I 'spect you right. In fact, he must hate colored folks considerable if he'd go all that way just to avoid 'em. Find Mayor Sawyer and Judge Cale. Ask 'em to drop whatever they're doing and come here."

"What's happened?"

"I'll explain it to you same time I explain it to them. You know where Amos Fulton is?"

"Last time I heard, he was up in Langston."

"Send him a telegram. Tell him he better get on down here soon's he can. We got trouble."

Late that afternoon Sheriff Alva Harriman and six deputies rode into town, accompanied by Lester Tully and his daughter. The group came riding in from the north at a slow trot. Tully followed in a dilapidated buckboard pulled by two bony plow horses, partially obscured by eddies of dust blown along the empty street. The only signs of life in the town were the horses and mules tied to hitching rails and a ribby dog sniffing along the wooden sidewalk.

Gypsy stepped casually out of his office and leaned against a gallery post. In his left hand he held a double-barreled sawed-off shotgun. His right thumb was hooked beneath his cartridge belt near his Colt.

The riders, made nervous by the town's emptiness, approached Gypsy slowly and seemed to stop in front of him as if by indifference or coincidence. Sheriff Harriman was not a corpulent man, but his body seemed fat because his flesh had a dropsical, flaccid look. He had a turkey wattle under his chin that wobbled when he spoke.

"Gypsy Smith, is it?"

"Marshal Gypsy Smith," Gypsy corrected, and added, "At yo suhvice, suh," mimicking the sheriff's Deep South drawl.

"*The* Gypsy Smith?" the sheriff said. "Well, I declare! I've heard about you. I hear you're one of the few darkies 'round these parts that can read. So I assume you read the telegram I sent, and you know why we're here. As you can see"—jerking his head toward the Tully wagon—"we brought the victim along to make identification. If the boys you're holding are the ones who so brutally violated and beat this young girl, we'll be taking them back to Guthrie with us to stand trial. Now, if you'll just bring 'em out. . . ."

"Well, Sheriff, I 'spect you can read, too," Gypsy said, amiably condescending, "so you know the telegram I sent you said we was going to keep the boys here. We'll give 'em a fair trial, and if they be proved guilty, why, we'll just take 'em out and hang 'em. You got my word on it."

"Your word? Nigrah, your word don't mean a damned thing to me. That badge you're wearing don't neither. Now I hope I don't have to educate you on matters of legal jurisdiction, boy, but you better realize one thing. I'm the sheriff of this county, and the territorial courts are in Guthrie, and that's where those boys'll be tried and hung—if proved guilty," he added, as if amused to think there could be any doubt about it. He leaned sideways in the saddle, preparing to dismount.

Gypsy snapped the order: "Don't get down."

The sheriff's body froze for a moment in imbalance as he glared at Gypsy. Then his body slowly settled back down into the leather-creaking saddle, and his hand moved tentatively toward his holstered gun. His indignation caused him to flush and breathe in asthmatic gulps. "Now, you listen to me, boy—"

"No, you listen to me." Gypsy raked his eyes across the other riders, who, following the sheriff's lead, were making tentative motions toward their guns. "Each one of you's in the sights of a gun right now. If any one of you so much as pulls a gun, none of you'll ride out of here alive. Better take time to think about that."

Their eyes darted here and there, searching out the hiding places of the alleged guns. None was anywhere to be seen.

"You're bluffing," Sheriff Harriman said.

"Am I?" Gypsy raised his voice enough to be heard at a distance above the rustling of the dust-swirling wind. "All right, men, show y'selves."

From behind the false-front parapets atop the two-story buildings on both sides of the street, men rose with rifles and shotguns in their hands. From around the corners of nearby buildings, from behind second-story balcony doors, from the catwalks on the water tanks at both ends of town, men stepped into the open with weapons aimed at the sheriff and his party. There were probably thirty men in all, all positioned to catch the sheriff in a crossfire.

"That look like a bluff to you, Sheriff?"

The sheriff's pursy body trembled with stifled fury. "Nigrah, do you have any idea what you're doing? This is insurrection, boy, pure and simple. This'll get you hung."

"Maybe so. But at least you'll have to hang me before you hang them two boys for something they didn't do."

"Didn't do! Why, goddamn you, look at that girl. You can see what they done. They brutally raped and beat that girl, and for you to aid and abet them makes you and all these here gun-toting Nigrahs as guilty as they are."

Careful not to make any quick movements, Gypsy stepped off the gallery and approached the buckboard on the side on which the girl huddled on the seat, a shawl draped over her downcast head and face.

"Missy?"

She didn't lift her head, but he could see her deeply pock-marked face framed in the dust-covered shawl and a frizzle of corn-colored hair. He could see the bruises on her face, the black eye, the swollen mouth. The deep pockmarks and frizzled hair gave her a slatternly look, but the way she held her head was almost angelic.

"Missy, did them boys beat you? Or was it your pa?"

"Get away from her, you black bastard!" Tully said. "My daughter ain't talking to no black niggers. Get away from her!" He made a threatening move toward the shotgun lying at his feet on the floor of the buckboard.

"Tully!" the sheriff barked.

Tully's hand pulled back. "Then tell that black bastard to get away from her!"

One glance at Tully's face told Gypsy that the man was on the edge of insanity, a loss of control that could bring on a calamity. Stepping away from the buckboard, he chanced to see the legs of one of the horses in the rear of the group. It had three white stockings, one in front, two in back. Gypsy's eyes fastened on to the horse's rider, a young man with long blond hair and blue eyes and a sly, mischief-loving demeanor.

Going back to the gallery, Gypsy announced, "If that girl wants to file charges against the two prisoners, I'll be happy to oblige her, and I guarantee they'll be brought to trial." He paused briefly. "But they'll be tried right here in Freedom, by a jury of their peers, as the saying goes, in the court of the Honorable Judge Willoughby J. Cale, Esquire. Everybody'll be welcome to attend, of course, and if the prisoners are found guilty, why, you'll all be invited to the hanging." After another brief pause he added, "Till then I reckon there ain't nothing else to say. So if you gentlemen'll just be on your way now, we'll all get on back to our chores."

"Well, they told me you was a crazy Nigrah, but I declare, I had no idea you was *this* crazy. Why, you 'bout the craziest Nigrah I ever did see. You think we won't be back?" He snorted with contempt. "Well, you just start counting the hours, black boy. You don't have many of 'em left. By this time tomorrow you'll be dead."

"Maybe so, Sheriff, but you can count on one thing: I'll take a lot of men with me when I go."

The sheriff swung his horse around with a jerk of the reins and kicked it into a gallop. The other riders fell in behind him, leaving the Tully buckboard to bring up the rear. And as they galloped out of town, the last thing Gypsy could see through the billowing red dust was Lester Tully standing up in his buckboard, whipping his plow horses into a run, as if terrified of being left behind.

Once the hoofbeats faded in the distance, the possemen started coming down from their vantage points and a few people began to filter out of the doorways along the street. Among them was Rufus Margrave, who emerged from the marshal's office still clutching a shotgun. Gypsy noted that Rufus had the sweaty, scared look of a man who had just had his courage tested and been found wanting.

"What d'you think they'll do now?" Rufus asked.

"That deputy with the long blond hair—know anything about him?"

"A little, I guess. Name's Sonny Boy something or other. Reeves, I think. Yeah. Reeves. Big Mama'd be the one to tell you 'bout him. He sneaks into town once in a while to see one of her girls."

Gypsy was taken aback. "*Here?* He comes *here*?"

"To Big Mama's place, yeah. She's the one who told me about him. I saw him sneaking into town one night and followed him to her place. He ties his horse out behind her house and sneaks in the back door. Why? What about him?"

"He's a Klansman."

"What?"

"Pretty sure. That horse of his was among them ridden by the Klansmen the night they burned Eula Rasmussen's place."

"A Klansman? Lord Jesus," Rufus said.

Some of the possemen and the townspeople, talking among themselves, were forming into a loose crowd in front of town hall. Buck came through them, his rifle resting on his shoulder, and joined Gypsy and Rufus on the gallery.

"Buck, I'm going to Big Mama's for a minute. While I'm gone, I want you to put three guards out here in front and three in the back and make sure they're in plain sight all the time. The rest of you men," he said to those gathering in the street, "can relax for a while, but don't wander off too far. They'll be back."

Bending his head against a gust of stinging sand, Gypsy went down a side street to Big Mama's hoodoo parlor and sporting house, a false-fronted two-story unpainted building sitting off by itself in a weedy lot behind Cooley's livery stable. A tumbleweed blew against his legs and he kicked it out of the way. As he mounted the squeaky steps to the porch, Big Mama, who had been watching through the window, opened the door before he knocked.

"Is they gone?"

"For now."

She quickly shut the door against the wind and dust. The small parlor was a maze of claptrap furniture and geegaws and the esoteric paraphernalia used by Big Mama in her profession as a hoodoo woman. As a sideline she kept four girls in the house. Three of them, dressed in their tawdry whore's finery, were in the parlor.

"Rufus tells me you got a white boy comes here sometimes, a deputy from Guthrie?"

"Yeah. Sometimes he sneak in the back way to see Lulu Belle."

"Which one's she?"

"She in her room. You wants to talk with her?"

Big Mama led the way in her flapping house slippers down the hallway to the last door, the room closest to the back entrance. Lulu Belle, dressed in a flimsy soiled chemise, was lying facedown on a rumpled bed. A homely coffee-colored girl with uncombed hair, she did no more than look up at them until Big Mama barked, "Lulu Belle! You get out that bed! Lord God, girl, you the laziest thing I ever did see." To Gypsy, she said, "I swear that girl'd lay there in bed if the house was burning down 'round her ears."

Lulu Belle heaved her body into a sitting position and planted her feet on the bare floor. She was maybe twenty years old but looked forty, and one side of her face was disfigured by a razor scar. The room was cloying with the smells of sex and stale perfume.

"What's y'all want?"

"I want you to tell me what you know about a white deputy sheriff—name's Sonny Boy?—comes here to see you sometimes."

"What's you wanna know?"

"Whatever you can tell me about him. Like, why's he come here to see you?" And to avoid an obvious answer, he added quickly, "I mean, you, a colored woman. He ever say anything about hisself?"

"He don't come to talk. He come frig wid me, what's you think? Don't talk. Only talking he do, he like to say, 'Nigger, nigger, nigger,' while he frigging me. Shiyut. White sumbitch, I don't care. He got a dollar, I frig wid him, even he do like to say, 'Nigger, nigger.' "

"He ever beat you?"

"Him! Shiyut. White sumbitch, he hit me, I cut 'im wid a knife. That's what I do."

"He ever mention the Ku Klux Klan?"

"He ax me once was I ever whupped by the Klan. Shiyut. Ain't no Klan gonna whup me. I cut 'em wid a knife. That's what I tell 'im. He just laugh. He say maybe he whup me someday. I tell 'im, he do, I cut 'im good."

Gypsy said to them both, "Look, if this boy ever comes back here, I want to know about it immediately. You understand? The minute he comes in the door, I want you to send somebody to tell me."

On leaving the house, he took a deep breath. In spite of being heavily laden with dust, the air had a cleansing effect on the stale sweet cloying smells of Lulu Belle's room that clung to his nostrils.

Back at the town hall he once again found Rufus Margrave sitting at his desk in the lamplit office.

"You manage to locate Fulton?"

"In Langston, yeah. Said he'd be coming in on tomorrow's stage."

"Send him another telegram. Ask him to check with his spies in Guthrie, find out everything he can about this Sonny Boy Reeves." He opened a drawer of the desk and rummaged around until he found a small black notebook, which he handed to Rufus. "Use that code he dreamed up case some of the telegraph operators along the way are Klansmen."

Rufus got up to go. "She's here," he said, jerking his head toward the door leading down into the jail cells. "Miss Drusilla. She brought the boys some supper."

Nodding, Gypsy turned once again to the wall maps. From the county map he refreshed his memory about all the different combinations of intersecting back roads that could be used to connect Freedom with Guthrie.

Drusilla's footsteps came up the stairs from the basement jail. Wearing an apron and a dusting cap, she entered the office carrying an empty wicker basket. Gypsy's presence brought a small quavering smile to her lips, but at the same time her eyes moistened with a grief that she could no longer contain.

"I brought the boys something to eat."

"You shouldn't be here," he said sternly, but relented, adding, "But the boys have to eat. How are you?"

She came to him and lightly, awkwardly touched his forearm. "Not very well, to tell the truth. I'm tired. I'm just so very tired and so afraid and so damned mad."

"Here. Sit." He guided her to the chair behind the desk.

"Those men . . . Rufus said one was a Klansman."

"Rufus talks too much."

She stared into the lamplight, her eyes glistening with tears. "They came here to lynch the boys, didn't they?"

"I 'spect so." He sat on the edge of the desk, reached out to touch her shoulder. "But don't you worry none. We ain't gonna let nothing like that happen."

She placed her hand on his, pressed it, and murmured, "Thank you, Gypsy. Thank God for you." She was making an effort to keep from weeping.

He placed a hand on her shoulder.

"I'm sorry," she said. "It's just that I'm so tired. How long are we going to have to run, Gypsy? Where can we go to get away from them? Why do they *hate* us so much? What'd we ever do to them that they should *hate* us so much? Why won't they ever leave us *alone*?" The tears were streaming down her face now. "Why do they want to kill our *children*?"

"I don't know. I got no answers."

Struggling to get control of herself, she dug a handkerchief from the pocket of her apron, wiped her swollen eyes, making an effort to regain composure. Lifting her head, she even managed a small apologetic smile. "Well, if you got no answers, how about a comforting hug?"

"Got plenty of them." He opened his arms, enfolded her, and said, "It's gonna be all right. You'll see. Everything's gonna be all right."

She seemed to believe him. She snuggled against him, and he felt an intense shudder pass through her body, a sort of convulsion that seemed to empty her of all violent feelings. After that, arms around each other, they stood, slightly swaying, and not another word was said until she, in a small voice muffled against the folds of his shirt, said, "Thank you, Gypsy. I feel safe here. In your arms, I mean. All my life it seems, ever since I was a little girl, I've been looking for someone—a God, a daddy, a husband—someone who'd take me in his arms and tell me everything was going to be all right and make it so." She lifted her head and gave him a searching look, then took a deep breath, as if summoning up all her courage and determination. "Gypsy Smith, would you marry me?"

He chuckled. "Why, Miss Drusilla, honey, I thought you'd never ask."

"I'm serious," she said, once again disconcerted by the levity with which he seemed to treat all matters of love and marriage.

"Well, I certainly hope so. I'd sure hate to think you was trifling with my heart."

They looked at each other for a moment across that small gulf of attitudes. She, a good Christian, always thought of love as something very serious, even somber, while he, who had come of age among heathen Indians, always associated love with laughter. What was sacred to her was delight to him. But she realized suddenly—and at last—that his lack of seriousness didn't mean that he wasn't sincere, and with this realization she finally leaped that gulf. With a small cry of joy she threw her arms around his neck, and in a jumble of words, as they covered each other's faces with kisses, she said, "You will?" and he said, "Sure," and she said, "When?" and he said, "Why, tomorrow'd be just fine with me," and she cried, "Tomorrow!" and he, in a more sensible tone, said, "Well, as soon's this business is over with anyway. I'll have to talk with Preacher Pangborn, get it all arranged," and she said, "I love you," and he said, "I love you, too, Drusilla, darling," and for a moment it seemed they were already hearing wedding bells.

It was the fire bell. Somebody had begun to ring the bell in a series of three rapid clangs, rest, three rapid clangs, rest.

"The signal for the men to assemble," Gypsy said. "Something's up. Come on, we got to get you home."

He snatched the shotgun off the desk and ushered her hastily out onto the gallery, where they saw the dark shapes of men coming out of lighted doorways and dashing toward the town hall building. One of them, thumping hurriedly along the broad sidewalks, almost ran into them as they stepped from the office. It was Rufus Margrave, panting and sweating.

"They're coming!" he said.

"How d'you know?" Gypsy asked in a voice so calm that it seemed almost indifferent, his instinctive way of counteracting panic in another person.

"The telegraph wires've been cut."

"Both ends of town?"

Rufus nodded. "I had a message coming in from Amos in Langston when the line went dead. A few minutes later the El Reno line went dead, too. They must be on their way."

"I 'spect so. Here, you, Abe!" he called to a man who was just driving up in a buggy. He escorted Drusilla to the buggy. "Take Miss Drusilla home, will you, Abe?" He helped her onto the buggy seat beside Abe and said, "Go home and stay inside. I'll send a couple of men up to guard the school, seeing as how them Ku Kluxers love to burn down schoolhouses."

"Isn't there anything I can do?"

"Well, you might get started making y'self a wedding gown, seeing's how you'll be needing it soon's this thing's over with."

She touched his face. "God bless and keep you, Gypsy Smith."

The buggy pulled away. He stood and watched as it was swallowed up by the darkness and the dust, savoring for a moment the lover's feeling of being blessed, of being the luckiest man alive.

CHAPTER TWENTY-SEVEN

HE WAS BROUGHT BACK TO REALITY BY A SHARP GUST OF wind that flung sand stinging against his face. He stepped back up on the gallery and faced the crowd of men gathering in the street. Some of the men were on foot, others on horseback, a few in vehicles, some with lanterns, all with weapons. Congregating on the gallery near the door of the marshal's office were some of the town's leaders: Mayor Sawyer, Judge Cale, Ike Jones, and Moses Webster. In order to counteract any panic that might be growing in the crowd, Gypsy spoke as if the situation were little more than merely routine.

"Use some wagons to make barricades at both ends of Main Street," he told Buck. "Put about twenty mounted sentries around the town, two guards each on the schoolhouse and the churches, and spell 'em every four hours to make sure nobody falls asleep. Keep 'em supplied with hot coffee. And, listen," he shouted to the other men, "don't start shooting till you know what you're shooting at, y'hear?" Then he turned to the nucleus of the leadership group. "I want to move the boys out of here to a good hiding place somewhere here in town. Anybody know of one?"

"They're not safe here?" Mayor Sawyer asked.

"The Klan could never get 'em out of here with guns, but what if they manage to set fire to one of the buildings on this side of the street? In this wind, wouldn't take long for it to reach us, and then we'd have to take the boys out, and that's when they might try to grab 'em. Be better if they was hid somewhere. We'll keep a heavy guard around this building, so the Klan'll think they're still here. So how about it? Anybody know of a good hiding place?"

Ike Jones said, "Well, how about my storm cellar? They'd be safe there, I should think, even if a cyclone blew up and the whole town burned down."

"Sounds good." To Rufus, who was standing on the edge of the group looking a little shamefaced and useless, he said, "Fetch the boys up."

Carrying lanterns and shotguns, Gypsy and Rufus, accompanied by Ike Jones and a guard called Geezer, escorted the frightened boys from the jail to the storm cellar in a weedy lot behind the street-fronted building that served as both Ike Jones's home and newspaper plant. The roof of the cellar was formed by a big mound of earth, and the entrance was through a steeply inclined wooden door. Gypsy left the boys in the moldy-smelling cellar with instructions to stay inside, with the door closed, until someone came for them.

"And don't worry," he told them. "Ain't no way in hell them Klansmen'll ever know you're here."

Just to be safe, however, he left Geezer, a teamster with a reputation for toughness, to stand guard outside the cellar. Then he and Rufus and Ike went back to town hall to await events.

About an hour later Buck Tyson hurried into the office with the news that the Klan had been spotted. With his false teeth clicking he announced, "Man on the north water tower saw 'em riding this way. Says he couldn't tell how many there was, but there was a bunch. They turned off the road about a quarter mile outside town, heading west." To Gypsy, he said, "Thought I'd take a ride out that way, do some scouting, see can I find out what they're up to."

"You alerted the sentries?" Gypsy asked, and when Buck confirmed that he had, Gypsy told him to go ahead.

The men in the office moved out onto the gallery, where they waited to see what would happen next. With his sawed-off shotgun dangling from his left hand, Gypsy leaned against a gallery post and calmly smoked a cigarette. Rufus paced back and forth on the gallery, a rifle cradled in the crook of his arm. A few times in his pacing he stopped near Gypsy and looked as if he were going to say something, but he turned away each time to continue his clump-clump pacing. At last he worked up enough courage to say, "Looky here, Gypsy, some-body ought to go for help, don't you reckon?"

"Volunteering, are you, Rufus?"

"I'd go, sure," he said, as if he wouldn't shirk his duty should such a desperate venture be required of someone.

"And who you gonna ask for help?"

"Well," Rufus said, groping for an answer. "Well, the army at Fort Reno."

And Gypsy, in the lackadaisical voice of a man reiterating the obvious: "Soldiers won't come without orders from Washington. Washington won't give the order unless the governor declares martial law in the Territory. Governor ain't gonna de-clare martial law till something happens that the territorial mi-litia can't handle. Territorial militia ain't gonna come to take care of something that ain't happened yet." He glanced at Rufus from the corners of his eyes, unable to conceal the pity he felt for the man's growing fears. "You seen anything happen yet? You gonna send the governor a telegram saying, 'Declare martial law, some Ku Kluxers are riding around our area'?"

Rufus nodded, grudgingly accepting Gypsy's argument, and went back to pacing.

After another half hour they heard a shout from the man on the water tower at the south end of town, and, almost simultaneously, shouts from the north end water tower: "Fire! Fire to the west! Prairie fire!" And through the spaces between the westward buildings Gypsy and the others could see, low on the horizon, the first yellowish glow of the fire.

"Yeah," Gypsy said. "That figures."

"God Amighty," Mayor Sawyer groaned. "With a wind like this, we'll be damned lucky if we can hold it at the firebreaks."

The fire bell began a continuous clamoring peal, and people rushed out of the lamplit doorways of the buildings and houses along Main Street to see what was happening.

"And those Klan bastards are gonna make sure it's a big one," Gypsy said.

Staring wide-eyed at the rapidly swelling dome of fiery brightness on the horizon, Rufus said, "Dammit, Gypsy, we got to let somebody know what's going on here. I could ride down to Andersonville, use the telegraph there. Let the federal marshals know, anyway. Not that we'll get any help, but they ought to know."

"All right," Gypsy said, knowing that Rufus would be worthless anyway if it came to a fight with the Klan. "Go ahead."

With unseemly haste, Rufus bounded from the sidewalk to his horse at the hitching rail, still justifying: "Well, you know, if the whole town burns down, we'll need relief supplies and things like that, won't we?" Without waiting for confirmation, he swung into the saddle. "I'll be back soon's I can." He dug his heels into the horse's sides and galloped off down the street, heading south.

The bell on the fire wagon clanged as the wagon pulled out of its shed behind town hall. It came around the corner onto Main Street with four horses straining in harness. Alongside the wagon, with its red water tank and coils of hose, trotted a number of volunteer firemen, and on the wagon seat next to the driver was Moses Webster, the fire chief. The wagon came to a halt in front of the marshal's office. Moses climbed down from the seat and said to the driver, "Take the wagon out to the end of Hally Street and stand by to protect the structures there. You men," he shouted to the volunteer firemen accompanying the wagon, "spread out through town, turn everybody out. Tell 'em to bring hoes and shovels and wet sacks."

The firemen began darting here and there along the streets, making megaphones of their hands and shouting, "Turn out! Turn out! Prairie fire! Turn out!"

"What can we do?" Mayor Sawyer asked the fire chief.

"Well, we got to turn out the whole town," Moses said. "We gonna need everybody who can swing a hoe or a wet sack, and we need wagons to carry folks out to the fire line. We'll try backfiring from the firebreaks this side of Spence's farm, and if we can't stop it there . . ." He shook his head.

Mayor Sawyer and Ike Jones looked questioningly at Gypsy.

"Go ahead," he said, "I'll hold down the fort here."

"What if the Klan comes in while we're out fighting the fire?" Ike Jones asked.

"Long's they don't know where the boys are, they won't get what they came for."

"And what," Mayor Sawyer asked, "if it's you they come for?"

"Well, they won't have no trouble finding me."

"If we hear shooting in this direction, we'll come back with some men," Mayor Sawyer said, stepping off the gallery to join the fire chief.

Left alone on the gallery, Gypsy watched the streets come alive like a disturbed anthill, watched, too, the fire on the horizon as it spread and raged and roared toward town in front of a gusting wind. From the looks of it, it was probably no more than a half mile away, and coming fast. He could already smell the smoke.

Buck Tyson returned from his scouting trip, riding fast on a lathered and blowing horse, and was on the ground by the time the horse skidded to a stop at the hitching rail. Stiff-jointed from the hard ride, he toiled up the steps to the gallery, saying, "Well, I got a look at 'em. Counted sixteen, in all. Come on inside, I'll show you on the map."

Inside the office Buck jabbed the Freedom township map

with a gnarled dirty finger. " 'Bout here, on section ten, Palmer's place. Twelve of 'em at first, and then in a little while, four more rode up from the south to join 'em. All of 'em dressed up in them damned bed sheets. Even their horses. Then they had a powwow and broke up into three groups, took off in different directions. I followed one bunch, the ones that started the fires. Tied bundles of grass to their lariats, they did, and set the bundles on fire, and dragged 'em across Palmer's wheat field. Headed in both directions, cutting fences as they went. Looks like they're making a half circle of fire around town. Sweet Jesus, this's gonna be one hellish night."

Within an hour the fire had reached the outskirts of town. Though perhaps as many as five hundred people were fighting the fire, they couldn't stop it. They slowed it down by backfiring from plowed firebreaks, but strong gusts of wind swirled the fire into small cyclones of sparks, scattering the sparks over large areas of unburned prairie grass or crackling dry wheat behind the firefighters. The firefighters, nearly suffocating from smoke and dust and ashes and heat, swarmed over the area with their wet sacks, beating at the small fires that leaped up from the sparks. Sometimes the sparks dropped on the firefighters themselves, setting fire to their hair and hats and clothes. Sometimes a long gust of wind would reach speeds of over twenty miles an hour as it roared across the tops of wheat and barley fields, sending the firefighters in front of it scurrying for their lives. And sometimes they would almost have it stopped when a jackrabbit or a coyote would dash out of the burning grass with its fur on fire, spreading the fire like a living torch through the unburned areas.

The firefighters kept falling back to form new lines of defense, until the fire had reached the edge of town. It had spread north and south on a two-mile front by this time, but the firefighters had gradually closed ranks as they retreated, until they were fighting virtually shoulder to shoulder in some places along a quarter mile front west of the town, trying to keep the flames from reaching the outlying houses and barns.

They tried to save the buildings by splashing buckets of water on the sides and roofs; but some of the drought-dry wells ran out of water and soon the structures on the outermost edges of town were ablaze.

Gypsy had remained at his post on the gallery in front of his office, watching. By now Main Street was thronged with many of the immigrants who had fled their campgrounds outside town, bringing with them their livestock and wagons and hastily loaded belongings. Most of the immigrants, both men and women, had left their old folks and children with the wagons and gone off to help fight the fire, and when the fire had come close enough to cast a pale flickering glow over the town, and when the hot wind surged through the streets in clouds of suffocating smoke and dust, Gypsy saw the agitated fear that was working its way toward panic in animals and people alike. Horses and mules plunged in their harnesses and reared against their tethers, children cried, old people fell on their knees and prayed.

The fire wagon came careening through the crowds on Main Street a few times, looking for water. On one of its runs Gypsy, wearing a red bandanna over his nose and mouth to filter the dust and smoke and ashes, stepped off the gallery and stopped the fire wagon and asked Moses if they were going to be able to hold it.

"Don't know." Moses's clothes were soaked with sweat, and ashes had adhered to the sweat on his exposed skin, giving him a grayish ghostly look. He and the firemen clinging to the sides of the fire wagon and the horses pulling it looked as if they were ready to drop from exhaustion. "We pretty much got the grass fire stopped on the west side, and if we had some water, or if this damned wind'd die down a little, we might be able to hold it. If not, if it gets into these buildings, this town's gone, and that's all there is to it."

"How many buildings on fire now?"

"Six or seven, last time I counted. Four houses, three or four barns, some outbuildings. If we could find plenty of water, we could stop it at Geezer's place, I 'spect. We on our way to Cooley's well now. He says he maybe got enough to fill the tank once or twice."

Gypsy waved him on. Moses lashed the exhausted horses into motion.

Buck rode up on his lathered mount. Reining to a stop, he turned his face away from a gust of dust- and ash-laden wind, and slumped in the saddle, his forearm resting on the saddle horn. Hawking to clear his throat of dust, he spit with such force that his upper plate was almost ejected with the spittle.

"Oldfield just got back from a scouting trip south of town," he said. "Says he saw sixteen Klansmen in a bunch about two mile out of town, whupping some colored man they'd caught and tied to a tree. Says he couldn't get close enough to see who it was, but he says they was beating the hide off the poor bastard."

Acting on nothing more than a vague apprehension, Gypsy said, "Get down and rest your horse for a while. Hold down the fort here while I go over and check on the boys. Heard some shots over that way a few minutes ago—probably somebody shooting at a white cow, or something like that, but I best go see. Geezer's house's on fire. I doubt he'd stay at his post and watch his house burn down."

"Well, I could use a cup of coffee, for sho."

With the bandanna over the lower part of his face, Gypsy crossed the street and strode along the board sidewalk, keeping to the darker areas to avoid being recognized by the people he met on the way, panicky people who would only delay him with requests for news and reassurances. But suddenly from out of the darkened doorway of the Jones building a woman burst forth, screaming in a voice loud enough to be heard all the way to town hall, "Marshal! Marshal!"

It was Lucille Jones, Ike's plump wife, who was ordinarily a dignified middle-aged woman with a soft voice; now she was in the grip of hysteria, running as fast as her heavy legs could carry her, headed for town hall, screaming, "Marshal! Marshal!"

Gypsy stepped in front of her. She bumped into him and recoiled, and because she saw the badge on his chest at her own eye level, another scream that had already begun in her throat was suddenly cut off.

"Marsh—oh! It's you! Thank God! The Klan! They just left! They shot out the light in my kitchen!"

Gypsy jerked the bandanna off his face, grabbed Lucille's hefty shoulder and gave her a quick shake to startle her into silence.

"The boys! What about the boys?"

"I don't know! I didn't see! Lord have mercy, when they shot through my window, I fell down on the floor, didn't get up till they were gone, 'cause they yelled that they'd shoot me if I came out of the house 'fore they were gone and—"

Gypsy was already running. Darting into the weedy alley-way between two buildings, calling, "Geezer!" before he even rounded the rear corner of the building. The cellar's inclined door had been smashed open and flung aside, and Geezer was nowhere in sight. His shotgun was in both hands, ready for use, as Gypsy leaped down the cellar steps.

The lantern was overturned on the floor. Jars of preserved fruit had been knocked from shelves to smash on the hard clay floor. The boys were gone.

Gypsy didn't even have to wonder what had happened, how the Klansmen had found the boys. He had only to concentrate for a moment, and the answer bubbled up from some deep well of intuition: Rufus! They caught him. He told them. Then, "Goddamn," he said, and whirled to dash back up the steps and out of the cellar, running again.

Buck was standing guard on the gallery, his form silhouetted against the lamplit office window.

"Get the posse together!" Gypsy shouted to Buck as he ran to the hitching rail and shoved the sawed-off shotgun into the center of the bedroll behind the saddle on his tethered Appaloosa. "They got the boys." He jerked the reins loose and vaulted into the saddle.

Buck stammered, "What? How? How'd they find—"

"Had to be Rufus. They caught him and whipped it out of him." The Appaloosa, sensing the urgency in Gypsy's body, pranced in the dust and jerked at the bit, ready to run. "I'll try to pick up their trail south of town. I figure they'll swing around east to get back on the main road to Guthrie. Get some men, head north fast as you can, try to get between them and Guthrie."

"But, Gypsy, the men, they're trying to save their houses. Ain't likely I can get many of 'em to ride out and leave the town to burn down."

"Do what you can, but don't waste any time trying to convince anybody. 'Less we catch 'em quick, those boys ain't got long to live." He slacked the reins and slammed his heels into the Appaloosa's sides, causing the horse to leap from a prancing standstill into a full gallop within a few strides.

The grass fire had been allowed to blow unimpeded across the fields of dead sorghum and wheat and prairie pastures south of town. The firefighters had swung inward like the flank of an army to allow the fire to pass at both ends of town. They were backfiring on a farm road just south of town, and because the wind here was at right angles to the front of the fire, the firefighters were succeeding in stopping the spread of the fire toward town. But the front of the fire, completely out of control, was blowing on east and south across the drought-dry land in sheets of flames, roiling in cyclones of sparks spiraling upward from groves of burning blackjack trees, blowing through gullies of long-stemmed grass with the crackling roar of a dragon, pouring undulating clouds of smoke and dust into the sky, blotting out the moon and stars completely, raining ashes. Gypsy rode the Appaloosa down the road at breakneck speed, while the ash and tiny stinging sparks from the blazing tumbleweeds now and then whirled around horse and rider like swarms of angry insects.

He stopped and dismounted at each intersecting farm road. It was impossible to pick up the trail of the Klansmen on the El Reno road, mingled as the many hoofprints on the road were, but he finally found what he was looking for: the hoofprints of many horses turning off the main road onto a little-used section road, heading eastward. In the light of the burning fence posts along the road, he saw that the hoofprints were sprinkled with ashes, indicating that the riders had passed this way before the fire. It meant they were probably at least twenty to thirty minutes ahead of him.

The tumbleweeds piled up against the fence along the section road had all burned away, leaving most of the cedar fence posts ablaze. Like torches fluttering in the wind, the fence posts lit the way for Gypsy to ride fast along the road for about two miles. But by then he was on the road running northward, and the burning fence posts fell behind. And when he reached the old burned-over area of the fire the Klan had started on Eula Rasmussen's place, he left all the flames behind and entered an area of total darkness. The fire-blackened land even seemed to absorb what little light filtered down from the moon and stars through the dark pall of smoke in the sky, but after about an hour he came out from under the cloud of smoke and set the Appaloosa at a pace that grew faster as the road became easier to see in the hazy moonlight. When he reached the main road and swung toward Guthrie, he was able to travel at a gallop for a few miles, far enough to put him outside the burned area entirely.

But here the speed of the pace became doubly dangerous. Here the road converged with Cottonwood Creek and ran parallel to the creek for about three miles, making the trees and bushes in the creek bottom perfect cover for an ambush. Under other circumstances Gypsy would have ridden slowly through such terrain, his eyes constantly scanning the surroundings for signs of an ambush, but now he didn't have time to be cautious, even though he had begun to doubt that there was any longer a chance to save the boys.

It was at Five-Mile Ford that he found them. It was about four o'clock that morning, when the moon was going down. He slowed the Appaloosa only slightly as he headed into the creek bottom, and he had already passed the huge cottonwood tree when he realized that he had glimpsed something strange in the moon-soft shadows beneath the tree.

Putting the horse into a spinning turn, he saw, silhouetted against the red blaze of the setting moon, the two bodies swinging by ropes from one of the tree's lower limbs. He had to ride to within a few feet of the naked bodies to recognize the boys, with their faces twisted grotesquely above the hangman's nooses, their hands tied behind their backs, their eyes bulging, mouths agape, their naked bodies splashed with blood from a multitude of knife slashes. The initials *KKK* had been carved into their chests, and their dangling legs were covered with blood that had spurted from their loins.

Gypsy had seen sexual mutilations before. Years ago, when battles between whites and Indians were matters of the most frenzied hatred, he had seen battles in which white soldiers castrated and mutilated dead Indian warriors, and Indians had been known to do the same thing to white men they had killed. But never had he heard of it being done to boys, to mere boys. And the sight of these two mutilated young dark bodies, dangling from ropes, illuminated by the dim red glow of a dying moon, stirred within him an old amazement, an appalled wonder at man's profound and dark and sinister capacity to brutalize his own kind. Had this been done by a single man, that man would have been called insane. Were the killers any less insane because they were in a group? And were the members of the group any less insane because they were honorable

men? Churchgoers, no doubt, and good citizens all, with children of their own? And since they were surely insane, why,
then, the very species itself must be insane.

The first indication that he had ridden into an ambush was
from his horse. A snort, ears pricked up, a toss of the head indicated other horses close by. And then Gypsy heard from
somewhere behind him the faint wind-muffled metallic *click-
click* sound of a gun being cocked. Instantly he drew his own
revolver and jerked around in the saddle to fire at a glimmer
of white that he saw in a thicket of trees near the creek.

And just as instantly his shot was answered by a fusillade of
bullets from a dozen or more muzzle-blazing guns concealed
in the thicket. Three of the bullets struck Gypsy. One grazed
his head, one struck him in the right chest, another went
through his upper right thigh. He was knocked from the saddle
and crashed facedown in the dust. He was unconscious for an
unknown time, though it couldn't have been very long, for
when he regained the hazy glimmerings of consciousness, he
could hear the hoofbeats of the riders coming toward him.
He tried to move, to find his gun, but he couldn't move, and
he had no gun.

The bullet that had grazed the right side of his forehead, ripping away the skin and shattering the skull bone, streamed
blood across his face and eyes, blinding him, but he couldn't
wipe the blood away because he couldn't move his arms. He
couldn't move any part of his body. He could hear the horses
coming toward him in the darkness, but he couldn't move.
There was some terrible force in him—a force like pain, like
death, like darkness, leaving his muscles and bones without
enough will or strength to move his arms or legs—against
which he had to struggle with all his will and strength. But he
could still hear, and when he blinked away the blood that matted his eyelashes together, he could see. Through the dust
churned up by the hooves of many horses, he could see the
hooded and robed Klansmen on their caparisoned horses as
they moiled around his body. Out of the confusion of sounds,
he could hear the fragments of voices, words.

"I knew the sonofabitch'd come. Didn't I tell you he'd
come?"

The force within him was trying to pull him down into ob-
livion, into nothingness, darkness, death. He struggled against

it. He struggled to blink away the blood and see. With the right side of his face pressed against the ground, the dust, he could see the legs and hooves of the horses as they churned around him, and he could see among them a horse with three white stockings. The man on the horse with three white stockings was slumped forward in the saddle, holding his side. On his white robe was a huge stain of blood. Voices in the vicinity of the slumped man were saying, "He's bleeding pretty bad. . . . Put a compress on it, take him on to Guthrie. We'll catch up. . . . That nigger shore could shoot."

Two men had dismounted. They stood over Gypsy's body. One of them clutched his shoulder and turned him over. He was looking up at the night sky through slitted lids. The two men bent over him.

"Is he finished?"

"Shot in the head."

"What d'you want us to do with him?"

"Cut him. I want the rest of those Nigrahs to see what happens to any black bastard who's got the balls to wear a lawman's badge. Cut 'em off."

One of them ripped his badge off.

"Let me have it. I think I'll start a collection of nigger lawman's badges."

Gypsy saw the knives. He heard his clothes being cut. He tried to reach out, but he couldn't move. He struggled for consciousness. Then he could feel the knives cutting into his flesh. One was cutting into his chest, another cutting into his groin. He could hear the knives cutting. He could see the men bending over his body, cutting, and he could hear the knives, cutting, and these were the last things he saw and heard before he dissolved into darkness.

CHAPTER TWENTY-EIGHT

AFTER MAXWELL STRAPPED THE TRUNK TO THE LUGGAGE rack of the surrey, he helped Rachel into the backseat. The surrey's driver, one of the agency's Indian wranglers, sat on the front seat beside the two carpetbags. Eula handed Maxwell a big basket filled with food for their journey, and he climbed in beside Rachel. The surrey pulled out of the agency, the wheels lifting little streamers of dust to be carried away by the hot wind.

They had gone about five miles when Maxwell, from the corner of his eye, caught sight of something in the dust-blurred distance: a rider traveling along the crest of a low treeless ridge about a half mile away. The ridge ran parallel to the road for some distance. Though the rider was too far away to be identifiable, it was clear that he was an Indian, and the bay horse he rode caused Maxwell to suppose that the rider was Corby. He wiped the dust from his spectacles with his handkerchief, but even then he couldn't be certain that it was Corby. But when Rachel saw him cleaning his eyeglasses and squinting at something in the distance on his side of the surrey, she leaned over to see out from under the surrey's tassel-fringed top and immediately cried, "It's Corby!" She threw herself across Maxwell's lap so she could lean out of the surrey and wave and yell, "Corby! Corby!"

The rider didn't respond.

"Maybe it's not he," Maxwell said. "There's more than one Indian who has a bay horse."

"Oh, of course, it is!" Rachel said, dismayed by his lack of comprehension, and again yelled, "Corby!"

"Here! Rachel! Get off me. Get back in your seat. You'd better start acting like a lady, or you—"

"Stop!" She pushed the driver's shoulder. "Stop the horses! Let me out!" She jumped down before the wheels had come to a full stop and ran around to the other side, where she could be sure that the rider could see her. She waved both hands. "Corby! Corby, come here!"

The rider stopped when the surrey stopped but still failed to respond to Rachel's frantic waves and yells.

"He can't hear you."

"Oh, Daddy, you tell him! Tell him to come down here this minute and stop being a sulky Indian."

"If he wants to come down, he will. If not, why require him to? Come on, now, get back in. We'll be late for the train."

"Oh, Corby," she said in a normal voice, as if he were only a few feet away, "I do wish you'd at least come and say good-bye." But he obviously wasn't going to, so she waved to him once more, this time in a sad, resigned way, and said in a small voice, "Bye, Corby. Bye . . ."

Then the rider raised his hand and made the sweep-the-sky signal of the Plains Indians that meant "Go in peace."

Delighted to have a response at last, Rachel waved again, signaling the rider to come to her, but he didn't, and finally, at Maxwell's insistence, she got back into the surrey, and they resumed the dusty, jolting journey to El Reno. Twice she leaned across Maxwell's lap to peek from beneath the surrey's top, and once more she waved, but the rider just kept riding along the crest of the ridge, pacing the surrey, and when she looked again he was gone.

They arrived in El Reno at noon, an hour before the sched-uled departure of the train that would take them to Caldwell, Kansas, where they would transfer to the Santa Fe for the re-mainder of the trip to St. Louis. There was no guarantee, how-ever, that they would even be able to get aboard the train at El Reno. Coming out of Texas, the train would be filled with set-tlers on their way to make the run into the Cherokee Outlet. "But they'll all be getting off at Kingfisher or Hennessey," the clerk said, "so if you can stand the squeeze until then, you're sure to get seats from Hennessey onward."

After checking Rachel's trunk into the baggage compart-ment, they found seats on a bench in the crowded hot malodor-ous fly-swarmed whites-only waiting room, where they ate cold fried chicken and biscuits from the basket Eula had pre-

pared. Afterward they drank from the whites-only drinking
fountain and visited the whites-only privies, with Maxwell
muttering more and more to himself about the disgraceful
damned foolishness of a race that would go to such elaborate
lengths to keep persons of a different race from pissing into the
same hole. This was his usual indignant reaction whenever he
was required to conform to the Jim Crow laws recently enacted
in the Territory, but today he found such laws especially gall-
ing when he contemplated what would have happened if Corby
had decided to go to Carlisle. As a "colored" he wouldn't have
been allowed to use the whites-only facilities. Maxwell would
never have tolerated such nonsense and therefore would have
made himself and Corby subject to arrest for using the same
waiting room, drinking fountain, railroad coach, or privy. *This*
was the civilization that the Indians were being forced to accept in exchange for their own heritage? No doubt Corby was
right to be reluctant to join a society in which he would be
subject to arrest and imprisonment for eating in a public café.

But Maxwell's present perturbation was mild compared with
what he felt after a barefooted newsboy came through the station hawking the latest edition of the *El Reno Dispatch:* "Klan
raid on colored town! Three lynched! Lawman shot! Read
about it here!"

Maxwell was quick to buy a paper and, with a deepening
sense of shock and shame and horror, read about the fire and
the lynching of "two colored youths who had gone into hiding
after being accused of molesting and brutally beating a white
girl" and the critical gunshot wounds suffered by Gypsy Smith,
the "well-known Negro gunfighter and lawman." There were
reports, the story said, that Marshal Smith had been badly mutilated and left for dead by the Klansmen, though "the doctor
in charge of trying to save the marshal's life refused to disclose
the nature of any such mutilations."

"Oh, my God," Maxwell said under his breath.

"What is it?" Annoyed by his preoccupation with things
other than herself, Rachel snapped open the fan that she carried tied to her wrist on a tasseled cord and began to fan
herself.

But he went on reading the newspaper with the same urgency he would have given to reading a telegram, and he had
read parts of the story two or three times before he got up and

said with the confused frown of a man who has forgotten to do something important, "I have to go to the telegraph office. This"—he rattled the newspaper—"concerns a friend of mine. You remember Gypsy Smith?"

"Of course, I—"

"He's been . . . I ought to send . . ."

But the newspaper had said that the telegraph and telephone lines to Freedom were still down. Anyway, even if he were able to send a telegram to Gypsy, what could he possibly say? "I'm sorry"? "My sympathies"? How pathetically inadequate every conventional reaction seemed! What he felt he should do was get down on his knees to Gypsy and say, "Forgive me for being of the same race as those who did this to you." Only that, impossible as it was, wouldn't even begin to assuage the guilt and shame he felt for being a member of the race in whose name this thing had been done.

"You can't," Rachel said, getting up. "The train's coming."

The train's whistle blew to announce its arrival, and a continuous ringing of its bell began as it pulled into the station and came to a steam-hissing stop alongside the loading platform.

The train wasn't as crowded as Maxwell had feared it might be. Every seat was taken, and passengers squatted and sprawled in the aisles and recesses, but at least it was possible for Maxwell and Rachel to squeeze aboard with their carpetbags, and the other passengers—boisterous Texas cowboys, mostly, on their way to the Cherokee Outlet—moved aside and made room for them near the dead potbellied stove at the front end of the coach. Then a young cowboy jumped up from a nearby bench and offered Rachel his seat.

"For the young lady," he said, with a flourish of his widebrimmed hat. He was half drunk and playing the fool for his friends, though there was nothing insincere or ironic in his gallantry toward Rachel. He was probably no more than twenty years old and had never before seen such a pretty girl.

And, indeed, Rachel was pretty, in spite of the thin layer of dust that had powdered her and her pretty new dress, a dress of lilac crinoline with yellow chiffon ruffles and ruchings. The Texas cowboy seemed very impressed and acted as if she were a great lady. But the real source of Rachel's prettiness at the moment was the radiant look of excitement in her uncertain smile. Never before had she been called a lady. Never before had a man offered her his seat. She glanced at Maxwell for guidance, and he signaled her without words that it would be all right to accept the cowboy's gentlemanly offer, and Maxwell could have sworn he saw her flutter her eyelids as she gave the cowboy a breathy "Thank you."

Then the cowboy in the other seat on the same bench, the seat next to the opened window, got up and offered it to Maxwell. This cowboy, too, was about half drunk, and barely old enough to shave, and exaggeratedly polite. "And you, sir, can have mine," he said.

"No, I couldn't," Maxwell said.

"Sir," the cowboy said in a tone that hinted he might be offended if Maxwell refused his hospitality, "sir, in Texas we're raised up to respect our women and our elders."

And though his attitude, like that of the first cowboy, was partly horseplay, there was no disrespect or irony in his tone, so Maxwell, in order to forestall any further blandishments, resigned himself to being considered elderly and took the seat beside Rachel. Through the opened window came a steady stream of hot air laden with dust and smoke and the oily smells of hot machinery. He shoved the two carpetbags beneath the seat. Rachel held the food basket on her lap until she was relieved of it by the first cowboy, who said, "Here, miss, let me put that on the rack for you."

The overhead luggage rack was crammed with all sorts of bags and saddles and bedrolls, but the cowboy shoved things aside to make room for the wicker basket, then turned back to compete for Rachel's attention. Alternately bashful and boisterous, the cowboys made inane and trivial remarks. At first, out of politeness and respect for their elders, they made attempts to include Maxwell in the conversation but gladly gave up when they saw that his eyes were riveted to his newspaper.

It was as if the newspaper story were some scene of carnage from which Maxwell couldn't turn, even though the sight stirred within him a mixture of shame, guilt, bafflement, fear, and that old feeling of impotent indignation. What could he do? He thought once again of sending a telegram to Gypsy but still could think of nothing appropriate to say. He thought of visiting Freedom on his way back from St. Louis, but what would that accomplish? According to the newspaper, Gypsy had suffered a head wound that left him in a deep coma, and the doctor attending him hadn't given him much chance of surviving, so Maxwell might not even get back from St. Louis in time for the funeral.

The train lurched into motion. Next stop Kingfisher, then Hennessey, where virtually all the settlers would get off, leaving the train to a handful of passengers as it continued on across the Cherokee Outlet to Kansas. And as far as Maxwell was concerned, that couldn't come too soon. His nerves were attuned to brooding and contemplation, not to the exuberance of a bunch of high-spirited cowboys.

This feeling was reinforced by the way Rachel responded to the cowboys. Being the center of attention of four or five young men had fairly taken her breath away. She caught the fan that dangled from her wrist and snapped it open and fanned herself rapidly, beaming with satisfaction, fluttering her eyelids in a way that could only be called coquettish. Where had she learned it? And where had she learned to say just the right thing, with just the right tone to keep her cowboy suitors interested and admiring? If this was her first flirtation, she certainly seemed to come by it naturally, with the astonished delight of a duckling's first discovery of water.

It was uncanny. It was also disappointing. Maxwell had taken it for granted that Rachel would be shocked, or at least concerned, about what had happened in Freedom, but at the moment such thoughts seemed farthest from her mind. Also disappointing was her failure to rebuke the cowboys when they started referring to Indians as "red devils."

"You mean," one cowboy asked after Rachel revealed that she had gone to school with Indians, "you mean to tell me them red devils can actually learn to read and write?"

To her credit Rachel said in a slightly scolding voice, "Of course, they can." But she smiled when she said it, as if to forgive him his ignorance. Maxwell had thought that her loyalty to Corby would have caused her to bristle with resentment at such a remark. Was she, then, willing to sell her loyalty for a compliment?

This was a trait that had always bothered Maxwell about her, the way she could be distracted from serious matters by a bauble or a pretty dress or a party. It was true that she always recovered her sense of values in time, as she did now when she suddenly seemed to feel some sense of betrayal and guilt. Flushing, she fanned herself rapidly and said more forcefully, "And they're not 'red devils.' My goodness, they're just like us."

"Well, little sister, I shore can't agree with you there," said a cowboy sitting across the aisle. He was older than the others, maybe thirty, and hadn't said anything to Rachel until now. "Just like us? Shoot! They ain't even human. Ain't no human beings woulda done what them Comanches done to my folks, back yonder. Had a sister, was about your age. Scalped her. My mother, too. And that ain't all they done to 'em neither. So don't tell me about them redskins, little sister. I know 'em. Like my old daddy used to say, 'The only good Indian's a dead Indian.' "

Rachel fanned herself and glanced at the other cowboys, the younger ones, with a look that said, "Let's disregard that grouch, shall we?" She wanted to be amused. As a way of leading the conversation back into a more convivial vein, she fanned herself and said, "My goodness, it's hot! Does it ever get this hot in Texas?"

"Hot! Why, bless you, miss," the first cowboy said, "hit's kinder chilly here, compared to Texas. Why, in Texas it sometimes gets so hot the hens lay hard-boiled eggs."

"Oh, sure," Rachel chided coquettishly.

"That's a fact."

"Oh, sure."

Being a witness to all this made Maxwell feel strangely insecure. Rachel was growing up so fast, changing so eagerly he couldn't help wondering what she would be like when next they met. That wouldn't be for at least ten months, and the thought of how much she might change by then made him afraid that he was losing her forever.

CHAPTER TWENTY-NINE

DEXTER HAD RECEIVED A LETTER FROM RACHEL ASKING HIM please to meet her train at Hennessey Station so they could say good-bye. He was living and working in Guthrie these days and would not have made the forty-mile ride to Hennessey just to say good-bye to Rachel; but he had to be in Hennessey on that date, anyway, because he was going to make the run into the Cherokee Outlet nine days hence as a runner for the Oklahoma Land Company, and he needed to scout the route into the Outlet and find the allotment he had been assigned to claim.

When Dexter left Agency, he had gone straightaway to the Hornbeck Building in Guthrie, where he found the clerks and cartographers who had bribed him to give them information about certain Indian allotments. They had promised him a job if he got fired for helping them, and they proved to be true to their word. Granted, it wasn't much of a job. In fact, it amounted to little more than being an errand boy. Dexter believed that he was meant for better things than being a courier, or passing out handbills on the steps of the territorial legislature, or policing voting booths to make sure that no colored people were allowed to vote, but he realized that he was only being tested. Shelby Hornbeck had said as much. If he proved himself to be loyal and willing to serve, well, who could tell? Maybe he would soon be given a job as a territorial tax collector or even be appointed as a county deputy sheriff or maybe—it was just possible—a deputy U.S. marshal.

In the meantime, the cost to his pride in being little more than a flunky was more than made up for by a new source of pride he had found in a new belief: the supremacy of the white race. Not that he had ever believed otherwise, but it wasn't until he moved to Guthrie that he became conscious of the pride inherent in the proposition "The White Man Rules the World." That was the title of a handbill that he distributed at a White Citizens' rally one day, and nothing he had ever heard or read had had the impact of that pure and simple creed.

He read the handbill avidly many times, memorizing it the way an acolyte would memorize Holy Writ. To him it was the gospel of a new religion, and Shelby Hornbeck was its minister, and Shelby Hornbeck was everything that Dexter Bingham had ever wanted to be: rich, powerful, handsome, smart, aristocratic, a born leader.

This adulation on Dexter's part didn't go unnoticed by Shelby Hornbeck. As a born leader he knew a born follower when he saw one. So as soon as Dexter proved himself to be both reliable and obedient, Shelby saw to it that he was moved up the ladder from flunky to tax collector, a job in which Dexter proved particularly adept, especially when it came to collecting taxes from Negroes and Indians. He was good at kicking down doors, as was often necessary when one tried to collect taxes from the inferior races.

Like most other tax collectors, Dexter worked not for a salary but for a percentage of the delinquent taxes collected, and he did all right for himself. It wasn't enough to make him rich, but it kept a roof over his head, food in his belly, and a good horse under his butt. Besides, it wasn't his only source of income. He was still called upon now and then to do special jobs for Shelby Hornbeck or one of the many organizations associated with him, such as the Oklahoma Land Company. His current assignment, for instance, was to be one of more than three hundred young men who would make the run into the Cherokee Outlet and claim preselected homesteads and later relinquish them to the Oklahoma Land Company.

The two-ten from El Reno pulled into Hennessey Station right on time. As it chuffed to a hissing stop alongside the platform, Dexter pulled out his new gold watch, ostensibly to check the train's arrival time but really to show off the watch in case Rachel and Maxwell could see him from the train.

They could. Rachel leaned across Maxwell's lap and waved through the opened window to Dexter.

Dexter merely nodded his recognition. He was twenty-one years old now, a grown man. Though he dressed well, and wore a derby hat, and carried a .44 Colt high on his hip, he was a rather average-looking young man, neither handsome nor homely, with a flabbiness about the waist that bespoke a future paunch.

Rachel and Maxwell emerged with the last of the passengers. Maxwell was carrying the food basket, leaving Rachel free to push her way through the crowd to embrace her brother, an embrace that left both of them feeling awkward and uncertain.

"Well, look at you!" Rachel said, stepping back. "You look like a bigshot! Doesn't he, Daddy?"

The greeting between Maxwell and Dexter had been in the nature of grunts and nods, and now Maxwell said, "A bigshot? Sure."

Dexter detected an edge of sarcasm in Maxwell's tone, but he let it go. "Well, I'm doing all right," he boasted. "And you? Off to school, huh?"

"Yes, isn't it wonderful! Oh, I'm so glad you could come and say good-bye. I was afraid you'd be too busy, you being a bigshot tax collector, and all that."

"Well, I had to be in Hennessey today, anyway," Dexter said, unwilling to give Rachel the satisfaction of thinking that he had come all this way just to see her. "Have to get a certificate at the Land Office. I'll be making the run into the Outlet."

"Oh," Rachel said. "Yes, I see. Well, the conductor told us we'd be here for an hour, with them loading and unloading things, so we thought we might all have lunch together."

Dexter pointed out that food of any kind would be hard to find that day in Hennessey. A small, ten-building town on the southern border of the Cherokee Outlet, Hennessey had become a staging area for what would become known as "the Run of '93," and thousands of settlers were turning it into a sprawling, teeming tent metropolis.

"Never mind, we have food here," Rachel said. "Let's find a place and have a picnic, shall we? Got some fried chicken and yams and mincemeat pie." On seeing Dexter's frown of distaste, she chuckled and said, "Oh, you remember my fried chicken, do you? Well, don't worry, *I* didn't cook it. Eula did. She's a great cook." And in response to his frown of mild puzzlement, she added, "She's the new woman who's keeping house and looking after Mother. She's wonderful. But let's find a place to eat. I'm starving."

With Rachel in the middle, the three of them left the station and strolled toward some trees on the banks of Turkey Creek, about a five-minute walk to the east. The banks all along the creek in both directions were crowded with tents and wagons and livestock and people, and a haze of dust hung over the countryside, giving the sun a hot reddish hue. There seemed little hope of finding a picnic spot near the creek, but that didn't dampen Rachel's spirits. As they walked, she chattered on, telling Dexter everything she had heard about Miss Finwick's Young Female Academy, taking it for granted that anything that concerned her was bound to be of interest to everyone else.

"So what d'you think?" she asked. "About me going to school?"

Dexter shrugged. "I reckon that's what Mother would've wanted, for you to be among others of your own race 'stead living around them red niggers all your life. Must be expensive, though, a school like that in St. Louis," he added in a tone heavy with implications. On one level it was an accusation of favoritism against Maxwell, who, after all, had never offered to send *him* to school. On another level it conveyed his belief that the money would only be wasted on her, a female. What need had she of schooling? And on still another level it was an expression of his resentment that she, not he, was going to live in the big city of St. Louis. He had fond memories of St. Louis, of the young years when he lived alone with his widowed mother in a house filled with bric-a-brac and doilies, a house with running water and an inside toilet. He had always resented Maxwell for having dragged them off to live in a harsh dusty land filled with rattlesnakes, grasshoppers, and heathen Indians.

"And Mother?" he asked. "What about her? You don't think your leaving'll make her worse?"

"Now, don't start that," Maxwell interrupted in the tone of a schoolmaster admonishing a pupil. "Nora's in good hands, and Rachel's got her own life to live. Besides, seems to me, since you're so worried about your mother's welfare, you might come around to visit her more often. It's been—what?— six months now?"

Dexter flushed with anger. It was just like Maxwell to cut the ground out from under him at every opportunity, as if he took some sort of satisfaction in making Dexter feel small. It had always been like that, and Dexter had always been forced to stifle his anger, as he did now, because Maxwell somehow always seemed to be right and Dexter somehow always seemed to be wrong.

"Yeah? Well, I been busy," he mumbled, agitated by conflicting feelings of guilt and self-righteousness.

"Here, now, how's this?" Rachel said, diverting their attention to a willow tree whose shade was presently unoccupied.

The tree had recently been used as a campsite by settlers who had left behind many mementos of their passing: tin cans, garbage, horse dung, and flies. But there were logs to sit on, and the shade was deep, promising relief from the September sun. From the other campsites crowded along the creek came the sounds of children shouting, dogs barking, the occasional whinny of a horse or bray of a burro, and the constant heat-muffled drone of people talking.

Rachel and Maxwell sat on a log. Dexter sat on a stump, facing them across the ashes of a dead campfire. Rachel brought from the wicker basket a piece of fried chicken and a bacon grease biscuit for each of them. Once they began eating, she tried to make conversation by saying to Dexter, "So! How is it? Eula's chicken, I mean."

Dexter tossed a gnawed chicken bone away, then pulled a white linen handkerchief from his hip pocket and wiped the grease from his fingers and mouth. "What about her?" he asked. "Who is this woman you hired to stay with Mother? And what makes you think you can trust her to be there when you get back?"

"If I didn't have confidence in her, I wouldn't be going, would I?" Maxwell was annoyed by Dexter's self-righteous skepticism but then reminded himself that Dexter, after all, had a right and a duty to be concerned about his mother, so he added in a conciliatory tone, "She's a good woman, Eula is, good with your mother. Very reliable. But," he added, unable to resist needling Dexter a little, "why don't you go on down and see for yourself? Be a good excuse to visit your mother again. After all this time."

Rachel attempted to head off their growing argument by

turning attention to herself. In a sprightly, chatterbox way, she said, "Eula Rasmussen, you might've heard of her, the woman whose house was burned down by the Ku Klux Klan over near Freedom a couple of weeks ago? It was in the newspapers. She's . . ." Seeing the look on Dexter's face, Rachel faltered, wondering what she could have said that would cause such a sudden scowl of disgust.

"*That* woman?" Dexter glowered at Maxwell. "*That* woman? Jesus Christ, is *that* who you hired to take care of my mother? A notorious nigger lover!"

Maxwell was poised for a moment between laughter and scorn, unable to decide whether Dexter was harmlessly ridiculous or dangerously ridiculous. He cleared his throat and said, "Well, now, Dexter, I'm not sure I know what you're implying by that melodramatic epithet. But if you're implying that Eula's some sort of degenerate miscegenist—you know what that word means, don't you, Dexter? Well, if that's what you think, you can set your mind at ease. Eula's the last person in the world I'd ever suspect of doing anything improper."

Dexter got to his feet. "Yeah? Yeah? You call sleeping with niggers proper?"

Making a supreme effort at self-control, Maxwell said in a taut but reasonable voice, "What makes you think she was 'sleeping with niggers'?"

"That's why the Klan burned her out!" Dexter was appalled by the depth of Maxwell's obtuseness.

"Oh, that's ridiculous. She lived near Freedom, yes, which is an all-Negro town, but what you're implying is a lie."

"Oh, for Christ sakes, you think the Klan'd burn her out if they didn't know for sure she was a nigger lover?"

Maxwell hooted with derision. "Ha! The Klan! Oh, yes! Those noble Knights of the Invisible Empire! Those self-appointed guardians of our racial purity, who go around at night in hoods and robes to burn the houses of helpless women and lynch and emasculate kids! Oh, yes! The noble Klan! As rotten a bunch of sonsofbitches as ever walked the face of the earth."

Dexter's whole body shivered with anger, like an attack dog plunging against its chain, totally inarticulate save for the bark, "Yeah? Yeah?" But after looking around as if to ask sympathy from an unseen audience, he found some more words and flung them at Maxwell with the force of long-suppressed hatred: "Well, you wanna know what *I* think, old man? I don't think you know *anything*. You think you know so goddamn much, but you don't know *anything*, old man. You're stupid."

"Dexter!" Rachel cried.

Dexter had started to leave but stopped after only a few steps and whirled around. "You know something, old man? You better watch out. You're just the kind of nigger lover the Klan likes to take care of." Then he strode away.

Maxwell was stunned not only by the virulence of Dexter's reaction but by the reason for it: why should he take Maxwell's ridicule of the Klan so personally? It was as if Maxwell had, by cursing the Klan, cursed Dexter himself. And the answer struck him with the shock of revealed truth: "My God . . . he's one of them."

CHAPTER THIRTY

IT SEEMED TO DR. UPCHURCH THAT HE HAD SLEPT FOR ONLY seconds, but the room was suddenly flooded with morning light, and someone was knocking urgently on his door.

"Doctor? It's Marshal Smith," said Nurse Deever through the door. "You said to let you know if there was any change."

"Yes?" Dr. Upchurch said, prepared for the announcement that Gypsy Smith was dead. "What change?"

"He's coming to, looks like."

Dr. Upchurch bounded out of bed. Scrambling into his scattered clothes, he left the room without even stopping to wash the sleep from his eyes, rushed downstairs to the operating room, where he found Gypsy Smith alive—barely alive, it was true, and only semiconscious, but at least alive and able to respond to stimuli. That in itself, Dr. Upchurch thought, was a small miracle, for which he felt an almost gleeful sense of relief and triumph, a swelling sense of pride. And why not? Gypsy Smith had been at death's door and now had come back.

But the Gypsy Smith who had been to death's door was not the Gypsy Smith who came back. This became uncomfortably apparent during the days and weeks following the operation as Gypsy slowly recovered his senses and reflexes. Those who came to see him, to help him, to love him were soon sent away with—at best—comatose indifference and—at worst—snarls of aversion. His first coherent sentence to Dr. Upchurch was an order concerning the people who came to see him: "Keep them the hell away from me," a prohibition that even included Drusilla.

So it soon became apparent to everyone that the Gypsy Smith who lay on a bed in the infirmary, shielded from the view of other patients by a standing screen around his bed, with his head, chest, thigh, and groin swathed in bandages, was not the Gypsy that most people had always known. For this man there would be no more jokes, no more laughter. This Gypsy Smith was as grim as a corpse, sullenly indifferent to everyone, taciturn to the point of rudeness, and he never once gave the slightest indication that he was grateful to be alive. On the contrary, his expression, from the moment he learned to refocus his eyes, was one of cold accusation, of steely outrage.

"He won't see anyone," Dr. Upchurch had to tell the people in the reception room who came for news of Gypsy's condition. Among them were three out-of-town reporters—one black and two white—who wanted to know when they could talk to him.

"Never," Dr. Upchurch said. "That's what he said: never."

It was also Dr. Upchurch who had to tell Drusilla that Gypsy refused to see her, and she, hurt and baffled, made him promise that he would convey her plea to Gypsy that she be allowed to see him, and he kept the promise, only to be rebuffed in a most startling way.

It was on the eighteenth day of Gypsy's recovery. His right arm couldn't be used because of the bullet injuries to the muscles in the right chest area, but he could still use his left hand, which he demonstrated when he pulled a Colt .44 from beneath the corner of the sheet and placed the muzzle against the end of Dr. Upchurch's nose and cocked the hammer.

"You want to live?" he asked in a matter-of-fact voice, with that expression of a man talking not to his doctor but to a worm.

Although startled, Dr. Upchurch had the presence of mind to murmur, "Of course."

"Then mind your own business. When I want your help in my personal affairs, I'll ask for it."

After that Dr. Upchurch would be the bearer of no more pleas from Drusilla. He wouldn't even take Gypsy a note she had written to him. He tried to assuage Drusilla's baffled pain by telling her that Gypsy was still in a state of shock and probably wouldn't relent in his refusal to see anyone until after he had somehow come to terms with what had happened to him. Until then, for him, for a man of his pride, to see pity for himself in the eyes of others would only deepen his humiliation.

The only person Gypsy finally consented to see was Amos Fulton. Fulton had tried to see him a number of times and had always been told by Dr. Upchurch that Gypsy refused to see anyone. But one day near the end of Gypsy's third week of recovery Fulton sent him a note by way of Nurse Deever, telling him that he had some news about the KKK that Gypsy might find of interest, and he was soon ushered into Gypsy's presence behind the standing screen. Fulton sat in a chair beside Gypsy's bed, hoping for a friendly conversation, but Gypsy not only didn't return his greeting, he didn't even make eye contact with him. Rather, he stared fixedly at the ceiling throughout the entire visit.

"Well, first of all," Fulton said, already discomfited by Gypsy's death mask countenance, "I want to say . . . for—for everybody how sorry we are that—"

"Cut the bullshit."

Fulton was surprised as much by Gypsy's tone as by the remark. Had the tone been bitter and brooding, Fulton could have understood. But if Gypsy's inflectionless tone reflected his feelings, then he had no feelings at all.

"Yes. Well," Fulton stammered, "I've had some information I thought might interest you. Our informants tell us that Sonny Boy Reeves was admitted to the hospital in Guthrie on the morning after the lynching. Gunshot wound in his side. I'm told there was one bullet fired from your gun. Did you get a shot at the Klansmen?"

Gypsy seemed not to have heard him for a moment. Then the flat metallic voice had a small edge of grim satisfaction as Gypsy said, "Sonny Boy Reeves," and the silence that followed was becoming awkward by the time Fulton realized that Gypsy had said all he was going to say.

"Did you shoot him?" Fulton prompted, but when Gypsy finally responded in a croaking whisper, it concerned somebody else.

"Rufus?" Fulton said, trying to get the drift of what Gypsy wanted. "He's dead. They killed him. His body was found a few miles south of town, swinging from a tree."

Another long silence.

"We assume," Fulton went on, trying to keep the talk going, "that they got the information about the boys from him. If so, he certainly didn't gain anything by it. He was beaten pretty badly and mutilated, too. There was a sign pinned to his back. . . ." His words faltered when he saw that Gypsy had closed his eyes. He paused for a moment, waiting for Gypsy to show some sign of interest. When it appeared that he had gone to sleep, Fulton said, "Is there anything I can do for you, Gypsy?"

"Yes."

"What?"

"Go away."

Flustered, Fulton nodded his head and got to his feet. He had a number of other topics he wanted to discuss with Gypsy, but such matters would just have to wait for a more appropriate time. Now Gypsy was like a wounded animal that had crawled into some dark hole to lick his wounds. Things having to do with life would have no more interest for him until he came out of the hole.

Two weeks later, after Gypsy had learned to walk on crutches, he left the infirmary. Under cover of darkness, still dressed in his pajamas and bandages, with his .44 Colt strapped around his waist, attended only by Big Mama, who carried his few belongings in a paper bag, he made his way, grimacing with pain, from the infirmary to Big Mama's house, where he took refuge in one of the second-story front rooms overlooking the street, there to do his convalescing. Dr. Upchurch visited the room at regular intervals to treat Gypsy's injuries and change his bandages, but other than the doctor and

Big Mama herself, who brought his meals and carried out his chamber pot, no one was allowed to enter the room.

Drusilla tried. Just as she had regularly returned to the infirmary, to be told repeatedly that Gypsy refused to see her, so did she go to Big Mama's house after learning that Gypsy had taken up residence there, only to be told by Big Mama, who met her at the door, that Gypsy still wouldn't see anyone.

"It ain't just you, honey," Big Mama said to her on her first visit to the house, trying to console her. "He don't see nobody."

"Could you ask him? Please? Or just let me go to him?"

"Oh, no, honey. He say he skin me alive do I bring anybody to his room. Huh-uhh-h-h-h, honey, not Big Mama. He trust me."

Still, she felt her heart go out to the girl, a feeling that increased with each succeeding visit until on the fifth visit, wearing a bright kimono and smelling of incense, Big Mama came out of the house, and put her arm around Drusilla's shoulder, and said, "Honey, you got to realize this here ain't doing you no good. Looky here, honey, now I tell you what. You go home now, do yo' schoolteaching, and when Gypsy say he want to see you, why, I run all the way to the schoolhouse myself, give you the message. Now, wouldn't that be better'n coming here every day fo' nothing?"

Drusilla's lip trembled like a child's. "I don't understand. Please." She took one of Big Mama's pudgy hands between her work-hardened ones and squeezed it to communicate her desperation. "Please, let me go to him. Maybe he'll be upset at first, but when he finds out how much I want to help him, to love him, why, he won't be angry with you."

Big Mama was not just skeptical, she knew it was hopeless, but such was the sympathy she felt for this very decent and very disturbed young woman that she gave it a moment's thought. "I tell you what. I go speak to him, tell him you here to see him."

"Would you, please? I'd be very grateful. Thank you. Tell him . . . tell him . . ."

"I let you tell him, if he wants to see you. You stay here."

Agitated and afraid, Drusilla turned her back on the door as if to deny herself any unrealistic hope of entering it. She stepped to the porch railing and swept the town and the sky with random glances, searching for something to distract her attention while she waited. But there were no birds anywhere in the bright October sky, and only a few people and horses were on Freedom's dusty streets since the immigrants had all left for the opening of the Cherokee Outlet, and the burned-over landscape beyond the town was a uniform sooty black. From where she stood she could see the small graveyard north of town. The fire had passed over the graveyard, burning the drought-dead shrubbery and grass and the wooden crosses, leaving it blackened like the surrounding land. The only way Drusilla could distinguish the graveyard from the surrounding countryside was by the five new mounds of raw red earth that protruded above the soot black ground—five new graves, one of them Clarence's.

Then she heard his voice. From inside the house, probably from the upstairs corner room, she first heard Big Mama's muffled voice, talking in normal conversational tones, and then Gypsy's voice answering in one or two words. Drusilla couldn't hear what was being said, but she knew it was Gypsy's voice, and the effect of it was like a trigger for an irresistible impulse. She turned and opened the screen door and went into the house. Without looking right or left, she passed through the parlor, where two young women were lolling about, and went straight to the staircase. She climbed the stairs under the bovinely curious gaze of the two young women and then tiptoed down the uncarpeted hallway toward a door that had been left slightly ajar, whence came the sound of Big Mama's voice, saying in an idle tone, "You sho you don't want me to make this here bed now? Only take a jiffy."

There was no response from Gypsy. Evidently Big Mama hadn't as yet told him that Drusilla was waiting to see him. Presumably she intended to lead the conversation around to that subject while making the bed, but Drusilla couldn't wait.

Big Mama turned from the unmade bed with a startled and reproachful look when Drusilla entered the room, but Gypsy didn't turn to look at her directly. Dressed in rumpled pajamas, he sat in a cushioned chair near the window, his Colt revolver and cartridge belt hanging from the back of the chair. The head wound was covered by a patch of gauze now, not the turbanlike bandage of earlier days, and both his head and his chin were covered with a month's growth of glossy astrakhan hair. He had been exercising his right arm when Drusilla entered the room, a movement that stopped immediately, though there was no other indication that he was aware of her presence.

Big Mama snapped, "Lordy, girl, didn't I tell you—" But she abruptly fell silent, realizing how trivial were her reproaches in an atmosphere charged with weightier matters.

"Hello, Gypsy."

A long silence ensued, and then he said in that inflectionless voice, "What d'you want?"

Big Mama made a tactful and unobtrusive exit from the room.

"What do I want!" Drusilla said, as if the question were absurd. "I want—I want to help you. I want you to let me love you and help you. Gypsy, please don't . . ." Her voice faded into futility and silence when she saw that her words were having no effect at all. He was as cold and unresponsive as a corpse.

But at last he slowly turned to look at her, and Drusilla couldn't hide the effect his face had on her. He had become gaunt and drawn. His cheeks were hollow, his eye sockets cavernous, and the fire of life had gone out of his eyes, eyes with the depthlessness of ashes. And as if in uncanny confirmation of her thoughts, he said, "I'm a dead man." He paused for a moment, giving her time to consider that, and then slowly turned back to the window. "Say you buried me along with Clarence and the others. Forget me. I'm a dead man."

Drusilla desperately sought within herself some way to reach him. She considered everything from helplessness and hysteria to anger and accusations, but in the end she knew nothing would work. He was unreachable. Still, she couldn't find it in herself just to turn and walk away, so she lingered, saying, "Please, Gypsy. Please don't do this. Don't send me away."

But his answer was one of unfeeling finality: "Good-bye."

With a deep sigh of regret she turned to leave, then turned back again and, holding her hand outstretched, approached him as cautiously as she would have approached a wounded animal. She put her hand lightly on his shoulder, half expecting him to flinch, but he didn't respond at all.

"Go with God, my friend," she said, and turned and left the

room. The tears didn't begin until the door was closed behind her. She stopped for a moment to dig a handkerchief from her skirt pocket.

Big Mama appeared from a nearby room. Her ambivalence was reflected in the way her tone shifted from sympathy to censure and back again within a few words as she said, "Oh, you po' child, why you do this? I knows you suffering, honey, but you get me in trouble, sneaking up here like that after I told you not to come up till I say so. You get me in trouble, you po' thing."

"I'm sorry, it's just that . . . I had to see him, don't you see? It won't happen again."

With her heelless slippers flip-flopping, Big Mama lumbered down the carpetless hallway alongside Drusilla, saying, "Oh, of co'se, honey, I understands, and I don't blame you none. Why, if it was up to me—"

"I know. It's all right. It won't happen again."

Big Mama put her arms around Drusilla's shoulders and they descended the stairs together. "That's the spirit, child. You do like he say, you forget Gypsy Smith, get on with your life. You young yet, they'll be other men. That young doctor, now, everybody knows he sweet on you, girl, and I couldn't think of a man who'd make a better husband—naw, and I ain't the only one thinks so, neither. Why, just this morning, I heard old Miz Crawford say, she say, 'Wouldn't they make a fine couple, now, that pretty young schoolteacher and that handsome young doctor?' That's what she say, and everybody say, 'They sho would, wouldn't they?' Tell you the truth, I 'spect that's what Gypsy himself'd want, too. Might help him to know you was happy and not grieving fo' him."

"Grieving?" They faced each other on the porch, but Drusilla's eyes kept wandering off into distances as if looking for something. "No. I'm all out of grief. I only want to help him. If there's ever anything I can do . . ."

"Help him?" Big Mama seemed amused by Drusilla's innocence. "Honey, how you gonna help him do what he got to do?"

"Do? What is it he's got to do?"

"Well, it ain't hard to figure, is it? You think he gonna let them Klansmen get away with what they done?"

"Killing? There's going to be more killing?"

" 'Deed," Big Mama said with gloomy relish, "I 'spect the real killing ain't even begun yet. Huh-*uh*." She smiled, flashing two gold teeth, and, as if envisioning the wonders to come, shook her head. "Lawd, Lawd, when that man gets well, look out. Them Ku Kluxers better give they souls to God, honey, 'cause they asses gonna belong to Gypsy Smith."

CHAPTER THIRTY-ONE

ON HIS VISION QUEST CORBY WENT OUT AND SAT ON A MOUN-tain for three days and four nights, without food or water or sleep, but no vision came to him, no Spirit. His thoughts were mostly about food and water and sleep.

He was neither surprised nor particularly discouraged by the failure. He realized that his white education put limitations on him that he would have to overcome before he would be vouchsafed a vision. He would have to learn how to do it, learn the magic chants and rituals of the old Indians for calling up his own special Spirit, and even then there was no guarantee of success. After all, Indian youths who had never been to the white man's school often failed to have visions, even though they tried repeatedly.

So he came back from his quest without a new name or a sacred medicine bundle. But he would try again, and to learn what he must do next time, he began visiting some of the Indian villages, talking to those who'd had visions, seeking out the medicine men who could tell him how it was to be done.

At first they didn't take him seriously.

"You think you can have a vision while your hair is cut like a white man's and you wear white man clothes?" said *Nakoemoxse*—Bear-smelling-sweet-grass—the old medicine man of the Sand Hills village. "You must be crazy. Also, you

are too young. Come back in two winters, and I will teach you
the things you must know."

He let his hair grow. He sometimes wore nothing more than
a breechclout and moccasins while he was staying with the Indians, but whenever he returned to the agency, he always
dressed in his agency-issue clothes so that he wouldn't be an
embarrassment to Maxwell. It wouldn't look right, as Maxwell
hinted, if Corby, an honors graduate from the school and a
known favorite of the school's superintendent, became a walking repudiation of everything that the school was trying to
teach the other Indian children, would it? So Corby, out of
gratitude and respect for Maxwell, always dressed in white
man's clothes while he was at the agency. He slept in his old
room in the barn, ate the food that Eula brought to him, and
performed his old chores: hauling wood, carrying water, feeding the livestock, repairing harnesses, grooming horses.

He had changed. He and Rachel had once romped through
their chores and had plenty of energy left over for pranks, but
now Corby went about his chores in a joyless way, and his
aloofness kept everyone at a distance. It was as if Rachel had
been his vital link to life. He was very much alone and very
lonely.

Rachel's letters helped. She wrote both Maxwell and Corby
each a letter at least once a week during the first few months
she was gone, and it was these letters that kept bringing Corby
back to the agency. Whenever Maxwell or Eula took one of
her letters out to the barn, he would stop whatever he was
doing and go off by himself somewhere to devour it as a starving man would devour food.

At first the letters were filled with laments of how lonely
and homesick she was, and how she wanted to come back
home, and how much she missed him, the most wonderful
friend any girl ever had.

It is as if I left a part of myself there. One of our teachers
here, the nursing teacher, Miss Lee, she says there is a
thing called phantom feelings. She says it is like when a
man gets his leg cut off and still reaches down to scratch
his toe that is no longer there. That is what I feel like. I
feel like I left a part of myself there.

All this was balm for Corby's own painful feeling of severance, and he had hopes that her unhappiness might soon bring her back home.

But within a couple of months the tone of her letters began to change. Rather than laments of homesickness and nostalgia, they gradually became epistles of excitement. She talked about her new friends and new fashions and her adventures in the big city.

> Oh, Corby, you should see the opera house here! All 9th grade pupils were taken to the opera last evening to see an opera by a German man named Wagner. The name of the opera was *Tristan and Isolde*. Oh, Corby, I cannot begin to tell you how beautiful it all was! The people were beautiful in their fine clothes, the music was beautiful, the opera house was beautiful! I felt just like a princess in a palace! I thought I was in Heaven! Oh, Corby, do please think about going to Carlisle. There is a wonderful world out here that we never dreamed of!

These letters left Corby apprehensive and bitter. He had feared that he would eventually lose her to the outside world, and his fears were coming true.

Her letters began to be shorter and less frequent. There was a flurry of letters and exchange of gifts at Christmas, but then her letters to Corby dropped off to about one a month. She continued to write Maxwell fairly frequently and always asked him to give her regards to Corby, but by the spring of the following year her communications with Corby himself had dwindled to random notes or picture postcards, on which she sometimes scribbled nothing more than "Wish you were here!"

With the lack of Rachel's letters to lure him back to the agency, Corby began to wander farther and farther afield and stay away for longer periods of time. His wanderlust often took him as far south as the Red River. Westward he wandered as far as the Blue Hills of Mendota. To the north he followed the Cimarron out of No Man's Land, now called the Panhandle, to the Glass Mountains.

Whenever he had a chance to race Big Red against Indian ponies, he always won. The best of the Kiowa, Comanche, and Cherokee ponies were brought out against him, but none ever beat him, and when the races were over, Corby pocketed his winnings and rode on. The Comanches gave him a new name, by which he became known among most of the other tribes: *Nakoni*—Wanderer.

CHAPTER THIRTY-TWO

LAMP IN HAND, BIG MAMA TIPTOED UP THE STAIRS AND TAPPED lightly on Gypsy's door. Identifying herself to the grunt from within, she said, "He's here."

Gypsy slipped the bolt and opened the door. He had a .44 Colt in his hand. "He?"

"That white deputy. He down in Lulu Belle's room, slobbering drunk. She know not to say nothing."

Jerking his pants on over his winter underwear, Gypsy said, "Send somebody to the stable, tell 'em to saddle my horse and bring him around back, quick."

When she left, Gypsy lit the kerosene lamp on the bedside table. Moving quickly, he dressed, strapped on his gun, and packed his saddlebags. During the first few weeks of his convalescence he had kept from going crazy by looking forward to this moment, knowing that it would come someday, laying his plans. After he had got well enough to ride a horse, he often made journeys into the countryside, journeys that lasted for days, a week, always riding out before dawn and returning after nightfall, and if he happened to meet any early-morning risers or late-night carousers who knew him, he ignored them. He seemed to want the townspeople to think of him as dead. And those few who caught glimpses of him riding in or out of town in the darkness might indeed have wondered if they were seeing a ghost. The weight he had lost during his convalescence had left him a gaunt man with deep-set, lackluster eyes and a look that forbade all familiarity. He wore his hat low over his face, low enough to cover the jagged bulge of scar tissue over the metal plate in his skull.

Wearing his heavy winter coat and a scarf and gloves, carrying a 30.06 rifle, he stepped out of his room and into the dark hallway. Big Mama, lamp in hand, was puffing up the stairs.

"They gonna have yo' hoss out back in a few minutes." They faced each other at the top of the stairs. "What's you fixing to do? You ain't going away, is you?"

"Yes. And I probably won't be coming back. So . . . thank you, Big Mama. Thank you for everything. I left some money on the table, but I figure I still owe you plenty. If you ever need me for anything . . ."

"Oh, hush now. Owe me? No. You's family. You just take care a y'self, y'hear?" For a moment she was on the verge of hugging him, but his grimness discouraged her from doing anything other than touching his arm and saying, "God bless."

Descending the stairs quickly and quietly, he went to the front door. A gust of cold wind carrying a few flakes of grainy snow swirled around him as he stepped out onto the front porch. He turned the collar of his heavy wool coat up around his ears and took in the town with a glance. At this time of night, on this kind of night, the dark streets were deserted save for a few horses tethered to the hitching rail in front of the Blackjack Saloon. Only a few lights could be seen here and there. From far across the frozen prairies came the yipping and howling of a coyote, and from somewhere another coyote answered, and a few dogs in town answered the coyote calls with barks and howls of their own. A half-moon glowed dimly through a layer of clouds.

Gypsy took stock of all this in the few seconds it took him to stride quietly across the porch and turn the corner of the building. He kept to the darker shadow close to the building on his way to the rear of the house, where he found the sorrel with three white stockings tethered to the newel-post of the back door steps. It stood with its tail toward the wind that had speckled its rump with snowflakes.

Gypsy gave the shivering horse a pat on the neck, then took the rifle from the saddle scabbard and flung it away into a patch of frozen weeds. He checked to make sure the saddlebags contained no weapons, then stealthily mounted the stairs to the back door and stepped into the dark hallway. Lulu

Belle's door was the first on the right. A dim light shone beneath the door. Gypsy could hear sounds from inside, the groans and gasps of a climaxing rut. He tried the doorknob, found it unlocked, and nudged it open an inch or two at a time. He feared the squeak of a hinge, but the squeaks in the bedsprings obscured the sound of the hinge, and there, in the light of a sooty table lamp, two bodies on a bed bounced beneath the covers. Or at least the top body was bouncing; the body on the bottom wasn't doing much, and her face reflected only a sort of long-suffering disgust as Sonny Boy Reeves, his long blond hair falling about his face, panted into the throes of orgasm.

Then, with one climactic groan, he collapsed on top of her. When Lulu Belle caught sight of Gypsy creeping into the lamplight, his rifle pointed at the bed, her eyes widened. Gypsy put a forefinger over his lips and advanced on the bed so quietly that Sonny Boy, his face sunk into a pillow, didn't realize that Gypsy was in the room until he felt the cold muzzle of the rifle press against the nape of his neck. He tensed, his heavy breathing stopped, and he abruptly flung himself onto the other side of the bed, and found himself looking down the barrel of the 30.06.

"Get up," Gypsy said.

Sonny Boy, terrified, cowered away from the rifle, and his terror increased as he assessed his predicament, and the first sound that dribbled from his mouth was a whine: "What— what're you . . . ?"

"You know who I am?" Gypsy asked.

Sonny Boy nodded vigorously, as if Gypsy might be mollified by recognition.

"Then you know you better do what you're told. Get up."

Sonny Boy thrashed out of bed. After turning up the lamp, Gypsy picked from among a pile of clothes on the floor Sonny Boy's Colt revolver, shoved it into the deep pocket of his own heavy coat, and then tossed the pants, shirt, and long underwear to Sonny Boy, who, either bashful to be seen naked by another man or reluctant to die without his boots on, scrambled to get into his clothes, panting, "What're you gonna do?"

Grimly silent, Gypsy noticed that the closer Sonny Boy got to being completely dressed, the more he regained his composure, and by the time he pulled on his boots, he was becoming assertive, even combative. Drunkenly slurring his words, he said, "You'll never ... whatever you gonna do, you'll never get away with this, boy. Better think twice about what you're doing."

"Get your coat on."

But Sonny Boy, growing cocky, balked at putting on his coat and even blustered a little. "Now, you listen, boy—"

Holding the rifle in both hands, Gypsy slammed the butt into Sonny Boy's solar plexus. With all his wind expelled in a cry of pain, he fell to his knees and clutched his chest in convulsive efforts to regain his breath. With his gloved hand, Gypsy clutched Sonny Boy's long straw-colored hair and jerked his head upward so he could glare into his grayish blue eyes.

"Now, have I got your attention, buckra?"

Sonny Boy blinked. His eyes flushed with tears, his body shook with shock and fear.

"Then listen to what I tell you. From now on you gonna be living from minute to minute, and the minute you give me any trouble, I'll kill you." He shook Sonny Boy's head. "Got that in your head, buckra?"

Sonny Boy made a few affirmative noises. Gypsy gave his head a contemptuous shove as he turned loose his hair.

"Get up. Get your coat on."

Sonny Boy obeyed, with all the alacrity that his drunkenness, fear, and pain would allow. But he did groan a small protest when Gypsy took a pair of handcuffs from his coat pocket and cuffed his hands behind his back. After slamming Sonny Boy's hat onto his head, he nudged him toward the door with the muzzle of the rifle.

He ushered Sonny Boy out into the night. His Appaloosa was tethered in the backyard, tail turned toward the stinging wind. Gypsy helped Sonny Boy struggle into the saddle on the three-stockinged sorrel, then mounted the Appaloosa and led Sonny Boy's sorrel in a gallop through the frozen, crackling weeds of a trash-strewn vacant lot, angling to intersect with the road leading out of Freedom toward the Cimarron.

Riding head-on into the blue-cold northern wind, the two men hunched forward in their saddles so that the brims of their hats protected their faces against the occasional swirls of ice-crystal snow. The horses resisted running into the wind, but

Gypsy kept them going at a pace that would bring them to the Cimarron before daybreak. Arriving at the frozen Cimarron River on schedule, they then turned northwest to follow the river's floodplain. There were no roads on the floodplain, nor any farmsteads or settlements, and on a December day as cold and dark as this one, no working parties were likely to be cutting logs on the plain, no hunting parties looking for game. The likelihood of the two riders' being seen was small. Even so, Gypsy kept to the cover of the leafless cottonwoods and willow thickets as much as possible, and at noon, with a sickly pale sun filtering through a sky of dark gray wind-driven snowclouds, he stopped in a cottonwood copse.

So stiff and exhausted was Sonny Boy that he couldn't stand on his feet when Gypsy pulled him from the saddle. Crumpling to his knees, his teeth chattering, he pleaded, "Build a fire."

After unlocking one of the cuffs, Gypsy half dragged him to a nearby lodgepole pine sapling, then snapped the opened cuff onto the tree. Sonny Boy jerked angrily against the sapling, whining curses under his breath, but Gypsy went about his work. He took the sawed-off shotgun from the middle of his bedroll, then jerked the bedroll itself off the saddle. One of the blankets from the bedroll he tossed to Sonny Boy. The other, along with the sawed-off shotgun, he dropped at the base of a big cottonwood tree.

"Build a fire," Sonny Boy begged. "Can't you build a fire first? Jesus, I'm freezing to death."

"No fires."

"No fires? Jesus! I'll freeze!"

"Suit y'self."

He took the bridles off the horses and tethered them on lariats to the young cottonwood trees, then took some strips of jerky from one of his saddlebags. He offered some to Sonny Boy, but he, with the blanket wrapped around his shoulders, turned his nose up.

"Suit y'self."

Wrapped in his blanket, Gypsy sat huddled against the trunk of the cottonwood and gnawed on the strips of cold hard beef as he surveyed the floodplain to the southeast. It was unlikely that anyone would be following their trail, since the wind had already blown sand and snowflakes skittering along the ground to lodge in their tracks and obliterate them, but he wasn't going to risk a surprise.

Sonny Boy crouched down at the base of the sapling, whining his misery. "Say, looky here, what's this all about? Where you taking me? What'd I ever do to you?" Gypsy, gnawing on the jerky, ignored him completely until Sonny Boy, growing testy, asked, "Goddammit, what d'you want with me?"

"You gonna tell me the names of the other fifteen Klansmen."

Sonny Boy was speechless for a moment, then sputtered, "What? Klansmen? What Klansmen?"

"Them that rode with you on that lynching raid."

"Raid? What lynching raid?"

"Freedom."

Sonny Boy was flabbergasted. "What? *Me*? What the hell you talking about? Jesus! You got the wrong man! I don't know nothing about no Klansmen's raid on Freedom." He was very relieved, almost to the point of laughter. "Well! So this is all a mistake! I'm glad we got this cleared up."

Gypsy tugged his blanket tighter around his shoulders and snuggled into it to try to get a catnap, while Sonny Boy, outraged at Gypsy's indifference to his protests of innocence, became even more insistent on claiming that he hadn't been involved with the Klan or any raid on Freedom, until Gypsy said, "Shut up. I'm trying to sleep. You better, too. Long night ahead of us."

"But you don't understand! Ain't I told you? I'm not the man you think I am. I don't know nothing about no Klan."

"If you don't shut up, buckra, I'll put a gag on you."

Sonny Boy lapsed into a silence of misery and frustration.

A steady snow began falling later that afternoon. Gypsy roused Sonny Boy, who had fallen into a sort of torpor of deep misery and shallow sleep. Gypsy once again clamped the handcuffs on Sonny Boy's wrists before putting him on his horse, but this time he allowed him to have his hands in front so he could hold on to the saddle horn.

They left the woods shortly after the snow started falling. They rode northwest, with Gypsy in the lead, picking his way along the river-bottom trails in the darkness and blinding snow flurries. Driven by a moaning wind, the snowflakes piled up in drifts against arroyo cut-banks and logs and thickets of dark leafless trees.

They rode all night. The snow stopped after midnight. The half-moon emerged from behind the scudding clouds to shine and twinkle on the wind-scoured snow, and at dawn a pale red sun rose in an ice crystal sky and gave the snow a rosy hue.

Sonny Boy had managed to stay in the saddle. Though he often swayed precariously during moments of deepest torpor, he always caught himself before falling by grasping the saddle horn with frozen fingers, alternately whining and cursing. But shortly after sunup, as the horses were plunging through a belly-deep snowbank at the bottom of a gully, Sonny Boy, too weak and cold to care anymore, toppled out of the saddle. Gypsy wheeled the horses around and rode back to where he sprawled in the snow.

"Get up."

"I can't," Sonny Boy pleaded. "I can't go no farther. I won't."

Gypsy dismounted and pulled Sonny Boy's own .44 Colt from the pocket of his snow-encrusted coat. He put the muzzle of the revolver into Sonny Boy's ear, so that the metallic *click-click* of the hammer being cocked would resonate through Sonny Boy's skull.

"You've picked your place to die, then, have you?"

"No. Please. I'll—I'll . . ."

Gypsy picked up Sonny Boy's hat, shoved it down on his head, and helped him to mount.

To avoid being spotted, Gypsy had planned to hole up during the day and finish the trip at night, but it soon became obvious that Sonny Boy couldn't make it much longer without a fire, so Gypsy pushed on until he came in sight of the mountains. Named for the selenite that veined their surfaces, the Glass Mountains glittered diamondlike in the sun. Gypsy swung away from the Cimarron and headed southwest and entered the mountains by the middle of the afternoon, the weakening horses staggering and plunging through the snowdrifts in Wild Horse Canyon. Twice more Sonny Boy fell out of his saddle and Gypsy helped him to remount.

Just before sundown they reached Wild Horse Plateau, one of the stair-step plateaus near the top of the mountains where there was a spring and a frozen pond and an old cabin made of gnarled dwarf timbers.

The cabin had been built perhaps fifty years before by trappers and had since been used by wild horse hunters and outlaws. Supplied with fish and water from the nearby pond and deer from the mountains and rustled beef from distant ranches, the outlaws had fared uncommonly well in the cabin and had kept it in a decent state of repair. Now that the outlaw gangs were mostly gone, however, the cabin had fallen into disrepair. The adobe chinking between the gnarled logs had fallen out, allowing the icy wind to moan through the cracks, and the roof had begun to sag, and the corn shuck mattresses on the bunks had long since been chewed to rags by generations of mice.

Gypsy half helped, half dragged Sonny Boy into the cabin and then locked his hands around the oak center pole that held up the cabin's smoke-blackened log rafters. Sonny Boy collapsed on the dirt floor at the foot of the center pole, shivering and moaning, while Gypsy started a fire in the old iron stove. Then he went outside to unsaddle the horses and tether them in a cottonwood grove near the pond, where they could feed on the bark of the young trees. He kicked a hole through the ice on the pond so they could get water.

Within an hour he had a lantern burning in the cabin and a pot of stew simmering on the stove. The stew had come from a can in a cache of supplies he kept in a hole in a red clay bank behind the brush corral. To get at the cache, he moved aside a huge boulder that had hidden the hole, then brought forth not only the cans of stew but also a canister of coffee, a canister of flour, and a lunch bucket that contained frozen bacon, sugar, salt, pepper, and a sack of tobacco. From the hole he also took a long roll of frozen rawhide that contained his old Sharps buffalo rifle. Among the things remaining in the cache hole was a Comanche bow and a quiver of arrows, as well as many boxes of ammunition of various kinds and calibers.

When the stew and coffee were ready, Gypsy took chipped enamel plates and tin can coffee cups from the jumble on a shelf behind the stove. After wiping the plates clean on his sleeve, he dished up stew for both of them. His own plate he placed on the warped plank table. Sonny Boy's he placed in front of him on the dirt floor.

"I would let you eat at the table, but I 'spect you wouldn't want to eat with no nigger, and I sure's hell wouldn't want to eat with no buckra Klansman."

"Look, Marshal, you got me all wrong," Sonny Boy insisted. Ravenously hungry, he scooped up a spoonful of the stew before it was cool enough to eat. He grunted with pain, but managed to swallow the food, and then reached for the tin can filled with coffee, which was too hot to hold. Desperate to get some of the hot liquid into his bone-chilled body, he alternately blew on it and slurped it, saying between blows and slurps, "I mean, I ain't got nothing against niggers. Nothing at all. And I ain't one of them Klansmen neither. You got me all wrong, I tell you."

Sitting on a bench at the lantern-lit table, Gypsy finally said between bites of stew, "Cut the bullshit, buckra. I saw that scar on your left side. It's where I shot you the night you and them other Ku Kluxers raided Freedom and lynched those boys."

"A bullet scar!" He snorted. "What's that prove? Hell, I know lots of men got bullet scars."

Gypsy had laid his coat on the bench beside him. From its pocket he pulled a soiled white book. "I don't suppose this's yourn, neither? Found it in your saddlebag. *The Revised and Amended Prescript and Edicts of the Grand Order of the Ku Klux Klan, Knights of the Invisible Empire.*"

Sonny Boy bristled when he saw the book in Gypsy's black hand but stifled his outrage. "Hell, anybody can read a book. Don't mean nothing."

Dropping the book on the table in a gesture of contemptuous indifference, Gypsy resumed eating, and ignored Sonny Boy's continued between-bites assertions that he didn't have anything against niggers and that Gypsy had better think twice about what he was doing.

"You'll never get away with this, you know," he said as he was finishing his coffee, and by now his voice carried a sort of blustery threat, as if by regaining his physical well-being, he also regained some courage and contempt.

Gypsy continued to ignore him. When they both had finished their stew, Gypsy rolled himself a cigarette and puffed on it while he finished his second cup of coffee.

"Say," Sonny Boy said. "Say, how about letting me have some tobacco? I could use a smoke."

Gypsy got up and crossed to where Sonny Boy sat on the dirt floor and offered him the half-smoked cigarette.

Sonny Boy recoiled, one side of his mouth raised in an involuntary expression of disgust. "I'll roll one of my own. I don't need your spit."

"Disgusted by nigger spit, are you, Sonny Boy?" Gypsy placed the cigarette between his thumb and middle finger and flicked it into Sonny Boy's face. The fire end of the cigarette exploded into sparks.

Sonny Boy yelped and jerked backward, scrambling to his knees, tugging against the center pole with his handcuffed hands, trying to brush the sparks off his face, saying, "What're you— What the hell— You burned me!"

"Oh, does it burn? Here, I'll put it out." He spit into Sonny Boy's face.

Sonny Boy recoiled. Rattling the handcuffs, he wallowed his head from side to side, trying to wipe the spittle off. "You black bastard, you'll pay for this, you!"

"Oh"—still in that tone of mock solicitude—"I forgot. You can't stand nigger spit, can you? Here, I'll wipe it off."

But instead of wiping it off, he reached out and smeared the spittle all over Sonny Boy's face, rubbing it in with an insolence so profound that Sonny Boy became paralyzed with dread. He seemed fully to realize for the first time that he was in the hands of a man who was not just a killer but a madman capable of the most humiliating torture. So rather than try to prevent it, Sonny Boy closed his eyes and mouth tightly against the smeared spittle.

When Gypsy saw that the fight had gone out of Sonny Boy, he stopped playing. It was time to get down to business. He unlocked one of the handcuffs and pulled Sonny Boy to his feet and jerked his arms behind him and once again handcuffed his wrists together. He then crossed to where he had dropped the saddles, got his lariat from his saddle, and, knocking Sonny Boy's hat off, dropped the slipknot over his head.

"What? Jesus, what're you—"

Sonny Boy's voice was cut off when Gypsy tossed the coil of rope over one of the smoke-blackened rafters and pulled it taut. To prevent being strangled, Sonny Boy backed under the rope, and Gypsy kept tightening the rope until Sonny Boy had to stand on the tips of his toes to keep from being choked.

Then Gypsy tied the loose end of the rope around the center pole, leaving Sonny Boy half hanging, half standing, squirming, making strangled moaning sounds, edging toward panic.

"Now, you're gonna stand there like that till you tell me the names of all the Klansmen with you when you lynched those boys," Gypsy said, "or until you can't stand on your toes anymore and hang yourself. Take your time. I'm in no hurry."

"I can't goddammit." He dropped at last all pretense of innocence. "I can't! I swore an oath! I'd die first!"

"Suit y'self." Gypsy ambled back to the table and sat down on the bench. "Agonizing way to die, though, slow suffocation is. Gives you time to think about things."

"Oh, Jesus," Sonny Boy moaned, doing a little dance on the tips of his toes to keep his balance. Anytime he let himself down as much as an inch, the noose cut into his windpipe, cutting off his words as he pleaded, "Oh, Jesus, don't—I can't—I took a sacred oath! They'd kill me. Let me down. Please! They'd kill me if I told."

As Gypsy casually rolled a cigarette, he said, "And if you don't, you'll die right where you are. And it ought to be clear by now that you got a hell of a lot better chance of getting away from them than you got of getting away from me."

"Getting away? You'd let me? Get away?"

"You tell me what I wanna know, I'll put you on your horse and give you a head start. Till dawn, say. If you're good enough, who knows? You might get to Mexico or California and live awhile longer before I catch up with you again."

"But I don't know this country, and it's snowing. What kind of chance is that?"

"A better one than you gave those boys." He ripped a page from the KKK handbook, held it to the fire in the stove, and lit his cigarette from it.

"Look. Let me down. We'll talk. All right?" He choked. "Take the rope off, we'll talk." Then he sagged back into the old fear and beggary as he said, "Please! I got to—goddammit, I got to piss! Let me down!"

Gypsy smoked and warmed his hands at the stove.

"Please!" Sonny Boy cried. "I'll piss in my pants!"

"Suit y'self."

Sonny Boy's feet and legs were beginning to cramp under the ordeal of standing so long on his toes. He writhed, groaned, cursed, and tears began to trickle down his face as the urine stain, beginning at his crotch, soaked downward to become a puddle at his unsteady feet.

When Gypsy finished his cigarette, he dropped the butt into the stove, and then, slowly, as if deliberating his next move, drew from the buckskin scabbard on his belt his big-bladed bowie knife. He stepped up to Sonny Boy and held the knife in front of his bloodshot, tear-filled, bulging eyes.

"The time's come," he announced in a tone of grim finality. "Know what I'm going to do now?" He paused, giving Sonny Boy time to wonder. "I'm going to do to you exactly what you did to me." He pushed the flaps of Sonny Boy's coat aside and began unbuckling his belt.

"Oh, Jesus! No!" Sonny Boy screeched, but the words were strangled to silence when the tugging on his belt caused him to lose his precarious balance. The noose tightened, and his horrified face began turning a bluish white color before he managed to get his toes back on the floor and relieve the weight of his body. By then Gypsy had jerked Sonny Boy's pants and underwear down around his shaking knees, exposing his genitals.

Sonny Boy's breath was coming in gasps. "Oh, Jesus! Not me! I didn't do it! I swear to God! Oh, please don't!"

"Who did?" Gypsy touched the point of the knife to Sonny Boy's skin just above his straw blond pubic hair. "Who done the cutting?"

"Oh, Jesus! It wasn't me! I swear! Please! *Please!*"

Gypsy increased the pressure of the knife until the skin was punctured and a few drops of blood trickled down into Sonny Boy's pubic hair.

"Who did?"

"It was ... oh, Jesus!" he moaned, and then broke. The words spurted out like water through a crack in a dam. "It was Pinkerton! Tully and Pinkerton! Don't! Please don't! I've told you! It was Pinkerton!"

Gypsy withdrew the knife. "Well, that's two of 'em. You might as well tell me the rest."

Tears dripped from Sonny Boy's eyes and mucus from his nose. "Ye—ye ... I'll tell! Lemme down!"

Gypsy stepped to the center pole and jerked the rope loose. Sonny Boy collapsed on the dirt floor. With his pants and un-

derwear bunched around his knees, he writhed on the floor in
the puddle of urine, sobbing, trying to reach his cramping legs
with his handcuffed hands.

"The handcuffs!" he pleaded. "Take off the handcuffs!"

"No. Better leave you like that for a while, case I have to
string you up again."

He slipped the knife back into its scabbard as he crossed to
a shelf above the bunks along the cabin's west wall. On the
shelf were many odds and ends left by the cabin's former oc-
cupants: a fruit jar filled with rusty nails, a mouse-gnawed Bible, the tattered remains of a child's school tablet. It was the
school tablet that Gypsy wanted. He took it back to the table.
From his vest pocket he took the stub of a pencil, touched it
to the tip of his tongue, and held it poised over the tablet.

"All right, let's have the names."

For more than an hour he sat scribbling in the tablet. He put
down not only the full names of the other fifteen men who had
made the raid on Freedom but also where they lived, where
they worked, and their physical descriptions. He kept pumping
Sonny Boy for information long after Sonny Boy, crying and
begging to be freed from the handcuffs, protested that he knew
no more about the raiders.

"I've told you everything I can. Now keep your word and
let me go."

Gypsy took the lariat off Sonny Boy's neck and unlocked
the handcuffs and stood over him as he, groaning with blessed
relief, massaged his cramped legs with one hand and his rope-
burned neck with the other.

"Now, you listen to me, buckra, and you listen good. I'm
gonna give you till sunup, like I said, and you better light out
for parts unknown, 'cause I'm gonna let the Klan know who
squealed on 'em, so if I don't get you, they will. Your only
hope is to ride as fast and far as you can, and it might be a
good idea to keep looking over your shoulder. Who knows?
Someday you might see me there, just before I kill you."

When Sonny Boy had at last managed to stagger to his feet
and pull his pants up and buckle his belt, Gypsy said, "If you
want to take time to saddle up, there's your tack." He nodded
toward the saddles in the corner. "But if I was you, I don't
think I'd lose a second getting out of here."

Sonny Boy sputtered, "My gun! You gonna send me out

into strange country without no food? Without even a gun to get game? What kind of a chance is that?"

"Like I said, a lot better chance than you gave those boys."

Sonny Boy limped to where his hat lay on the floor. "Jesus! Some chance! Some chance!" He put his hat on and staggered to his saddle, but before picking it up, he turned once again to Gypsy. "Just a little food? A can of beans or something? Some jerky?"

"Your time's running," Gypsy warned.

"Jesus!" Sonny Boy snorted, tugging at his saddle, once again on the verge of bitter tears.

Gypsy picked up the lantern and followed him outside, where snow had begun falling again. He lighted their way to the horses and held the lantern while Sonny Boy, fumbling in his frantic haste, finally got his horse saddled.

"You might at least tell me which way to get out of here," Sonny Boy said plaintively as he struggled into the saddle. "How'm I supposed to find my way in this goddamn snow?"

"That's a problem, all right," Gypsy conceded. "But I wouldn't curse the snow if I was you. By morning your tracks'll be covered, so you might actually get away, for a while, anyway—a day, a month, maybe even a year or two. But no matter how long it takes, or how far I have to go, someday I'll find you, buckra. I'll find you, and I'll kill you."

He slapped the sorrel on the rump, sending Sonny Boy plunging into the snow-swirling darkness. He waited there for a few minutes, listening to the horse's snow-muffled hoofbeats fading into the canyon.

After adding a few sticks of wood to the dwindling fire in the cabin, he took the long roll of now-unfrozen rawhide from among his bundle in the corner. He carried the rawhide bundle to the table and unrolled it, revealing his "Big Fifty" Sharps buffalo rifle wrapped in oily rags. Also in the roll was a Y-shaped shooting stick, a cleaning rod, and a buckskin bag filled with .50 caliber cartridges.

Gypsy began cleaning the rifle in the light from the rusty lantern, using the oily rags, working slowly, admiring the rifle's bigness and beauty, the simplicity of its single-shot mechanism, its awesome power. The rifle had been chambered for a monster shell case carrying 170 grains of powder and 700 grains of lead. With it Gypsy had once dropped a buffalo bull at a distance of over a mile and a half. And once, back in the days when he was a buffalo hunter, before he gave up the profession in shame, he had been able to kill 242 buffalo in one day. His two skinners had had to pour water over the rifle barrel to keep it cool as Gypsy, lying prone on a grassy hill, with the muzzle of the rifle resting in its shooting stick, fired into a milling herd of buffalo, killing an average of 20 an hour from sunup to sundown. It was on that day that the jubilant skinners, following the tradition among frontiersmen of giving special names to special rifles, named Gypsy's buffalo rifle the Grim Reaper.

Having lovingly cleaned and polished the long-unused rifle, Gypsy blew out the lamp, but remained sitting at the table for a while, smoking a cigarette, watching the little flickers of flame through the cracks in the stove, imagining tomorrow, wondering how long it would take to bring Sonny Boy into the sights of the buffalo gun.

But the next morning when he rode out to kill Sonny Boy, he found him where he had fallen in the snow, frozen stiff. By the signs Gypsy guessed that Sonny Boy had sunk into a torpid sleep and fallen from the saddle as his horse was plunging through a snowdrift. Sonny Boy had floundered around, trying to catch the horse, and finally, exhausted, must have sunk once again into sleep and died within hours. He was hardly visible beneath the snow and hoarfrost, which, smooth as marble, had encased his face and head.

CHAPTER THIRTY-THREE

NORA DIED IN LATE MAY 1894, SO WEAK AND WASTED THAT hardly more than twelve hours elapsed from the time Dr. Gresham first diagnosed pneumonia to the time she breathed her last. Eula dressed her for burial, and Reverend Poggemeyer said the funeral services in the Mennonite Missionary Church.

Dexter, wearing a shiny new deputy sheriff's badge, was among the mourners, but Rachel wasn't. Maxwell had purposely delayed sending her a telegram until it was too late for her to get back home in time for the burial. What was the sense in her coming all the way from St. Louis on the train, unchaperoned, just to attend the funeral and then turn around and go back? Nearing the end of her spring term, she would be studying for her final exams and no doubt involved in all sorts of other year-end activities.

Anyway, Nora's death wasn't a great sorrow for Rachel or anyone else. For those who knew her, Nora had died years ago, so her funeral was more a ceremony of relief than of grief. As Mrs. Poggemeyer had said when told of Nora's death, "Oh, the poor soul. Well, it's a blessing, I reckon."

In his funeral eulogy Reverend Poggemeyer didn't go so far as to call it a blessing, but he did say that Nora's suffering had earned her a place at the right hand of God, and one should not mourn for a poor woman who had been released from suffering and attained heaven, "where she shall walk upon streets of pure gold," he said from the pulpit, and cocked his ear toward heaven, as if straining to hear the very sound of Nora's footsteps treading those streets.

Actually, what he was listening to was the rumble of distant thunder. Everyone had been hearing it for the last few minutes, and a sort of restlessness had swept over the mourners, who dared not let themselves hope for rain. Too many times they had seen big banks of rain clouds moving up out of Texas and the Gulf and allowed themselves to hope that this was the rain that would end the drought, only to have the clouds spatter the earth with a few raindrops, then hurry on to some other place, and the sun would come out again, scorching hopes as surely as it scorched the meager stalks of corn and sorghum that had been coaxed up from the dust.

Still, they and the reverend were restless to leave the church and see what was happening on the horizon, and so, cocking his ear toward the distant thunder, he murmured, "Glory be," and cut the eulogy short. The pallbearers and mourners left the church as hurriedly as decorum permitted.

What they saw was an enormous bank of blue-bellied thunderheads boiling up over the southern horizon, flickering with lightning, thunder rumbling. And gathered at the grave site, listening to Reverend Poggemeyer commit Nora's body to the earth, dust to dust, they kept glancing up at the oncoming clouds and sniffed the air for moisture.

As the thunderheads began to loom over them, the first gust of wind swirled across the graveyard, flapping the men's trousers against their legs and making them grab for their hats, rustling the women's skirts and tugging at their bonnets. Tumbleweeds bounced rolling across the graves. Then a long streak of jagged lightning crackled across the darkening sky, sending waves of thunder rumbling across the land.

And just after Maxwell and Dexter each tossed a shovelful of red dirt down upon the coffin, causing small puffs of dust to rise out of the grave, a spatter of raindrops swept across the land. Warm and as big as marbles, the raindrops made little craters in the dust and splattered across the pages of the reverend's opened Bible.

"Glory be, folks," he said, "looks like we might get wet."

People all over town were beginning to emerge from their offices and houses and places of work to have a look at the dark lightning-flickered underbelly of the thunderheads, and when the spattering rain swirled over them, they let the raindrops splash on their upturned faces. Small children, with cries of delight, frolicked here and there, trying to catch raindrops in their mouths.

Then, with a terrific clap of thunder directly overhead, the clouds opened up. The rain swirled across the land in sheets and showers, and the land, because it had been so dry for so long, at first repelled the rain, sending it gurgling into crevices and depressions, where it collected to become rivulets rushing into gullies and dry washes, gathering up red dust as it cascaded into bigger gullies, then poured into the ravines leading down onto the floodplain of the South Canadian River, into which it emptied in roaring walls of red muddy water.

The two Indian gravediggers began hurriedly filling in Nora's grave before the rain could turn the dirt to mud. And now that the rain had begun in earnest, many of the mourners scurried for shelter, making joyous noises. Even Reverend and Mrs. Poggemeyer, though constrained by the decorum required by their calling, gave a few skips as they hurried toward the church, the reverend croaking with unaccustomed delight as he said with every skip, "Glory be! Glory be to God!"

Eula, who had been standing among the mourners on the rear fringes of the gathering, lifted the hem of her skirt and dashed for the house to close the windows.

Maxwell was one of the last to leave. He didn't mind getting wet. Dr. Gresham fell in beside him as they left the graveyard.

"Well," he said lightly, as a way of testing Maxwell's readiness to talk, "think the rain'll hurt the rhubarb?" And he judged from Maxwell's response—a snort of appreciation—that he was amenable to conversation, so he said as they walked along through the rain, "Listen, John, I'd like to have a word with you sometime."

Maxwell glanced at him through the small waterfalls that were pouring off the brims of their hats.

"About your housekeeper," he said.

"What about her?"

"Nothing urgent."

They had reached the edge of the town square. Here their paths would diverge toward their respective residences, but Maxwell, feeling the warm rain running down his body beneath his clothes, stopped and, reluctant to part from the doctor without an explanation of his enigmatic reference to Eula, turned to face him.

"She'd make a good nurse," Dr. Gresham said somewhat evasively. "The way she worked with Nora . . ."

"Yes, I don't know what I'd've done without her."

"There's something you might want to mention to her."

"Yes?"

"Her mouth. It doesn't have to be that way, you know?"

"What? What d'you mean?"

"There's a surgeon in Philadelphia who's perfected an operation to correct harelips. He has an article in the latest *Journal of Modern Medicine.* It's in my office if you want to come by and take a look at it sometime."

"An operation?"

"Sort of expensive, I'm afraid, but the results are very gratifying, I'm told. Have to look really close even to see the scar. Well, it's not hard to imagine what such an operation could do for a young woman like Eula, is it? Probably mean a whole new life for her."

"My God," Maxwell said, trying to imagine it. He hardly knew what Eula looked like beneath that bonnet. He knew she had grayish green eyes and a small button nose, but he had caught glimpses of her face so seldom that he hadn't been able to form an indelible impression of it. "Expensive?"

Rain streamed from the ends of Dr. Gresham's scraggly beard as he smiled and said in a tone that terminated the conversation, "Come by the office sometime. I'll give you all the information I have." He angled across the square, slogging through the mud, toward his house.

In the middle of the square some Indians crowded under wagons to escape the downpour, but one of them, a woman with a baby, stood out in the rain, her calico dress plastered wetly to her body, and held the naked baby up at arm's length toward the sky, letting the warm rain pour over its squiggling body.

Preoccupied as a man contemplating a moral conundrum, Maxwell strolled on across the square toward his house. That medical science had progressed to the point of being able to correct a congenital deformity such as a harelip wasn't surprising to him. What was surprising was the enormous impact such an operation would have for someone like Eula. Why, it would be a little like giving sight to a person who had been blind since birth. And while that prospect made him glad for Eula, he instantly foresaw the dangers it held for *him*. Eula—a young woman in her prime, hardworking, a woman with an enormous store of grit and goodness—why, without the harelip, she would be snapped up as a wife by some young cowboy before you knew it. And he didn't want to lose her. What he had said to Dr. Gresham was true, he really didn't know what he would have done without her. She'd been a godsend, and the harelip was the only reason she was there. So maybe he shouldn't even tell her about it—a thought that caused him to flush with shame to realize how monstrously selfish he was being. Even to think of depriving Eula of a chance for a normal life simply because he wanted to keep her as his housekeeper was shameful. And yet he would surely hate to lose her. . . .

"Drought's over, looks like," he announced as he stepped into the house. He could hear Eula in the kitchen, but she didn't respond. On the neatly made bed in the front room she had laid out for him a towel and some dry clothes. But before changing, he glanced into the kitchen. Eula, at the stove with her back toward him, continued to work as if he weren't there. He sensed that she was gripped by some sort of tension, and he didn't have far to look to find the cause: Dexter was in the house, in Nora's room, going through Nora's things.

"What're you doing?"

"I'm taking some of Mother's things," Dexter said, ready to take offense. He had placed an opened carpetbag on a chair and was stuffing it with mementos: a Bible, a jewelry box, a matching silver hairbrush and hand mirror set, other things.

"So I see. But for your information I'm Nora's next of kin, and in the absence of a will, her belongings become mine, and I don't think you should be taking things without at least asking me first."

Dexter shoved one of Nora's old scrapbooks down into the bag. "Well, for *your* information, I'm only taking things that belonged to her *before* she married you. This brush and mirror set? A present from my father to her on their fifth wedding anniversary. And what about her wedding ring? The one my father gave her? You saying *that* belongs to you, too?" He took the scrapbook from the bag. "And what about this? This's my baby scrapbook, you gonna try to tell me it belongs to *you*?"

"For myself, I don't care if you take these things, but Rachel might. She might want some for herself."

Dexter shoved the scrapbook back into the carpetbag. "Like I said, I'm just taking things that belonged to Mother before she married you. If Rachel wants any of 'em, we'll settle it between us." He strapped the bag closed. "At least they'll be safe with me."

"And why wouldn't they be safe here? What're you insinuating?"

"Well, with the housekeepers you bring in here, who can tell?" Dexter spoke loudly enough for Eula to hear. "Wouldn't be the first time one of 'em run off with some of Mother's things, would it?"

"But because one housekeeper stole some of her things doesn't mean all housekeepers steal, and I particularly resent your insinuation that Eula might. I think you owe her an apology."

"You just go ahead and resent all you want to." He moved

to the door, and when Maxwell failed to step aside and let him pass, he, in a roosterlike display of power, drew himself up to his full height and expanded his chest.

They stood staring at each other for a moment, and it was Maxwell who at last acknowledged the foolishness of their posturing. He moved aside. Stepping back into the kitchen, he watched Dexter with a cold eye as he stepped out of Nora's room and headed for the front door, where he stopped and turned to face Maxwell again. As if loath to leave the house without at least one more gibe, he said, "Oh, yeah. Speaking of lawbreakers, that teacher's pet of yours? Corby White?"

"All right, spit it out, what about him?"

"I got reports he's in the peyote cult now. But I suppose you don't know anything about that?"

"No. And I don't believe it either." Maxwell began taking off his wet shirt as though the information were of no consequence.

Dexter snapped, "Yeah? Well, I guess you'll believe it when I come to arrest him one of these days. The Indian police've been told to crack down on the peyote eaters, and we're gonna give 'em a hand. It's a sure jail term for any peyote eater we catch."

"You're all heart, Dexter." He dropped the wet shirt on a chair, then grabbed the towel from the bed and began to dry his neck and shoulders. "Now, if you'll excuse me, I'd like to get out of these wet pants."

"Well, don't say I didn't warn you."

"I'll never do that, Dexter. I'll never say you didn't warn me."

Dexter was still reluctant to leave without having the last word, but unable to think of anything, he left the house and dashed through the pouring rain toward the Bixby Hotel. For a moment Maxwell pondered the vicissitudes of fate that had given him for a stepson Dexter Bingham, an abrasive white-supremacist bullyboy deputy sheriff. What had he done to deserve that?

As for Corby, who had been more of a son than Dexter had ever been, had he really joined the peyote eaters? Maxwell wouldn't be at all surprised. The massacre of the Sioux Ghost Dancers by the U.S. 7th Cavalry at Wounded Knee in 1890 had ended, once and for all, the dreams of the Ghost Dancers, had convinced most Indians that there would be no messiah for them, no flood to wash the white man from the face of the earth. The Indian dead would not come again, the buffalo would never return. The Indians were finished forever. And now, in place of the Ghost Dance, a religious cult had been spreading rapidly throughout the Plains tribes, in which the eating of peyote was a sacrament. Called the Native American Church, it was a religion that allowed the Indians to accommodate themselves to defeat. It allowed them to see the world differently without having to make it different.

Naturally the white authorities saw the peyote cult as something that had to be stamped out. So a bill had passed both houses of the territorial legislature prohibiting the use of peyote, and thereafter any Indian accused of participating in a peyote ceremony was subject to arrest and prosecution. And that was what Corby had to look forward to if, as Dexter claimed, he had joined the peyote eaters. As far as Maxwell could tell, Corby hadn't completely gone back to the blanket yet, but that was only a matter of time, unless Maxwell could find some way to turn him around.

But, then, why should he even try? After all these years that Maxwell had seen young Indians stripped of their heritage and sent out either to compete in a white world that didn't want them or to return to a reservation where they felt alien and ashamed, his confidence in the rightness of his life's work had eroded to the point where he could hardly blame anyone for backsliding. Indeed, there were moments, more and more frequent of late, when the weight of failure lay so heavily upon him that he wondered if he had deluded himself into thinking all these years that he had been a friend and helper to the Indians when, in fact, he had been doing the work of their worst enemy. How better to assure their defeat than by stripping them of their identity and sending them off, full of hope and knowledge and civilized manners, to certain failure because he couldn't give them the one thing that was necessary for success in the white world: a white skin?

CHAPTER THIRTY-FOUR

DEXTER RETURNED FOR CORBY A MONTH LATER. MAXWELL was at his desk in his office. Dexter knocked and entered without waiting to be asked. Nodding curtly, he said, "Where's that teacher's pet of yours? I got a warrant for him."

Maxwell leaned back in his swivel chair. "Why, they're all my pets. Which one do you mean?"

"You know which one. Corby White."

"Ah, yes. On what charge?"

"I don't have to discuss that with you." Chewing a toothpick as a token of his nonchalance, Dexter stood in front of the desk, his thumbs hooked carelessly under his gun belt, his bowler hat tipped rakishly back on his head.

"No, you don't. But unless you do, you can just get out of my office. You've got neither warrant nor invitation to be here, and I've got work to do." He returned to the papers on his desk.

After a moment of resentful silence Dexter said, "Peyote eater."

"Ah. And what evidence do you have?"

"Got an informer, willing to testify in court. Where is he?"

"I take it you've checked the barn already, or you wouldn't have come to me."

"He's not there. Horse's gone. You know where he is?"

"Might. But I don't think I'll tell you. As a county deputy you have no jurisdiction here on federal land."

Dexter took the toothpick from his mouth and pointed it toward the agency's headquarters building. "Maybe you'd like to go over and talk to Tanner? He knows I'm here, and he knows what I'm here for, and he's given me the authority to do it.

Now, where is he? If you don't tell me, you could be charged with harboring a fugitive."

Maxwell slowly rose and leaned across the desk. "You're threatening *me*, Dexter? *Me?* Why, goddamn you, I'm the man who put a roof over your head and food in your mouth for how many years? And you come around here threatening to arrest *me*? Listen, boy, you may think that badge and gun make you a big man, but you're just another bullyboy asshole to me."

"Yeah? Yeah?" Dexter sputtered, nearly speechless with indignation. "Asshole, am I?"

"No," Maxwell said, disgusted with himself for having wasted his contempt on someone who was beneath it. "I take it back. An asshole is at least part of a man." And then, to divert Dexter's rage: "Let's go see Tanner."

"Yeah," Dexter said, as if it had been his idea, as if he had finally thought of a way to give Maxwell his comeuppance, "let's go see Tanner."

Maxwell saw the wagon cage as soon as he stepped outside. At first he couldn't tell what it was and then, recognizing it, couldn't quite believe his eyes. It was a circus wagon that had been used in the Run of '92. Enclosed with iron bars and a gingerbread roof, it had once served as a moving cage for some circus animal. In the run it had been filled with circus performers who wanted to be homesteaders, pulled by a team of Clydesdale performing horses. Now, parked in front of the agent's office, it was hitched to two teams of mules and filled with Indians.

"Now, what the hell is *this*?" Maxwell asked as they approached the cage.

"An arrest wagon," Dexter said condescendingly.

A cluster of Indian policemen had come out of their barracks to get a look at the unique conveyance. Another group of people, mostly clerks, had formed around Orville Snipes, the agency's chief clerk, who held a clipboard in his hands and appeared to be writing down the names of the prisoners. Beside him was Dexter's cohort, a young deputy named Roscoe Brown, who was identifying the prisoners for the chief clerk. Some of the prisoners were sprawled on the floor of the cage, passed out, while others sat with their backs against the bars. Still others stood and stared through the bars like jail-house inmates.

"Water! Water!" cried an old woman. She had been one of the drunks passed out on the floor of the cage, and the sun streaming in through the bars had cooked the alcohol out of her. "Water! Guts on fire." She had urinated on herself. Nearby another drunk had vomited. Flies buzzed sluggishly in the hot cage.

Maxwell whirled on Chief Clerk Snipes. "Does Mr. Tanner know about this?"

"About what?" asked Snipes. In the green shadow of his celluloid eyeshade, his eyes blinked with calculated naïveté behind the thick lenses of his horn-rimmed glasses.

"These prisoners. The way they're being transported. In a circus cage."

"A-yep. Thought it dandy idea. Good advertisement. Shows lawbreakers what'll happen when caught. Why? Don't approve?"

Orville Snipes was officious, a stickler for detail, a dough-faced little man with thinning gray hair and a paunch. He wore garters on his sleeves and celluloid cuffs on his wrists. Late of Mississippi, he had arrived with the locusts in '86, went to work as a warehouse clerk, worked his way up to become chief clerk within three years, and now, serving under an agent who was too old and ill to be bothered with the details of running the agency, he had become the agency's de facto ruler.

"Where is he?"

"Mr. Tanner? Taking nap. Not to be disturbed. Something I can help you with?"

"I'd like to know why these county deputies are being allowed to arrest people on federal land."

"I understand," Snipes told him. "The Indian boy. Works for you. You're upset. I understand. But. Well. Have to cooperate with local authorities, don't we? Bureau's orders. Too bad about the boy, but can't play favorites, can we? How'd it look? Half them in cage have been arrested for peyote. Must stamp out barbaric customs, mustn't we? Not going to be trouble, I hope."

Maxwell knew then that he wasn't going to be able to prevent Corby's arrest. He hadn't had much hope in the first place, but when Snipes started talking about stamping out barbaric customs among the Indians, he knew the chief clerk had taken a stand on lofty principles and couldn't be budged.

"There'll be trouble, all right," Maxwell said, "if you send these deputies after him. Corby won't surrender to this one"—indicating Dexter with a jerk of his thumb, as if he couldn't bring himself to speak Dexter's name—"without a fight."

"Ah. I see. Well? What d'you suggest? Has to be brought in. Can't play favorites, can we?"

"Then I'd better be the one who goes and gets him. Tell these deputies to stay here. If he's where I think he is, I'll be back within an hour."

Maxwell hurried to his barn and saddled his strawberry roan and took the wagon road to Arapaho, a small new town on the banks of the South Canadian about two miles downriver from the agency. With a few stores, a post office, a Methodist missionary church, and a racetrack, the town served as a place where the Arapahos from the choice allotments along the river could come together, just as they did in the old days, to raise hell and go to church. The racetrack was the town's main attraction. Indians and a few whites came from miles around to make bets on the races. Gambling had been outlawed for Indians, but bettors had little fear of being arrested at the track because neither Indian police nor the white constabulary was foolhardy enough to try to arrest two or three hundred Indians, many of whom were armed, some of whom were drunk, all of whom would have resisted.

Maxwell rode to the windmill that marked the racetrack's start and finish line, where he found Corby accepting the admiration of the spectators and collecting his winnings from a bareback race he had just won. He was stuffing a wad of bills into the pocket of his jeans when Maxwell rode through the crowd.

"Won again, did you?" Maxwell said.

Someone shouted that another race was about to begin, and the crowd fell away from Corby, surging back toward the starting line. A small Arapaho boy was struggling to bring Corby's saddle and saddle blanket and shirt to him.

Corby gave Big Red's neck a pat. "Never lost yet," he said, and glanced around for an explanation of Maxwell's presence. "Not often we see you here at the track. Something wrong?"

"Dexter's at the agency. Got a warrant for your arrest."

"What for?" Except for a slight tightening of the facial muscles, Corby didn't seem bothered by the news.

"Says he's got somebody who'll swear you're a peyote eater."

Saying softly, "Ho, Big Red, easy, boy," Corby took the saddle blanket from the hero-worshiping Arapaho boy and tossed it over the nervous stallion's back. To Maxwell, he said, "Thanks for warning me."

"I didn't come here to warn you." Maxwell shifted his weight in the leather-creaking saddle. "I came here to get you. Now, dammit, Corby," he added hastily when Corby gave him a quick questioning look, "if you're thinking about running away or resisting arrest, don't. That's what he'd like you to do. That'd be a much more serious offense than the one you're charged with now. Don't make it worse on yourself."

Corby adjusted the saddle on Big Red's back, then hung the stirrup on the saddle horn and tightened the cinch. "I'm not going to let him put me in jail."

Maxwell swung down from the saddle. "Listen to me, *naha*. I'll do everything I can to get the charges against you dropped. I'll hire a lawyer. I promise I'll do everything I can to see you don't go to jail. But," he added emphatically, "even if you do have to go to jail for taking peyote, it'll only be for thirty days. If you run away, he'll come and get you, and they'll put you in prison for maybe six months. And if you resist arrest, they'll put you in prison for a long, long time, and if you give him any justification, he'll kill you, or you'll have to kill him, and then they'll hang you." He took off his hat and slapped it against his leg in exasperation. The movement and sound made Big Red jerk sideways.

"Ho, boy. Easy, boy."

"For Christ's sake, don't give him the satisfaction of ruining your life. Like I said, I'll do everything I can to get you off, but . . . well, hell, if worse comes to worst, do the thirty days. It won't kill you. Resisting will."

Once the saddle was on, Corby turned to take the blue cotton shirt from the outstretched grubby hands of the Arapaho boy. *"Haho,"* he said to the boy, causing the boy to blush with pleasure. As he put the shirt on, he seemed to think the matter over.

"Listen," Maxwell continued, "trust me on this. I know

what I'm talking about. Just come on back to the agency, give yourself up, and I'll ride with you to El Reno and do everything I can to help."

Without meeting Maxwell's eyes, Corby made a curt nod of assent.

They rode back together. The spectators around the wagon cage had thinned out. Chief Clerk Snipes and his underlings had gone back into the administration building. Dexter and the other deputy, Roscoe Brown, had gone into the dining room at the Bixby Hotel. They came out when they saw Maxwell and Corby ride by.

Corby's revulsion at the sight of the cage increased considerably when Dexter, sucking on a toothpick, approached and ordered Corby to get off the horse and into the cage. Deputy Roscoe Brown brought a huge key from his pocket and opened the cage door.

"Is that necessary?" Maxwell demanded. "He gave himself up, so why can't you trust him not to run away? I'll make sure—"

"No. Get down and take off the knife," Dexter ordered. "You ride in the cage just like everybody else."

Corby seemed to be having second thoughts about giving himself up, but Maxwell said in an undertone, "Do what he says. I'll bring your horse. Give me the knife, and I'll put it in your saddlebag."

"Water! Guts on fire," said the old woman.

"Shut up," Deputy Brown told her. "You'll get water when everybody else does, and not until, so just shut up."

Corby's and Maxwell's eyes met and held for a moment, and then Corby slowly swung down from the saddle and handed the reins to Maxwell. He unbuckled the belt on which he carried a hunting knife and shoved it into his saddlebag.

"Search him," Dexter told Deputy Brown.

Although it was obvious to everyone that Corby was carrying no more weapons, he submitted sullenly to being searched, then caught one of the iron bars and swung up into the cage. After locking the door, Deputy Brown climbed up into the driver's box and unwrapped the reins from the brake lever.

Dexter unhitched his horse from a nearby rail. "He'll appear before Judge Slater in the morning if you want to go his bail," he told Maxwell as he mounted.

"I'm coming with you," Maxwell said.

Dexter shrugged. "It's a free country."

"Is it?" Maxwell asked, glancing at the wagon cage. "Is it, indeed?"

Dexter ignored the gibe. He rode to the front of the wagon cage, told Deputy Brown, "Move out," and took the lead as the wagon cage began laboring along the muddy road to El Reno.

Riding the strawberry roan and leading Big Red, Maxwell rode alongside the wagon cage, close to where Corby stood at the bars. He tried now and then to make eye contact with him, to assure him that he wasn't alone, but Corby continued to stare with a sort of dreamy rage toward the far horizon.

Maxwell could sense the humiliation he was experiencing, and his own shame—the shame of being a member of a master race bullying a weaker one—was hardly less acute. By now this was a familiar feeling, and he had never found a way to resolve it. That the Indians, in order to avoid extinction, had to learn to live in a white man's world he had no doubt (except in those moments when he doubted that the white man's world was worth living in); but he was worm-eaten with doubts about the means by which this assimilation was supposed to be achieved, and doubts turned to shame and disgust at times like this, when laws that had been made to force the Indians to change their ways of living were used instead to victimize them.

He had no illusions about why the Indians in the wagon cage had been arrested. It wasn't because they had broken the law and had to be punished to discourage others from doing the same; it was because each Indian in the cage represented a twenty-five-dollar fee to the arresting lawmen. So the lawmen usually brought them in by the wagonloads. It didn't matter that the Indians were often guiltless of any crime, the deputies had only to produce them before a territorial judge or a U.S. commissioner and charge them with anything at all in order to collect the twenty-five-dollar fee and mileage expenses.

Dexter was making a good living. This load alone would bring him and Deputy Roscoe Brown a tidy six hundred dollars. At this rate they would both be wealthy men by the time they were forty—if, that is, they lived to be forty. Deputy Brown, as it happened, didn't.

It happened as they were passing through a stretch of barren land that was unsuited for homesteading, a place called Gypsum Flats. Suddenly, before anyone even heard the shot, Deputy Roscoe Brown jerked backward in the driver's box and gave a strangled cry, a cry punctuated by the puffy, faraway *crack-boom* of a rifle. As if by reflex, he jerked to a standing position in the driver's box, holding himself erect by pulling back on the reins, causing the mules to stop. Then he pitched forward out of the driver's box and fell crashing onto the wagon's whiffletree and tongue. He landed facedown in the gypsum mud beneath the wagon's front wheels, blood gushing out of an exit hole in his back.

Both Maxwell and Dexter wheeled their horses and sprinted to the south side of the wagon cage, frantically scanning the countryside to the north, the general direction from which the distance-muffled shot had come. Dexter was going so fast by the time he reached the protection of the wagon cage that he had to yank his horse back onto its haunches to keep from going beyond the wagon. He came to a skidding stop in the mud, saying in a voice made singsong with fury and fear, "Goddamn! Goddamn!"

Maxwell leaped to the ground and dropped to one knee beside the wagon cage. Dexter jerked his rifle from its scabbard as he swung out of the saddle and fell on one knee beside Maxwell. "Where are they? You see 'em?"

Maxwell could see a distant thicket of creosote bushes on a ridge about a mile away, which was too far away to be in accurate range of a rifle. And yet it was from those bushes that the shot had come, *had* to have come, since there wasn't enough cover between the wagon cage and the bushes to hide a jackrabbit, let alone a man. But what kind of rifle could have fired accurately from such a great distance?

"Haven't seen anybody," he answered.

"Where'd it come from?"

"Those bushes yonder is my guess."

"Shit," Dexter sneered. "No damn rifle could shoot that far."

"Buffalo rifle. I've heard they can shoot that far."

"Buffalo rifle? Goddamn," Dexter groaned through clenched teeth. "What the hell's going on here?"

They kept watching the bushes, waiting for another shot. The Indians in the cage stirred restlessly, afraid that they, too, might be shot, exposed as they were in the cage; but then a man's reassuring voice among them said in Cheyenne, "Do not fear. It is not we he came to kill."

When it became reasonably apparent that the sniper wasn't going to fire again, Maxwell crawled beneath the whiffletree and caught Deputy Brown's body beneath the arms and tugged it to the edge of the wagon. Dexter caught hold and helped drag the body out into the open, leaving a smear of blood across the whey white mud.

Maxwell said of the exit wound in the deputy's back, "Big as a man's fist. Must've been a buffalo rifle, to make a hole like that."

Hearing a chuckle from the Indians who had crowded together at the bars to get a look at the dead man, Dexter shook his rifle at them and barked, "Laugh, you bastards! Go ahead, laugh! But you won't get away with this. You hear? You'll pay, goddamn you!"

"Take it easy. They didn't have anything to do with this."

"What? You crazy? It's some friends of theirs, trying to rescue 'em."

"I don't know. If it's somebody trying to set 'em free, when's he going to make his next move? My guess is, he got who he wanted, then took off."

Dexter considered that possibility, then said, "Goddammit, I got to go get some help." But he spent the next few moments in a frenzy of indecision about how to accomplish that. He glanced around, muttering curses, and finally came up with an idea. He scurried to his horse.

"You stay here," he said, snatching up the reins and shoving his rifle back into its scabbard. "I'll make a fast run to El Reno, bring back a posse." Holding the reins under the horse's neck, he caught hold of the saddle horn with his left hand. "I'll be back in three or four hours." He crouched behind the horse's neck and withers and nudged the animal into movement, using the horse's body as a shield. He kept up with the horse's slow trot by holding on to the saddle horn.

Maxwell wouldn't have been surprised to see the horse drop in its tracks at any moment, but it soon became apparent that the sniper had either left or had no intention of killing Dexter. This must have become clear to Dexter, too, but he wasn't go-

ing to take any unnecessary chances. He kept trotting alongside
the horse until he was out of range of the buffalo rifle.

"Key," one of the Indians in the cage said, pointing toward
the deputy's body. "Key."

Maxwell turned the deputy's body over and reached into a
pocket and brought out the key to the cage door. The prisoners
murmured with excited approval as he unlocked the door and
swung it open. The livelier ones jumped to the ground running.
Most of them headed back down the road toward the agency,
but a few of them took off across country. They seemed to
have no fear of being shot by the sniper.

Corby jumped down from the cage and took Big Red's reins
off the saddle horn of Maxwell's mount. He turned back to
speak to Maxwell but was interrupted by the old woman, who,
as she was crawling out of the cage, asked Maxwell in Cheyenne if he had any water.

"No," Maxwell said, giving the old woman a hand to steady
her as she stepped down. "I am sorry, grandmother, I do not."

"My guts are on fire," the old woman said again, and
then—quite unexpectedly for an old woman who seemed so
mild—she delivered a swift kick to the side of the deputy's
dead body. "*Veho,*" she sneered and spit on the body. "This
white man sells me whiskey and then arrests me for drinking
it. The buzzards will revenge me." Sighing and straightening
her shoulders, as if summoning up all her strength, she turned
and shuffled off down the road after the others.

"I'm going to drive this rig on to El Reno," Maxwell said
to Corby. "I don't suppose it'd do any good to ask you to
come along? Be best if you turned yourself in, make it easier
to get that charge against you dropped. Otherwise it'll just be
hanging over your head."

"No," Corby said, flatly refusing Maxwell for the first time.

"Thought not. Well, then, help me get him onto the cage,
will you? Can't leave him here in the road."

"Why not? Like the old woman says, leave the *veho* to the
buzzards." But Maxwell's hurt look persuaded Corby to loop
Big Red's reins over the nearest wagon wheel and help Maxwell tug and wrestle the deputy's body into the cage.

"Listen," Maxwell said, wiping blood from his hands with
his handkerchief, "I'll do all I can to get that peyote charge
against you dropped. Till then, might be best if you go out and

stay with the Hehyo band for a while. Just long enough for me to get this mess straightened out. Then you can come on back. We've got to do something about your life before you throw it away."

Without touching the stirrup, Corby vaulted into the saddle. "If I throw it away, it'll be as my father threw his away." He wheeled the horse around to the other side of the wagon cage, where he stopped, facing the faraway bushes, and jerked his rifle from its scabbard and held it horizontally above his head.

"Haho naheto!" he shouted, though the sniper, if he was still in the bushes, was too far away to hear Corby's thanks. "Whoever you are, you are my friend!"

Then he spun Big Red around and galloped back down the road, leaving Maxwell at the wagon cage alone, save for the three bodies—one dead deputy and two drunk Indians— sprawled on the vomit- and urine-fouled floor of the cage.

CHAPTER THIRTY-FIVE

SHERIFF ALVA HARRIMAN HAD A REVELATION ABOUT THE KILL- ing of Deputy Brown. It was only one in a series of mysterious deaths that had occurred during the last few months in Logan County. At first there seemed to be no connection between them, but Deputy Brown was the second man known to him personally who had been shot with a buffalo rifle. This led Sheriff Harriman to obtain from the coroner a list of all the people within the county who had met violent deaths within the last year, and from this list he compiled the names of seven men whom he had known personally. Six of these men had died violently within the space of a few months, but by such different means and under such different circumstances that no one had as yet connected them.

First there was Brod Clemmens, the owner of a Guthrie

grocery store. He often stayed late at the store, and on December 14, 1893, he left at ten o'clock with the day's receipts in a canvas bag. He was shot in the head with a .44 at close range by someone who had been waiting for him outside. The killer took the bag of money. Sheriff Harriman put the death down to robbery. The robber was never caught.

Twenty-five days later, during a snowstorm, Potter Gibbs, a cowhand on the Olanco Ranch, was found with four arrows protruding from various parts of his body. They were Comanche arrows, but no Comanches had been reported in the area.

On February 10, 1894, Justin Williams, another cowhand at the Olanco Ranch, was ambushed and blown out of his saddle by a monstrously big .50 caliber slug that could only have come from a buffalo rifle. But the buffalo rifle allowed the ambusher to kill from such a great distance that his place of ambush and his tracks could never be found.

A few weeks later a county tax collector named Pat Buchanan, while riding through some hills north of Guthrie, fell from his horse, caught his foot in the stirrup, and was dragged to death. Pat Buchanan had been a good horseman, so it was difficult to believe that he would have died in such a misadventure. The sheriff's investigators found the hoofprints of a second horse running alongside the dragging body, but the prints were soon lost in a creek.

Next came Clifford Arnette, a clerk for the Land Commission office in Kingfisher. He got up in the night of March 15 and went to the privy but didn't come back. His wife found him sitting on the hole, his throat cut from ear to ear. A butcher knife lay at Arnette's feet, so suicide had to be considered, though his wife had never before seen the knife. Anyway, Sheriff Harriman wanted to know, whoever heard of a man killing himself while taking a shit?

But there was never any doubt that Lester Tully, the next man to be killed, was murdered. On the night of April 7, Tully's house had been set afire. When Tully and his family ran out the front door, Tully was shot in the chest with a slug from a 30.06. The force of the slug knocked him back into the house, where his body was burned. Tully's hounds hadn't alerted the family to the arsonist because they all had been poisoned with strychnine-laced meat. The killer left no clues or tracks, and nobody could say who did it, or why.

Then came the killing of Deputy Roscoe Brown, the second man to be killed with a buffalo rifle, and Sheriff Harriman had his revelation: all the men on the list had been murdered by one man, and he knew who that man was.

"God Amighty," he murmured with an asthmatic wheeze, and reached for the telephone on his desk. He had the operator at the city switchboard connect him with Shelby Hornbeck's office and left a message that he was coming over immediately. He hurried down the street to the new Hornbeck Building, where he found Hornbeck waiting for him in his walnut-paneled office. Harriman showed him the list.

"Know what all these men have in common? Besides being dead, I mean?"

"Members of the brotherhood."

"What else?"

Hornbeck's face registered the answer almost immediately. "Freedom."

"That's right. Sixteen men made that raid on Freedom last year. Since then seven of them's been killed. Somebody's got a list. I'd say somebody's out to kill every man who was on that raid. And if it's who I think it is, we're up against one smart, tough, cold-blooded sonofabitch."

"Gypsy Smith," Hornbeck said.

"Who else? That black bastard! I knew we should've gone back and finished him off soon's we heard he was still alive, no matter how hard it would've been to get in and out of that niggertown."

"He should've been finished off the night of the raid."

"We thought he was. He was shot in the head, all of us thought he was dead."

"Well, what we have to do now is find him and dispose of him before he has a chance to kill anybody else. Any idea where he might be?"

"I hear different things. Some say he's living down in Mexico, others say the Comanche reservation, and somebody says he was up in the Panhandle not too long ago. Probably keeps moving. For all I know, he might be hiding out in any of these niggertowns hereabouts."

"Find him," Hornbeck ordered. "Kill him."

The sheriff reached for the telephone. "I'll put out an all-points bulletin on him right now."

"No," Shelby said, leaving the sheriff with the receiver halfway to his ear. "Keep it in the Klan. The newspapers mustn't find out about this. That black bastard knows who we are. If he should be arrested somewhere and brought to trial, we'd all be exposed, and my chance for the governorship would be jeopardized."

Harriman replaced the receiver.

"What we'll do is," Shelby continued, "we'll get the word out to all the Dens in the Territory and in Texas. With thousands of Klansmen looking for him, and a five-thousand-dollar reward on his head, he shouldn't last long."

" 'Less he holes up in one of these niggertowns hereabouts, where we can't get to him."

"We'll get him. There's always a Judas. But the first thing we have to do is find out who the Judas is among *us*. If this Smith has a list, he had to get it from one of the men on the raid."

"If it's who I think it is, he's already dead or long gone."

"Reeves?"

"The killings started a couple of weeks after he disappeared last year. It has to've been him."

"Well, a man doesn't just 'disappear' off the face of the earth. If he's alive, I want him found and brought back to face Klan justice. If he isn't, I want to know where he's buried."

Harriman was about to ask Shelby how in the world he could be expected to find, in all the vast miles of the Oklahoma Territory, the very place where Sonny Boy Reeves's bones might be moldering, but Shelby silenced him by tapping the list with the tip of one finger.

"And he must have spies among the niggers who work for us. Janitors, maids, cooks—some of them must be keeping him informed of our whereabouts. Find out who they are, and the brotherhood'll take care of them. Also," he added as Sheriff Harriman rose to leave, "call a meeting of the Den for tonight. The others'll have to know about this before somebody else gets killed."

But at that very moment another of the sixteen raiding Klansmen had come into the sights of Gypsy's rifle. As the owner of a small slaughterhouse just outside Guthrie, Roy Pinkerton sometimes had to make trips into the countryside to find herds of prime beef. While he was traveling to the Blondell Ranch southwest of the Glass Mountains, Pinkerton, as usual, took a shortcut trail that led over the mountains. He had shed his coat and was wearing a bright white shirt with a black string tie and a shoulder holster that held a .38 revolver. At the caprock plateau of the southernmost mountain, he stopped to take a drink from his canteen.

Crouched behind a bush about a hundred yards ahead, Gypsy squeezed the trigger at the same instant Pinkerton lowered the canteen. The bullet hit the metal, was deflected downward, and tore a hole in Pinkerton's side. He was knocked out of the saddle. When he hit the ground he lost the canteen and his hat and the .38 revolver from its shoulder holster. Frantically he thrashed toward the protective cover of some nearby rocks and bushes, scurrying away on his knees and then on his feet, crouching, with his right hand grabbing for the missing .38. As he threw himself behind the nearest rock outcropping, Gypsy's second bullet ricocheted off the rocks.

"Shit," Gypsy said. "Gut shot."

Pinkerton's horse galloped away, trailing its reins on the ground, and disappeared in a grove of cedar trees, heading north along the caprock.

Leaving his horse tethered in a mesquite thicket, Gypsy walked to where the canteen, hat, and pistol lay in the dust. He picked up the revolver, shoved it into his hip pocket, and surveyed the terrain. Bushy and rocky, it offered many places for a man to hide, but how far could Pinkerton get? It was obvious from the way he had scrambled for cover that the bullet had struck no vital organs, so the best Gypsy could hope for was that Pinkerton was bleeding to death.

However, as he followed Pinkerton's trail and studied the distance between the footprints made by Pinkerton when he had left the first hiding place, he saw that Pinkerton had actually sprinted away. A trail of blood drops accompanied the footprints, but nowhere did he see a big splash of blood that would indicate a fatal hemorrhaging. He went back to get his horse, a new buckskin mare named Girl, as all his mares were named. Having had no water since last evening, she was getting restless and would resist going after Pinkerton, but the closest drinking water was at Sweetfern Spring, a two-hour ride down to the foot of the mountain and back, and Gypsy didn't think he could give Pinkerton that much time to make an escape. He considered letting Pinkerton go for now, but after wounding him, he knew he might never get another chance at him, and this was the man Gypsy had been looking forward to killing for a long time. This was the man who had mutilated him, and he wanted to see this man dead, now.

After checking his canteen, he poured some water into his hat for the mare. He himself took a small swallow, just enough to wet his mouth and throat, then patted the horse's forehead. Glancing up at the blazing noonday sun, he said, "Don't worry, Girl. We'll run him down in plenty of time to get back to the spring before dark."

That estimate was based on the assumption that Gypsy, on horseback, would have the advantage, but Pinkerton neutralized the horse's advantage by keeping to broken ground and dense brush where the horse couldn't follow. He climbed ravine walls that a horse couldn't scale and ducked under low-hanging branches of thorny mesquite trees. Having to follow on foot and lead the buckskin, Gypsy often lost the trail on shaly hillsides or in thorny thickets. But the constant movement kept Pinkerton's wound open and bleeding, and Gypsy always picked up his trail again by the drops of blood he found.

Gypsy had cursed the punishing sun more than once that day, but when he realized it was getting close to going down, he cursed it for deserting him. He and the horse had shared the last water in the canteen, his throat was parched, he had nothing to eat, and his guts were grumbling as he lay down just after dark.

The mare spent a restless night tugging against the picket rope, and in the morning she wanted to head down into the canyons to water. But Gypsy gently forced her on, stroking her neck and saying, "It won't take much longer now, Girl. Another hour or two, we'll have him."

He found where Pinkerton had spent the night, and there was something about it that was amiss—something Gypsy sensed without being able to name. There was only a shallow body depression under a bush and, maybe twenty-five yards away, a small pile of human feces. Had he not been confused by the sun and heat and thirst and dust, he might have figured it out, but whatever was missing from the scene escaped him for the moment.

By late morning he had lost Pinkerton's trail entirely. He floundered around, backtracked, and discovered that Pinkerton had doubled back on the trail. He found the place where Pinkerton had waited in a clump of bushes not twenty yards away from where Gypsy and the buckskin passed through a clearing.

The sonofabitch was tough and smart. Gypsy had to admit it.

He put a pebble in his mouth and rolled it around to try to work up some spittle to swallow, but there was hardly enough moisture in his mouth to wet the stone.

"Well, he can't keep it up," he argued aloud to the mare. "He needs water as much as we do."

Then suddenly, without any deliberate figuring, he realized what had bothered him when he inspected the place where Pinkerton had spent the night.

"He's drinking his own piss!"

Nowhere during his tracking had he seen where Pinkerton had stopped to urinate. Not that he would have had much to urinate, but Gypsy, in spite of having had very little water during the last twenty-four hours, had urinated twice.

"That's how he's doing it," he's drinking his own piss!" he said to the mare, angry with himself for not having realized it before. "And you!" he said accusingly to the mare. "When're you gonna piss?" He made a mental note to keep an eye on her, and anytime she showed signs of preparing to urinate, he would see if he could catch some in his hat.

It was early afternoon when Pinkerton made what seemed to be his first serious mistake. He doubled back on his trail again, but this time it took Gypsy only a few minutes to understand what had happened. He leaped into the saddle and kicked the mare into a loping run.

When Gypsy caught sight of him, Pinkerton was going down an embankment too steep for the horse to follow, making a dash for the cover of a cedar copse, holding his side, limping on his left leg. Without time to dismount and take a steady aim, Gypsy swung the rifle on him and fired. The bullet kicked up dirt as Pinkerton plunged into the cedars. In frustration Gypsy fired three more shots into the cedar copse.

"I'll get you," he said, his tongue and lips so dry that the words were unintelligible even to his own ears. He raised his voice, attempting to compensate with volume for his thick tongue, and cried, "I'll get you!" But still the words had no clarity, so he yelled as loudly as his parched throat would permit, "I'll get you! You hear me?," shouting across a vast heat-shimmered wasteland. "I'll get you!"

He felt on the verge of tears. In all his life he had never felt so close to utter failure yet never so determined not to fail. But at what cost? His own life? He had to wonder that now. He was dizzy and weak with thirst and weary to his very bones.

By midafternoon the buckskin had begun to stagger and stumble, too weak to carry Gypsy any longer. He tied the reins to his belt and led her, and twice, trying to break away, she pulled him off his feet, dragging him, then stopping, wild-eyed and trembling, as Gypsy got to his feet and mumbled through swollen and cracked lips, "Easy, Girl. Easy, now."

The main thing that saved him from panic was the thought that he could always kill the mare to save his own life. In his youth he had learned that Comanche raiding parties kept from dying of thirst on the waterless plains of Texas by taking extra horses with them on raids, and when pursued by white men, they would strike out across areas of the country where they knew there was no water. The white men would eventually have to turn back or die. But the Comanches drank the blood of their extra horses. They would open a vein in a horse's neck and put their mouths over the spurting blood.

By late afternoon Gypsy was close to losing consciousness, and he knew that he must soon have the horse's blood. He had even begun pulling his knife from its scabbard, eyeing the place on the mare's neck where he would be most likely to puncture the jugular vein. But he knew he would have to hobble the mare's legs to keep her still, and the effort that would require caused him to postpone his take from minute to minute, while he kept going, taking heart from Pinkerton, whose condition he supposed was even worse than his own. The man was amazing. Even drinking his own piss, how could he keep going? A grudging admiration for the man grew in proportion to Gypsy's frustration at being unable to hunt him down and kill him. And for one dizzy, feverish moment in the blindingly hot sun, as he was following the trail out of a rocky, cactus-choked arroyo, he thought he would like to know the man.

This was one tough sonofabitch. Smart, too. But nothing was going to save him.

"You're a dead man, Pinkerton!" he shouted as he staggered and stumbled out of the arroyo, though the shout was no more than a dry grunting sound emitted through his cracked and swollen lips as he staggered through a landscape of sun-baked desolation.

Later he found himself on an immense alkali flat. No trees or grass grew in the sterile soil. The only vegetation within sight was a thorny thicket of greasewood and mesquite brush.

Pinkerton's tracks were clearly indented in the powdery white dust, and Gypsy had no difficulty following them until they disappeared into the thicket. He tied the mare's reins to a bush and circled the thicket. He found no tracks leading out of it.

"Well, I've got you now," he rasped to the thicket.

He fired a few shots into the thicket, trying to flush Pinkerton out, but there was no sign of movement. Maybe Pinkerton's last violent efforts to get away had left him hemorrhaging and too weak to leave the thicket. Maybe, in fact, he was dead already.

Gypsy went into the low dense tangled mesquite brush, scooting on his buttocks so that he could have the rifle ready, but soon the brush became so impassable that he had to get on his hands and knees, sometimes even on his belly, and pull the rifle along as best he could. The thorns and limbs cut at his skin and clothing, and the prickly leaves on the ground punctured and scratched his hands and knees, but he kept following Pinkerton's drag marks in the alkali dust under the shrubs until he found that the tracks began to wander everywhere, crisscrossing and circling in a strange pattern. Why would Pinkerton enter the thicket only to walk and crawl around in circles?

"Well, I'll be goddamned," Gypsy moaned.

He scrambled out of the thicket and made another quick circle around it, and sure enough, there they were: Pinkerton's footprints leaving the thicket only a few yards from where the other prints had entered it. So he had gone in and left a maze of tracks for Gypsy to follow, then hidden near where he had entered it, and when Gypsy had entered the thicket, Pinkerton had left.

Gypsy didn't bother with the horse. With his legs wobbling

from weakness and feet dragging though the dust, he followed
Pinkerton's tracks westward across the alkali flat and entered a
shallow draw between two small barren shaly ridges. The setting sun cast the eastern slope of the western ridge into twilight
shadows, so Gypsy didn't quite trust his eyes when he saw the
form moving among the shadows, an indistinct shape laboring
up the ridge toward the descending disk of the sun. With all
the painful tension of a clenched fist, Gypsy brought the rifle
to his shoulder and waited a few seconds until the shape was
at the farthest point from any possible cover. He fired. The bullet ricocheted off a rock above Pinkerton's head, sending him
into a desperate scramble toward the top of the ridge. Without
pausing to curse the man's charmed life, Gypsy dropped behind a boulder and rested the barrel of the rifle on it. Pinkerton
was about halfway up the ridge now, plunging in the loose
shale, a blurred shape. Gypsy took aim, but not directly at Pinkerton. Instead he aimed into the sky at the crest of the ridge,
at the place where Pinkerton would top the ridge, which was
also the exact spot where the sun was about to sink below the
ridge. The terrific glare made his eyes water and sting, but
he forced himself not to look away.

When Pinkerton finally pulled himself onto the crest of the
ridge, he paused for an instant to regain his balance, and for
that split second he was sharply silhouetted against the sun.

Gypsy fired. The bullet hit Pinkerton between the shoulder
blades. He toppled backward, crashed into the shale on the
slope, and his momentum hurtled him into another backward
somersault. He came to a stop on his back at the bottom of the
ridge.

Gypsy ran in a stagger up the draw to where Pinkerton's
broken and convulsing body sprawled in the dirt and shale. As
he approached, Pinkerton tried to move his head to look at
him, but there was only a twitching of nerves in his paralyzed
body. Blood was oozing out of his agape mouth, and his eyes
rolled wildly in their sockets as he tried to get a look at Gypsy.
His face was terribly blistered, his lips swollen and cracked,
his eyes bloodshot and swollen.

Gypsy dropped the rifle and jerked his bowie knife from its
sheath. He knelt, and as Pinkerton continued to gaze at him
with unblinking wonderment and horror, Gypsy plunged the
knife point into Pinkerton's throat. A stream of blood squirted

out of the puncture hole at each weakening heartbeat. Gypsy put his mouth to the hole and drank.

When he pulled away, Pinkerton was still staring at him, eyes filled with wonder and horror, as his breathing and his blood slowly came to a stop. A cloudy film of death, like breath blown on a cold windowpane, slowly covered his eyes.

CHAPTER THIRTY-SIX

ON THE DAY THAT MAXWELL DROVE THE WAGON CAGE ON TO El Reno, he found a judge who, for a bribe of fifty dollars and a few drinks of whiskey, was willing to see that the peyote charge against Corby was dismissed. Even so, Maxwell expected that Dexter and the other lawmen would want to question Corby and the other wagon cage prisoners to see if they had any connection with the sniper. To his surprise, the lawmen acted as if they already knew who the sniper was, and so urgent were their efforts to find him that Dexter forgot about Corby for the time being.

The newspaper stories said that the killer's identity remained a mystery, but rumor named Gypsy Smith, a rumor that was given credence by the fact that Gypsy soon became the most hunted man in the Territory. Lynch mobs, sometimes led by lawmen, combed the country looking for him. One posse, led by U.S. Marshal Silas Renfro, with Deputy Dexter Bingham at his side, rode through Agency a few days after Deputy Brown had been shot, asking about Gypsy Smith.

"Why're you looking for Gypsy Smith?" Maxwell asked Marshal Renfro, but got no answer. The posse rode away, headed for the Comanche-Kiowa reservation, where someone reported recently having seen Gypsy.

"Oh, the poor man," Eula murmured that night. "To be run down by lawmen and lynch mobs and die in a shoot-out or by a hangman's rope." Sitting in a straight-back chair, slowly and absently smoothing her dress down over her thighs, her head bowed, she seemed to be visualizing the scene. "The poor man. He was right kind to me over in Freedom."

Maxwell had always valued Eula highly as a housekeeper, but it wasn't until he saw how deeply she sympathized with Gypsy's outcast state that he fully realized how fond he had become of her as a person. It was uncanny how she, who never touched him physically, so often touched his heart. And this realization brought with it a new rush of guilt about his own selfishness. So reluctant had he been to lose her as a housekeeper that he had delayed telling her about the operation that could repair her mouth, and even when his conscience finally forced him to tell her, he had merely conveyed the information about the operation, rather than encouraged her to have it.

She seemed to have been struck dumb by the idea. It was as if the idea held consequences for her that were too profound for her to comprehend. As usual when upset and in need of contemplation, she sat down and began slowly and absently smoothing her dress down over her thighs or picking imaginary lint from her clothes.

"Dr. Gresham mentioned that it'd cost about three hundred dollars," Maxwell said. "With, say, seventy-five or so to get you to Philadelphia, and that much to get you back, that's about four-fifty. With another fifty or sixty dollars to live on while you're there, I'd say five, six hundred ought to do it."

"No, sir," she said, "I better not," and got up to go back to work.

"If it's the money . . . ?" Maxwell was sitting at the table, having a cup of after-dinner coffee and a pipe. "I could lend it to you."

"No, thankee," she said from beneath the bonnet. "I couldn't be beholden."

Maxwell let it go at that. But he got very little sleep that night, and when he came to breakfast the next morning, he said to her, "Sit down. I want to talk to you."

Surprised by the order, Eula quickly sat down, and as soon as he brought up the subject of the operation again, she began absently smoothing her apron down on her lap.

"If it's just the money, don't worry about it," he said as he poured hot syrup over his pancakes. "I'll give it to you as an advance against your salary. How's that? You can work it off over the next year or two." He thought that was a clever idea, because it made it less likely that he would lose her after the operation to some wife-hunting homesteader.

"I got nearly two hundred dollars," she said. "I been saving it up for my homestead, so I could go back and work it again"—this said in a tone of lament, since she no longer had a homestead. To qualify for ownership, homesteaders had to live on their claims for at least six months out of every year for five years, and as soon as Eula had been gone from her allotment for six months, the Olanco Ranch had filed on it as an abandoned claim. Now her homestead was part of the Olanco Ranch.

"Well, there you are," he said. "Maybe it was fate that caused you to lose it, so you could spend the money on this."

She smoothed her apron. "You don't think it'd be just vanity?"

"Vanity? Oh, for pity's sake, Eula, if you had a clubfoot and could get it fixed with an operation, you'd do it, wouldn't you? What's the difference?"

"I'll think on it."

Another few days passed before Maxwell sat her down again and said, "Well? Shall I tell Dr. Gresham to wire that doctor in Philadelphia and make a date for you?"

"But there's so much to do here. Who'd take care of the house while I was gone?"

"Don't worry about that. Rachel's coming home for the summer. She can take care of things around here till you get back. So? What d'you say? Wouldn't you like to do it?"

Eula got up and went to the stove to stir a pot of beans. "I don't think so. I'd be too scared, I reckon."

"Why? What's there to be scared of?"

"I reckon I done got used to being the way I am, and if I was some other way, I wouldn't know how to be."

Maxwell nodded understandingly. "I know a lot of Indians who feel the same way." He shrugged. "Well, if you change your mind, the money's always available."

"Thankee kindly. You're a right good man."

Impulsively he reached out to pat her shoulder, just as he would have patted the shoulder of a student who was in need of encouragement, but with quite different results because now there was fondness in his touch, too. Both of them felt it, and both were left a little disconcerted. She made a small breath-catching sound in her throat, and he jerked his hand away as if the touch had been a mere inadvertence.

A week later he went to St. Louis to bring Rachel home for her summer vacation. It was the middle of June by then, and summer had begun with a heat wave. As long as the train on which they were riding kept moving, the hot wind coming through the opened windows at least kept the passengers from suffering heat stroke, but when the train stopped in stations or was shunted onto sidings to let other trains pass, the metal cars sweltered in the sun. Babies cried from heat rashes, passengers were grumpy from lack of sleep, the dining car was covered with dust, sand got into the food, the food was bad, the short-tempered conductors paid little attention to passengers' complaints, and there were no young cowboys on the train to flirt with Rachel. She was bored and hot and uncomfortable, and before she even got back to the agency, she began to wonder if coming home had been a mistake. She had been invited to spend the summer with Melvina Rhodes, her best friend at school, whose family owned an enormous country estate on Lake Wappapello, where they would spend the summer under parasols in canoes, or playing croquet on vast green lawns, or listening to chamber music quartets play sweet melodies in the cool shade of an ivy-covered gazebo. And she had declined the invitation for *this*?

Although still a gangling girl of fifteen—"nearly sixteen," she would have said—Rachel had acquired at Miss Finwick's Young Female Academy a certain amount of grace, not to mention impeccable manners, a softer way of speaking, and a snobbish attitude toward backwoodsy ways. But her ladylike demeanor vanished entirely when a man sitting in front of her spit a long stream of tobacco juice out the window, some of which blew back into Rachel's face.

"Listen, mister," she snapped, "if you're going to chew that stuff, why'n't you go on back to the observation platform, like the rest of the spitters 'stead of spitting all over us?"

The spitter got up and skulked away.

That incident seemed to set Rachel's disposition for the summer, and it even got worse when it began to appear that Corby wasn't coming back to the agency anytime soon. Max-

well had sent word to Corby at the Hehyo village that the peyote charge against him had been dropped and he was no longer
subject to arrest, but by then Corby had gone with Chief
Hehyo and a small band of Cheyennes on a visit to Wyoming.
It wasn't supposed to be a summerlong visit, but when a
month had gone by and there was still no sign of Corby, Rachel gave up all hope of having any fun that summer. She
seemed to resign herself merely to enduring the hot, dusty, fly-
buzzed, malignant monotony of the place.

She tried to find some of the girls she had known before she
left, but prissy little Mary Poggemeyer was studying to be a
saint. Peggy Howard, the blacksmith's daughter, had married a
local homesteader and was, at the age of sixteen, about to give
birth to her first child. And Bonnie Blue Hand, the daughter of
Black Kettle Woman, Rachel's old wet nurse, had recently
graduated from the agency school and gone to work in the
agency's slaughterhouse.

This slaughterhouse had existed for a few years now—ever
since the Bureau of Indian Affairs had decided that the
monthly beef issue to the Indians should not be conducted as
a mock hunt. To allow them to shoot and butcher their cattle
only encouraged them to remember the old days of the buffalo
hunts. So the Bureau formed a cooperative slaughterhouse,
where the cattle would be killed and butchered and issued to
the Indians in pieces, rather than on the hoof. The slaughterhouse had been built about a mile west of the agency—far
enough away so that the prevailing westerly winds would prevent the agency from being suffocated by the stench.

When Rachel grew desperate for some form of distraction,
she decided to ride out to the slaughterhouse to see Bonnie
Blue Hand. She put the sidesaddle on the strawberry roan, and,
protected from the fierce sun by a lacy parasol, rode out to the
slaughterhouse, where she was met by a stench so disgusting
that she considered turning around and going back without
even seeing Bonnie. But then she noticed the young man who
was working the killing chute. For a moment she thought it
was Corby. He was a very handsome young man of about
eighteen or nineteen, his blue-black hair held in place by a
rolled bandanna. He wore only a breechclout, his body glis-
tened darkly with sweat, and the muscles in his shoulders and
arms rippled with sensuous strength as he, straddling the chute

above the cattle as they were driven up the chute, raised the sledgehammer high in the air, and brought it down on their skulls. *Whock*, one would drop, and, *whock*, another, and, *whock*, another. The stunned cattle fell down a ramp leading into the building, where they were raised on pulleys to hang head down over the processing table, there to be skinned and gutted and butchered.

For a long while—she wasn't sure how long; maybe as long as a minute or two—she stared with mingled fascination and revulsion at the young man as he wielded the sledgehammer, and she couldn't turn away until somebody said, "You want something?"

He was an Indian, a boss of some sort, to judge by his clothing and his clipboard. When Rachel told him she had come to see Bonnie Blue Hand, the man nodded toward a tin-roofed shed next to the butchering building. "In there. But you don't want to go in there."

Bristling at being told what she wanted or didn't want to do, she dismounted and demanded to know, "Why not?"

"Too much not nice," the man warned.

Brushing aside his warning, Rachel entered the first shed. The stench was overpowering, and the heat of the sun on the tin roof had turned the place into an oven, the air alive with swarms of flies. It was the gut-cleaning shed. Indian women, dressed in oilcloth aprons and rubber boots, their heads wrapped in bandannas, stood at a table and scraped the guts of the slaughtered cattle clean of their contents. The contents were ladled into tubs alongside the table, and the guts were thrown into a tank, to be cleaned and used for sausage casings. The women cleaners were flecked with fecal matter, and Rachel didn't recognize Bonnie Blue Hand among them until one of the gut cleaners stared at her with amazement and said, "Rachel? Is it you? My God, what you doing here?"

The Indian man with the clipboard had followed Rachel and now said, "Get her out of here. Don't want no white girls fainting here, bringing doctors and such around. Outside."

Bonnie Blue Hand dropped her work on the table, briskly washed her hands in the water of the gut tank, and rushed to Rachel, who, using the closed parasol for support, was sweating profusely and clenching her teeth in an effort to keep from fainting.

"Come on." Bonnie led her out of the slaughterhouse. They stopped at the hitching rail where Rachel's horse was tethered, and Bonnie asked, "What in the world you doing here?"

Clutching at the horse for support, Rachel muttered, "I thought I'd drop by and see you. I didn't know where you lived." Then she blurted out, "My God, Bonnie, how can you *stand* it?"

Bonnie shrugged. "You get used to it. You can get used to anything if you have to."

They were standing where they could see the young man with the sledgehammer on the killing chute, and Rachel found herself staring at him again with that strange feeling of mingled fascination and revulsion. And she gave a little gasp when the young man, while waiting for some more cattle to be driven into the chute, waved at her. At least she thought for a moment that the wave was for her, and it set her heart to pounding, but then she realized that Bonnie had returned the wave.

"You know him?" she asked, relieved.

"Him? Sure. My boyfriend. Tom Jefferson. You don't remember him? Couple grades ahead of us in school."

"*That's* Tom Jefferson? Well, he certainly has changed, hasn't he? He looks . . . very strong."

"Real strong. Sure makes good boom-boom in the bushes."

"You go into the bushes with him?" Rachel couldn't believe that Bonnie, being a Christian and educated, after all, and only a few months older than her, could be going into the bushes at night with young men.

A sly expression played on Bonnie's sweat-drenched and excrement-flecked face. "You wanna go sometime? He got friends who like white girls."

Rachel found the stirrup and lifted herself onto the sidesaddle. Snapping the parasol open, she said, "I can't imagine why you'd make such a suggestion to *me*."

"The way you look at him." Bonnie made a soft and knowing sound.

"I was just looking at him because he's so . . . disgustingly dirty." And as she looked at Bonnie, Rachel concluded that she, too, looked disgustingly dirty. "G'bye," she snapped, and turned the horse toward home.

"Disgustingly dirty" was a phrase she had sometimes heard

her mother use when talking about Indians. She had dismissed
it then as the prattle of a bitter old woman and had completely
forgotten it until she heard it from her own mouth. Now she
wondered for the first time if perhaps her mother had been
right after all. Riding back through the trash-strewn area of tepees and log cabins in which lived the agency's Loafer Indians, Rachel had occasion to use the phrase more than once,
and used it with particular vehemence when she saw a small
naked Indian boy squat and defecate in a ditch and a ribby old
dog waited to eat the excrement.

"I want to leave here," she told Maxwell when she came up
from the barn and found him sitting in his rocking chair on the
back porch, fanning himself and drinking iced tea. "I want to
go back to St. Louis. I can't stand this place any longer. I'm
serious. May I go back? I just got a postcard from Melvina last
week. They'll be at Lake Wappapello until September first.
That would give me a whole month there. May I go, Daddy?"

"What is it? What's the matter?"

"I *hate* this place."

To him she seemed very much like her mother at that moment. "Why, Rachel, how you've changed!" His disappointment was real, though his tone was one of mock surprise. "I
never heard you complain about it before."

"Sure—before I knew anything else existed. And anyway,
that was when Corby was here. But who knows when he might
come back or even *if* he's coming back? Anyway, I'm tired of
waiting. I want to go back to St. Louis."

The impatience in Maxwell's voice betrayed his own feelings of being disprized when he said, "Well, what am I supposed to do? Just jump up and take you back to St. Louis
anytime you get bored and take it in your head to leave? I
have things to do. I have to make plans ahead of time when
I'm going to be gone."

"I can go on the train alone. For goodness' sakes, Daddy,
I'm old enough to travel without a chaperon."

"No, you're not, young lady, so let's hear no more about
that. I'll give it some thought. If I can afford the time to take
you back early, I'll let you know. Otherwise you'll just have to
stay here till September, as we planned."

Rachel flounced inside.

In a few minutes Eula came out onto the porch. Drying her

hands on her apron, she stared absently out across the heat-shimmered land.

Automatically trying to enlist her sympathy, Maxwell said, "You heard that? Wants to go back to St. Louis! As if I didn't have anything else to do except chaperon her around the country."

"Well, I reckon I could."

Maxwell rattled the ice in his tea glass. "Could what?"

"Ride with her to St. Louis. If you really don't mind her going back early, I mean."

"*You*? Go to *St. Louis*?"

"I'd be going through there, anyway, wouldn't I, on my way to Philadelphia?" After a brief pause she continued, "I been thinking 'bout that operation, you see, and I'm thinking, maybe so. Maybe I ought to try it. I mean, if you still don't mind loaning me the rest of the money, and all."

"Mind? Why, I'd be delighted." But at the same time he felt a quiver of apprehension. "Why, that's wonderful! What made you change your mind?"

"Well, I just got to thinking it wouldn't be no more scary than me coming out here to get myself some land in the first place, would it? I mean, it ain't like I got anything much to lose."

"No," Maxwell wanted to say, "it'll be I who'll be losing—losing the services of my housekeeper and the company of my daughter, all at the same time." But he neither said it nor begrudged them the excitement and joy they both felt when, two weeks later, he took them to the train depot in El Reno.

He waited until it was almost time to board the train before he gave Eula the envelope containing the money.

"There's a little something extra in there. Since you're practically going to be a new woman, and all, I thought you might like to buy yourself a new dress or two."

He thought for a moment that she was going to embrace him, but she restrained herself, saying only, "I don't know how to thankee, Mr. Maxwell. You're a right kind man." Then she rushed aboard the train.

As the conductor was calling, "All aboard!" the first time, Maxwell and Rachel embraced. Her eyes puddled with tears as she said, "Oh, Daddy, I'm sorry I've been such miserable company since I came home. Eula's right, you're a good man. You deserve a better daughter than me."

"Now, now, you're the best daughter a man could have. Go on, get aboard. Be good, now, and mind Eula, you hear?"

She turned in the doorway to wave to him as the conductor picked up the steps and shouted, "Boooooard!" for the last time before the train, with a sudden hissing release of steam and a chattering of spinning wheels, began to pull away from the station. Eula, with one hand covering her mouth, waved to him from a window. He walked along the platform for a few steps, keeping pace with the train, and waved and called to both of them, "Good luck! Good luck!," feeling in some strange way that he was saying good-bye forever to both of them, feeling that he was sending them both away, each to her own transformation.

CHAPTER THIRTY-SEVEN

THE SMALL BAND THAT ACCOMPANIED CHIEF HEHYO TO WYO-ming hoped to reach the reservation of the Northern Chey-ennes before the chief died. He had been getting weaker and weaker during the trip, until finally he wasn't even able to get out of the tattered overstuffed chair in which he rode. Corby and the other young men helped him in and out of the chair. He made the journey with his eyes closed, saving what little sight he had left so that he could once more feast them on the vistas of the ancestral hunting grounds of the Human Beings.

At night around the campfires the chief told Corby the old stories about Sweet Medicine Man and the Sacred Arrows, and about the Thunderbird, and about the Sacred Mountain where the Human Beings were born. Corby listened carefully, even though the old chief often got the characters and places mixed up, or forgot where he was in the stories, or couldn't seem to tell the difference between what was story and what was real, and sometimes he even forgot whom he was talking to. The chief's own name for Corby was Boy-who-rides-the-bay-horse—usually shortened to just Boy—but sometimes he called him Red Eagle, the name of the chief's firstborn son, who had died many years ago.

Water Bird Woman, the old chief's granddaughter, Red Eagle's youngest daughter, scolded him. "Grandfather, this is not Red Eagle. What is the matter with you? Have you lost your mind?"

"I have no objection to being called Red Eagle," Corby told her.

The condition of the chief continued to deteriorate as they drew closer to the Wind River country and to the place on top of the Bighorn Mountains where the old chief planned to open his eyes. He had described to the driver of the wagon exactly where he was to stop, a place where he would be able to see the valley of the Wind River and the trees and the mountains and the fat-grass prairies where millions of buffalo used to feed.

When they finally reached the place—at dawn about three weeks after they had left the reservation in Oklahoma Territory—it was Corby and the medicine man, Iron Shirt, who helped the old chief out of the wagon. With his eyes shut tight, Chief Hehyo allowed the two to position him so that he was facing west, with the Wind River valley stretched out before him in all its springtime splendor. Then he took a deep breath and opened his eyes.

Although completely covered by the milky film of cataracts, his eyes widened as though he had been vouchsafed a view of paradise. His old skin-and-bones body shook with excitement as he threw up his hands and cried, "Look! They have come back!" And so great was his joy that he jerked out of Corby's and Iron Shirt's hands and tottered a few steps toward the valley. It was obvious from the way he stumbled over rocks and bumped into bushes that he could see nothing, yet he held his arms out toward the valley and cried, "They have come back! The buffalo! They have returned! Look! Buffalo beyond counting!"

When he tottered and fell, Water Bird Woman rushed to pull him to his feet. "Come along, grandfather. There are no buffalo there. You have lost your mind as well as your eyes. Come back to the wagon."

"Leave him alone," Corby said.

Resentful of his interference, Water Bird said, "He is an old man. He might fall and break a bone."

"Leave him alone," Corby said again, and helped steady the tottering old man in an upright position.

"You see them, don't you, Boy?" Chief Hehyo cried. "You see the buffalo?"

"Yes, grandfather, I see them."

"Buffalo beyond number! You see them, don't you? As far as the eye can reach! Ha! I knew they would come back. I knew the white man could not kill them all. And here they are. Look!" He flailed his arms and crowed like a doddery old rooster greeting one last sunrise. But suddenly he drew himself up to his full height, assumed a grave demeanor, as befitted a great chief of the Human Beings. "Alert the dog soldiers, Red Eagle," he commanded. "The Crows and the Pawnees will be following the herds." Then, just as suddenly as he had assumed his chiefly demeanor, he abandoned it, and once again like an old rooster, he flapped his arms and did a little dance. "The buffalo have returned, Boy! We will never again have to go hungry! Think of that! Never again will our children cry with empty bellies!" He sighed then, a long deflating sigh, a sigh of mingled weariness and contentment. "Now I can die a happy man. I have lived to see the buffalo return. Now I can die."

And as if to set the process in motion, he slowly collapsed. Corby and Iron Shirt carried him back to the wagon. They lowered him into the old chair. The caravan continued on its way toward the Wind River reservation, but the first time they went down a steep hill they found that the old chief no longer had the strength even to hold himself in the chair. They had to tie him in with a rope.

Some of the chiefs from the Northern Cheyenne and Shoshone tribes, having heard that the legendary Chief Hefollows-his-father's-ways of the Southern Cheyennes was on his way to visit them, rode out to meet him. They had even planned some welcoming festivities in his honor, but it soon became apparent to them, as it was to everyone by now, that the old chief was more in need of a burial than a banquet.

But to everyone's surprise he lived for another two months.

Bedridden and blind, toothless and senile and shrinking, he seemed to die by degrees in a process of regression: first he became a child, then an infant, and then one day in August he curled up into a fetal position and stayed that way until he stopped breathing. Corby was with him when he breathed his last.

"Good-bye, grandfather," he said to the old chief. "*Nimeaseoxzheme*—May your journey to the Spirit Land be a good one."

The older chiefs wanted to dispose of the body according to ancient Cheyenne custom—wrapping it in blankets and depositing it on a scaffold—but there were Indian policemen about who required the tribal elders to follow the white man's law and put the dead body in a hole in the ground. So that was where they buried him. But in spite of the white man's disapproval, they did follow the old burial custom of the Human Beings when they sacrificed the two pinto ponies that had pulled the old chief's wagon. They led the ponies onto his grave and shot them. This was done so that the old chief would have ponies to ride on his journey to the Spirit Land.

CHAPTER THIRTY-EIGHT

THREE MONTHS AFTER MAXWELL SAW EULA OFF AT THE EL Reno railroad station, he once again stood on the platform. He watched the passengers disembark, but she wasn't among them. Had she missed the train? Had he got the information wrong? He was sure the telegram had said the twelve-forty from Wichita.

Among the passengers remaining on the platform, exchanging greetings and gathering luggage, was a young woman who seemed to be waiting to be recognized—waiting for *him* to recognize her, apparently, since she was looking directly at him. But his glance glided past her completely before being jerked back by a shock of recognition. Squinting from behind his spectacles, as if looking at something miles away, he said, "Eula?"

She was a woman of about Eula's age, all right, plainly but prettily dressed, with ash blond hair brushed upward and bundled on the crown of her head, topped by a small hat that bobbled wax cherries. She had hazel eyes, a small button nose, and a smiling mouth. But it wasn't until she brought her hand up to cover her mouth in that old gesture of shame and self-consciousness that he said, "My God, it *is* you!"

"Yes, sir, it's me."

He stepped closer to get a better look at her mouth. She hung her head. He put a finger under her chin and lifted her face. Her mouth had an unusual shape to it when she smiled, but other than that and a pink thread of a scar running from the base of her nose to her lip, one would never have known that she had once had a harelip.

"Well!" he said. "Well, well, well!" It was one of the few times in his life that he had been at a loss for words. "Wonders will never cease! Eh?" He wanted to relieve her self-consciousness by averting his eyes, but he couldn't. "My goodness! Well, welcome back!"

"Thankee."

"Well, then, shall we be on our way?"

When both reached down to pick up her carpetbag at the same time, they bumped heads. Their hats were knocked askew. Embarrassed, they straightened up, chuckled, straightened their hats.

"Allow me," he said, and picked up her carpetbag and started for the buggy. And when he noticed that she had, from old habit, fallen in behind him, he took her arm and escorted her to the buggy and helped her in.

"Thankee."

One more look at her face before he went around and climbed onto the seat beside her left him shaking his head with wonderment at the change in her.

On their way back to the agency he tried to make conversation by asking her to tell him about Philadelphia, but all she said was "It's a right big place."

"Think you'd like to live there?"

"Oh, no, sir, not me. I best stay right here. I've et so much Oklahoma dust already, I done become part of the place."

It was as close to a jest as Maxwell had ever heard her utter and was as close as she would let herself come to expressing the joy she felt at having been transformed from a harelipped drudge in a sunbonnet to a good-looking young woman in a cherry-bobbling hat.

Slapping the reins against the horses' rumps to nudge them into a faster trot, he said, "Well, I wouldn't be truthful if I didn't tell you I'm really glad you're back." He had started to say "back home" but caught himself.

"Thankee. I'm right glad to be back."

He chuckled with delight, and when she glanced at him for an explanation, he said, "I was just wondering what their faces are going to look like when the folks in Agency get a look at you."

He naturally assumed that they would be as astonished and pleased as he had been, though he was to realize over the course of the next few days and weeks that his was a very special astonishment. It would take him awhile yet to realize that his astonishment wasn't entirely due to Eula's transformation, but to his own. He found himself tingling with a new enthusiasm for life. His walk, which for years had been degenerating into an old man's shuffle, took on a new and sprightly bounce. He surprised people with the cheerfulness of his greetings, with the renewed optimism of his outlook, and with the new energy with which he tackled his work. Why, he was almost like a young man again. He was happy. He was excited.

He was in love. That was fairly apparent to everybody else, but he didn't know it until about three weeks after Eula's return when, from his office window, he saw her on the sidewalk in front of Simon's store conversing with a young cowhand. Eula had come out of the store carrying a number of parcels, and the cowhand had offered to help her. Eula shook her head, refusing his help, but the offer alone had suffused her face with delight.

That look stabbed Maxwell with a terrible dread. It was as he suspected: sooner or later he was going to lose her to some young cowhand or homesteader. And it was then that he had to admit to himself what many other persons around the agency already knew—that he was in love with Eula—and that realization made the prospect of losing her even more painful.

It was true that Eula seemed perfectly content to remain as his housekeeper. She was naturally flattered by the attention she now received from young men, but she didn't even know how to flirt, let alone have any inclination to, and besides, all her attention was saved for Maxwell, out of a profound gratitude to him for having saved her from a life of ugliness and shame. Without him, she would surely have ended up as a harelipped old hag, alone and unloved, never having known what it was like to smile back at someone. So she couldn't do enough for him in repayment. She made his favorite foods, saw that his reading lamp was always free of soot, listened raptly whenever he read to her at night from a book or a newspaper, and always spoke to him in the tenderest of tones.

Still, Maxwell knew that gratitude alone wouldn't always hold her. He knew with dreadful certainty that she would someday meet a young man for whom she felt something stronger, and on that day he would lose her. And what could he do?

It was Mrs. Poggemeyer who suggested the solution. Busybody that she was, she came to see Maxwell in his office at the school one day and hinted to him that it wasn't fitting for him—a respectable man and the superintendent of the school, after all—to be living alone in a house with a pretty young woman who wasn't his lawful wedded wife. It was different, she said, before Eula got her mouth fixed because nobody would think anything might be going on between them, but now things were different. People were beginning to talk.

"And what am I supposed to do," Maxwell protested, "fire her?"

"Fire her? Heavens, no," Mrs. Poggemeyer said. "Marry her. Oh, I know it's none of my business, Mr. Maxwell, but it's just as plain as the nose on your face that you're plumb gone on that girl, and she obviously worships the ground you walk on, so why not?"

Maxwell could think of about a dozen reasons why not, not the least of which was the great difference in their ages, but he didn't confide that to Mrs. Poggemeyer. Her question, however, and her assertion that Eula worshiped the ground he walked on caused him to rethink the whole thing, only to find that he couldn't think his way out of it. It wasn't until he stopped thinking that he resolved the situation.

It happened one evening when he came home from the office and found Eula kneeling beside a wooden box that she had placed on the floor near the kitchen stove. Within the box on a nest of hay were a half dozen fluffy yellow peeping chicks.

"A coon got their mother last night," she explained. "I thought I'd bring 'em in here for a night or two, keep 'em from being cold and afraid out there in the barn without a mother to protect 'em." She held one of the chicks cupped in her hand. She put some bits of crushed corn on her palm, and the chick pecked at it, peeping between pecks. She smiled. "Feels funny. Wanna see?"

He knelt on one knee beside the box. Eula took some more crushed corn from a can, dropped it on his outstretched palm, then took one of the chicks from the box and put it in his hand. The chick peeped a couple of times and began pecking at the corn. The little beak made pricking sensations against his skin.

"Eula, would you marry me?"

He hadn't meant to ask that question. He hadn't planned it at all. It just popped out—not blurted, because, being unplanned, he hadn't had time to become nervous about it. He just asked her in a casual way, as if asking for the time of day.

Perhaps that—the casual way he asked it, without even taking his eyes off the chick in his hand—was what gave her such a start. She flushed a deep red and stammered, as if she couldn't quite believe what she thought she had heard, "What? What did you—"

"Oh, I know, I know," he added hastily, trying to mitigate his foolishness and forestall the humiliating refusal that was certain to come when she recovered from her shock. "I know that, well, I'm fifty-one years old now, and you're what? Twenty-eight? A big difference." He replaced the chick in the box and brushed the crushed corn from his hands. "So I can understand if you don't want to. It's just that . . ."

That what? Afraid now that he had made a fool of himself, he tried to make his proposal seem a merely reasonable idea by saying, "Well, you see, there's some talk around the agency. Seems folks are beginning to wag their tongues about our living here alone like this, so I thought ... well, if we were married ..."

Recovering her composure at last, Eula replaced the chick in the box, brushed the corn from her hand, and sat back on her heels.

"I'd be right honored," she said.

At first Maxwell was incredulous. "You mean it?"

"Yes, sir," she said, and fell silent, unable to meet his eyes. Never before having been a lover, she didn't know what lovers were supposed to say or do next, so she reverted to her old habit of hanging her head and slowly, absently smoothing her dress.

And Maxwell, who hadn't been a lover for more years than he cared to remember, was also at a loss. But then, with a nervous chuckle, he said, "Well, then, I suppose you could stop calling me sir, couldn't you? And Mr. Maxwell? My name's John."

"Yes, sir," she said, but smiled and quickly corrected herself, "I mean, yes, John."

He stood up. "Well, we'll need to make some plans, won't we? I mean, like when? And where?" He reached down and took her hands and helped her to her feet. He would have continued pulling her into his arms after she was standing, but she was so nervous and embarrassed he released her hands, thinking he would give her more time to get used to the idea before plying her with his affections. "And a honeymoon! I'll get some maps." He started for the front room but turned. "Where'd you like to go? New Orleans? San Francisco? I've always wanted to go to—" He stopped his nervous chattering when he saw that something was wrong. "What is it?"

In an agony of embarrassment she said, "There's something ... afore we get into all that, there's something I'd like to—" She couldn't finish.

He took a few steps back toward her. "Yes? What is it? Don't be afraid. You can tell me."

She shook her head. "No. I can't. You go on."

He moved to within arm's reach of her. "Of course, you can. You can tell me anything. Is something wrong?"

Lowering her face the way she used to do when hiding under the bonnet, she methodically smoothed her apron down for a moment, then abruptly looked up at him. "Well, y'see, I ain't never been kissed."

He looked at her blankly. Had he not been in an agitated state himself, he would have understood immediately, but his mind was racing too fast for him to see the obvious.

"And I—I've always wondered, you know, what it'd be like, and since we're going to be married, I was wondering if . . ."

Smiling with a sudden rush of relief, he took her in his arms and kissed her lips. At first she was unresponsive, her arms hanging stiffly at her sides, but by the time the kiss was half over, she had begun to relax a little and her lips returned some of the eagerness of his own.

"So that's what it's like," she said, delighted. "All these years I been wondering. . . . Why, it's right nice, ain't it?"

CHAPTER THIRTY-NINE

AFTER THAT FIRST SUMMER VACATION SPENT AT HOME, RACHEL decided that she would stay in school through the summers, thereby enabling her to graduate in three years rather than the usual four. This decision was made easy for her when Maxwell wrote that Corby, after his summer with old Chief Hehyo in Wyoming, had gone back to the blanket—had, in fact, gone to live on the Comanche reservation as an acolyte in the Native American Church. Rachel wrote to Corby, begging him not to give up on going to Carlisle, but she had no address for him, and letters sent to him in care of general delivery at the Comanche agency at Fort Sill were returned, marked "Unclaimed—Return to Sender."

It grieved her to know he was throwing his life away, but what could she do? She had her own life to live. So she stayed in school, spent her short school holidays at Lake Wappapello with her best friend, Melvina Rhodes, or as the guest of other classmates or teachers, and was graduated from the academy in June 1896. When she returned to Oklahoma Territory at last, she was eighteen years old, she had been gone from home for more than two years, and she had changed. No longer a gawky girl, she had filled out to pleasing proportions—nothing in extremes—and was of medium height, had fashionably coiffed auburn hair, a complexion that had lost its freckles but none of its healthy glow, and bright hazel eyes that had retained their flecks of gold.

Maxwell traveled to St. Louis to attend her graduation and to bring her back home. Eula had been feeling poorly and therefore didn't accompany Maxwell on the trip, for which Rachel was sorry. She was eager to see the results of Eula's operation and to tell her how pleased she was to have her for a stepmother. It was true that she hadn't wholeheartedly approved of the marriage. She thought it showed a definite lack of ambition on her father's part to have married an uneducated and unsophisticated domestic. Still, she had always liked and admired Eula, and if Eula made her father happy, why, that was all that really mattered.

The train stopped for two hours in Guthrie. Rachel had wired Dexter to meet her at the Guthrie station, and he was there on the platform when the train pulled in.

Their greeting was confused and awkward, especially on Dexter's part. He had no idea how to greet a sister he hadn't seen in three years, a sister for whom he had never had much affection in the first place. But Rachel handled the situation adroitly by giving him a quick sisterly peck on the cheek and petting his shoulder with her white-gloved hand as she said, "My, how handsome you've become. I'm surprised you're not married yet. You must have to beat the girls off with a stick."

Dexter managed a smile as he grunted with gruff but good-natured skepticism. "Not really. But look at you. You're all growed up. Pretty dress," he added, just to have something to say.

"You like it?" She stepped back to give him a better look at her lined, boned, padded, ruched, and bustled gray cheviot dress and basque. She wore a Robin Hood hat of dark gray velvet with a plume of white egret feathers sweeping back from its crown, and she carried a lacy pink parasol.

But her bid for admiration elicited no more compliments

from him. "Two hours, huh? Well, what'd you like to do?" He spoke as if their meeting were a chore he wanted to get done with.

"I don't know about Daddy," Rachel said, glancing at Maxwell, "but I'd like to stretch my legs a bit. Maybe you'd show us around your little town?"

"Little!" Dexter snorted. "Well, I guess it's not so much compared to St. Louis, but we got an opera house now and electric streetlamps, and our downtown streets are all paved."

"Really! Daddy, did you hear that? Electric streetlamps! Would you like to go look at them?"

Maxwell had been standing apart. "You two go ahead. I'm going to get myself a cold beer. But don't forget, the train leaves at three-twenty."

Without Maxwell present, Dexter seemed a little more congenial as they strolled along the brick sidewalks of Harrison Street. She put her gloved hand through the crook of his arm in a display of affection that discomfited him at first, but when he saw the admiring attention that she was getting from the men along the street, he felt himself swelling with pride. It did Dexter good to be envied.

"So! You're a deputy sheriff now," she said admiringly.

"A special deputy," he boasted. "I'm one of the bodyguards assigned to Shelby Hornbeck."

"Shelby Hornbeck? Do tell! And why, may I ask, would Shelby Hornbeck need bodyguards?"

He glanced at her to see if she was being a fool or a tease. "Are you kidding? Men don't get as rich and powerful as him without making enemies along the way. And a lot of Radical Republicans'd like to kill him, I reckon, 'cause they know there ain't no other way of stopping him from becoming governor, once we get to be a state. There"—nodding toward a three-story brick building across the street—"that's his. The Hornbeck Building. Biggest office building in Guthrie. All the most important men in the Territory got offices there. There's a steam room in the basement and a two-story brick privy out back—only two-story privy in the Territory, far's I know."

"Fascinating," Rachel said.

"It's true. Would you like to see it?"

"The two-story privy?"

"The building. I could show you through it."

"Oh, would you?" she begged.

They crossed the street toward the building, but before they reached the marble entrance steps, Dexter's attention was diverted by a buggy approaching.

"That's Mr. Hornbeck's buggy," he informed her.

It was a fancy yellow-wheeled leather-hooded buggy pulled by a matching team of blue roans and driven by one of three bodyguards. The other two bodyguards, mounted on sleek horses, were escorting the buggy as it came to a stop near Dexter and Rachel. The driver jumped out and tied the team's tether line to one of the black-jockey hitching posts embedded in the sidewalk. The bodyguards exchanged nods and grunts of greetings with Dexter, and the one who had been driving the buggy said, "Well, Dexter, where's your manners? Ain't you gonna introduce us to the young lady?"

But all talk ceased when Shelby Hornbeck himself emerged from the Hornbeck Building and hastily descended the marble steps to the sidewalk, pulling on yellow kid gloves. Ordinarily Shelby would have passed Dexter without even a nod, but this time he stopped and said, "Howdy," speaking to Dexter but glancing at Rachel.

"Mr. Hornbeck," Dexter said, disconcerted and deferential, like a sergeant speaking to a colonel. "Do you need me for anything?"

"Is *this* the young lady you referred to as your kid sister?"

Flattered by such unusual familiarity, Dexter stammered, "This's her, all right. My sister, Rachel. Growed up some since I last saw her. Rachel, this here's Mr. Hornbeck."

Shelby touched the brim of his dove gray Stetson. "Miss Bingham."

"Maxwell," she corrected. "We're half sister and brother, Dexter and I."

"Miss Maxwell," he said. "When Dexter asked to be relieved from duty this afternoon so he could meet his kid sister at the depot, I had a vision of a twelve-year-old with pigtails and freckles."

"Sorry if I've disappointed you," Rachel said, smiling.

"Disappointed?" he said, to the surprise of the onlookers, who weren't used to hearing him banter with young ladies. "Why, how could you possibly be a disappointment to anyone?"

"Thank you, sir, you pay a pretty compliment." She had once read that phrase in a Jane Austen novel and had been waiting a long time for a chance to use it.

"I'm showing her around town," said Dexter, who wanted to be included in the conversation. "I was about to show her your building."

"That so? Well, I'm just on my way out to Kingstree." To Rachel he said, "Kingtree's the plantation house I'm building just southeast of town. If you're sightseeing, you might be interested in it."

"That's kind of you, Mr. Hornbeck," Rachel said, "but I'm afraid I have to get back to the depot before three-twenty. My train—"

"Why, that gives you plenty of time." Shelby pulled a gold watch from the watch pocket of his pants and sprung the lid. "It's only ten minutes from here. I could have you back in plenty of time to catch the train." He replaced the watch. "That is, of course, if you'd like to. . . ."

"Oh, sure," Dexter said. "Sure, we'd like to, wouldn't we? Don't worry. If Mr. Hornbeck says he'll get you back on time, you don't have to worry."

And it wasn't entirely to please Dexter that she nodded her assent. She was dazzled by the man. At thirty-five not only was Shelby Hornbeck strikingly handsome, rich, powerful, and—as far as she knew—unattached, but he had the courtly manners of a southern aristocrat and a drawl as sweet as honeydew.

Having folded her parasol, Rachel sat between Dexter and Shelby on the padded leather seat, and as the buggy made its way toward Kingstree, Shelby made no attempt to carry on a conversation. It was Dexter who babbled on like someone who was afraid of silence.

"Kingstree was the name of Mr. Hornbeck's family plantation back in South Carolina before the War between the States," he informed Rachel, trying to ingratiate himself with Shelby by speaking for him. "Isn't that right?" he asked Shelby.

"Yes," Shelby said.

"Before the damned Yankees burned it down," Dexter continued to Rachel, though the remark was also meant for

Shelby's ears, a reiteration of the covenant between them: Shelby's enemies were Dexter's enemies.

The three bodyguards rode one on each side of the buggy and one behind, their rifles drawn, their eyes constantly scanning the countryside. Rachel assumed from the presence of the bodyguards that Shelby Hornbeck must be in great fear for his life, though he showed no sign of being afraid. Indeed, it was hard to imagine the man ever having allowed himself to feel an emotion so base as fear. Rachel supposed that even in front of a firing squad, Shelby would be very much the same as he was now: reserved and respectful, a man who would be courteous even to his enemies, every inch a gentleman. His demeanor was that of a man who knew exactly what he wanted to be. Everything about him seemed exact, inevitable, perfect, even to his looks: his well-groomed corn silk hair, his cornflower blue eyes, his handsome, unblemished, and clean-shaven face, his expensive suits, his yellow kid gloves, his boots of Spanish leather.

"I'm sorry," Rachel said. "About your house being burned, I mean."

"It's kind of you to say so. I am, too, naturally. It was a beautiful old house. But the new Kingstree will be beautiful, too. At least *I* think it will be. I hope you agree."

She did. When she first saw the house—a mansion, really—standing on a hill overlooking the Cimarron River and its floodplain to the north, she said, "Oh, my! Yes, I agree. It *is* beautiful."

She had seen grander and more stately mansions in St. Louis, it was true, but Kingstree, raw and unfinished though it was, was at least more impressive than any other house she had ever seen in Oklahoma. Two-storied, with a veranda running all the way around it, built in straight lines and sharp angles, made of beige brick and red alabaster, with four huge white columns in front and four in back, many-windowed, it stood on the hill, stark and imposing like some sort of ancient temple—a Roman temple, say, built in the wilds of a conquered land as a symbol of dominance and power to the conquered peoples.

The place was abuzz with activity. Alongside the graveled lane leading from the main road to the house, laborers with mule-drawn tank wagons were watering two rows of recently transplanted rowan oaks. There were drayage wagons loaded with lumber and crates of furniture and piles of supplies, carpenters and laborers busy building barns and sheds and stables, landscapers digging and planting and leveling everywhere about the place. A barefooted black boy, dressed in livery copied from a black-jockey hitching post, held the team of blue roans under the portico as Shelby helped Rachel down from the buggy.

They were met on the steps by a middle-aged woman dressed in black. Shelby introduced her as his widowed aunt, Mrs. Bertha Dolph, who had kindly agreed to serve as Kingstree's housekeeper and hostess "till the house has a mistress of its own," he said, and by this remark Rachel gathered that Shelby wasn't yet a confirmed bachelor. He apparently still had plans—hopes, anyway—of one day having a wife. And Rachel wondered what it would be like to be that wife. It was rather difficult to imagine, for she knew him not at all, but it wasn't difficult for her to imagine being the mistress of Kingstree.

"Like it, do you?" Shelby asked, pleased by her exuberance.

"Oh, I love it! You're so right to be proud of it. My goodness, it just goes on and on, doesn't it? How many rooms did you say?"

"Twenty-two."

"With a fireplace in every room?"

"Just about."

"Well, we haven't got time to see them all, but I'm certain this'd be my room, if it were my house." They were in one of the second-story rooms in the east wing of the house. Pointing with her folded parasol, she said, "A vanity there. A full-length mirror there. Chandeliers with prismed globes."

"You're very decisive for someone your age," Shelby observed approvingly. "You seem to know exactly what you want."

"Oh, I do," she boasted. "I certainly do."

French doors led from the room out onto the second-story veranda, from which Rachel could see the Cimarron River in one direction and Guthrie in another.

"Which one is the Hornbeck Building?" she asked.

Pointing, Shelby said in his mellifluous accent, "That one there," and Rachel said, "The one with the funny roof?"

"Look down my arm, sight on my thumb."

She put her face against his shoulder, squinted one eye, and sighted along his arm. A few minutes ago she had been a decisive and self-assured young woman; now she seemed to be a confused girl who needed his help to find the biggest building in town. Their heads were only a few inches apart when she abruptly lifted her face from his shoulder, looked up, and caught him staring at her. His breeze-ruffled golden hair shimmered in the sunlight, and his blue eyes met her gaze for a moment, their faces still only inches apart, and it struck her then, once again, that Shelby Hornbeck was quite possibly the most handsome man she had ever seen. Indeed, if he had a fault, it was that he was *too* handsome. Such perfection gave his face a look of blandness, a look of characterless innocence, a face incapable of registering either ecstasy or horror.

"Mr. Hornbeck!" A messenger on horseback came galloping up the graveled lane toward the house. Coming to a skidding stop beneath the veranda, he shouted, "O'Keefe's called a quorum on bill three twenty. Speaker Wallace wants you back quick as you can."

As the messenger galloped away, Shelby said to Rachel, "Politics. Some people want the capital moved to Oklahoma City, and their representatives are trying to pull a fast one on us. I'm afraid we'll have to go back in a hurry."

"Suits me," Rachel said. "I love a fast ride."

When they were settled in the buggy, Shelby took the buggy whip from its socket. "Ready?"

Rachel nodded. Dexter nodded, too, though Shelby hadn't been speaking to him.

Shelby barely flicked the whip at the pair of blue roans to set them into a gallop, a rather slow gallop at first, for Shelby was a prudent driver, but Rachel asked, "This is as fast as they'll go?"

Shelby smiled at her naïveté. "I was thinking of your safety. You're not afraid to go faster?"

"I'd like to."

When they turned onto the main road, accompanied by the three mounted bodyguards, Shelby flicked the team into a fast gallop. The buggy bounced and jolted along the rutted road, streaming dust onto the bodyguards, who rode behind, and Shelby glanced to see how Rachel was reacting. Most of the

women he had known in his life would now be babbling with
fear and holding on for dear life, but the only thing Rachel was
holding on to was her egret-plumed hat, and the look on her
face was one of exhilaration.

"Faster!" she cried above the noise of the galloping hooves
and the rattle and bang of the buggy. She jostled against him
as the buggy careened over the ruts, and cried out once with
frightened delight, like a child on a carnival ride, when the
buggy skidded around a corner on two wheels, almost over-
turning. Dexter had been frightened and on the verge of jumping out.

Shelby slowed the team down after that, first to a slow
gallop and then, entering the outskirts of town, to a brisk trot.

"Thank you," Rachel said. "That was fun."

"I'm glad you enjoyed it. Perhaps we can do it again sometime."

"I'll look forward to it."

CHAPTER FORTY

RACHEL INTRODUCED MAXWELL TO SHELBY WHEN SHELBY RE-
turned her to the train depot in Guthrie. Maxwell shook hands
with him and muttered the responses required by common
courtesy, but it was obvious that he had to exercise great self-
control to keep from making some disparaging remark to
Shelby about his politics.

When they were on the train, unable to contain himself any
longer, he told Rachel, "That's the man who's responsible for
all the Territory's Jim Crow laws. That's the man who's made
it against the law for me to sit on a public conveyance with my
students or Indian friends or to eat with them in restaurants.
That's the man who made it against the law for teachers of one
race to teach the children of another."

Her seeming lack of outrage only incensed him further. "He took you for a tour of his house, did he? No doubt built with the money he and his business cohorts have bilked out of the Indians."

Rachel stared at her father, wondering if he could be talking about the same Shelby Hornbeck with whom she had just spent a pleasant and exciting hour. She knew nothing about business and politics, and didn't want to know anything about them, but she thought she knew something about the man who had just given her a tour of his new home, and she couldn't bring herself to believe that he was anything other than what he appeared to be: a gracious and honorable man, a gentleman, innocent perhaps to the point of being dull. Where was the cruel, thieving, cynical rascal that Maxwell was describing?

"Politics," she said. "Daddy, you know very well that when you meet a Democrat, you're at once disposed to turn your back on everything good in him and see only what's bad."

Maxwell was dumbfounded for a moment, not only because of the injustice of the accusation but because he saw that Rachel had taken a shine to the man.

"Now, Daddy," she said, "let's not get into a tiff before I even get home, all right? Let's talk about something else." She put her arm through his and snuggled up to him on the rail-rocking wooden bench. "Tell me more about Corby. He came by to see you last year, you say? How tall was he? Taller than you? My goodness! Imagine that! Oh, I do wish I could see him again!"

"For the sake of being agreeable, my dear, I suppose I ought to allow you to change the subject, but I can't if you're going to talk about Corby. Don't you realize that if he were on the train with us now, he'd have to ride in the car reserved for coloreds?"

"Then I'd go ride with him," she declared, which mollified him somewhat, for he knew it was true. She was like her mother in that way: issues of social justice and civic ethics seldom entered her head unless they affected her in some personal way.

Still, she didn't dismiss Maxwell's opinion of Shelby Hornbeck lightly. She had seldom known her father to be wrong about anyone. She had come to realize, however, during her years in Miss Finwick's that this was because she had always seen things from his point of view. Now that she was eighteen, and had been away to school for three years, where she had proved herself to be a bright and emancipated young woman, she felt she was permitted to have a point of view of her own, and in her opinion Shelby Hornbeck was a prince.

That was the word she would have used to describe Shelby to her schoolmates back at Miss Finwick's. In years past, during whisper-giggle sessions in their rooms at night after the lights were out, they would discuss the opposite sex, and a male who met their sharp-eyed standards of approval was usually placed in one of three hierarchical categories: a squire, a knight, or a prince. And Shelby Hornbeck would have been a prince, most definitely a prince. Who but a prince would have said, "Why, how could you possibly be a disappointment to anyone?"

And just like a prince in a fairy tale, he even invited her to a ball, a real ball, the Commemoration Ball to celebrate the grand opening of Guthrie's new opera house. She received the gold-trimmed invitation on the fourth day after her return to Agency, and it was Dexter who brought the invitation. He rode horseback all the way from Guthrie to Agency during the night to deliver it to her.

"Do you have any idea how lucky you are?" he asked Rachel in the voice of a nervous salesman. "This'll be the biggest social event ever in Guthrie, and you've been invited to be a guest in Mr. Hornbeck's private opera box on opening night. And go with him to the Commemoration Ball afterward. Why, there's not another unmarried woman in Oklahoma who wouldn't give her eyeteeth for such an invitation."

"But where would she stay?" Maxwell wanted to know. "Who'd look after her?"

"Me, of course," Dexter said. "I'll get her a room near mine at the boardinghouse. It's perfectly respectable, run by a preacher's widow. I'll be her chaperon. I was thinking of asking her to come to visit me anyway. Spend some time together. Get to know each other again, like brother and sister ought to. That's what Mother would've wanted."

They were in the front room of the house. This was the first time Dexter had set foot in the house since the day of Nora's funeral, and though his attitude had changed, being under the same roof with Eula still made him uncomfortable. Eula had tactfully gone to the barn to do chores while the three of them talked, but still, when Rachel urged him to sit, Dexter said he had been riding all night and would just as soon stand, thanks just the same.

"Well?" he said to her as he shuffled from one foot to the other. "Will you come?"

To placate Maxwell, she would have probably declined had she not become so bored with life in Agency. When she first got home, she had sent a letter to the Quahadi Comanche village where Corby was last reported seen, to let him know that she had returned from school and would like to see him. There had been no response. The letter wasn't returned this time, but she assumed that he hadn't received it, for it was difficult for her to believe that he, the beloved friend of her childhood days, could be within a hundred miles and deliberately stay away if he knew she was home. And without him Rachel had quickly become bored with life at Agency, just as she had during that aborted summer vacation two years ago. Indeed, she now felt the malignant monotony of the place even more profoundly than she had then. So, fingering the gold-trimmed beribboned invitation, she said, "Yes. Yes, I will. It'd be fun. Tell him I accept."

Dexter sighed with relief. "Well, that's settled then. Let me know which train you're coming in on. Well, I better go. Gotta get some sleep before I start back tonight."

"Sleep?" She was puzzled by Dexter's hurry to be gone. "Well, if you need sleep, there's an extra bed here."

"No, no," Dexter interrupted, with a contemptuous look toward Maxwell. "I'll get a room over at Bixby's. Don't worry 'bout it."

After he was gone, Rachel said, "For heaven's sake, what's the matter with him? Can't the two of you even spend a night under the same roof?"

"You'd better ask him. The fact is, not only won't he sleep here, but this is the first time he's set foot in this house since your mother died. It's Eula. Oh, it's me, too, I suppose. He hates me, that's plain. Mainly, though, it's Eula. Being under the same roof with her makes him nervous."

"Why? What'd she ever to do him?"

"I think the more appropriate question might be 'What's he done to her?' "

"Well?" she demanded. "*Has* he ever done anything to
her?"

Maxwell mused on the question for a moment, clicking his
pipe stem on his lower teeth. "There are ... well, rumors,
that's all I can call them, but I heard that ..." He paused for
a moment to puff on his pipe to keep it going. "Well, did you
ever wonder why Shelby Hornbeck never goes anywhere without bodyguards? And did you ever wonder why Dexter, who's
one of his bodyguards, travels cross-country only at night?"

"Yes. Why?"

Maxwell knocked the dottle from his pipe onto the lip of the
potbellied stove. "To keep from getting ambushed. Somebody's out to kill them. I hear people say it's Gypsy Smith. They
say he's got a list of all the Klansmen who did that to him and
those two boys three years ago, over in Freedom. Remember
that Klan raid? Took place the night before you left for school.
Remember? They say quite a few of the men who made the
raid are dead already, and Gypsy's hunting the others down,
one by one."

"*Dexter?* Oh, Daddy, you can't mean that *Dexter* was one of
them!"

"I don't know. I have my suspicions, but I don't know. If he
was, though, it's likely the same bunch that burned Eula out."

Rachel's eyes snapped with anger. "Burned Eula out? Dexter? My God ..." This was the kind of injustice she could re-
late to, the kind that touched her personally. "I can't believe
Dexter would do a thing like that. I'll ask him."

"If it's true, you expect him to admit it?"

"Maybe not, but I want to hear him deny it." Dropping the
gold-trimmed invitation on a side table, she left the house and
marched down to the Bixby Hotel, where she found Dexter sitting at a table by himself in the nearly empty dining room.

"Dexter, I want to talk to you." Taking a chair, she lowered
her voice as if asking for a confidence. "I want to know if you
and Shelby Hornbeck were in that bunch that burned Eula's
house."

"That's ridiculous," Dexter sneered without blinking an eye.
"I guess there's no need to ask who told you that. *He* did!
Well, it's a damned lie."

Stymied by the force of his denial, she hesitated a moment.

"Dexter? Tell me the truth. Do you and Shelby Hornbeck belong to the Ku Klux Klan? I want the truth, now."

The waitress, an Indian girl dressed in a soiled apron and gingham dress, came to stand beside their table, a pencil poised above her order pad. Dexter was petulant as he gave her his order, and as soon as she was gone, he glowered at Rachel.

"No, I do not belong to no Ku Klux Klan. Neither does Shelby Hornbeck. Now, are you satisfied? What a dumb question! Who d'you think you are, coming around here questioning me like this? Did *he* put you up to this?"

"Nobody 'put me up' to anything. I've got a mind of my own, you know."

"Well, then, use it, stop asking dumb questions."

"You swear?"

"Look, Rachel, I answered your question. I'm not gonna sit here and try to convince you of anything, so don't push me."

"I have to know before I go to that ball"—instinctively reaching for a weak spot, which immediately succeeded in making him conciliatory and civil.

"Now, look, Rachel, I'd like us to try to get along. Try to be family, you know? I'm gonna be real proud to introduce you around Guthrie as my sister, and I'd like you to be proud of me, too, and have some faith in what I say, without questioning me like I was some sort of damned criminal. This ain't the way Mother would've wanted us to be."

Rachel studied his face for a moment longer before she dropped her gaze. "Yes. Well, all right." She got up. "I'm sorry, but I had to know." And though she felt a creepy kind of dread, she pronounced herself satisfied that Dexter had told the truth. She wanted to believe him and had no reason not to. Her father had only heard rumors, after all, and in any case, she couldn't bring herself to believe that Dexter, a deputy sheriff, sworn to uphold the law, and Shelby Hornbeck, a prince of a man if there ever was one, could be involved in anything so cowardly and cruel as burning poor Eula's house.

As she was leaving the building, a voice from behind said, "Rachel?"

It was the Indian waitress from the dining room.

"I been looking for a chance to speak to you alone," she said in a hurried whisper. "I'm Molly Iron Shirt. I got a message to you from Corby."

At the mention of his name Rachel felt a surge of love and longing. "Corby! Where is he? I'm very angry with him. Why hasn't he come to welcome me back?"

Molly Iron Shirt's eyes glanced about furtively as she said in a low voice, "The Native American Church is having what the Indians call a *vessemataveanatoz*. A peyote ceremony. A few miles from here, in a hidden place. Corby asks if you can come."

"A peyote ceremony?" Rachel was slightly shocked and thrilled by the idea, scornful yet fascinated.

"It's a church service," Molly Iron Shirt said defensively, taking umbrage at the implication in Rachel's tone that there was something scandalous about it. "I know. I thought the same thing when I came back from Carlisle. I was raised a Christian, and I'm still a Christian, but Corby helped me see that peyote is just another way of worshiping God—the Indian's way, not the white man's way—and there's nothing sinful in that." With another look around to make sure nobody was eavesdropping, Molly said, "Corby says not to tell Mr. Maxwell. He says he shouldn't know, it'd only upset him. Peyote's against the white man's law."

Intrigued, Rachel said, "But how would I find him?"

"I can take you there. Soon's my shift's over, two o'clock, I'll be going there. If you want to go, meet me behind the building."

Without realizing that she had already made up her mind, Rachel said, "Thank you, I'll think about it," and she thought about it all the way back to the house, where, in response to Maxwell's interrogative stare, she was recalled to the purpose of her outing.

"He flatly denied it. He claims he's not a Klansman, and neither is Shelby Hornbeck, and they didn't burn Eula's house."

"And is he telling the truth?"

"I think so, yes. I have to think so, don't I?"

"Only fair to give him the benefit of the doubt, I suppose, even if he is a liar." He took his coat and his hat from the rack near the door. "Eula's out gathering eggs. Tell her I'll have lunch in the dining hall, will you? No need for her to fix anything." He paused at the door. "And you? Do you really intend to go to that ball with Hornbeck?"

"I'll have to go through my old dresses, see which one I can fancy up, so I'll have something to wear"—her way of telling him yes, she planned to go, regardless of his objections. "Look, it's just a diversion, Daddy," she said in response to his frown of disappointment. "The truth is, I'm beginning to understand now why this place drove Mother crazy."

Alarmed by the remark, he said, "Look here, young lady, I think it's time we talked about your future. Seems to me you're obviously not going to be happy here at Agency, so we'd better figure out what you're going to do, where and how you're going to be living, till you meet someone you want to marry."

It was taken for granted that Rachel's goal was to get married and have a family. That's what respectable girls did. Barring a flight to New York City to become an actress or an opera singer, she had very few choices. She could become a schoolteacher or maybe even a nurse, but she had no interest at all in such occupations, so it was taken for granted—even by Maxwell, who could have been persuaded to support her in just about anything she wanted to try—that her next important step was to start looking for a husband. Actually there was only one man she had ever met whom she would even consider marrying, but there was no use mentioning that to Maxwell, for he didn't approve of Shelby Hornbeck.

"Yes, well . . . in the meantime, please don't be angry with me if I go to the ball."

He recognized that prohibition would only provoke defiance in her, so he shrugged resignedly and left the house.

Rachel went to her room and spent the next few hours examining, modeling, and modifying dresses, wondering how on earth she could possibly let herself be seen in *this* tacky old thing or *that* old rag. But as two o'clock drew nearer, she grew bored and restless and couldn't continue the task. She snatched up her wide-brimmed straw hat and tied its ribbon beneath her chin as she left the house. She went to the barn and put the sidesaddle on Maxwell's strawberry roan and rode to the windmill behind Bixby's. Molly Iron Shirt was on foot, carrying a small bundle in her hand. She swung up behind Rachel and sat sideways on the horse's haunches, her legs dangling off the same side as Rachel's.

"Take the trail upriver about five miles," she said.

Rachel wondered if Molly Iron Shirt and Corby were sweethearts. As they rode along, she said, "You two must spend a lot of time together."

"No," Molly said regretfully. "He never stays in one place very long. That's why he's called 'Nakoni.' "

"Nakoni?"

"It's what the Comanches call him."

"What's it mean?"

"Wanderer."

"Nakoni," Rachel said, and smiled. "Beautiful name. Sounds like him, doesn't it? Nakoni."

It took only a few more casual questions for Rachel to conclude that Corby and Molly weren't lovers. For some reason that she didn't quite understand, this conclusion came as a relief to her. She had somehow naturally taken it for granted that Corby would never get married. He seemed to be meant for something grander than the life of a breadwinner with brats to feed. But what? She had no idea. But she knew it would be grand, whatever it was.

CHAPTER FORTY-ONE

THE PEYOTE CEREMONY WAS TAKING PLACE IN A VALE through which ran a small creek. On the high ground around the area stood lookouts. In each of five canvas tepees were gathered about fifteen worshipers, seated in circles around the peyote altar and the peyote priests. The priests were beating drums, rattling gourds, blowing whistles and flutes, and chanting with monotony sufficient to induce a trance.

Molly Iron Shirt said that this congregation of peyote worshipers was larger than usual, due to the presence of Chief Quanah Parker, the most famous of the peyote priests, who had come to proselytize for the Native American Church among the Cheyennes and Arapahos.

"You stay here," she told Rachel in the tree-shaded place where the worshipers had parked their wagons and picketed their ponies. "I'll go get him."

"Can't I come?"

"No. Only those who take part are allowed to see the ceremony. You stay here. I'll send him to you."

Rachel tied the strawberry roan to the picket rope. Relieved to be in the shade of a huge cedar tree, she took her hat off and fanned herself with it. She looked the area over carefully and was surprised to see that no one was dancing. In all the other ceremonies performed by Indians at the agency, dancing had been the most important part, but here there was no dancing, no revelry, no painted faces—not even any debauchery. She had certainly expected debauchery. Whenever whites spoke of the peyote cult, they always hinted at unmentionable practices, so that Rachel had come to think of a peyote ceremony as little more than a debauch of dope fiends. But here all seemed calm and decorous. A few women were about the area, some carrying pails of water from the creek to the tepees, others cooking over open fires, and a few children splashed about in the nearby creek.

When Corby emerged from the center tepee, a flute in his hands, she couldn't be sure it was really he, so tall had he grown. And rather than hurry to meet her, he began playing the flute as he moved toward her like someone out for an afternoon stroll, again causing her to wonder if it were really he. But when he got far enough away from the tepees for her to hear the music he was playing, she recognized the song. It was something she had often heard him play years ago, a haunting melody that was at odds with the drumming and chanting coming from the tepees.

He had grown into a handsome young man. His glossy black hair hung in two braids down his bare chest. He wore only moccasins, buckskin pants, a beaded Indian necklace, and a headband made of a rolled red bandanna. His eyes were heavy-lidded, but to Rachel's relief, he showed no sign—no lurch or stagger—to indicate that he was under the influence of a drug. On the contrary, he seemed serene and self-possessed.

Restraining an impulse to run to him, Rachel waited in the

shade of the huge cedar until he reached her and stopped playing the flute, and said, "*Vahe*, Rachel. Welcome home." There
was in his eyes and smile a look that she had never seen before, a sort of bliss—not the bliss of satiety or inebriation but
a sort of beatific bliss, a look of intense but quiet reverence.

Unable to control herself any longer, she threw her arms
around his neck and clung to him for a moment, pressing her
face into the hollow of his sweat-damp shoulder, smelling the
aroma of sage and cedar smoke on his skin.

"Oh, Corby, Corby, how I missed you! But *you*!" she said
in a suddenly reproachful voice, pulling away from him. "You
haven't even come to see me. I've been home four days now,
and you haven't even come to say hello. I was beginning to
think you'd forgotten me. My goodness," she said then, as if
she had just noticed, "how *Indian* you've become."

"And how white you've become." He touched her powdered
cheek. "Sweet, like icing on a cake, and your words are birds
that fly away in fright."

Rachel blinked. This whimsicality of speech was something
new to him. Amused, she said, "Are you drunk?" But then she
said, "Oh. It's the peyote then."

"Of course. How else could I see sounds?"

"See sounds? Peyote allows you to *see* sounds?"

"Yes," he said, feeding her amused disbelief. "And hear
sights. Did you ever hear a sunrise? Touch a rainbow?"

"No. Sounds fascinating, though. Is it fun?"

"Fun," he said, mulling the word. "If you mean 'joy,' then,
yes, it makes everything *voese*—joyful. It makes everything
beautiful. Lets you see-hear-taste-touch-smell God in everything, and since God is beautiful, everything is beautiful."

"Listen, do you think it might be possible for me to attend
a peyote ceremony sometime? Just to see what it's like?"

"No, Rachel. At a peyote ceremony no spectators are allowed, and you can't take part unless you belong to the Native
American Church, and for that you have to be Indian."

"Quanah Parker himself is only half."

"But he chose to be Indian—not that he had much choice
in the first place, of course. But he chose to follow the Indian's road, rather than the white man's."

"And you? Is that what you've done? Chosen the Indian's
road?"

"Well, I could say I've chosen, I suppose, but I can't be sure that I've *been* chosen. For that I'd have to have a vision quest."

"You've not had a vision quest yet?"

"Not yet."

"Why not?"

"You wouldn't understand."

"You might try me. We used to understand each other."

"When we were children, yes, but you've changed. We've changed."

"Sure, but we can still try to understand each other, can't we? We can still be best friends, can't we?"

"Friends? Is that all?"

She tilted her head back, searching his face for meaning. And though she felt a slight panic when she saw the kiss coming, she didn't stop it. She even returned the kiss for a moment, so sweet and gentle and loving was it, a kiss made all the more thrilling by that slight panic, causing her to feel once again that impish excitement of a child doing forbidden things.

Drawing away, he said, "What we always felt was the love of mates, not the love of friends."

He kissed her again, and this time the kiss quickly became passionate. Rachel joined in the passion for a moment but then came to her senses sufficiently to say, "No, we mustn't."

"Why not?"

"Because," she said. "Please. Let me go."

He released her with a readiness that not only surprised her but disappointed her a little, too, because she had never in her life experienced anything more sensually exciting than those kisses, and she pulled away only because her more sensible self told her that playing such dangerously daring childish games could have consequences beyond her ability to control.

"Because," she said, as if trying to convince herself as well as him, "other things do matter. I mean, my God, what if . . . something happened?"

"Whatever happened, it'd be all right, as long as we were together."

It was only then that she began to comprehend the full dimension of what he was suggesting. Confused and excited and appalled all at the same time, she thrashed around within herself for a moment, trying to find some solid ground on which to stand, and finally found it. "You mean . . . go off and *live* together?"

"Yes."

"Are you out of your mind? We'd be outcasts. We'd be beggars."

"We'd be together."

"In some tepee somewhere?"

"Nothing wrong with a tepee."

"Not for *you*, maybe." She was surprised by the cruelty she heard in her own voice. "But can't you just see me living in a tepee somewhere up a muddy creek? Sleeping on a dirt floor? Cooking rabbit stew over a campfire? Good God, Corby, I'm not a *squaw*."

By now the peyote bliss had vanished from his face, replaced by a sort of withdrawn sullenness.

"Oh, do be sensible," she said in a placating voice. "We'd be *outcasts*. We'd be *beggars*."

"How little you know me," he said grimly, "if you think I'd ever beg for anything."

"Oh, it's just a figure of speech. I didn't—"

"As for being an outcast, what's it like *not* to be?"

"Oh, I'm sorry. I didn't mean . . ." And again, prompted by sympathy, she felt herself drawn to him. In spite of her fear, she found herself wanting to touch him again, to kiss him, to surrender to that pull of nostalgia back to the days of childhood, when they had seemed to share instantaneously all sensations, thoughts, and desires. But she managed to resist the pull. "I have to go. It's getting late, and I want to get back before Daddy gets home."

"Then go."

"Look, I'm sorry, I didn't mean to hurt your feelings, but don't you see? We mustn't let this happen."

"See? Yes. I see the sounds you're making, and the words don't look anything like your voice. Your words say one thing, your voice says another. They even have different colors and feel different. White words, red voice. The words have sharp edges and cut me; your voice licks the wounds."

They could hear the distant drums and chants from the peyote ceremonies, and the distant laughter of the children swimming in the creek, and the song of a mockingbird in the cedar tree overhead. She waited for some sign of release from him.

He raised the flute to his mouth. "There's an old Cheyenne courting song that goes like this." He played a few notes on the cherry wood flute, then asked, "You like it?"

"It's beautiful. Does it have words?"

"No, but it has a meaning. It was made up a long time ago by a Cheyenne warrior who was trying to get a captive Cherokee woman to be his mate. But she thought the Cheyennes were savages. Well, what else could she think? They'd killed and scalped her people and taken her captive. And even worse, the warrior who wanted her—who d'you think it was? The same one who'd killed her father. So he was a special savage to her. But he began courting her in the Cheyenne way, with a flute. He sat outside her tepee at night and played love songs for her." He illustrated by playing a few notes from a sprightly love song. "But she wouldn't come out. She thought the songs were pleasant enough, but she was afraid.

"Well, he almost gave up. After playing all the love songs he knew, he decided to play just one more, a song he'd made up just for her, and if she didn't like it, he would quit." Again he played a few notes. "And what d'you think? When she heard it, she was finally convinced he wasn't a savage after all. Anybody who could play a flute like that, how could he be a savage? So she became his woman."

"And they lived happily ever after?" But she repented her sarcasm and added in a sincere voice, "Well, she was right, anyone who played that song as beautifully as you do couldn't be a savage."

She moved to the horse. After putting the flute away in a buckskin sheath he carried on his belt, he interlaced his fingers, making his cupped hands into a stirrup, and hoisted her onto the sidesaddle.

"So it's not because I'm a savage that you're afraid of me?"

Settling into the saddle and arranging her skirt, she smiled at him with gentle irony, then reached down to touch his cheek with her fingertips.

"My darling Corby, don't you understand yet? It's not the savage in *you* that I'm afraid of. . . ."

CHAPTER FORTY-TWO

A BOUQUET OF RED ROSES WAITED FOR HER IN HER ROOM AT the Simpson Boardinghouse in Guthrie, the first flowers she had ever received from a man. Once in St. Louis a boy had given her a nosegay of posies to wear to a graduation picnic, but posies from a boy were quite different from roses from a man—and not just any man, either, but Shelby Hornbeck.

Dressed in her prettiest dress, she greeted Shelby promptly at six, thanked him for the roses, told him he looked dashing in his dark evening suit with its high stiff collar and white silk vest and swallowtail coat, and marveled when he blushed.

"I'm only thankful I don't have to dress up like this more than once or twice a year," he said.

She had been afraid that she might appear to be a schoolgirl on her way to her first grown-up ball, so she was grateful that he pretended discomfort in order to set her at ease. Or *was* he pretending?

He'd brought along a chaperon, Aunt Bertha, who sat in the backseat of the surrey in her widow's weeds, like a totem in whose presence no hanky-panky could ever take place.

Being whisked through the evening traffic toward the opera house, escorted by the ever-present trio of bodyguards on horseback, one of whom was Dexter, Rachel felt herself flattered by the attention of the townspeople they passed along the way, most of whom knew Shelby, none of whom knew her, and in whose eyes were the questions, Who is she? Who is that girl?

The lobby of the opera house was festively decorated and lit by electricity, and by its novel light Rachel was ogled by the women of Guthrie society. For Shelby Hornbeck to have brought this chit of a girl to the opera house to meet the most important and respectable people in the Territory, chaperoned by a respectable widowed aunt, clearly indicated that his intentions toward her were serious and honorable.

Rachel was delighted to find herself the center of attention. Shelby introduced her to some of the Territory's most important men, including Territorial Governor William C. Renfrow himself. She also met a United States senator, a justice of the territorial supreme court, a number of self-made millionaires, a banker or two, and a few others whose names and occupations she didn't catch. She charmed the lot. How to be charming and graceful she had learned in classes at Miss Fenwick's Young Female Academy, but on her own she had discovered that by pretending to be a vivacious but self-possessed young woman, she became one. Hers was the ability of a good actress to become the role she was playing. And it was obvious to everyone that Shelby, for one, was very pleased with her performance. Here was a man who had never before been known to be affectionate to a woman in public, who had never before been seen to touch another person except in a formal way, but who now was seen to touch Rachel's elbow lightly a few times, guiding her here and there, and when curtain time was announced and they left the lobby to take their seats, he was actually seen to put his arm lightly around her waist as he guided her down the hallway toward his private box. What were they to make of it?

Dexter stood guard outside the door. Aunt Bertha sat behind Shelby and Rachel in the box. Not having seen an opera in nearly a year, Rachel had been looking forward to tonight's performance of *Lucia di Lammermoor*. She had read the Sir Walter Scott novel on which the opera had been based, and she knew well the story of the star-crossed lovers: Lucia, frail and soft-hearted, destined for madness and an early grave, manipulated by a wicked brother into marriage with a rich man, while her beloved—dark and gloomy, a proud sufferer, an outcast—wanders in foreign lands. Lucia stabs and kills her detested bridegroom on their wedding night, and goes mad, and dies, covered with blood, singing her heart out. And her beloved, the proud sufferer, the outcast, on learning of Lucia's death, kills himself with the hope of being reunited with her in heaven.

Rachel enjoyed the opera immensely, and even cried,

"Brava! Brava!" a few times, but very few others in the audience seemed to share her enthusiasm. Most of them could not understand a word that was sung, let alone appreciate the singers' finer flourishes. Indeed, the singers might as well have been singing lullabies, so soporific were the results: by the time the performance was half over, there were many yawns amid the polite applause, and even the snort now and then of a snore being cut short by an elbow in the ribs.

Aunt Bertha was one of the victims. But she didn't snore loudly enough to disturb anyone, so Shelby let her snooze, and Rachel welcomed her lack of vigilance. It gave her a chance, during the less compelling moments of the opera, to watch Shelby from the corner of her eye without herself being watched. And not only was she once again dazzled by his handsomeness, she was also fascinated by his strangeness. He wasn't at all what she would have expected a man of such wealth and political power to be. He acted more like, say, a successful minister. He had that look of rectitude about him, a look of unassertive but self-confident moral superiority. And the simile of the religious minister carried over to the ball later that evening, where Rachel learned to her surprise that Shelby didn't dance.

"I'm sorry. You'll excuse me, I hope? I just never liked doing it well enough to learn how," implying that he'd had better things to do in his life. "But if you like to dance, please do. I'm sure you won't lack for partners." It was as if he were encouraging a spoiled child to run along and play.

So Rachel accepted the request for a dance from Governor Renfrow himself—how could she refuse the governor, after all?—and thereafter was invited to dance by many of the young bachelors. She often glanced at Shelby, and twice she caught his eyes following her as she danced by, and she was reminded of the appraising and approving gaze of a horse trainer watching the paddock workout of a beautiful new thoroughbred filly. More often, however, her glance found him talking to one or more of the men who congregated around the punch bowl, most of whom were older men with big cigars and big paunches. Shelby, who was young and had neither, stood out among them like a prince among burghers, but he seemed very comfortable with them, to judge by the animation of their conversations.

These conversations always seemed to falter when Rachel returned. Once she asked Shelby what they had been talking about.

"Politics. Nothing to bother your pretty head about," he said. "Enjoying yourself?"

"Oh, yes," she said breathlessly, fanning herself with the fan she carried on a cord around her right wrist. "I've never danced so much in all my life. If I could just have a sip of your punch?"

"Would you like—"

"No, a sip's all I want. I'll just take it from yours, if you don't mind." She pointedly turned the cut-glass cup around so that she could drink from the same place on the rim where his lips had been, all the while looking at him to make sure he noticed.

The intimacy of the act seemed to stir something in Shelby. For a moment he seemed slightly discomposed, an unusual condition for him, as if he were on the verge of saying something of life-altering importance. But that pregnant moment passed, and what he finally said was, "Would you like to get some fresh air?"

"Oh, yes! What shall we do? Go for a midnight ride?"

He smiled apologetically. "I'm sorry. I'm afraid I promised Aunt Bertha I'd have her home by twelve o'clock. But what about tomorrow? Would you take a ride with me then? There's something I want to ask you," he hinted, and then hurriedly added, "We could have a picnic," as if coaxing a child with visions of sugarplums.

"Without Aunt Bertha?"

"Without Aunt Bertha," he replied. "I'm afraid I've put her to enough trouble as it is. It's long past her bedtime. I should be taking her home soon. Do you mind?"

With old Aunt Bertha sitting in the backseat of the surrey and with the bodyguards riding close by, Rachel knew that kisses were unlikely, but she felt that an evening as grand and eventful as this one should end with a kiss or two or at least a furtive embrace in a shadowed corner of her boardinghouse hallway.

But all Shelby did was to escort her to the front entrance of the boardinghouse, take off his top hat, shake her hand, and say, "Good night," and, "What a pleasure it's been," and, "I trust you enjoyed yourself," quite as if he were a boy who had been coached on how to say good night on his first date, and finally, "Well, good night, then. Till tomorrow?" He stepped away, leaving her to go upstairs to her room.

This was not the way she had envisioned being wooed. If he was—as his actions seemed to indicate—attracted to her, was a formal good-night handshake the way to show it? She could not have imagined a more unusual man. While brushing her hair, she tried to fantasize about being married to him and even spoke aloud the name Rachel Hornbeck to discover how it sounded. But what would her answer be if he should someday actually ask her to marry him? She hadn't the slightest notion.

The next day they had their picnic under an old lightning-scarred oak tree high on the escarpment overlooking the Cimarron River basin. The bodyguards carried the heavy wicker hamper from the boot of the yellow-wheeled buggy and put down the picnic blanket, a service that surprised and pleased Rachel but that Shelby seemed to take for granted. It made her feel pampered and important to have people do that sort of thing for her, although she knew it was Shelby, not her, they were doing it for. Never before had she seen Dexter so eager to be of service to anyone. And like good servants, as soon as the picnic was prepared, Dexter and the other two bodyguards took up protective positions at a discreet distance from the picnic site.

Rachel anticipated their spending an hour or so eating and laughing and talking, getting to know each other by whiling the afternoon away, but she soon realized that all the laughing and most of the talking would have to be done by her. Shelby never laughed, apparently had very little sense of humor, and no one would have called him a conversationalist. Politics and power were the only subjects that seemed to interest him, yet those were subjects he thought women shouldn't bother their pretty heads about. He talked about his politics of white supremacy, but only grudgingly and because Rachel required some explanation of her father's charges against him.

"It's something I'm proud of," he said when she seemed to expect him to defend himself guiltily. "Every white man is a white supremacist at heart—even your father."

Rachel hooted. "I doubt he'd agree."

"He may not admit it, but how could it be otherwise? Dexter tells me he's trying to teach the Indians the white man's ways. Why would he be doing that if he didn't believe that the white man's ways are superior? If the Indians were the superior race, we'd be trying to learn their ways. No, being white is a gift of God, and we shouldn't be ashamed of God's gifts."

That sounded reasonable. And though he became a little testy when she asked him if he was a member of the Ku Klux Klan, as if he thought it were none of her business, it was a testament to his regard for her that he condescended to deny it. As for his personal background, he seemed willing enough to talk about his father—a Confederate major, killed at the Battle of Shiloh—but of his mother he would say only that she, too, had died in the War. When Rachel tried to find out how, she noticed a fleeting look of alarm in his eyes, as if he were afraid of something.

He seldom turned the questions back upon her. He seemed to know all he wanted or needed to know about her and to be satisfied just to sit in silence and look at her, as if spellbound. And even after he was caught staring, he sometimes continued for a few seconds before the spell was broken, at which time he would become slightly flustered and avert his eyes. It was as if he contemplated—were on the verge of—diving into dangerous waters but couldn't quite bring himself to take the plunge. Perhaps he was thinking about taking her in his arms and kissing her but was stymied by—what? Bashfulness? Fear?

Once she allowed herself a daring flight of fancy to probe the meaning of his spellbound stares. "You know what your eyes remind me of? A sonnet by Shakespeare, something we studied in school."

> Thou blind fool, Love, what dost thou to mine eyes,
> That they behold, and see not what they see?

But seeing his discomfort, she let the words trail off and die and asked apologetically, "Have you ever read the sonnets?"

"Never had much time for poetry"—implying again that he'd had better things to do in his life.

But if there was no poetry in Shelby's soul, there was certainly something in his eyes, something that made her feel very special, and she decided to busy herself throwing pebbles over the escarpment into the Cimarron River below and let him look as long as he liked. In a few minutes he approached her, saying as if to a child, "Don't go too near the edge. You might fall."

And she, as if to provoke him, walked out onto the very edge of the bluff. "Would you care?" she asked.

"Very much. I wouldn't want to lose you."

"But I'm not yours to lose."

"I'd like you to be," he confessed.

But her quizzical gaze caused him to avert his eyes again for a moment, as if he didn't want her to see what was in them.

"In what way?" she prompted.

"In what way? What do you mean?"

"In what way would you want me?" she asked, with just the right amount of coyness. "As a friend?"

"Well, now that you mention it," he said in a businesslike way, "there is something I want to say to you. I don't suppose it would come as a surprise to you to learn that I haven't had much experience with women. But that's only because I never found one that I liked and admired enough to—to want her to be the mother of my children." He gave her a straight look. "Until now." Giving her a moment to register that fact, he went on to say, in the voice of an adult coaxing a child, "I could make you happy, Rachel."

"Why, Shelby Hornbeck, is this a proposal?"

"Yes. If you'd consent to be my wife, I could give you everything you ever wanted. I could take care of you, keep you safe."

Keep you safe—what a strange thing to say! As if she had ever cared about being safe. "You make it sound a little like a business proposition. What would I be expected to give you in return?"

"A son," he said without hesitation. "I want a son."

She looked up at him for a moment in silence. Actually she was waiting for him to take her into his arms and cover her face with kisses and declare his undying love, but he just stood there, waiting for a reply, his blond hair shining in the sun. And she couldn't answer because she couldn't imagine agreeing to marry a man whom she had never kissed.

So she kissed him. When she moved against him and put her arms around his neck, she saw once again that fleeting look of alarm in his eyes, as if he were afraid of something, but then, as soon as she raised herself up on her toes and put her lips to his, he dropped all restraint. Like an eager and awkward boy, he grasped her around the waist and pressed his mouth against hers, his lips stiff and unyielding to the point of causing pain.

It had never occurred to her that a thirty-five-year-old man wouldn't know how to kiss. But she could teach him that. She could teach him how to kiss, and how to dance, and how to laugh. She could even teach him poetry. But love? She felt none of that in his touch. There was desire in his touch, and possessiveness, but no love, and she wondered if she would have to teach him that, too.

CHAPTER FORTY-THREE

"DO YOU KNOW WHAT YOU'RE DOING?" MAXWELL ASKED.

"Oh, Daddy, I do hope you're not going to start that stuff about politics again." She glared at him across his desk.

"It's not just politics," he protested. "It's exploitation and murder. And after all the years on this reservation, seeing how the Indians have been treated, you should certainly know the difference."

"Oh, for goodness' sakes!" She threw up her hands in despair. "Murder? Where d'you get such ideas? He may be a white supremacist—all right, he admits it, he's even proud of it—but *murder*? How can you think that?"

"All right, maybe not, maybe not," Maxwell conceded, fearing that his careless charge might have pushed her further into opposition. "But even if he's just a white supremacist, how can you marry someone who thinks Indians are an inferior race?"

"And you know what he says? He asks why you're teaching the Indians the white man's way if you don't think our ways are superior." Seeing that he had no ready answer, she softened her remarks by adding, "Now, Daddy, you know I don't think Corby is inferior to *anybody*"—personalizing the issue, as usual. "And as far as that goes, Corby seems to think the Indians are superior to the white man. Should I be offended by that? Should I call him an Indian supremacist and never associate with him again? To me this is all just politics—men talk. You men get to run the world and decide such things. You don't even let us vote. What business is it of mine?"

"Well, maybe it should be your business when they burn down people's houses and lynch kids."

"Oh, Daddy, he's not in the Klan, if that's what you're still thinking. He didn't burn down Eula's house."

"You're sure?"

"Of course, I am! I asked him. He said he wasn't in the Klan, and I believe him." She leaped up from the chair and took an aimless turn about the office as she said, "I'm sure when you get to know him, you'll see how wrong you are. Why—why, for heaven's sakes, he's a *gentleman*! And a church deacon!" she cried in triumph. "What's more, he doesn't drink, smoke, gamble, or chew tobacco. He's not a woman chaser, he takes good care of his widowed aunt, and Dexter tells me he supports four or five families of widows and orphans in Guthrie. My goodness, it seems to me I'm describing the very man every father would *want* his daughter to marry—and yet you don't approve!"

"Well, my dear, I don't doubt that everything you say about him is true, and those are qualities any man would admire in another. But allow me to point out that none of those qualities precludes him from being a Klansman. I'm sure most Klansmen are churchgoing, God-fearing men who honor their fathers and mothers, love their country and their families, and don't kick their dogs. But that doesn't mean they don't go out and lynch a Negro now and then."

"Oh, for goodness' sakes," she said, and for a moment she reminded him of Dexter, with that look of defiant intransigence, a repudiation of everything that stood in the way of her desire. "We're obviously never going to agree on this. I might as well go."

"All right, all right," he replied hastily, and threw up his hands in surrender. "I'll try to give him the benefit of the doubt. But I still don't see why you can't wait. My gosh, you just met the man, and you're going to marry him in a *month*? What's the hurry?"

"*He* wanted to wait. It was *I* who didn't. I made it a condition, in fact, that we get married within a month, and d'you know why? Because I knew you'd just keep trying to get me to change my mind, and I didn't want to spend months or years arguing with you about him. Is that reason enough? Or should I tell you how sick to death I am of this place and how I'd give anything to be mistress of my own house—in Guthrie."

While these reasons seemed fairly persuasive, Maxwell was left with obvious reservations, reservations that probably would have been nullified had Rachel chosen to share with him one of her most urgent reasons for wanting to be married, whether to Shelby or someone else: her feelings for Corby. Since the day of the peyote ceremony, when she had found herself responding to his kisses with a passion equal to his own, she knew that she must find some barrier to put between them. Time had not succeeded. During the years she had spent in Miss Finwick's, she had managed to hold her love for Corby in abeyance—out of sight, out of mind—but as soon as she had seen him again and felt his kisses, all of the old feelings of love had come back, and so strong were they that she couldn't trust herself to resist them for long. What was needed, then, was a barrier, and what better barrier than a husband?

But she couldn't confide this to Maxwell, so she thought to end the discussion by saying, "Daddy, I know what I'm doing. I'm not a child anymore."

"No," he agreed in a wistful voice that had an edge of irony. "No, you're not a child anymore."

"I know what I want."

Maxwell smiled to show he meant no criticism when he said, "And judging from that greedy look in your eyes, I think I can guess what it is you want: pretty clothes to wear, fine horses to drive, and a mansion to live in."

"And what's wrong with that?"

His shrug was barely perceptible. "Nothing—except they're not very good reasons for getting married. What about love? I haven't yet heard you say you love the man. Do you?"

"Of course, I do. Yes, I do. I love him." She crossed to Maxwell and stood beside his chair and put her arms across his shoulders. "And you'll like him, too, I know you will, as soon as you get to know him. You'll see." She gave his shoulder an affectionate and reassuring shake. "Why don't you come with me to Guthrie next week? I have to go get some material for my wedding dress and some things for a trousseau. Why don't you come with me and talk to him?"

"Well, if he's such a southern gentleman," he teased, "why doesn't he come here to ask me for your hand?"

"He wanted to, but he has to be at the capitol every day for the next two weeks. They're having a big political fight over some bill or other, and he can't come here—"

"The Negro School Funding Amendment, if I'm not mistaken," Maxwell interjected.

"Is that it? I wouldn't know. But he—"

"Radical representatives want to bring Negro schools into the territorial school system, and he opposes it."

"Does he?" She spun away from him to sit on the edge of his desk, her arms folded across her breasts. "Well, then, maybe that's something you two'd have in common to talk about. How many times have I heard you say you weren't sure that Indians should be educated?"

"Rachel! It's not the same thing, and you know it. I've had my doubts about educating Indians, sure, but only because, once they are educated, the white world doesn't want them. *He* doesn't want to educate Indians and Negroes because he wants to keep them ignorant and dependent. He wants to make sure they're kept in their place."

Her haughtiness fell away to reveal mere peevishness. "Well, what about Mother? As I remember, she was another one who thought coloreds should be kept in their place, but that didn't stop you from marrying *her*, did it?"

He had to admit defeat on that point. "And I don't suppose it'd do any good to argue that you should profit from my mistakes?"

"Mistakes?" she echoed, ready to be shocked. "Are you saying your marriage to Mother was a mistake?"

"No, no, no. Look, Rachel, I just don't want you to marry someone who's a bad man, that's all."

"And how you can think he's a bad man is simply beyond me! Mistaken, maybe, on the subject of race—all right, I grant you that—but so was Mother, and that didn't make her a bad woman, did it? My goodness, Shelby Hornbeck is almost too good to be true, yet you keep trying to make him into some sort of villain. We're not seeing the same man at all."

At least he could agree with her on that. She was seeing what she wanted to see. However, he finally consented to go to Guthrie and spend some time with Shelby. He was determined to try to like the man, for her sake. And indeed, as he watched him on the floor of the legislative assembly chamber, he found qualities in the man that he had to admire, however grudgingly. From his seat in the gallery overlooking the assembly floor, Maxwell studied the young man as he coolly went about the business of presiding over a debate on the controversial amendment currently under consideration. The Negro School Funding Amendment had been attached as a rider to the General Education Appropriations bill by some Radical Republicans, and the Democrats were trying to defeat it.

Unlike the other legislators, Shelby didn't seem to sweat. Electric fans hanging from the ceiling just managed to stir the air in the chamber, and most of the tie-loosened legislators mopped their faces with handkerchiefs as they went about the noisy, fractious, and contentious business of debating the Bill. But not Shelby. In front of a huge American flag stretched across the back wall, he sat behind the speaker's lectern at the chairman's desk, gavel in hand, recognizing speakers, admonishing members who were out of order, keeping speakers to their allotted times, and never seemed to sweat, even though he was one of the few in the chamber who had not shed their coats.

"Isn't he wonderful?" Rachel said. She sat beside Maxwell, fanning herself, leaning forward in her seat, resting her elbows on the gallery railing.

Wonderful? Well, hardly. Still, he had to concede that Shelby's composure and authority, the way he managed men, were qualities to be envied and admired. But he cringed with embarrassment at the racial demagoguery of some cracker Democrats who opposed the funding bill, the more so since he was sitting directly across an aisle from Negro spectators, who muttered protests when one of the speakers kept referring to Negroes as "black baboons."

Maxwell's was an aisle seat in the whites-only section of the public viewing gallery. Across the aisle from him was the colored section, a very small portion of the gallery's seating space. All the seats in the colored section were occupied, and a few Negroes were standing against the back wall behind the colored section seats, while in the far larger whites-only section a few seats were still empty.

This—the fact that Negroes had to stand while there were empty seats in the white section—was also a source of self-consciousness for Maxwell and actually caused him to consider leaving the chambers in protest, but when Shelby turned the gavel over to another man and stepped to the speaker's lectern to address the crowded assembly, Maxwell found that his attention, almost in spite of himself, became riveted on him.

"I'm against the amendment" were the first words out of Shelby's mouth, and his voice, with its mellifluous South Carolina tones, rang through the chamber. Holding up a folded copy of a newspaper, he said, "Here, I'm sorry to say, is the result of teaching Nigrahs to read and write. This newspaper is published for and by Nigrahs in the all-Nigrah town of Freedom, only a few miles from where we are. Here on the masthead is the paper's slogan: 'A good Democrat statesman is a dead Democrat statesman.' That's the slogan. Well, since I myself might be considered a Democrat statesman, does anyone think that I should vote to educate people who advocate my death? That I should help finance my own death?

"I'm genuinely sorry to say it, but it must be said: money put into efforts to educate Nigrahs will be repaid with insurrection." He shook the newspaper. "God made them as they are, and we must accept them as they are. As long as they can't read, they are not eligible to vote. If you give darkies the vote, they will elect darkies. And those among you who lived through the dark days of Reconstruction in the South know well what I mean. Those of you who never had to suffer the humiliation of living under Nigrah rule had better heed my warning. It will not be a pretty sight to see darkies occupying these seats of honor, I can tell you. I have seen it happen. The Yankees installed barefooted darky field hands in our governing bodies throughout the capitals of the Confederacy, and they became drunk with power. I am sorry to say it, but they and their white-trash carpetbagger patrons didn't—"

This brought a few boos from the legislators on the Republican side of the assembly floor. The acting chairman banged his gavel for silence, and Shelby, stern and dignified, went on with his remarks. "I realize that many people do not like to hear what I'm saying, but I speak only of what I have seen with my own eyes. As God is my witness, when the carpetbaggers and former slaves took power in my home state of South Carolina, what followed was a reign of terror against southern whites, the likes of which you would have had to live through to appreciate. And what could white people do in their own defense? Nothing. In their helplessness and humiliation they could do nothing. I have seen this."

After a long dramatic pause his voice took on the authority of an Old Testament prophet exhorting the multitudes when he said, "As God is my witness, I will not see it happen here.

"No," he said, summing up. "We must accept the Nigrahs as God gave them to us and see that they are put to some good use in society. Rather than spend the taxpayers' money to educate them, we should teach them according to their capacities to be laborers and domestics, as servants of the superior race. This, it seems to me, is God's will, and I will do everything in my power to see that God's will be done."

Had demonstrations of support been allowed in the chambers, Shelby probably would have received a standing ovation from the whites in the gallery. As it was, he received scattered applause, which was quickly gaveled to silence by the acting chairman, who then adjourned the proceedings for lunch.

As Maxwell and Rachel and the other spectators were leaving the gallery, Rachel said giddily, "My goodness, with such powers of speech, do you think he could be president someday?"

She and Maxwell were among the white spectators who mingled with the Negroes as they made their way up the aisle and out into the second-floor foyer. Maxwell could sense the tension and outrage among the Negroes and figured that now was hardly the time to discuss Shelby Hornbeck's political possibilities.

As soon as they reached the foyer, their attention was caught by a uniformed page who was walking among the white spectators saying, "Mr. Maxwell? Paging Mr. John Maxwell." Identifying himself to the page, Maxwell was handed a note from Shelby Hornbeck, asking him and Rachel please to meet him in five minutes at the cloakroom downstairs and join him for lunch. Maxwell passed the note to Rachel, who had been craning her neck to see what it said.

Among the Negroes leaving the colored section of the gallery were a young woman in a maternity dress and her husband. When they heard Maxwell identify himself to the page, they stopped and spoke quietly to each other, and after Maxwell handed the note to Rachel, the young Negro man, well dressed and well groomed in the manner of a professional, with a neat goatee and black horn-rimmed eyeglasses, approached Maxwell.

"Pardon me, sir," he said. "Mr. John Maxwell? My wife"—indicating the young woman who kept her distance—"wondered if you might be the Mr. John Maxwell of Agency, who married Miss Eula Rasmussen?"

Maxwell's face brightened at the sound of Eula's name. "Why, yes, indeed, I am. You know her?"

"My wife was acquainted with your wife when she lived near Freedom. I'm Dr. Homer Upchurch. This is my wife, Drusilla. Your wife would've known her as Drusilla Pointer, I believe."

Dr. and Mrs. Upchurch were observing all the subtle nuances of an elaborate racial etiquette. When introducing himself and his wife, he didn't offer to shake hands until Maxwell himself extended his own and said, "Of course! Well, what d'you know!" He shook hands with Drusilla. "Yes, I've heard Eula speak of you affectionately many times. Pleased to meet you. I only wish Eula were here. She'd love to see you again."

"She wrote me about the operation," Drusilla said, "and sent me an announcement about the wedding, but I haven't heard from her since. I owe her a letter, I'm afraid. My apologies to her. It's just that I've been very busy—with this sort of thing," she added pointedly, indicating by a glance and a tilt of her head that "this sort of thing" meant the proceedings in the assembly.

"Daddy?" Rachel stepped to his side, touched his arm to get his attention, and said, "Excuse me," to Dr. Upchurch and Drusilla, then, "Daddy? I'm going on down to the cloakroom," and, without waiting for a response, hurried away.

"My daughter," Maxwell explained lamely. "Well, look, maybe you could come and visit us someday? You and your husband. We can always find room. You'd be most welcome."

He was sincere in the invitation, but he was aware of the empty formality of the words. He was aware that in these days and times in Oklahoma black folks didn't go around paying social calls on white folks. They both thanked him, however, not in acceptance of the invitation but for the gesture, and began taking their leave, when Maxwell said, "Wait."

They stopped and turned at the head of the stairway leading down to the exit for coloreds.

"Look, I feel bad about this sort of thing"—using Drusilla's phrase and gesture to signify what had gone on in the assembly. "I realize that apologies must be awfully weak balm for all this and the things you folks have been through over in Freedom, but I want you to know that I don't—"

"We know you're not one of them," Drusilla said. "Gypsy Smith spoke well of you."

"Gypsy," Maxwell said with mingled tribute and nostalgia, then lowered his voice: "Anybody have any news of him? Is he all right? I've lost track of him completely."

"Everybody has," Drusilla said. "He seems to've dropped off the face of the earth. Well, good-bye again. Tell Eula I'll write her someday soon, I promise."

Maxwell would have liked to continue the conversation, but they had people waiting for them, and he did, too, so he let them go. Taking a deep breath, he went down the whites-only stairway to meet his future son-in-law.

CHAPTER FORTY-FOUR

RACHEL AND MAXWELL WERE ON THE TRAIN TO KINGFISHER, where they were to change trains for El Reno. Rachel sat next to the open window, holding her hat in her lap, the wind blowing her hair. The luggage rack above the seat was crammed with parcels.

"What did you tell him?" she asked.

"I told him I'd think about it."

"My goodness, what's there to think about?"

"His motive, for one thing. I think he's trying to buy my good opinion." Maxwell chuckled. He was still a little tipsy from the brandy he'd had with Shelby at the Commercial Club, the most exclusive and prestigious dining establishment in Guthrie. After luncheon Dexter had escorted Rachel shopping, leaving Shelby to ply Maxwell with cigars and brandy and the offer of the position of vice-chancellor at the University of Oklahoma.

"What's funny?" Rachel asked.

"I was just thinking—a rent-free house comes with the job, you know? Brick." He smiled grimly. "I was just thinking what an irony it'd be if Shelby, in spite of his denials, were in fact a Klansman, maybe even one of those who burned Eula's house. Well, wouldn't it be ironic?"

"Daddy"—almost pleading with him now—"do you still think he's lying about that?"

He became serious. "I'm not at all sure what to think of the man. He denied being a Klansman but admitted being a Klan sympathizer. Said the Klan was what saved the South from the chaos after the War, and for that it had his undying gratitude. But when I told him that my wife had less reason to be grateful to the Klan, he said he deplored the Klan's burning her house. Huh! I thought I had him there. Pointed out that the Olanco Ranch took over Eula's homestead as an abandoned claim and that the Olanco is owned by the Oklahoma Land Company, of which"—chuckling again—"Shelby Hornbeck just happens to be chairman of the board. Well, what do you think? He denied knowing anything about it. Apologized. Offered to give her back her claim. With compensation."

"There, you see? You see what a fair and generous man he is?"

"But *is* it generosity? Or just another way to try to buy my good opinion?"

"You know, Daddy, sometimes I worry about you. When're you going to learn to take advantage of situations to get ahead in the world? Or do you even *want* to get ahead? Are you going to be satisfied staying in that dirty little Indian agency for the rest of your life?"

"So you think I should take the job?"

The subject brought to her face an avaricious expression like the one he had so often seen on her mother's face.

"Even if it means I have to become a Democrat?"

"Of course," she chided, as if she had never heard such a silly question. "Well, it isn't as if you've ever given a hoot for any political party, is it? What was it you used to say? That political parties are just the system for dividing the spoils? Well, I think it's high time you got yourself some of those spoils. Take the job." She gave him an affectionate pat on the shoulder. "And just think! If Shelby gets to be governor, as everybody seems to think he will, why, then, I'll be the governor's wife, and you know what? I'll bet I could get him to name you *president* of the university. How'd you like *that*?"

"Not very much, I'm afraid."

"Oh, Daddy, haven't you ever had *any* ambition?"

At that moment she seemed the very reincarnation of Nora.

"You would have me sell my soul to the devil?" he asked with a provocative levity born of brandy.

Exasperated, she turned away from him to gaze out the window at the passing scenery, but he took her hand and pressed it lovingly, saying, "A mere figure of speech, my dear, a mere figure of speech," and she turned back to him to ask in a pleading voice, "But you do like him a little, don't you? He's not a bad man, is he?"

He made an effort to become sincere and sober. "To tell the truth, I don't know what to make of the man. He's probably the most opaque person I've ever met. An enigma. A man of secrets."

Rachel sighed with defeat. But after a moment she seemed slightly rueful when she said, "You really think so? Well, he is very secretive, I'll have to agree with you there. Even so, he's a good and kind and generous man, and I'm going to marry him, so you might as well make up your mind to that."

During the month preceding her wedding date Rachel made her own wedding gown. She had help from Miss Clarksdale and Eula, but she did most of the work. It gave her something to do. She went back to Guthrie four more times during that month. She enjoyed herself on each occasion and especially enjoyed the governor's birthday banquet and the party celebrat-

ing the completion of Kingstree. But whenever she came back
to the agency, she found she had time on her hands and nothing much to do except work on her wedding gown.

Against her better judgment she had hoped each day to see
Corby again. Molly Iron Shirt told her that he had gone off
with Chief Quanah Parker somewhere. The news left Rachel
both angry and sad. She and Maxwell often talked about
Corby, lamenting his going back to the blanket, though Maxwell usually ended up sighing and saying, "Well, maybe it's
for the best." One evening after supper, he said, "Being colored in a white society is a losing game. Who can blame him
if he doesn't want to play?"

And Rachel, suddenly defensive, snapped, "Well, it's not *my*
fault!"

Momentarily surprised by the tortured logic of that response,
Maxwell said, "Why, Rachel, nobody said it was." He looked
at her more closely. "What's the matter? You got a guilty conscience about something?"

"No. Why should I have?"

Maxwell shrugged. "I don't know, but every time you get
back from Guthrie, you seem a little touchier on the subject of
race. Could it be that Shelby's trying to make a white supremacist out of you?"

"I told you, we don't talk about politics," she said. The truth
was, she wasn't sure what was wrong. "I'm just . . . well, sort
of nervous, is all." Turning to Eula at the other end of the table, she said, "That's natural, isn't it, Eula? You were nervous,
weren't you? About getting married?"

Eula blushed. "Considerable. But I never doubted I wanted
to."

That touched the source of Rachel's nervousness. She was
having doubts, second thoughts, misgivings, not constantly
and about nothing specific that she could name, but a general
feeling of uncertainty caused her to become more and more
apprehensive as the day of the wedding drew near. She always managed to dispel such doubts and reaffirm her joy, but
sometimes she was pulled wildly between the two, a tug-of-
war that left her irritable and short-tempered.

Such was her disposition on the day before she was supposed to go to Guthrie, the day that she put the last touches on
her wedding gown and modeled it in front of the swing mirrors

on the dresser in the main bedroom. Maxwell and Eula had gone to El Reno to buy wedding presents, so Rachel had the house to herself and was glad for the privacy she needed to picture herself as the bride-to-be.

She wasn't pleased with what she saw. The gown and the gossamer veil made her look like the product of some confectioner's art, molded from a bland sweet icing, like an edible doll. She remembered Corby's saying how white she looked, like the icing on a cake.

But all thoughts of the wedding went out of her head when she heard what she thought were galloping hoofbeats that came to a stop in the backyard. She listened for a moment for the slam of the backyard gate, and when she heard it, she tossed the bridal veil onto the dresser and darted through the kitchen to the back screen door.

Corby had tied the sweat-lathered red stallion at the corral water trough and was coming up the footpath to the back porch. He was dressed in faded blue jeans and a flimsy dirty buttonless blue work shirt that was soaked with sweat at the armpits. He was hatless and wore his hair in braids.

She cried his name and stepped out to meet him on the back porch. She had an impulse to throw her arms around him but held back when she saw the look on his face. She had seldom in her life seen him angry, but she remembered the signs: the slightly hooded eyes, the slight but unmistakably scornful lift of the upper lip, the twitch of jaw muscles, the flaring nostrils.

"What is it?" she said. "What's the matter?"

"So it's true." He raked his eyes up and down the wedding gown. "Molly said you were getting married. I didn't believe her. But it's true."

"Yes. Sunday. I asked Molly if she could get a message to you, letting you know. I wanted to see you again before I left for good. Corby," she added with good-natured ridicule, "you're not going to be jealous, are you?"

Taking offense at the ridicule, he raised his voice to match his hostility. "And why should I be jealous? This"—scornfully gesturing toward her wedding gown—"is not the Rachel I loved. You know what you are now? A *vehoa*."

Already irritable and already resentful of his retreat into Indianness, she didn't spare the venom when she struck: "A white woman? Yes, and I'm proud of it! And who're you to

look down your nose at *me*? Just take a look at yourself. You
know what you've become, Corby? A dirty Indian, that's what
you've become. Look at yourself. Look at your hands, how
disgustingly dirty they are."

Moving with sullen slowness, Corby lifted his hands and
looked at them. They were black with charcoal from his last
campfire. And in a low voice he said, "So that's what I've become to you, is it? A dirty Indian, with dirty hands?"

She glared at him defiantly, saying the most hateful words
she could think of: "They would soil anything you touched."

Corby put his hands on Rachel's shoulders. "Then be soiled
by them," he said, and wiped his hands on the pristine white-
ness of the wedding gown. Then he spun around and left the
porch.

Glancing down at the two smudges of charcoal and dirt on
the shoulders of her wedding gown, Rachel cried out with
shock and outrage, and charged after him. She caught up with
him as he was going through the yard gate, and struck him in
the back of the head with her fist.

"Damn you, Corby! Damn you!" she cried, and struck him
again, and again. She was hitting him with the butt of her
hand, not with the knuckles of her fist, so the blows weren't
very painful, but they were nevertheless thumping good blows,
for she was as furious as she had ever been in her life.

The first blow caused him to flinch, but after that he let the
blows rain down on his head and shoulders without defending
himself. He strode toward the barn as she ran after him, pummeling him.

"Damn you, Corby! How dare you? Who d'you think you
are? How dare you ruin my wedding dress." But because he
took the blows as though he deserved them, Rachel's fury
foundered for lack of opposition, and by the time they reached
the barn she had ceased striking him, and her voice took on a
plaintive edge. "Answer me! How could you do such a thing?
Look what you did."

Grimly silent, Corby strode on into the barn, scattering
chickens before him, and into his room, with Rachel following,
demanding explanations. He went to the window at the foot of
his bed and stared out, keeping his back to her, refusing to
look at her, but finally he said, "I'm sorry," and then, sad and
repentant: "You were right. I'm jealous."

"Damn you! What right have you to be jealous?"

He jerked his head around to fix her with his suddenly accusing eyes. "Right? What right do I need? I love you. What rights does that give me?"

"None! None at all, unless I said I'd be yours."

"And you did, dammit, you did. You carved a sign in the tree by the river that said we were betrothed."

"For God's sake, Corby, we were *kids*. We're not kids any longer. And there can never be anything like man-woman love between us. You've known it for years, and it's time you faced the facts."

"Why not?" he asked, and in the face of her exasperated disbelief, he added, as though it were a perfectly feasible proposition, "Don't marry that man. Marry me."

She searched his face for signs of insanity or peyote but found neither. He seemed quite reasonable—excited by the possibilities and eager to act, with no signs of derangement. And yet she said, "What you're saying is plumb crazy."

"Maybe so, but that never stopped us before, did it? We always had fun doing crazy things, didn't we? Well, let's do the craziest thing in our lives. Let's go to Mexico and get married."

She couldn't help being caught up for a moment in the romantic vision, and though she resisted being thrilled by it, her hesitation in refusing him outright gave him the courage to kiss her.

She allowed the kiss for a moment and even enjoyed the sensual pleasure of it, but soon she pulled away, and he, rather than desist, grasped her by the shoulders and pulled her to him and kissed her again. She tried to turn her face away, but his lips followed, seeking hers.

"Stop it, Corby. Your hands! You're getting me dirty."

"There was a time when you liked being dirty."

"We mustn't do this." She was admonishing herself as well as him, but allowed him to kiss her again, and even while she returned the kisses, she tried to suppress the exciting turbulence that had begun to surge through her body. Though in direct conflict with her better judgment, her desire was stronger than her will to resist, which became weaker with every advance he made, as when he dropped his hands to her hips and pulled her tightly against him.

"No, Corby! Stop, now!"

"Why not? I have as much right to you as he does."

She tried to push him away, but he overpowered her. He pushed her against the wall and thrust himself against her, and she said, "We mustn't do this," but she didn't try to stop his kisses, no longer tried to stop him from thrusting against her, and soon even found herself responding with pressure of her own. But she truly meant to call a halt to it when he pulled her toward the bed. With both determination and hostility, she jerked against his grasp.

"Stop it, Corby! Now this's gone far enough, Corby. No!"

"Yes. Listen to your heart. What does it say?"

And without the least hesitation, as if he were certain that she was resisting not because she really wanted him to stop but because she wanted to avoid responsibility for the act, he gently forced her down onto the dusty bed. She wanted to say, "Stop! Don't!" But the words turned to throaty sounds of mingled protest and pleasure as he kissed her.

When he felt her resistance ebbing, when her arms slowly lifted to clasp him around his shoulders, pulling him close, he began tugging at clothes, shifting around, frantic and awkward, struggling to get the starchy voluminous folds of her gown up above her thighs.

It was then Rachel realized that she was no longer in control of her body. She could muster no more physical resistance. The only hope she had now of stopping him was by appealing to him, but even as she was murmuring, "Corby, we mustn't, please don't, Corby, don't do this," she continued to kiss him, to breathe his breath, to dig her fingers into his shoulders.

"I love you, I want you," he said, panting, tugging at clothes. "And you love me, and you want me, too. Don't you?"

"Oh, but we mustn't, we mustn't," she pleaded, but even her tongue was failing her now because she didn't hear the words. She spoke the words in her mind, but her tongue refused to form them. What her tongue was murmuring instead were not words that she had thought about saying: "Oh, Corby . . . my darling Corby . . ." These murmurs were interrupted by a sharp intake of breath and her small cry of pain when he entered her.

Afterward they lay in bed for a long while in a silence broken only by the sound of their breathing as it gradually subsided into sighs of satiety and sadness—that, and the rustling of clothes, the sounds of animals in the barn and barnyard. Then Rachel sniffled, and Corby, shifting his position so that he could see her face, used his thumb to wipe away one of the tears that overflowed her eyes.

"Tears?" he asked. "Why?"

"Oh, my God, Corby, what've we done now?"—whispering, as if afraid someone might overhear.

"Something we've always wanted to do," he said, and quickly added, "Had to do." And after another pause: "Were meant to do."

She shook her head as if shaking off a spell. Sighing again, she said, "No," no longer whispering, as if whispers were reserved for tender feelings and twilight. For denial and harsh reality a normal voice was required. "No." She began struggling to disentangle herself from their embrace. "We can't. Let me up."

Baffled by her abruptness, he shifted his position so that she could sit up in the bed, and before he could ask her what was so wrong about loving each other like this, she said, "Oh, damn." She had seen a spot on the gown, a pink wet spot on the gown's taffeta lining. "Oh, damn, it's ruined," she cried as reality began to rush back in upon her with all its terrible problems. She stood up and jerked the back of the gown around so that she could see it and then sighed. "Oh, thank God, it doesn't go all the way through. I can save it."

Corby struggled to revive. "What? Save it? Why?"

"What d'you mean, 'Why?' But oh, just look at it!" She was noticing the dark smudges on the arms and waist of the gown where he had held her. "My God, what'm I going to do?" Her face took on an absent look for a moment as she did some fast thinking. "I'll have to hurry and wash it before Daddy gets back."

Corby fastened his pants as he scooted off the bed, saying, "Wait. Wait a minute, now. You mean you're still going to marry. After *this*?"

"Of course," she said without hesitation.

With a glance toward where they had lain, he stammered, "But you—you said just now . . . you said you loved *me*."

She didn't contradict him.

"And yet you're going to go ahead and marry *him*?"

"Yes."

"Why? You don't love him."

"Yes, I do," she insisted. "It's different, that's all. But listen to me, Corby. Listen to me now. Even if I didn't love him, I'd still marry him, *because* I love you. Do you understand?"

"No."

"We can't be together anymore, not after this. We can't allow this to happen again. Because no matter how much I love you, I'm not going to run off with you and live as an outcast, a beggar, a *squaw*."

They stared at each other in silence for a moment, as if neither had anything left to say, and then Rachel moved to the door.

"I have to go. I have to see what I can do to save this gown." At the door she turned and said in a sadly resigned tone, "Good-bye then, Corby. I don't think we should see each other again until—until afterward."

He turned his back on her. "Go to hell," he said.

CHAPTER FORTY-FIVE

THE SOUTHERN METHODIST TABERNACLE IN GUTHRIE SAT ON the edge of town, across from wooded acres that had been set aside for a future city park. It was from the edge of the woods that Corby watched the wedding procession. Partially concealed by hackberry bushes in the shade of a butternut tree, he sat on Big Red and watched the tabernacle while the wedding took place and then watched as the bride and groom emerged from the church and got into the governor's ceremonial coach, amid a rain of rice and cheers, and were driven away toward town.

So it was done. Corby had needed to see it with his own eyes. Otherwise he was afraid he would never be able to convince himself that Rachel had actually done it. Now, faced with the finality, he rode out of the woods and onto the dusty road and headed south toward the Comanche-Kiowa-Apache reservation.

When he got back to the Quahadi village, he resumed preparations for a vision quest. His mentor and teacher was the venerable Comanche medicine man Three Rains, who had told Corby under what circumstances a vision quest could occur and had prepared him for all eventualities. The one thing Three Rains couldn't tell him was where and when the vision quest should take place. Three Rains spoke to the Great Spirit about it, but all the Great Spirit told him was "From the place of the dead, follow the wolf."

Corby found this very cryptic. He asked Three Rains if the Great Spirit couldn't be a little more specific, but Three Rains explained that the Great Spirit was not giving him directions, He was giving him a test, a way by which He—the Great Spirit—would know that Corby was ready for a vision quest.

"Look for the signs," Three Rains said. "From the place of the dead, follow the wolf."

Corby kept his eyes open, but weeks and months went by, and still he saw nothing that he could interpret as a God-sent sign. Whenever Chief Quanah Parker traveled around to different Indian settlements to spread the creed of the Native American Church, Corby always went along as a leader of the peyote ceremonies, and he never missed an opportunity to visit burial grounds along the way, but he never saw a wolf that he could follow from any place that might be called a place of the dead. Indeed, he never saw a wolf at all. Wolves on the Comanche-Kiowa-Apache reservation had been poisoned and trapped to the point of extinction by the white ranchers who had leased enormous tracts of rangeland on the reservation for cattle raising, and the wolves that had survived never ventured within range of a man's eyes. The only chance Corby had of seeing one was to come upon it by surprise, as finally happened one very cold day late in February 1897.

He had gone rabbit hunting. A recent blizzard had covered the ground with snow, and Corby, bundled against the icy blasts of northern wind in a capote, with its hood pulled over his head, riding Big Red, crisscrossed snow-whitened meadows, stopping at bunches of soapweeds or sagebrush to look for little airholes in the snow. These were breathing holes for jackrabbits hiding beneath the snow. When he found one, he poked a hickory stick into it, and when a rabbit jumped out, he killed it with the stick as it floundered in the snow.

He had got two rabbits that way and was searching for at least one more when he happened on a squatter's cabin. It was a plain board shanty of the kind being built by thousands of homesteaders who had begun entering the reservation in anticipation of the day when it, like the other reservations, would be taken from the Indians and opened for settlement. Such cabins were illegal, and the army was supposed to keep all squatters out, but what could they do? Denied the power to arrest and incarcerate the squatters, the army could only escort them to the borders of the reservation, and as soon as the soldiers had ridden out of sight, the squatters went back to their cabins.

Mounted on Big Red, with the cold northwest wind buffeting his back, Corby examined the squatter's shanty from a distance. No smoke came from the chimney. On the back side of the house the hard earth had been swept bare by the winds, but at the front of the building the snow, scoured to glittering brilliance by the wind, was piled about ten feet high, completely covering the front door. So nobody had gone in or out of the shanty since the blizzard ended two days ago. . . .

He rode down to the shanty and used his hickory stick to dig the snow and ice away from the front door on the unlikely chance that someone inside might still be alive. After half an hour he finally forced his way inside, then had to wait for a moment until his eyes adjusted to the dimness of the interior. A pale light seeped through the two snow-encrusted windows, but most of the light in the place streamed in through the opened door.

There was not a stick of furniture in the place. The small tin stove was covered with hoarfrost. The floor, too, and the walls were covered with frost. On the north and west sides of the room were little drifts of snow that had blown in through small cracks in the wall.

Then Corby saw, in the farthest corner of the room, a pile of bedding on the floor. Stepping closer he saw the three bodies: a woman and two small children, stiff in death, with hoarfrost in their hair and on their faces. Their eyes were closed as if in sleep. The mother had her arms wrapped tightly around the smaller child; the other child was clinging to her back.

Turning away, Corby glanced around the room, automatically reconstructing the bitter struggle that the woman had waged to stay alive. She had demolished every piece of furniture, every box, every picture frame that would burn and in the end had even burned the ax with which she had demolished the furniture. So desperate had been her plight that not a splinter was left anywhere, not a scrap of paper. She had even torn the labels off the empty food cans.

But no, there was one scrap of paper left. Corby saw it on a nail near the door, a page from a child's school tablet, and the words scrawled on it in pencil (the pencil, too, had been burned) seemed to have been written with a shivering hand:

My dear husband we et the last of the food yesterday and burned ever thing there is to burn even the Bible and now we are going to bed. We have prayed for you and for us ever day but we are afraid the storm is so terable you have become lost or will not come back in time. If that be true I pray that we will all meet again in Heaven. We are going to sleep now.

There was nothing to do but leave them there like that. If the husband was coming back, he should find them as they were. If not, a rescue party of white men would no doubt soon be making the rounds of the squatters' shacks and would give them a Christian burial.

Corby put the note back on the nail and went outside, closing the door behind him. After allowing his eyes to adjust to the bright snow-glittered sunlight, he swept the horizon with hand-shaded eyes. Everywhere there was crusted snow and bleak rocks blown bare by the northwest wind, but no signs of life.

He mounted and rode toward the south, the direction the squatter would have most likely taken, making for the nearest white settlement, the small town of Burkburnett, just across the Red River in Texas. And he had ridden no more than a half mile before he topped a small rise and, struck by what he saw, brought Big Red to a halt.

About a hundred yards away was a white wolf feeding on

something. As a child Corby had more than once seen packs of gray wolves in the Territory and had once seen a pair of brown wolves from a distance, but he had never before seen a white wolf, a wolf of the mountains, larger than the other wolves and more cunning, seen always alone or in pairs, never in packs.

As soon as Corby topped the ridge, the white wolf raised its head from whatever it was eating, saw Corby, and ran. Corby kicked Big Red into a plunging run through the snow, giving chase. But when he passed the place where the wolf had been feeding, he reined Big Red to a sudden stop.

It was a man's body—no doubt the body of the husband who had gone for help. Lying facedown, half covered with snow and ice, the clothes partially torn away, the frozen flesh of the shoulder and arm gnawed to the bone, the body was testimony to the foolishness and greed of the white man. To take another man's country and then be so foolish as to let that country kill you. . . . Still, he had been a brave man. Only a brave man would have left the shanty in a blue norther to go for help, no doubt knowing that he was going to his death.

Again Corby thought it was best to do nothing. The ground was frozen, so he couldn't bury the body. He might cover it with stones to keep animals from eating it, but why save it from the wolves and coyotes, only to give it to the worms? Besides, those who would come looking for him would want to know what happened.

So he left the body there and went riding after the white wolf with the excitement of one whose destiny was about to be revealed.

CHAPTER FORTY-SIX

IN THE FIRST FEW MONTHS OF MARRIAGE RACHEL HAD BUSIED herself with furnishing and decorating the house. After that she found she had nothing to do. It was Aunt Bertha who paid the bills, kept the accounts, hired and supervised the staff, decided what would be served for dinner, and kept the keys to the storehouse, as well as the keys to all the drawers and rooms and closets and cupboards that she wished to keep locked. She kept the keys on a ring that she carried on her belt. Rachel sometimes had need to go into the basement or into the storehouse, and Aunt Bertha was willing to go with her and unlock the doors, but she refused to give up the keys.

"I'm sorry," she said when Rachel suggested they be turned over to her. "Shelby has charged me with certain responsibilities in this house, and I mean to discharge them faithfully. If any changes are to be made, the instructions will have to come from him."

When Shelby came home late from a meeting one night, Rachel met him at the front door and accompanied him to his study, demanding to know why was it that Aunt Bertha was responsible for running the house, and not she.

"You don't like the way she runs it? Seems to me she does a good job." On entering the study, he switched on the electric bulbs that were hidden in the prismed crystals of the overhead chandelier, then strode to the fireplace, where embers still glowed. He went through the motions of warming his hands.

"That's not the point. Sure, she does, but I could, too, if given half a chance."

"What? Keep accounts? Make out the household payroll? Order hay and oats for the stock? Most women would consider themselves lucky not to have to do such things."

"Well, I'm not most women. In fact, sometimes I don't feel like a woman at all. Sometimes I feel like an empty-headed little doll that's been dressed up and put on a shelf and told to stay there until you get ready to notice me—which isn't often."

"Well, there's just so much work that I have to do. You know that. And as the next election gets closer, there's going to be even more work to do. I'm sorry, but"—gesturing toward his desk—"what would you have me do? I have responsibilities."

"And *I* don't have *any*. You've got your work, and I don't begrudge you that. But what've *I* got? I get up in the morning. I read the newspaper. I fix my hair. I go off with Aunt Bertha to the Ladies' Literary Society. I do a report on a novel by Jane Austen or Charlotte Brontë. And if the day is really full, why, I might even get to go to a tea given by the church's Ladies' Temperance Union and talk about ways to save the poor benighted drunks in Jessup Hollow. And always with Aunt Bertha along, of course, because you won't let me go out alone. And when I come home, I can't even change the sheets on our bed without asking Aunt Bertha to unlock the linen closet for me."

"Why would you want to change the sheets? That's the maid's job."

"That's not the point. The point is, I get treated like a guest in my own house, for God's sake. *I'm* the mistress here, not Aunt Bertha. That's the point."

A small indulgent smile played in the corners of his mouth. "All right. I'm sorry. I hadn't realized you were so dissatisfied. Tell you what, I'll ask Aunt Bertha to let you help her with some of the household accounts. But she's to remain in charge of the housekeeping. She's a very loyal person and efficient. Someday I'm sure you'll appreciate her as I do and realize that Kingstree couldn't get along without her. And if you'll be a good girl, I'll take you away on a long trip somewhere as soon as the elections are over. In the meantime, I have to get on with my work." He nodded toward his desk. "Financial reports from the Land Company subsidiaries."

"Tonight?"

"There's a board meeting in the morning." He stroked her shoulders. "Be a good girl. Go on to bed. I'll be up in a little while."

She snuggled her head against his chest. "And if I go to sleep, you'll wake me up when you come to bed?" And because he seemed hesitant to make that commitment, she tried to encourage him with a kiss, which he returned, though without enthusiasm. Sometimes she suspected that he really didn't like to kiss.

"I'll be up in a while."

Upstairs Rachel slipped into a nightgown, touched her neck and arms with perfume, and crawled into the downy comfort of the huge canopied bed, where she waited for Shelby, in case he decided to try once again to beget the son he wanted. She wasn't really optimistic, however, for he seemed to think that only an occasional deposit of seed should be sufficient to produce results, and always seemed a little puzzled and disappointed to learn that another month had passed and she hadn't become pregnant.

She hadn't the least idea how to help him, how to arouse him, to make him want her. Her one experience with Corby, so charged with passion and desire, hadn't at all prepared her for the possibility that a man like Shelby might actually need encouragement. It had been a shock to her on her wedding night when Shelby had been unable to consummate their marriage, but before their honeymoon was over, she came to believe that his failure was due to something more than mere ignorance or lack of experience. She sensed that he had, at some time in his life, been deeply hurt in his manhood.

So she decided to have faith that he could deal with the problem in his own secretive and self-contained way, and in time the marriage was consummated. Shelby seemed relieved, as if he had successfully completed an onerous task, got past some huge hurdle, and decided thereafter to rest on his laurels. After several months Rachel felt that she simply must talk to someone.

"As handsome as he is, women must have been chasing after him all his life," she said one day to Aunt Bertha. "Did he ever have ... an *experience* with one, do you think?"

Aunt Bertha responded with asperity, "If you want to know such things, you best ask him."

One cold December night when Rachel and Aunt Bertha were decorating the Christmas tree, Rachel observed that

Christmas wasn't really Christmas without children around. Aunt Bertha gave her a significant look.

"Well, maybe there'll be a few around in Christmases to come," she said.

Rachel's only response was a skeptical snort. "Huh!"

"Why, what's wrong?" Aunt Bertha asked with feigned innocence, as if she hadn't noticed how often of late Shelby had been sleeping in the small bedroom adjoining his study.

"I wish I knew," Rachel said. They were on opposite sides of the Christmas tree, hanging a long string of popcorn and cranberries. "I was hoping you might be able to shed some light on it."

"Shed some— On what?"

"On what's wrong with him."

"With Shelby? Why, is there something wrong with him?" Aunt Bertha was cautiously concerned now, as if she weren't at all certain that she wanted to hear more. A substantial woman in her early sixties, with her gray hair pulled back into a bun, with severe features and humorless gray eyes, Aunt Bertha had the look of a protective mother wolf trying to sniff out danger to her cub.

"There's no—no *joy* in him. You know something? I've never seen him laugh. I mean, really laugh. Have you? Have you ever heard him laugh?"

"Well, I don't know. I guess he's always been pretty serious, even as a boy, and no wonder, with the things that happened to him."

"What *did* happen to him? Other men say, 'When I was a boy, I did this or that,' but Shelby never mentions his childhood. Sometimes I wonder if he even had one."

Aunt Bertha stepped back to look at the tree. "Well, that may not be too far from the truth. He's had to be a man, and do a man's work, ever since he was eight. All of us were ruined by the War, and Shelby lost everything. He didn't have much to laugh about, let me tell you. But I've said all I'm going to. You want to know more, you best ask him."

Rachel looked for an opportune moment to do so, and found it one night shortly after Christmas when she and Shelby were sitting before the fire, and Rachel looked up at the portrait of his mother that hung above the mantel.

"She must have been very young when she died," she

mused. "What did she die of?" And she saw a sudden tension grip his body, as if he had gone on guard against a threatened attack.

"Why do you want to know?"

"Because I want to know about *you*. Don't you see? We've been married now for over six months, and I hardly know any more about you than I did the day we married. Please?" She was coquettish now in that little-girl way that so often won him over.

As usual, Shelby was taciturn and reluctant with his revelations, but Rachel, sensing success, was at her persuasive best as she led him, stumbling and still guarded, from specific bits of begrudged information into a sort of brooding introspection. Staring into the fire, he slowly, bit by bit, revealed to Rachel the very first memory of his life, the memory that became the first unspeakable secret in his storehouse of hatred, a memory that went back to the time when he was four years old, a memory that began with swirling flames and screams and cries of horror.

"Near the end of the War Yankees swept through South Carolina on a raid, gave the slaves firearms, told them to revolt against their masters, to burn the crops and plantations. They did. They went wild, drunk on whiskey and vengeance, became marauding bands. They burned Kingstree. My father was away in the War—dead, though we didn't know it at the time. Mother got us out, just the two of us, out of the house with our lives, but that was all. We hid in the woods, the two of us. No food. No blankets. Just the clothes we had on our backs. For days we stayed in the woods, dodging marauding bands of drunk niggers. We ate roots, frogs, berries, slept on the cold ground, running like hunted animals. And then . . . there were two of them. They found us, ran us down. 'Run, Shelby! Run!' my mother—"

He broke off, too distraught to go on for a moment, then cleared his throat. "They caught her, tore off her clothes. She told me to run. I tried to protect her. They knocked me down. I ran at them again and again, crying, hitting, trying to make them stop, but they just knocked me away. She told me to turn my head. She didn't want me to see . . . but I saw. I saw it all. And I swore I'd get back at them someday, those black apes, I'd make them pay."

When his words finally trailed off and died in a brooding, malignant silence, Rachel, her eyes filmed over with tears of sympathy, said, "Oh, Shelby, how awful for you! Your poor mother . . ."

"She died a few months later," Shelby went on in a less mesmerized tone. "She probably would've died the day it happened, if it hadn't been for me. She lived only long enough to see that I was safe and had a good home with Aunt Bertha, and then she turned her face to the wall and willed herself to die."

"The poor woman. And the men who—did they get away with it?"

"For years they did, yes. There was no law, nowhere to go to seek justice, until the Klan was formed."

"The Klan? Did they—"

"Yes, the Klan. In spite of what your father may think of them, Klansmen are law enforcers, not lawbreakers. The Klan was formed to protect the weak, the innocent, and the defenseless from the indignities, wrongs, and outrages of the lawless."

"What did they do?"

He hesitated, doubtful for a moment that he should go on, but finally continued, though no longer in a brooding reverie. Now his voice had a hard vindictive edge.

"My mother had given a good enough description of them to identify them as renegade slaves from a plantation in the next county. Some of our menfolk went after them, but they'd gone. It was four years after the War that the Klan got word that the two of them had been seen in the vicinity of the plantation where they'd once been slaves. The Klan caught them, brought them back to our county.

"I was eight years old when the Klan came to get me. About a dozen of them rode into our yard one night, dressed up in their robes and hoods, carrying torches. The leader explained that they wanted me to go with them, to see the niggers die. The leader put me up on the horse behind him and took me to the place where they had them. There were about a hundred Klansmen there, with a big cross burning. They had the two niggers tied to stakes, with firewood piled around their feet, wood soaked with coal oil. They'd been flogged, but they were still alive when I got there.

"The Klan leader asked me if I wanted to set the fires to finish them off. Some of the men didn't think that was a good idea, I was so young. The leader said I didn't have to do it, though I could if I wanted to, and offered me the torch.

"I took it. I practically grabbed it out of his hand. Took it and jammed it into the firewood. I watched their faces as they died, and their screams were sweet music to my ears."

"My God," Rachel murmured when he finished speaking. She was unable to look at him for a moment because the fire that flickered across his face made her imagine him as he must have been then, standing in the flickering glow of the burning pyre on which living men writhed in their death agonies, a little golden-haired boy, lovely as any angel, listening to the sweet music of dying men's screams.

CHAPTER FORTY-SEVEN

NEAR SUNDOWN CORBY FOUND HIMSELF ON THE NORTH BANK of the frozen Red River. He was about twelve miles from where he had first seen the wolf. The wolf had proved so difficult to track that it had taken him more than eight hours to cover the twelve miles, and now the sky was threatening more snow, so he decided to give up the chase for the present. Surveying the area for a likely place to spend the night, he spotted the opening of a cave about halfway up the side of the bluff.

He left Big Red tethered to a leafless cottonwood tree and made his way up the scree to the cave, the opening of which was about forty or fifty feet in diameter. In the last light of the sinking sun he saw the remains of recent campfires near the entrance, and there was even a cache of firewood piled near one recently used fire pit.

"Anybody here?" he called back into the dark shadows of the interior. No answer came, except the suspiring sound of his own voice echoing against the high-domed selenite ceiling.

He went back down to the river bottom, unsaddled and hobbled Big Red, and brought the two rabbits and his bedroll back to the cave. He put one rabbit into a snowbank, the other he skinned and roasted on a spit over a fire he built near the cave entrance, using wood from the cache of firewood left by some former occupant.

While the rabbit was cooking, he used a cedar faggot from the fire as a torch to explore the rest of the cave, looking for additional signs of recent occupancy. He found a few footprints, an empty whiskey bottle, and a small sump hole that someone had dug to collect the water seeping from a fissure in the wall near the back of the cave. But the signs of occupancy that surprised him most were not of recent origin.

On one wall of the cave, on a vast expanse of alabaster, about a hundred feet back from the entrance, he was surprised to find a number of pictures and symbols carved in the alabaster, pictures of animals and humans and mysterious markings reminiscent of those on tepees. Huge horned creatures that looked like buffalo, with small sticklike men attacking them with sticklike lances, ran across the wall. Many of the signs and symbols he had never seen before, but among those he recognized were a human hand, a winged animal of some sort, and a wolf. The figure of the wolf, at the far edge of the carvings, was sitting on its haunches, its head tipped backward, howling at a full moon.

"The Cave of the Ancient Ones," Three Rains said gleefully when Corby told him where he had spent the night. "*Haiya!* Medicine Bluff! Many bands of red men have been there, to the top of Medicine Bluff, to make medicine before raiding the enemy or hunting the buffalo. And a white wolf led you there! The Great Spirit was in the wolf. The cave will be the place of your vision quest. We must begin preparations at once."

Three Rains spoke with the Great Spirit and was told that Corby's—Nakoni's—vision quest should begin on the night of the next full moon. This meant a wait of nearly a month, but Corby had plenty to do in the meantime to purify himself and make himself worthy of a vision. He and Three Rains made many visits to the sweat lodge, where Three Rains used the tail of a buffalo as a ladle to splash water on the hot rocks and engulf their bodies in searing steam, all the while shaking a rattle made from a buffalo's scrotum and chanting many prayers.

Three Rains told Corby that he must not eat peyote until the vision quest was done. Three Rains had great respect for the efficacy of peyote, but vision quests achieved through peyote were too easy, too joyous. As in the days of old, a real vision quest must be accomplished through an ordeal of fasting and pain and sleeplessness.

"And you must not follow any of the girls into the bushes until you have accomplished your quest. There will be plenty of time for that when you come back. Then you will be a man, with a new name, and will want a lodge of your own and a wife to warm your bed and cook your food."

The month of preparation passed very quickly for Corby, and as the time of the full moon of March drew near, he was escorted to Medicine Bluff by Three Rains and two lesser medicine men, who, after doing a dance around a fire at the top of the bluff, gave him his last food and water. They took Big Red with them when they left.

As Corby stood motionless on the bluff, looking to the east while the sky grew light and the sun came up, his ordeal began. He looked into the sun as it climbed into the brightening sky, and by midmorning he felt as if his eyeballs were going to explode. It was all he could do to keep looking, even through eyes squinted so tightly that only a little of the fiercely bright light got through, and by noon his whole head seemed ready to burst with pain. His legs became so weak that he could hardly stand. Yet he went on staring and standing and silently chanting prayers.

With the occasional relief of some high clouds scudding across the sky, and with more determination than he thought himself capable of, he managed to fulfill his first requirement. He remained standing and looked at the sun until it went down.

Although blind from the fire and pain raging in his eyes and head and scarcely able to move on his shaky and cramping legs, he then crawled down the steep rocky face of the bluff to the entrance of the Cave of the Ancient Ones, carrying the parfleche that contained all the ritual paraphernalia he would need for his quest.

Following Three Rains's instructions exactly, he stopped in the entrance of the cave and turned around and around in a dizzying dance as he chanted a prayer, asking the Great Spirit to give him the strength to endure four days and nights without water, food, or sleep.

A few days previously a warm chinook wind had swept out of the southwest to melt the last of winter's ice and snow, warming the earth, turning the Red River into a muddy torrent, but the air inside the cave was still very chilly when Corby took off all his clothing. These—all made of buckskin, sewn with gut and hemp, so that they had nothing of the white man about them—he folded and placed like an offering in front of the sacred wall carvings. On top of the clothes he placed his only weapon, a hunting knife in a fringed and beaded sheath.

Next he built a small fire in which he burned braided sweet grass and crushed sage. He stood above the flames and caught handfuls of the purifying smoke to rub over his naked body.

Among the other ritual items in the rawhide parfleche were four small hollowed-out sections of elk horns, stoppered with wooden plugs, containing sacred paints that Three Rains had mixed from pigments and bear grease. With these he decorated his face and body in symbolic swirls of yellow and white and black, and he marked in red the places where he would insert the wooden skewers through folds of his skin.

Shaking the buffalo scrotum rattle and blowing a shrill whistle made from the wing bone of an eagle, he began a slow shuffling dance. He danced until the fire died out, and then, on the verge of collapsing from exhaustion, groped his way to the entrance of the cave. In the light of the full moon he sat down cross-legged on some boulders that formed a ledge in front of the cave, the rocks cold against his nakedness. With his left thumb and forefinger, he took hold of the folded skin above his left breast, touched it with the point of the knife, took a deep breath, and shoved the knife through the fold.

Gnashing his teeth until his head shook with the tension, he managed to suppress the scream of pain. Nor did he cry out when he forced a wooden skewer into the wound.

That night he put a skewer through a fold of skin above the right breast. The next morning he put a skewer through a fold of skin on his left thigh, and that evening he put one through the skin on his right thigh.

The pain kept him awake. He danced to keep the wounds open and oozing blood, until he was exhausted, shivering with cold, light-headed with hunger and lack of sleep, and by the third day, when he had been without food or water or sleep for three days and two nights, his light-headedness began to grow into hallucinations.

Standing before the sacred rock drawings, he felt himself fainting, felt the world swirl into dream shapes and dream sounds, a world of spirits. Feeling himself falling, he thrust out a hand against the alabaster wall, and his hand fell exactly into the outline of the hand carved by the Ancient Ones, and looking up, his eyes fell on the scene of the giant buffalo being hunted by sticklike men with lances. Then the wall gave way, and he felt the carved hand fold itself around the shaft of a lance, and he was running, panting, shouting. He had become one of the carved stickmen, who were no longer stickmen, but burly figures dressed in furs, painted for the hunt, and the giant buffalo had become hundreds of buffalo, thousands of buffalo, stampeding, driven by the hunters. On foot, dressed in wolf-skins, crouching as they ran after the panicked prey, the hunters stampeded the animals over a cliff and into a deep ravine. The buffalo piled up in the ravine, thrashing and kicking, as others poured over the edge of the cliff onto them, until the ravine was filled with the dead and wounded animals, and when the stampede ended, the man who had once been Corby and the other wolf-disguised hunters jumped with their flintstone spears onto the mass of writhing animals to finish off the wounded ones, stabbing into hearts and jugular veins, howling with triumph as they brought forth geysers of blood, until they and the death-quivering buffalo were covered with blood, awash with blood, wading in blood.

He was standing in the river. He didn't know how he had got there. He didn't remember leaving the cave and coming to the river, but in a sudden moment of undreamed lucidity, he found himself standing knee-deep in the rolling red waters of the Red River, and he heard the river say, "I am the blood of the earth. Drink of me and be strong."

He dipped his cupped hands into the bloodred waters and drank, and then he reached down into the water and brought up from the bottom the first pebble he touched. This pebble would be the first relic in his medicine bundle.

As he was climbing back to the cave, he saw a raven perched on the limb of a buffalo currant bush. Preening, the raven dropped a feather to the ground and said, "Take that for

your medicine bundle," and Corby was pleased to have a gift
from a bird that was a messenger between the earth and the
Great Spirit in the sky. Now he would have that power for
himself.

"There is a spider's web just inside the cave," the raven
said. "You will need his power, too."

Yes, the power of the spider would be his, too, the most in-
telligent of all creatures, sharing its name—*veho*—with chiefs
and white men. He found the web just inside the cave entrance,
a web that remained from last summer, left there especially for
him. He rolled it into a tiny ball.

These relics he placed inside the beaded doeskin pouch that
had been made for him by Sings-in-the-morning, a young Comanche woman who had given it to him as he was leaving the
camp. "For your medicine bundle," she had said with a shy
smile, and now, amid the mad swirl of dreams and thoughts
that disturbed his consciousness, he thought, Yes. After this I
will want a mate.

He put the things into the drawstring pouch. Then he picked
up a stone and went to the sacred rock drawings. He wanted
for his medicine bundle a chip of alabaster from inside the
carved outline of the howling wolf. He drew back the stone
and struck the alabaster.

The wolf howled. Corby believed at first that the howl had
come from the alabaster wolf, but when he heard it howl a second time, he realized that it came from outside the cave, a
strange howl—not a howl for a mate or a howl to warn an enemy away but a howl of being hurt, a howl for deliverance.

In his next moment of lucidity Corby found himself hunting
the wolf. Naked except for the rawhide belt strapped around
his waist, on which he carried the sheathed hunting knife and
the medicine bundle, he made his way through some woolly
buckthorn bushes on the riverbank and drew near a tamarisk
thicket, whence came the strange snarling howls of the wolf.
He drew his knife before entering the thicket.

Caught in a trap was a huge white wolf, a male, no doubt
the same wolf that had led Corby to the Cave of the Ancient
Ones. A smaller white wolf reluctantly slunk away, leaving her
trapped mate to face Corby alone.

The wolf growled and lunged at Corby, only to be brought
up short by the chain on the trap on its broken rear leg.

"You are finished, my brother," Corby said. "A wolf with such an injury cannot hope to live. Even if you escaped from the trap, you could no longer hunt and would soon die."

"I know," said the wolf.

"How is it you are caught in the white man's trap?"

"The Great Spirit blinded me for a moment," the wolf said. "I am to be a sacrifice."

Suddenly elated, as if everything had become clear to him in a flash, Corby said, "The white wolf is to be my animal helper?"

"Yes, if you can release me from this worthless body. But I warn you, it will not be easy. I will fight you to the last breath."

Corby hesitated. As weak and light-headed as he was, he realized he could not overpower the wolf. The wolf was huge— probably six feet from the tip of its nose to the tip of its tail and weighed as much as Corby himself—and would fight with the ferocity of a cornered demon. So Corby had need of something more than his knife and his depleted physical strength. In this act he would need intelligence, the power of the spider, which now, by virtue of the web he had in his medicine bundle, was at his disposal and served him well by directing him to find six sticks, all about an inch thick and sixteen inches long. He stripped the knife scabbard and medicine bundle from his belt and used the belt to lash the sticks to his left hand and forearm like splints. Then, with the knife in his right hand poised to strike, he advanced on the wolf.

The wolf backed up until Corby was within the striking distance allowed by the chain, and then, snarling ferociously, it lunged. Corby used his stick-encased forearm as a shield, and true to his expectation, the wolf sank its fangs into the sticks, cracking them like bones as Corby's right hand went under the wolf's head. In one quick slashing movement he cut the wolf's throat.

With a look of surprise and horror in its eyes, the wolf released Corby's protected forearm and jerked backward. As the blood gushed from the severed jugular, the wolf stood for a moment and looked at Corby, and then its legs began to wobble, and then it crumpled onto the blood-splashed ground, and the light of life slowly faded from its eyes. Corby chanted a prayer that would let the wolf's released spirit enter his own body.

> Give me your strength, O wolf.
> Give me your cunning, O wolf.
> Give me your fierceness, O wolf.

And when he felt a shudder run through him, a sort of convulsion of ecstatic strength, he knew that the wolf's spirit had entered him, and he knew—for the first time in his life—who he was.

"I am White Wolf."

To seal the covenant, he crouched and dipped two fingers into the blood puddled beneath the wolf's head, then drew the two fingers across his forehead, overlaying the streaks of red paint with streaks of the wolf's blood. He did the same to the streaks of red paint above his breasts and on his thighs that marked the places where the wooden skewers pierced his flesh. Then he jerked the skewers out. He winced but didn't cry out. New blood trickled from the four knife wounds to mix with the wolf blood markings.

After freeing the wolf's leg from the trap, he used the chain to hang the carcass from the low limb of an ash tree, where he skinned it and then cut out the heart. Roasted over a fire, the heart would be the meat with which he would break his fast. His vision quest was over.

The sun had gone down and darkness was descending over the land as he made his way up the scree to the Cave of the Ancient Ones and then on up the face of Medicine Bluff to the top. Reaching it, he was so exhausted that he had to lie prone on the ground for a long while, panting, fighting unconsciousness, before he finally regained enough strength to struggle to his feet. By then a giant red full moon had begun to rise out of the hills on the horizon.

Now, standing naked on the edge of the bluff, he carefully draped the still-bloody wolfskin over his head and back.

"I am White Wolf," he shouted to all the spirits that inhabited the earth and sky. "From this day forward I am White Wolf."

Then he thought he heard from somewhere nearby the long howl of a wolf. At first he thought the white wolf's grieving mate had followed him, but then he became aware that it was his own voice he was hearing. Naked save for the wolfskin draped over him, he stood on the topmost pinnacle of Medicine Bluff, facing the enormous rising red disk, and pierced the darkness with the sounds of a wolf howling its mastery to the moon.

CHAPTER FORTY-EIGHT

DEXTER AND SHERIFF HARRIMAN STRODE TO SHELBY'S STUDY at Kingstree, entered without knocking, and closed the door behind them. Sheriff Harriman slapped his hat against his leg in fury and frustration.

"We got to do something," he said. "Dammit, Shelby, we got to *do* something."

Saying, "Calm down, now, Alva, getting all riled up won't help anything," Shelby moved to the liquor cabinet. He gave them each a glass, filled their glasses with whiskey, and when they had gulped the drinks, he refilled the glasses. "All right, now, sit down, tell me what happened."

With his wet pendulous lower lip trembling, Sheriff Harriman related to Shelby what he himself had recently been told over the telephone: two more of the men who had made the raid on Freedom four years ago had been killed the night before, both shot from ambush as they were returning to Blucher's sawmill, where they worked as millwrights. They had taken a buggy belonging to the sawmill and ridden into town and had some drinks in the saloon, and when they were returning—

"The fools. How many times have they been warned? And yet they get caught alone, probably drunk, on an empty road at night. . . ."

"Yeah, they got careless," Harriman admitted, reaching for

the bottle on the desk, "but, goddammit, it just ain't possible for us to go on like this, year after year, and not get careless some time or other. We got our lives to live."

"Well, it fairly amazes me," Shelby said, "that the combined forces of more than five thousand men of the brotherhood scattered across the Territory can't find one pitiful nigger and kill him."

"Well, it amazes me, too, but the fact is we've always underestimated this man. This ain't just 'one pitiful nigger' we're dealing with. This is the toughest, meanest, smartest, cold-bloodedest, most determined sonofabitch any of us've ever come up against. He must travel only at night, and he knows this country like the back of his hand, and he's got us at a terrible disadvantage because we've got our lives to live, families to take care of, jobs to do, and he just lives for one thing and one thing only: *to kill us*."

He gulped another whiskey and wiped his lips with the back of his hand.

"And here we are," he continued, "the last three men left alive of all those who raided Freedom. Which one of us is gonna be next? I get up in the morning and ask myself, 'Is it me today? Is this my day to die?' And I don't mind telling you, it's getting to me. If I thought it'd do any good, I'd quit this damned job and head for Timbuktu, but I know, sure's hell, that black bastard'd find me, just like he found Harris in Louisiana. That man's a *devil*, I tell you, and he ain't gonna stop till he's killed every one of us. Now, it seems to me we got to go to the law. We got to make that sonofabitch the most wanted man in the Territory. Put his face on WANTED posters and tack 'em up in every post office, sheriff's office, train station, put 'em on every telegraph pole in the whole damned Territory. Put it in the newspapers. With a five-thousand-dollar reward on his head, dead or alive, we'll have every lawman and bounty hunter in the Territory on his trail like the hounds of hell."

"And what if he gets taken alive?"

"He won't be. Nobody's gonna take him alive, he'll see to that himself. And if he don't, I will."

Shelby considered the proposition for a moment, then dropped his hands on his desk in a gesture of resignation. "All right. Go ahead. But make damned sure you have a good story ready for the newspapers. And make sure that black bastard never comes to trial."

The first time Rachel saw Shelby leaving the house with the valise, she called down to him from the second-story veranda and asked if he was going to be gone all night. When he said he would be back by midnight, she asked him why he was carrying the overnight bag.

"Taking a change of clothing, just in case," he had said, and rode away with his bodyguards before she could ask, "In case of what?"

Another night, after he had returned home late with the valise, she observed him taking it to the basement. The next day she went to find it, tingling with curiosity to know what was in it. But the valise was nowhere to be found among the basement's stored furniture and provisions. That left only an antique wardrobe, which was locked.

Later that day, when she and Aunt Bertha were crocheting, she asked, "What's in that old wardrobe in the basement?"

"Wardrobe? What wardrobe?" Aunt Bertha was quite ruffled by the question, then, as if recollecting: "Oh. Just some things."

"Why's it locked?"

"Locked? Why, for the same reason that all closets are locked in this house. Locks make honest servants."

But one day in March, when Aunt Bertha was down with a bad cold and had been ordered by her doctor to stay in bed for a few days, Rachel was entrusted with the ring of household keys so that she could issue the cook her daily supplies from the storeroom. Aunt Bertha had ordered that the keys be brought back to her as soon as the chore was done, but Rachel went down into the basement to the wardrobe and fumbled through the keys until she found the one that fitted.

Unlocking the wardrobe door, she paused for a moment before opening it, trembling with mingled excitement and dread, then steeled herself, and jerked the door open.

A Ku Klux Klan robe hung from a hanger. A conical hood was folded neatly on the shelf above. Both were newly starched and ironed—no doubt Aunt Bertha's handiwork. On the floor of the wardrobe was the empty leather valise.

Rachel examined the robe and hood with both repugnance

and fascination. Grotesquely gaudy, the bleached linen robe
was trimmed with scarlet silk and had scarlet half-moons and
stars and a skull and crossbones embroidered on it. It had
black silk borders, from which hung a multitude of shimmering
red tassels, and tassels decorated the edge of the mask and the
havelock, while at the peak was fastened a long flowing white
egret's plume.

Acting on impulse, she left the door of the wardrobe unlocked and returned later that day to get the costume and take
it to her room. When Shelby came home that evening, she met
him at the bedroom door dressed in the costume. She stood in
silence, facing him, allowing the costume to charge him with
deception and dishonor.

For a moment Shelby seemed too stunned to react, but then
an expression came over his face that Rachel had never seen
before. Looking into his eyes was like looking into the eyes of
a coiled rattlesnake just before it struck. She jumped back,
stumbling over the hem of the robe.

Shoving the door closed, Shelby jerked the hood off Rachel's head with such force that the cloth rasped her face as he
muttered, "How dare you? How *dare* you?"

"I dared because you lied to me, that's why."

"Get out of that robe this instant."

Hurriedly pulling the robe off over her head, she said, "You
told me you didn't belong to the Klan. You told me a barefaced lie."

"You stupid girl." He snatched the robe from her hands.

"I'm *not* stupid! And even if I was, what's that got to do
with you telling me a barefaced lie?"

"If you weren't stupid, you'd know that a Klansman takes a
sacred oath to God never to reveal to anyone that he belongs
to the Klan. 'Anyone' includes you. And if you ever again do
anything so disrespectful and foolish, I'll . . ."

Unable to decide on an appropriate punishment, he turned
and started to leave the room, the costume clenched in his
hand, but he jerked around as if on a string when Rachel, in-
furiated by her inability to defend herself against the charge of
being a stupid girl, demanded, "You'll *what*?"

"I'll do what should be done to any disobedient and foolish
child. I'll take my belt off and give you a good licking—

something your father obviously neglected to do in the past. And if you don't think I will, you just try me."

"Oh, I don't doubt you're capable of it. After all, anybody who could beat a woman to death with a bullwhip is capable of just about anything, isn't he?"

He stared at her.

"Well, it's true, isn't it? You were among those Klansmen who took that black woman off the train that night near Edmond a couple of months ago and beat her to death, weren't you? You were their leader, weren't you? Not to mention all the other people you and your Klansmen have whipped. Sure, you must be pretty good at it by now."

"You keep on, you're going to find out."

"Well, I *am* going to keep on. I'm going to keep on till I find out the truth. It was you and Dexter and your other bullyboys who burned Eula's house that night, wasn't it?"

"I'm warning you for the last time."

But she couldn't have stopped now even if she had wanted to. It was as if she were running downhill and had to keep going faster just to keep from falling. "I'm not afraid of you. Oh, I know how mean and dangerous you can be. I know what you and your Klansmen did to those colored boys from Freedom. Oh, you must be proud of yourselves, mutilating *children*. Which one of you actually did it to them? You?"

He stared at her, his nostrils flaring, his eyes narrowing.

"But you made a bad mistake when you did it to Gypsy Smith, didn't you?"

He slapped her. It was a stinging slap, not a forceful one, meant only to silence her, not to hurt her.

"You bastard!" she cried, and tried to strike him with her fists.

He caught her wrist. She tried to hit him or claw him with the other hand, but he dropped the robe and caught that hand, too, and squeezed her wrists until she cried out with pain.

"What do you know about Gypsy Smith?"

"Let me go." She thrashed against him. "Let me go, damn you."

He shook her so forcefully that her head snapped back and forth. "What do you know about Gypsy Smith?"

In the throes of a needless fury, she cried, "No more than anyone else who's heard the rumors of what you did to him.

But even if you did take his manhood, he's still probably a better man than *you*."

She didn't even see the hand that struck her, that spun her around and sent her sprawling across a chaise longue. Hearing nothing but a loud ringing inside her skull and seeing only a multitude of small exploding lights, she was unaware that Shelby stood over her and had slipped the black leather belt from his pants. But she looked up in time to see him swing the belt. She tried to scramble away, but the stinging slash across her shoulders slammed her back down, paralyzed with pain.

Then he caught her dress at the collar and ripped downward.

She cried out, struggling against him, but her kicking and cries only increased his frenzy, and by the time he had her clothes stripped away and began lashing her naked flesh, bringing the belt down with fiery stings across her legs and buttocks and back, Rachel's instinct for survival told her to cease struggling. It had become apparent by then that he wanted her to struggle, that the greater her struggle, the greater would be his excitement in subduing her.

And then, after perhaps a dozen hard lashes, the blows tapered off in frequency and force, until he stood above her, the belt dangling from his hands. He was breathing heavily.

Then she became aware that he had dropped the belt and was unbuttoning his fly in a frenzy, tearing at the buttons. She tried once more to bolt when he fell upon her, but again resistance only increased his passion. He slammed her back down, holding her by the nape of the neck, shoving her face down into the chaise's cushions, causing her to struggle in fear of suffocation, and then he penetrated her, brutally from behind, his thrusts only a continuation of the whipping.

CHAPTER FORTY-NINE

AFTER THE ASSAULT, SHELBY, WITH AN ANGER SO PROFOUND that it could only be called insane, told her, "We made a bargain. I made you my wife and gave you everything a wife could want, and you were to give me a son in return. Well, when you fulfill that bargain, you'll have my permission to leave. I'll give you money, enough to live well on for the rest of your life, but you'll give me a son before you leave here."

"You bastard, you can't keep me here against my will."

"I can do anything I damn well please."

After he was gone, she threw all his things out of the east wing apartment into the hallway. She locked the doors and wedged straight-back chairs underneath the door handles so that not even Aunt Bertha, with her abundance of keys, could come in uninvited. She took a pistol from a bureau drawer and kept it under her pillow. It was a fancy little snub-nosed .32 revolver, nickel-plated and pearl-handled, with engraved scrollwork on the barrel, a gift from Shelby. He had taught her how to use it and urged her to take it with her for self-protection whenever she went out. Now she was prepared to use it as protection against him should he try to enter her bedroom again.

She had been afraid that the barricades would only inspire him to more violence, but in the days following the assault Shelby spent very little time at home and, as far as Rachel knew, never once ventured upstairs. She assumed that he was leaving her alone to ruminate on her predicament and come to terms with it.

But remaining a prisoner at Kingstree was never one of her options. She was going to leave Shelby, of that there was no doubt. The only consideration was how to leave without incurring more violence, more trouble. By the end of the first week behind the barricades she was still undecided, though the problem seemed to be made simpler when she began spotting. At first she was alarmed, fearing that Shelby had caused her some internal injury, but it soon became clear that it was the beginning of her period, which brought her a sigh of relief. At least she would not be having a child by Shelby Hornbeck, now or ever.

When she first heard the music—or thought she heard it, for she couldn't be sure, so faint and faraway it was—she was at her petite Victorian desk, writing a letter to Melvina Rhodes in St. Louis. Her Negro maid, who, with Aunt Bertha's permission, kept the barricaded apartment supplied with food and water, had agreed to sneak the letter out of the house and mail it for her, as she had already done with a letter to Maxwell. At first she thought the music was the sad sweet song of a night bird but soon realized that it was a flute she was hearing. But who was playing it? Knowing that Shelby was away from the house for the time being, she took away the chair from beneath the handle of the door leading out onto the veranda, unlocked the door, and went out into the unseasonably warm air of the late March evening. She cocked her head and listened. The sound was coming from behind the house.

With a wave of excitement sweeping over her, she rushed down the hallway to the French doors that opened onto the south veranda overlooking the backyard and corrals and barn and outbuildings.

"Corby?" she wanted to cry out when she heard the flute coming from the general direction of the barn, but she suppressed the cry for fear of being heard by Aunt Bertha.

She tiptoed along the veranda to the outside stairway leading down to the gardens and gazebo on the east end of the house and went down the stairs as silently as possible. But once on the ground she lifted the hem of her sateen skirt and raced across the backyard toward the shrubbery whence had come the sound of the flute, and then, when she raced past an oak tree, a hand suddenly reached out and grabbed her arm and swung her around, and she found herself looking into the barbaric face of an Indian warrior. She almost cried out with fright.

"My God, is it really you?" she said at last. The wolf pelt cloak and buckskin clothes he wore reeked of smoke and sweat and death. "What're you doing here? You could get yourself shot, sneaking around here in the bushes like that. And only God knows what Shelby'd do if he found you here."

"Where is he?"

"I don't know."

Aunt Bertha's voice came from the house. "Rachel? Is that you out there? What're you doing? Who're you with?" Her darkly dressed form could be seen in the shadows on the back veranda.

Rachel shoved Corby behind the tree. "Nobody! I'm just going for a walk. Can't I even go for a walk around here without being followed?"

"I thought I saw somebody out there."

"There's only me. I'm just out for a little walk."

She watched in silence as Aunt Bertha's silhouette passed in front of a lighted window and disappeared into a briefly lighted doorway; then she whispered, "Come on. We've got to get out of sight."

She took his hand and led him hurriedly toward the barn, in which burned electric lights, the lights being a point of pride with Shelby since no other barn in Guthrie had them. The colored stableboys always turned the lights on before leaving for the day, in order to deny ambushers a convenient hiding place in a dark barn.

Rachel pulled Corby into the barn, hastily closed the door, and turned to him, smiling now. "Let me get a look at you. Well, you didn't merely stop at going back to the blanket, did you? You went all the way back to skins."

Slipping the flute into the deerskin case on his belt, Corby touched with his fingertips the discoloration around her right eye. "What happened? Did he hit you?"

"No, I bumped into something. Oh, Corby!" Putting her arms around him, she pressed her face against the begrimed buckskin shirt and felt an old comfort and joy when he put his arms around her shoulders and pulled her tightly against him. "I'm so glad to see you. But what're you doing *here*?" She pulled back so she could get another look at him. "In this wild Indian getup! Sneaking around in bushes, playing your flute! Don't you realize you could get yourself shot?"

"I went to Agency to tell your father about my vision quest, and he let me read the letter you wrote."

"Then why did you come? I told him I didn't want any help. I got myself into this mess, I'll get myself out."

"Knowing how proud and pigheaded you can be, I thought maybe it was your way of asking for help. Was I wrong?"

"Yes," she said, and then, "No," and then said, "I don't know. I could use a little sympathy, I guess, but I don't want you or Daddy getting mixed up in this. Shelby can be a dangerous man." She touched the discolored eye.

"So he did beat you."

"He did once, but he'll never do it again. I won't—" She fell silent, suddenly on guard.

They could hear the hoofbeats of a few horses and the sound of wheels on gravel approaching the barn.

"Oh, my God, it's Shelby. They're bringing the buggy into the barn. Oh, damn! What're we going to do? Come on," she whispered urgently, and clambered up the ladder to the hayloft, Corby following close behind. Once in the loft they dropped down onto a pile of hay and settled into it, listening to the men enter the barn. Shelby had gone on to the house, leaving the bodyguards to put the buggy away and tend to the horses.

It was Dexter's voice they heard first. As he and the other two men went about unhitching the blue roans, putting them in their stalls and fetching oats and giving them quick rubdowns, they talked idly, discussing guard duty schedules. When they finished, the lights went out and the door closed, leaving the barn in darkness.

Rachel whispered, "Come on, we have to get you out of here. Soon's Aunt Bertha tells Shelby she saw me out here, he'll come looking for me, and there'll be hell to pay if he catches you here."

They had to crawl on hands and knees across the hay in darkness, feeling their way toward the edge of the loft until they reached the ladder.

"You first," she whispered. "Go on! Get out of here as fast as you can."

Corby descended rapidly, but rather than dash toward the door, he waited for her at the foot of the ladder and took her in his arms as soon as her feet touched the floor.

"No," she said. "We haven't got time to—"

"Come with me, Rachel."

"What? Now? Run away with you?"

"You said in your letter that you were going to leave him. Do it now. Come away with me."

"With only the clothes on my back? Don't be crazy. When I leave here, I'm not going to run back to the reservation. I'm going to St. Louis. I have friends there. They'll let me live with them till I come to terms with Shelby. Now, come on, we've got to get you away from here before they—"

But her words were cut off when all the lights in the barn suddenly came on. Just inside the door in front of the barn stood Shelby and Dexter; the other two bodyguards came in the back door. Shelby was carrying a double-barreled shotgun. Dexter and the other two had their pistols drawn, and all the firearms were pointed at Rachel and Corby.

Approaching them, Shelby said, "What's this red nigger doing here?"

Rachel stepped protectively in front of Corby. "This 'red nigger,' as you call him, is an old friend of mine. He came to visit me. He was just leaving. Go, Corby, leave."

"Stay right where you are." Shelby gripped the shotgun as if preparing to fire. "Put your hands over your head."

Corby hesitated.

Dexter jabbed him forcefully over the kidney with the muzzle of his .44 Colt. "You heard him, get your hands up."

With three cocked Colts and a shotgun aimed at him, Corby resisted the impulse to turn around and strike Dexter. But when he raised his hands, he did it slowly and contemptuously enough to show them that he wasn't afraid.

"Leave him alone," Rachel said.

Dexter jerked the horn-handled hunting knife from its sheath on Corby's belt, flung it away onto the floor, and then checked the flute's deerskin sheath to make sure it held no weapon.

"What're you doing?" Rachel demanded of Shelby. "I told you, he's a friend of mine from the agency."

"Is he, indeed?" He plucked a piece of straw from her hair and held it for her to see. "You were in the loft awhile ago when the men came in. With this red nigger. What were you doing?"

"Hiding, of course. What else would we do, knowing how you feel about 'red niggers'?"

"Get in the house," he said to her in a scarcely audible voice. "I'll deal with you later."

"Let Corby go, and I'll—"

"Do what you're told." He grabbed her arm and flung her toward the front door with such violence that she fell sprawling across the floor.

Corby's reaction was purely automatic: he lunged at Shelby and struck him with his fist across the face, a blow that knocked Shelby backward against the buggy, and then one of the deputies—Billy Blankenship—cracked Corby on the back of the head with the barrel of his revolver, knocking him to his hands and knees. The blow wasn't forceful enough to render him totally unconscious, but it did stun and blind him for a moment, and then the men grabbed his arms and jerked him to his feet.

Frightened and furious at the same time, Rachel had scrambled to her feet but didn't know what to do. Her impulse was to run to Corby, but the look on Shelby's face stopped her. As during his assault on her, the mask of his sculpted composure fell away to reveal a fury so profound that it became a sort of insanity. A small drop of blood trickled from Shelby's nose. Slowly raising his fingers to touch the drop, he looked at the smear of blood on his fingertips.

"You *struck* me? . . . You struck *me*?" It was as if Corby had committed some sacrilege beyond comprehension. Then he said, "Tie him up."

"What're you gonna do?" Rachel demanded. "Leave him—"

Her words were cut off with a slap across the face, a stinging slap that brought instant tears to her eyes.

"I told you to get in the house," Shelby said through clenched teeth. "Now, *go!*"

Rachel made a few futile, indecisive motions before she turned and dashed out of the barn.

"Tie him to the ladder."

While Deputy Blankenship held the muzzle of his Colt to the back of Corby's head, Dexter and Harry Dahl tied his hands above his head to one of the rungs of the ladder.

Shelby leaned the shotgun against the gate of a nearby horse stall, then crossed to the tack room on the other side of the barn and brought out a coiled bullwhip.

"We're going to teach this red nigger some manners," he announced. "We'll make sure he never again has the impudence to strike a white man. Strip him."

Eagerly obeying, Harry Dahl jerked the wolfskin cape off over Corby's head. Dexter took out his pocketknife and slit the buckskin shirt from collar to tail and drew aside the flaps to leave Corby's back naked.

With the solemnity of an executioner, Shelby positioned himself behind Corby at an angle that would allow maximum effect from the whip. He took a wide-legged stance and let the whip uncoil across the floor toward Corby, measuring the distance. And then, as if to give the proceedings a semblance of legality, he said, "For the crime of striking a white man, you're going to get twenty-five lashes, nigger, and as many thereafter as it takes to teach you to stay in your place."

"You sonofabitch," Corby muttered, jerking furiously against the ropes. "If you whip me, you better kill me 'cause I'll—"

The first lash of the whip silenced him.

"I see we're going to have to show you how to talk to a white man, too," Shelby said, and brought the whip down again across Corby's back, and again, and again. All the lashes left long red welts, and some cut through the skin, laying it open like the slash of a knife. Blood trickled down his back.

His body contracted convulsively at each lash and brought from him grunts and gasps, but he didn't once cry out, and he never stopped jerking against the rope that held him to the ladder. Like a wild animal in a trap, he kicked and cursed, and his struggling caused the ropes to cut into his wrists so severely that they, too, began to bleed.

By the time he delivered the fifth lash, Shelby had begun panting slightly with excitement, and as the lashes continued, his excitement seemed to increase. By the time he reached eight, he had slowed the lashes to a pace that made it seem as if he didn't want the experience to end. By the time he reached ten lashes, Corby's back was a swollen mass of welts and cuts, covered with blood, and he was very near losing consciousness. He still had moments when he struggled like a wild animal in a trap, but those moments were becoming less frequent as the whipping continued, until finally, by the time Shelby delivered the thirteenth lash, the shock and pain had made Corby almost insensible to more.

That was when Rachel burst into the barn, brandishing the pearl-handled .32 revolver that Shelby had given her. She was holding it in both hands, as he had taught her, and she was pointing it directly at him. He had raised the whip to strike again but now held it poised above his shoulder as if paralyzed by disbelief at what he saw.

"Stop it!" she cried, approaching to within ten or twelve feet of him. "Turn him loose." Her hands were shaking, and her eyes were filmed with tears.

Not one of the three bodyguards moved except to look back and forth between Rachel and Shelby, not knowing what to make of this turn of events: Shelby's own wife, pulling a gun on him and looking as if she might use it. And Shelby himself seemed so dumbfounded that he was unable to let the men know what he wanted them to do.

"Cut him down, damn you," she cried.

Her words seemed to release Shelby from his paralysis. He turned to face her, and on his face was that look of insane anger, an anger that made him heedless of danger, contemptuous of consequences. Still holding the whipstock above his head, he advanced on her. She took a few steps backward, stumbling, bumping against the buggy, keeping the pistol pointed at him with shaking hands.

"Shelby!" she cried as a warning.

He brought the whip flashing overhead to strike Rachel on the shoulder at the base of her neck, and the pain of the lash caused every nerve and muscle in her body to contract in a cringe. So close was the sound of the whip striking and the sound of the pistol that she didn't even realize she had fired the weapon until she saw Shelby standing there with the whip dangling from his right hand, clutching his chest with his left hand, blood pouring through his fingers. It was the sight of the blood and the cordite smell of the wisp of smoke rising from her pistol that finally made her realize that she had shot him.

With his face turning the color of cold ashes, Shelby looked down at the great stain of blood spreading across the front of his white shirt as though he were totally surprised and bewildered by it, as though he were trying to figure out how it got there. Then his body began to sway ever so slightly. He dropped the whip and clutched the wound with both hands, as if trying to stop the blood that was streaming from his chest and down his shirt and pants. Then, as the swaying motion increased to a stagger, he looked at Rachel in a peculiarly pleading way. He seemed to be asking her with his eyes to take it back, to go back a moment in time and not pull the trigger, and he continued to look at her that way as he crumpled to his knees. But by the time he collapsed on the floor, all the expression, as well as the light of life, had begun fading fast from his cornflower blue eyes.

In her confusion and horror Rachel's first impulse was to rush to him, but she held back, altered by movement among the bodyguards. It was Dexter who rushed to Shelby's side and dropped to his knees, saying, "What the hell've you done? What've you *done*?"

The other two made a move toward Rachel.

"Stay where you are," she warned. "I'll shoot you. I will!"

They stopped in mid-stride, exchanged questioning glances, each looking for guidance from the other. Had Rachel been a man, she would have already been dead, but the prospect of shooting a woman—Shelby Hornbeck's wife and Dexter's sister—left them irresolute and confused. Besides, she had a gun pointed at them and was obviously willing to use it.

"He's dead," Dexter said. "You killed him."

"Oh, Jesus," Rachel moaned. "Oh, Jesus . . ."

"Rachel!" Corby called. "My knife! Give me the knife."

Rachel responded with a stiffened backbone. Keeping the bodyguards always in the periphery of her vision and always in front of the pistol, she crabbed sideways to where the horn-handled knife lay. She picked it up, then moved cautiously to Corby. She reached up and placed the handle of the knife in his hand and kept her eyes and the pistol on the bodyguards as Corby, panting and cursing, cut the rope that bound his wrists together over a rung of the ladder.

With freedom came a renewed fury. With the pieces of rope dangling from his bloody wrists, he dropped the knife and lunged for the shotgun that Shelby had left leaning against the gate of the nearby horse stall.

It was then that Deputies Harry Dahl and Billy Blankenship were finally galvanized into action. Had Corby's release revealed him to be weak and defeated, as most men would have been after such a whipping, they would have continued biding their time, waiting for more favorable circumstances to act. But when they saw Corby break loose from the ladder like a wild animal escaping from a trap, they knew they would have to risk getting shot by Rachel in order to stop Corby from getting hold of the shotgun.

Harry Dahl was the first by a fraction of a second to draw his Colt, but it had not cleared the holster when the first blast from the shotgun hit him in the chest with such force that his body was lifted into the air. Billy Blankenship managed to get his gun clear of the holster, but before he could bring it to bear, the second blast of buckshot hit him in the right shoulder, tearing away his arm, spinning him completely around, and sending him sprawling across the floor.

As soon as Corby pulled the second trigger, he flung the empty shotgun away and, in movements that were continuous and unhesitating, snatched the .32 revolver from Rachel's hands. He crossed to where Dexter still knelt beside Shelby's body. He stopped in front of him, aimed the pistol directly at the middle of Dexter's forehead, and cocked the hammer.

"Don't shoot!" Dexter begged in a small voice, cringing, holding up his hands as if to ward off the bullet. "Don't kill me!"

Corby had already begun to pull the trigger. Rachel, shaking off the shock of having seen the two deputies die, flung herself at Corby and knocked his hand aside just as the pistol fired.

"No!" she cried. "Corby, you can't do that." As Dexter whined and cringed, she grabbed Corby's arm so that he couldn't aim. "For God sakes, he's my *brother*."

Corby shoved her away and brought the pistol back to bear, but hesitated. Panting, his nostrils flaring, his face contorted with pain and fury and hatred, he looked at Dexter for a moment, and the sight of him cringing there on the floor, pleading, "Don't shoot me . . . please . . . don't shoot," caused Corby's fury to subside into disgust.

"I've always known I'd have to kill him someday," he said. "It might as well be now."

"Let him go," Rachel pleaded. "For my sake."

Corby wavered. "He may be your brother, but right now he's the worst enemy you got. He's the only witness to all this. If we let him live, he'll put our necks in a noose."

"No, no," Dexter said. "I wouldn't do that. Honest, I wouldn't."

"Shut up," Corby snapped; then to Rachel: "You'd better think about it. If he lives, he'll get us both hanged."

Rachel actually seemed to give it some thought, much to Dexter's consternation, but she finally gave the only answer it was possible for her to give: "Let him go."

Corby took a moment to think what he was going to do, then told Dexter to stand up and turn around and take off his gun belt. Dexter readily complied. Corby took the gun belt and handed the .32 revolver back to Rachel, who looked at it as if she didn't know what she was supposed to do with it. After Corby had strapped Dexter's gun belt around his own waist, he jerked the fancy .44 Colt from its holster.

"You got off lucky this time, *veho*," he said, "but if you ever cross my path again, I'll kill you. You understand? I'll kill you," and without hesitation he brought the barrel of the revolver down on the back of Dexter's head with enough force to knock him sprawling unconscious across Shelby's body.

Then he snatched up his knife and wolfskin cape, saying to Rachel, "Come on, we've got to go."

Rachel was staring fixedly at Shelby's body. She had let the .32 revolver fall from her limp hand. "Go?" she said. "Go?"

"We haven't got much time."

Like someone trying to get her bearings, she glanced absently about the barn, murmuring, "My God, Corby . . . what've we done?"

"What we had to do."

"And what—what're we going to do now?"

"What we have to do," he said, clutching her hand and dashing toward the back door. Rachel allowed him to lead her, running, out of the barn and past the paddocks and down the sloping pasture toward where Big Red was tied in a distant darkness of trees.

CHAPTER FIFTY

THEY FOLLOWED THE CIMARRON WESTWARD. AROUND MIDnight a drizzling spring rain began to fall. The moon disappeared behind the clouds and Corby could no longer see where they were going. He let Big Red pick his own way slowly in the darkness. Dawn brought a short respite from the rain, but it began again before they left the river to angle southwest toward the Glass Mountains.

It was almost midday before they reached the old trapper's cabin on one of the stair-step plateaus near the top of the caprock mountain. It was a cabin that Corby had discovered during one of his wandering sojourns into the wilderness, a cabin made of gnarled dwarf timbers and brush and adobe.

Within a few minutes they had a fire going in the rusty iron stove, fueled by a cache of dry firewood that had been left by some former occupant.

"All the comforts of home," Corby said mockingly, trying to raise their spirts a little.

While he went out to tend to Big Red, Rachel hung the wet blankets on the smoke-blackened rafters and took off all her clothes except a cotton camisole. The clothes and the wolfskin she spread out on a plank bench near the stove to steam and dry.

Corby brought the wet saddle back into the cabin and dropped it in a corner near the door. He took the saddlebags off and tossed them on the plank table.

"Something to eat in there, and a little coffee."

She unpacked the saddlebags while he undressed. Ordinarily his nakedness would have made her uncomfortable, but so desperate and unhappy was their plight that any squeamishness about a lack of modesty would have seemed absurdly out of place. Nevertheless, she was glad to have the contents of the saddlebags to inventory as a focus for her attention, though when he turned his back, she stole a glance at him, and couldn't turn away.

"Oh, your poor back," she murmured. "What can we do?"

"Make some coffee. I'll get some water."

Barefoot and naked, he took a rusty bucket from a wall peg near the door and went out to the pond. Rachel found a bundle of beef jerky in the saddlebags, as well as a small sack of dried apricots, a pint fruit jar filled with coffee, a packet of wet salt, matches in a waterproof metal container, and a tobacco sack filled with what appeared to be dried buttonlike mushrooms. Also, there were a few small elk horn containers of ceremonial paints, a tortoiseshell comb, a can of gun oil, and a cleaning rag.

When Corby returned, his hair and body streaming rain, he took the wolf pelt and tied it around his waist like an apron. "I saw some Indian turnips out by the pond," he said, and began to make coffee in a battered saucepan he took from the box of cooking utensils behind the stove. "If it stops raining tomorrow, I'll see if I can catch us a rabbit, make some rabbit stew."

Rachel had been fighting back tears ever since leaving Kingstree, but at the mention of rabbit stew, the tears overflowed. "Oh, Corby," she said, sitting down heavily on the bench that was covered with wet clothes. Leaning forward, her elbows on her knees, she hid her face in her hands. "What's going to happen to us?"

"It'll be all right. Rain's washed out our tracks. Not much chance they'll find us here. Not many people know about this place."

"Maybe not now, but they'll keep hunting till they find us." She added in a voice heavy with foreboding, "We're going to die, aren't we?"

"With any luck, we'll get to Mexico."

"And if they catch us?"

"They won't." He put another stick of wood into the stove and left the stove door open so he could stare absently into the fire. "But if they do ... Well, there's something you better know, so you'll ... well, just so you'll know. I'm not gonna be taken alive." He gave her a moment to absorb that before

he added, "I'm not gonna let them hang me." But he tried to
ameliorate the gloominess of the pronouncement by adding in
a slightly mocking tone, "The Indians, they say if a man dies
by strangling, his spirit can't get out of his body to travel to
the Spirit Land. He has to wander the earth forever."

"You believe that?"

"I'm an Indian," he said flatly, his tone no longer mocking.

Her eyes flooded with tears. "What about *me*? What am *I*
supposed to do?"

"If you want to go back, there's a ranch headquarters about
fifteen miles from here. I could take you there. They'd see that
you got back to Guthrie."

"What for? To be sent to prison?"

He didn't deny it.

"I'd rather die," she said.

Later that night, she took off her gold wedding band and
dropped it into the fire.

For the next three days the rain continued in gusty showers,
the sky was low and leaden, the cabin dark and dank. They
made a bed by gathering all the straw and corn shuck stuffing
from the cabin's old mice-gnawed mattresses and then spreading the two blankets over the mound. But sleep for both of
them was light and fitful. He was very feverish those first few
days, and his back was so stiff and sore that he could scarcely
move. When his buckskin pants dried out, he put them on and
wore them constantly, but the festering wounds on his back
wouldn't allow him to wear a shirt, and he had to lie on his
stomach when he slept. They seldom touched or spoke ten-
derly to each other during those days and nights. Their
predicament had left them in different worlds, with Corby un-
consoling and Rachel unconsolable. Both seemed to feel that
intimacy of any kind would only have complicated their troubles.

The dried apricots and jerky were gone by the end of the
second day, leaving them nothing to eat. Corby offered to go
out in the rain and see if he could catch some frogs from the
pond, but she pleaded with him not to go. She went instead.
During a lull in the rain she took a willow fishing pole and a
red flannel jig that had been stored in the rafters. She had lost
one of her shoes in the mud on the first night at the cabin

when she went outside to answer a call of nature, so now she went everywhere in her bare feet.

She caught a big bullfrog, but when she tried to roast the legs over the fire in the stove, one of the legs suddenly seemed to come alive. It contracted and then straightened out so violently that it leaped out of her hand and fell on the dirt floor. And so startled was she by the lifelike movement that she dropped the other frog leg into the fire.

"Oh, damn!" Peering down through the lid hole in the stove, she saw that the frog leg was beyond retrieval. She pounced on the remaining leg on the floor, as if she half expected it to hop away. This time she tied it to a stick of kindling with a leather thong. She held it over the fire until it was black. She offered it to Corby.

"You eat it, I'm not hungry." He stood with his naked back toward the stove, letting the scabs of his wounds soak up the healing heat.

"But I ate the last of the jerky. This should be yours. You have to keep up your strength to get well."

"Really, I'm not hungry." But he sensed her reluctance to eat the frog leg as long as he was present, so he said, "I have to go out"—the code phrase for going to the privy, had there been a privy. He left Rachel in the lantern light staring at the frog leg on the tin plate in front of her, her sight blurred by the tears that once more spilled over and trickled down her face.

But suddenly she became disgusted with her self-pity. She wiped the tears from her face with the sleeve of her soiled blouse, straightened her backbone, and snatched up the frog leg. As her fried chicken had often been in the past, the frog leg was burned on the outside and somewhat raw in the center, and it was as tough as the leg of an old game rooster, but she ate it, every bite of it. She even thought about going out and getting another bullfrog, maybe even two more, but Corby averted that plan when he returned.

"Better put out the fire for a while. I heard some shots, might be signal shots. Don't worry, they were a long way off." He dashed water into the stove. "Probably down on the river. With all this mist and clouds, it's not likely they can see our smoke, but we better not take any chances, just in case it's a posse."

"But you said they wouldn't be able to track us in the rain. . . ."

"They're not tracking us. If it is a posse, they're just poking around, hoping to stumble across us." But even as he spoke, he strapped the gun belt around his waist, then took the rifle from its scabbard and pulled back the bolt far enough to see the round in the chamber.

"Is there going to be shooting?"

"If it's a posse and they find us, yes, there'll be shooting. But you needn't be involved. I'll make sure you get a chance to give yourself up before any shooting starts." He gave her a long look of inquiry, asking her what she was going to do.

Actually, she didn't yet know what she was going to do and didn't want to think about it. The choices were too terrible to contemplate.

"I'll go outside, look around," he said.

He didn't come back until dark. By then Rachel had combed her hair, washed her face and hands and then her feet in a pan of water, then gone to bed, fully clothed.

"If it was a posse," he said, "they've holed up somewhere for the night. Go to sleep. I'm going to sit up all night."

"Then they are out there."

"No. Go to sleep."

But she couldn't sleep. Afraid that a posse with guns blazing might storm the cabin at any moment, and hungry, and guilt-ridden, and confused, she lay staring into the darkness. Hearing a mouse rustling around in the corn shucks beneath the blankets, hearing the rain dribbling off the roof, she lay on the bed in what seemed to her the very nadir of her life, trying to reconcile herself to dying.

But the sun came out the next morning, and the world was reborn. The earth steamed in the bright sun, the roof of the cabin steamed, the pond steamed. Rubbing sleepy eyes, Rachel and Corby emerged from the dark cabin and into the glittering sunlight like two animals awakening from a winter's hibernation, to behold a transformed earth. The dogwoods around the pond were in bloom, the pussy willows were putting forth their furry buds, birds sang as they built their nests, and geese in V formations were flying northward in a cloudless sky. Frogs croaked in the pond, and three deer drank at its edges.

The deer—a buck and two does—bounded away as soon as

they saw Corby and Rachel. Corby was tempted to shoot one of them but knew he couldn't risk a shot being heard.

Rachel stretched herself in the warm sun like an animal. Big Red in the brush corral nickered, anxious to be let out to graze.

"I'll saddle up and take a look around," Corby said. "But soon's I get back, I'll dig some worms. We'll have fish for breakfast."

After watching him ride down the trail that led off the plateau and into Wild Horse Canyon, she turned and went back into the cabin to get the fishing pole. If Corby could catch fish, so could she.

While she was looking around outside for something with which to dig some worms, she jumped a rabbit, a plump cottontail, and gave chase. Dashing barefoot through the grass and mud, she felt the exhilaration of a hungry savage on the hunt as she chased the rabbit here and there around the cabin, until the rabbit went to ground, disappearing into a hole behind a boulder in the bank of red clay behind the brush corral.

Rachel dropped to her knees and thrust her arm into the hole, trying to reach the rabbit, but found to her surprise that the hole was the opening to a small cavern hidden behind the boulder. She tried to wrestle the boulder away, but it probably weighed at least 150 pounds, so she had to find a pole to use as a lever, and then, after much struggling and grunting and shifting of rock fulcrums, she succeeded in moving the boulder, revealing the entrance of the tiny cavern. But instead of the rabbit, what she saw just inside the cavern was a bulging parfleche, a rawhide bag commonly used by Indians. On top of it was an Indian bow, unstrung, and a quiver of arrows.

With her heart racing, she tugged the parfleche from the hole, pushed aside the bow and arrows, and hurriedly untied the rawhide thong that held the flap. She threw the flap back, and what she saw made her gasp with wonder: a can of coffee, two cans of tomatoes, a can of peaches, as well as three watertight canisters, one filled with cornmeal, another filled with dried beans, the third filled with a mixture of dried fruits and nuts. There was also a tin lunch bucket that held a small slab of salted bacon, a box of matches, some salt, some ground pepper, a sack of tobacco, three boxes of shells for three different caliber guns, and a bar of soap.

"Come see what I've found," she said when Corby returned.

He dismounted from the blowing stallion and squatted beside the parfleche. "Somebody's cache." He picked up the bow and quiver of arrows. "Comanche. War arrows and hunting arrows both."

"There's a difference?"

"The head of a hunting arrow is perpendicular to the feathers, so it'll go through the ribs of a buffalo or a deer. On a war arrow the head is horizontal, so it'll go through a man's ribs." He looked around. "But what's a Comanche doing here? How'd you find it?"

Rachel told him about the rabbit and leaned down to look into the hole. "And there he is." The rabbit was cowering against the back wall of the hole. "You want rabbit stew for dinner?"

"No, he's a good spirit who led you to this cache. Let him go. Anyway," he continued as he examined the bow, "with this I'll have us a deer before sundown."

"What about the posse?"

"Maybe forty or fifty men camped on the river last night. Probably a posse. I saw them ride on up the river, with Arapaho outriders looking for signs." He strung the bow and notched one of the arrows on the bowstring to test its strength.

"Are we safe here then?"

"Probably safer here than anywhere else—for the time being, at least. They've probably got every lawman and bounty hunter in the Territory searching for us right now. But they'll get tired looking in a week or two and call it off. Then we can head out for Mexico."

"A week or two in this place?"

"Maybe two or three. But that won't be any problem, now that we've got this cache, will it?" He was probing to see if she had decided what she was going to do.

"Problem?" she said gloomily. "My God, we're hunted killers. What could be a problem after that?"

Corby went hunting with the bow and arrows and brought back a buck. Rachel overcame her squeamishness sufficiently to help him skin and gut it, and by the time they were through cutting it up, she didn't even mind that her hands were covered with blood. They kept only enough fresh meat to last for a few days and cut the rest into thin strips and hung the strips on a rack above the stove to dry.

Rachel also cleaned the cabin: swept and dusted, arranged the food containers on a shelf, cleaned the ashes from the stove, aired the blankets. She even washed her clothes. One day while Corby was out hunting, she took the bar of soap to the pond, stripped naked, and waded into the chilly waters to wash herself and her hair and then her clothes. Shivering, she emerged from the pond and spread her clothes out on bushes, and combed her hair as it dried in the sun. Then she lay naked in the grass and soaked up the sun and smelled the earth and felt the wonder of being alive.

Corby brought back another deer—a yearling doe this time—and Rachel not only helped him skin and clean it, she even helped him tan the hides. He staked the two hides to the ground in the yard, fur side down, and showed her how to scrape off all the flesh, then rub the hides with a mixture of deer brains and urine and wood ashes. She even contributed some urine.

"When it dries, I'll make you a pair of moccasins," he said. "We'll make a squaw out of you yet."

With a long thong from the buck's skin, she mended the slit down the back of Corby's buckskin shirt, though he still wasn't able to wear it. His back was healing fast, and he no longer had nights of fevered weakness, but the scar tissue forming on his back was still too tender for him to wear a shirt, and he still slept on his stomach.

But he wasn't in bed when Rachel woke up that morning. This wasn't surprising in itself, for he still sat up at least some part of each night, or slept with his arms folded on the table to cradle his head, or went for walks in the moonlight. What surprised Rachel this morning was the sound of his flute. It was the first time since their arrival at the cabin that she had heard him playing it. The cabin door was open, and the sunlight streamed in, bringing with it the flute sound that was very much like the sunlight itself.

She tucked in the tail of her wrinkled and torn blouse, brushed bits of straw off her skirt, ran her fingers through her hair, and went outside.

Corby was sitting on a boulder near the pond, dressed only in the wolfskin, wearing it wrapped and tied around his waist like an overlapping apron. Beside him on the rock was his rifle. He was never more than arm's length from a firearm these days.

He stopped playing when she approached.

"Don't stop. What's that you're playing?"

"A song for a—a *vessemataveanatoz*. What the whites would call a peyote ceremony."

"Peyote? You're having a peyote ceremony?"

"Sort of, I guess."

"You've taken peyote?"

"A little. It's April first, a day of worship for the Native American Church. A little like the white man's Easter, I guess."

"I want some," she blurted out, not giving herself time to think about it lest she lose the impulse to adventure. She wanted to be a child again, to be happy again. "I want to find out what you mean when you say you can *see* sounds."

"Well, since you don't belong to the Native American Church, you can't be in a peyote ceremony, but I guess I can give you some peyote, if you want, so you'll know what it's like."

It turned out that the dried mushroomlike things he carried in the tobacco sack in his saddlebags were peyote buttons. From some of these buttons he made a strong tea over a fire on the cabin stove.

"What we need is a sweat lodge," he said, stirring the concoction with a stick, "so we could purify ourselves before we take it. But since we don't have one, I guess a swim in the pond might do. We'll take the pot with us, let it steep while we bathe." Using a piece of buckskin for a potholder, he took the pot from the stove and picked up his rifle. "Bring two drinking cans."

"Yes. All right. You go ahead. I'll be right out." She hung back, needing a moment to adjust to what was happening. She had bathed a few times by herself in the pond, always naked, but if she and Corby were going in together, should she be naked? Well, she certainly couldn't go in with all her clothes on. So she stripped down to her camisole and then wrapped one of the blankets around her, all the while savoring the feeling that something significant was about to happen.

Corby was already in the water, standing in the deepest part of the pond, almost up to his breasts, his face tilted upward, his eyes closed, as if he were saying a prayer.

Leaving the two rusty tin cans on the boulder next to the pot of peyote, Rachel went to the edge of the pond, dropped the blanket, and waded into the water, still wearing the camisole.

"Take that off," he said, and when she gave him a questioning look, he added, "This's supposed to be a purification bath," implying that both her camisole and her modesty were inappropriate to the ceremonial nature of the act.

"Oh. Well, then, turn your head."

But he had already tilted his face toward the sky again, as if he had more important things to do than see her nakedness.

She jerked the camisole off over her head, tossed it aside, and dived into the pond. The chill of the water was invigorating and impelled her into a swim across the lily-padded pond, but she stopped when she saw Corby lift his hands toward the sun. Then he began chanting in Cheyenne. And once again Rachel was struck by how Indian he had become, how serious he had become about things spiritual.

He finished the chant by splashing water over his head, then sloshed out of the pond, purposeful and strong, his bronze skin gleaming wetly in the sun, drops of water draining crookedly over the scars on his back. He tied the wolfskin around his waist like an apron and retrieved the rifle before going on up the bank to the boulder and the peyote pot.

While his back was turned, Rachel dashed out of the water and wrapped herself in the blanket, dried herself with it, and then joined him. She accepted the tin can filled with the dark brown dreggy-looking tea, which proved to taste as bad as it looked. She almost gagged on the first few swallows. It was what she imagined hot muddy swamp water would taste like. But Corby didn't seem to share her aversion, so she assumed it was something you got used to, though she was afraid that her growing queasiness might become outright nausea at any moment.

"Sometimes you might get a little sick," he said. "So if you can't hold it down, don't worry, we can always make some more."

But the thought of drinking more of the muck furnished her with the willpower to keep this dose down. When her gorge threatened to rise, she clenched her teeth, stiffened her backbone, and invited the tea to do its damnedest, she would *not* get sick.

"Sometimes it helps to move around a little," he suggested.

So she, hugging the blanket around her, moved about aimlessly for a while, stopping for a moment here or there to look at a dogwood blossom or a sumac bush, a bird, a cloud, or a blade of grass, but mainly concentrating on not becoming sick, and she soon found that her nausea was indeed abating, and then she began to feel the first tingling sensations of the peyote. It was as if little shivers of energy were spreading through her body, transforming her aimless movements into a sort of formless dance.

Corby played the flute again. He had sat down on the pond's grassy bank and begun playing what seemed to be random notes, following no tune at all, which was just right for Rachel's formless little dance.

"I'm feeling something," she announced. She stood still, taking stock. The tingling sensation wasn't at all like the dizziness produced by champagne. It had no effect on her coordination. But it did have an effect—a profound effect, as she soon learned—on the acuteness of her perceptions. Colors, for instance: never had she seen colors so vividly. Never had the blue of the sky, the yellow of a wild daffodil, the white of a dogwood blossom shimmered with such brilliance. It was as if her eyes had suddenly been opened and she were seeing colors for the first time. Then, stranger still, she began to see that colors had sounds, and sounds had shapes.

These were not things she could have described in words, because they were beyond the compass of words, experiences and sights for which words had never been invented, perceptions for which her senses were not prepared. The color yellow became a joyous cry, and that joyous cry became a bird, and the bird became air, and the air became sunlight, and sunlight became a daffodil, and the daffodil . . .

"My God," she murmured. "It's endless." She ran to Corby and sat down beside him on the grass. "Corby." He stopped playing the flute. "Corby," she said, "everything is *connected*."

"Yes."

And then, more astonishing still, she went on to see that not only was everything connected, everything was in harmony with everything else. All her life she had taken it for granted that the flight of a crow, say, and the flutter of a leaf were random and disconnected happenings, but now she saw that there was a harmony in all things. It was as if every sound, every color, every moment, every rhythm and shape were synchronized, as if every bird and rock and stream and tree and mountain and cloud and blade of grass, as if all, all were players in a gigantic symphony orchestra of Being.

"Corby!" she cried with the joy of revelation. "Everything . . . is . . . *everything is everything.*"

Corby was amused by the delight she felt in her discoveries, and as always, ever since they were children, he was pleased with her capacity to lose herself so completely in an experience, an adventure. And so completely had she lost herself in this experience that she failed to notice, or didn't care, that the blanket had fallen from her shoulders, leaving her naked.

CHAPTER FIFTY-ONE

HE DIDN'T SAY THAT HE HAD ALWAYS LOVED HER AND ONLY her, but she knew that was what he meant when he said, "You're the only one," and she confessed that she had never loved anyone else and had loved him most during those times when she was trying to put distance and time and another love between them. But now the battle was over. Doomed now, what did they have to lose?

But Rachel not only reconciled herself to the predicament in which fate had placed them, she finally said yes to it, welcomed it, loved it. It was as if she had been lost for years and finally found herself in a place where she had always wanted to be: in Corby's arms, on the earth, making love. Nothing else mattered. Let them be outcasts, let them be hunted fugitives, she no longer cared, as long as they were together. And if and when the hunters ran them down—

"We'll die together," she said.

But they didn't often speak of dying, though they did live every day as if it were their last. During the three weeks that they stayed in the cabin, lovemaking very nearly became an obsession with them. Sometimes it was done with trembling tenderness, sometimes with a sort of playful joy, sometimes with lustful abandon, depending on the mood at the moment, in which they shared an uncanny mutuality.

They went naked most of the time and slept outside at night, making their bed in different places around the plateau. This was partially a precaution against being taken by surprise by a posse, but it was also a matter of choice. Corby preferred sleeping outside, and Rachel found a new delight in making love under the stars.

They took peyote once more during their time at the cabin, and the experience proved to be as fascinating to Rachel as the first one had been, and even more fun. They went riding bareback, both of them naked. She rode behind him, her hair streaming in the wind as Big Red galloped across the caprock mountain. They laughed aloud with delight at the way their naked bodies moved in unison on the bare back of the bay stallion.

It was that day that Rachel decided she wanted to become an Indian. They were back at the cabin and she was trying on the moccasins he had made for her.

"Not very fancy," he said, "but they're double-soled, so they'll last till we get to Mexico anyway."

Naked except for the moccasins, she moved about the cabin. "Now if I only had a deerskin dress, I'd be a squaw."

"You think that's all it takes? Just clothes?"

"What does it take? I'd like to become an Indian. I'm serious, Corby, I would. Can't you adopt me into the tribe or something? Give me an Indian name?"

"Maybe. But the first thing you'd have to learn is that Indians attach a lot of meaning to a name."

"I know that."

"Then why do you keep calling me Corby? I've told you my name's White Wolf. I'm no longer Corby. A vision quest is a serious thing. If you had to go through it, you'd know. So the name given by the Spirits should be respected."

"You're right," she said, triumphantly chastising herself.

"You're absolutely right. And from now on—cross my heart— I'll make a very special effort to remember. White Wolf, White Wolf, White Wolf. But I hope you won't blame me," she added, moving to him and putting her arms around his neck, "if I forget and call you Corby while we're making love."

Neither of them wanted the idyll to end, but there came a day when their supplies were running low, and Corby—White Wolf—said they had better start for Mexico.

"Somebody's bound to stumble on to us here, sooner or later, and the posses are probably no longer beating the bushes for us. We'll still have to travel mostly by night, at least until we reach Texas, but we've probably got a pretty good chance. I'll see if I can get us another horse somewhere."

He thought he might be able to steal a horse or two from the Blondell Ranch headquarters, which was about fifteen miles southwest of the Glass Mountains. And it was while he was on his way to the ranch, dressed in his buckskins, with the .44 Colt strapped to his side and the rifle in its saddle scabbard, that he came across a fresh set of hoofprints about a quarter mile south of the cabin. The hoofprints appeared to be those of a shod mule, traveling west.

He swerved from his own path to follow the tracks. When he came to some scattered droppings, he crumbled them in his fingers. They were between twenty-four and thirty-six hours old. Then he found what he dreaded to find: a place where the tracks veered almost due north, in the direction of the cabin. He put Big Red into a lope, needing only a glimpse now and then of the mule's hoofprints to keep on the rider's trail. He was within sight of the cabin when he found the place where the rider had stopped. It didn't take him long to read the signs to know what had happened: probably hearing a sound from the direction of the cabin, the rider had dismounted, tied his mule to a blackjack tree, and climbed a small rise of rocky ground to hide behind some buckthorn bushes. From the same spot White Wolf saw Rachel swimming in the pond. He jumped up and dashed to the tree where the mule had been tied. Quickly he found the hoofprints leading away from the area, headed southeast. He leaped into the saddle and sent Big Red plunging down the slope toward the pond.

When Rachel saw him, she hurried out of the pond, her

suntanned nakedness streaming water, and met him on the bank.

"We've been spotted." He swung down from the saddle before Big Red came to a full stop. "One man, on a mule. He was laying up there sometime yesterday, watching us. Probably guessed who we are, or else he'd've come on down to water his mule, being this close. We've got to get a few of our things together and get out of here." He looked at the sun and calculated aloud: "Figure he was here yesterday morning and lit out for Kingfisher or Guthrie. Got there last night maybe. Couldn't get a posse together at night, so they probably left this morning. If they came fast, it'd put 'em here about anytime now. Let's grab a few things and go."

He tied Big Red to a post near the door of the cabin and jerked the rifle from the saddle scabbard before he went in. Rachel quickly got dressed in her rumpled and tattered camisole, blouse, and skirt. White Wolf grabbed his saddlebags and began stuffing them with jerky and boxes of ammunition and whatever other odds and ends of his possessions or foodstuffs he had room for, while Rachel folded the blankets and the wolfskin. Then they heard the voice.

"Hello, the cabin!" It was a man's voice, calling from a distance.

White Wolf grabbed the rifle. The cabin door stood open to let in the light of the lowering sun. White Wolf kicked it closed, then pressed against the wall and opened the door far enough to give him a field of vision that included the trail approaching the cabin from the direction that the voice had come, and now came again.

"Hello, the cabin, I'm coming in. Hold your fire. I'm a friend."

White Wolf aimed the rifle through the opening of the door toward the spot where a rider, coming up from Wild Horse Canyon, would gain the edge of the plateau and ride into view.

The man who did so, riding a big blaze-faced sorrel, was a black man.

"That's far enough," shouted White Wolf, his rifle aimed at the middle of the man's chest. "Who are you? What d'you want?"

The rider pulled up and raised his right hand in the Indian gesture of peace. "Gypsy Smith!" he called. "I bring news."

"You alone?"

"All alone."

"Come on in."

Rachel had been terror-stricken when she first heard the voice, but now she dashed to the door to get a look at the approaching figure.

"My God, it *is* him. It's Gypsy Smith."

White Wolf used the rifle to push the door open all the way. Relieved but still cautious, he waited until Gypsy reached the cabin before he and Rachel stepped out to greet him. And though they did recognize him, it wasn't the Gypsy Smith they had last seen over four years ago. He was gaunt now, almost skeletal, with a beard in which there were streaks of gray. He wore a plain dark worsted suit, not the flashy Comanche garb he used to wear, and a farmer's dark Sunday hat. He could easily have passed for a well-off middle-aged farmer, except for the sleek horse he rode and the many weapons he carried: in one saddle scabbard was a Winchester rifle, in another scabbard was a Sharps buffalo rifle, and on his person he carried two .44 Colts in hip holsters.

"Howdy. Long time no see." He leaned down to shake hands with White Wolf, touched the brim of his hat to Rachel. "Miss Rachel."

"News?" White Wolf said anxiously. "What news?"

Dismounting, Gypsy said, "There's a posse on its way here, 'bout four hours behind me. Marshal Renfro and maybe sixty men."

"Four hours?" White Wolf asked. "You sure?"

"I got pretty reliable sources of information. Seems you was spotted yesterday by somebody who's looking to collect that thousand-dollar reward."

"A thousand dollars?"

"You didn't know? You been hiding out here ever since you left Guthrie?" At White Wolf's nod, Gypsy said, "Yeah, you're worth a thousand, dead or alive."

"How about me?" Rachel asked.

"You?" Gypsy asked, tilting his head with puzzlement. "What about you?"

"How much reward did they put on my head?" she asked, as if it might conceivably be a matter of status.

"Reward?" Gypsy tilted his head the other way, as if seeing

it from another angle might help him understand. "You mean, ransom? Last time I heard, they hadn't received no ransom note."

"Ransom?" she said. "What d'you mean, 'ransom'?"

"Let's talk inside," White Wolf said, "so we can be getting our things together."

Looping the sorrel's reins over the hitching post beside Big Red, Gypsy followed White Wolf and Rachel into the cabin.

White Wolf snatched the parfleche off a rafter and dropped it on the table, saying to Rachel, "if we've got four hours, we better take time to pack the rest of the food. We're gonna be needing it."

Gypsy was watching them closely, tilting his head with puzzlement. "Ah," he said then, noticing the parfleche and the canisters they had begun shoving into it, "I see you found my cache."

"Yours?" Rachel said, and stopped packing.

"We didn't know," White Wolf said. "If I'd known . . ."

"Forget it." Gypsy moved to see the stove and touched the coffeepot for warmth. "In your place I'd've done the same thing." He took a tin can cup from off the shelf behind the stove and half filled it with the dregs of the lukewarm coffee. "But looky here, maybe you'd better let me in on what's happening. I come to warn you"—speaking to White Wolf— "about the posse and to help you get away if you want me to. And I must admit I was gonna try to talk you into letting Miss Rachel go. From the way things look, though," he said to Rachel, "I gather you wasn't kidnapped?"

"Kidnapped?" she said.

He sipped his coffee. "According to all the stories in the newspapers, Corby kidnapped you."

"That's ridiculous."

"According to the newspapers, he came to your house, killed your husband and two deputy sheriffs, then dragged you kicking and screaming away with him."

Rachel and White Wolf exchanged puzzled glances, and then she said, "That's not true. I'm the one. I killed Shelby. I didn't mean to," she added quickly. "I mean, I had a gun trained on him, and when he hit me with a whip, the gun went off. I didn't mean . . . Anyway, I'm the one that shot Shelby, not Corby—White Wolf—and I'm here with him because it's where I want to be."

"White Wolf?" Gypsy said, and White Wolf told him that he had been on a vision quest and now had a new name. Gypsy nodded. He knew the Indian custom and honored it. "In any case," he said to Rachel, "it was your brother who gave out the story."

Rachel and White Wolf once again exchanged puzzled glances. "Dexter!" she said. "Why would he lie?"

Gypsy shrugged. "Beats me, but from what I gather, he was the only eyewitness, and that's his story." After another sip of coffee he said, "Anyway, we'd better get going. You've only got the one horse? Well, if you want to ride with me, I'll take the parfleche on my horse. We'll head south for the Red, where I have another cache. Maybe we'll steal another horse along the way if we can do it without calling attention to ourselves. If not, I know some Comanches down on the Red who'll sell us a couple. From there we'll head out to Mexico."

"That's where we planned to go," White Wolf said, delighted with the prospect of having Gypsy Smith for company.

"We'll go together, then, if you want to. Have to travel mostly at night till we get to the Red. With you riding double, it'll take four, five nights of hard traveling. Maybe six."

"But why're you doing this for us?" White Wolf asked. "I mean, coming all this way to warn us about the posse? And willing to help us escape?" He handed the parfleche to Gypsy, then grabbed the saddlebags.

"Well, I was headed out for Mexico, anyway, when I heard about you two being up here, and I figured I owed you a favor." When they responded with only stares, he added, "For killing Shelby Hornbeck. But," he continued to Rachel, "you might've saved y'self the trouble. He didn't have long to live anyhow."

"I've heard you have a list," she said. "Was Shelby on it?"

"At the top."

"And Dexter? He's on it, too?"

Leading them out of the cabin, Gypsy secured the parfleche to the bedroll behind his saddle. "He's probably with the posse that'll be chasing us, and he won't know I'm riding with you. I 'spect Dexter'll have a little surprise in store for him if they catch up with us."

White Wolf put the saddlebags over Big Red's withers. Then, securing the blankets behind the saddle as a riding pad for Rachel, he said, "With us riding only at night, they're bound to catch us."

"Maybe not." Gypsy swung up into the saddle. "I got a way to throw 'em off our track for a couple of days."

Mounting, White Wolf reached down to catch Rachel's arm and swing her up behind him.

"In any case, though," Gypsy said, "figure on five or six nights of hard riding, with cold camps in the daytime, to get to the Red." He looked at Rachel. "You up to that, Miss Rachel?"

Getting comfortable on the blanket pad behind the saddle, she put her arms around White Wolf's waist, and said, "I'm up to anything."

Gypsy tipped his head with admiration. "Let's go then."

CHAPTER FIFTY-TWO

BECAUSE OF THE BLOWING SAND, A PERSON COULD WALK through the Little Sahara without leaving tracks. It was almost like walking through water. Headed northwest, they crossed the Cimarron and entered the Little Sahara about midnight. To save the horses, they dismounted and walked them, struggling and plunging, through the deep sand. At White Wolf's instructions, Rachel held on to Big Red's tail and was half pulled through the dunes.

While still in the desert, they turned due south and came out on the Cimarron near Slocum's Crossing, where a wooden bridge spanned the river. They recrossed the river and rode south on the road for a couple of hours, mingling the hoof-prints of their horses with those already in the dust, and then left the road and angled eastward across an area of open range.

"That ought to buy us a couple of days," Gypsy said. "With

any luck, they'll figure you two are heading for No Man's Land. Time they find out different, we'll be halfway to the Red."

About an hour after dawn they went into a dry gully to make a cold camp and spend the day hidden in a clump of post oak trees. They ate jerky and a few dried fruits and drank from a canteen. They spread their bedrolls in the thin shade of the small trees and got some sleep, with Gypsy and White Wolf taking turns at lookout duty, four hours on, four hours off. The horses were unsaddled and tethered on lariats within the clump of trees and allowed to forage on whatever vegetation came within reach of the ropes, which wasn't much, nor did they get any water except when Gypsy poured some from his canteen into his hat and let each of the horses have a swallow. They left at dark.

On the second day Gypsy took his binoculars and climbed to the peak of a small ridge to have a look at the terrain behind them. White Wolf and Rachel spread their bedroll under a mesquite tree.

"I been thinking," White Wolf said. They were on their hands and knees, feeling around to make sure there were no small stones under their blankets. He sat back on his heels. "I been thinking that ... well, since you're not a fugitive ... I mean, since they think it was me that killed your husband, and that you were kidnapped ... well, don't you see? You could wait here for the posse, and say you escaped, and go back to your old life."

She crawled across the blanket and took both his hands in hers. "Cor—White Wolf." She, too, sat back on her heels, their knees touching. "Listen to me, my love. I have no life to go back to. It's you and me now. All we've got is each other now, now and forever, you and me."

"But if they catch us ... like I said, I won't be taken alive, and Gypsy won't either, so ... Well, there's no need for you to ... And if I made it to Mexico, I could send for you."

"And if you didn't make it?"

He shrugged. "I'd be dead."

"And I wouldn't want to live," she said without hesitation or doubt.

On the third night of traveling, they crossed the South Canadian River; on the fourth night, the Washita River. And though they were now on the Comanche-Kiowa-Apache reservation, they still kept to back roads and wilderness trails and skirted all human habitations, making their way by the light of a waxing three-quarter moon, on and on, night after night, across open-range prairies and over hills and through valleys and woods and along dry washes, until the horses, deprived of sufficient forage and water, began to show signs of exhaustion.

"We'll let 'em rest up for a day or two after we get to the Red," Gypsy said, gnawing on a piece of jerky. "And we'll treat ourselves to a hot meal, too. I got a pretty good cache put away in a cave down there. We'll cook us up some beans and coffee and fried biscuits. Maybe even open a can of peaches for dessert."

"What cave?" White Wolf asked with more than idle curiosity.

"Medicine Bluff Cave. Indians call it the Cave of the Ancient Ones. You know it?"

"Know it! That's where I had my vision quest."

Gypsy and White Wolf were hunkered down on the creek bank at the edge of the water. Gypsy's hat was pushed back on his head, revealing on the right side of his forehead the bump made by the metal plate in his skull and the jagged scar tissue that covered it, revealing also the streaks of gray that had appeared in his hair. In one hand he held his canteen burbling beneath the surface of the water, in the other he held the strip of jerky. With his gray-streaked beard and gaunt face and eyes that had the depthless look of ashes, he appeared much older than his forty-seven years.

"That so?" he said, gnawing on the leathery jerky. "Well, it's always been a sacred place for Indians. That's why it makes a good hideout, none of 'em come around, 'cept to make medicine."

They both remained hunkered down near the water even after their canteens were filled, enjoying a moment in the morning sun, enjoying the stillness of their bodies after a hard night's ride. Rachel had waded out into the slowly flowing creek, still wearing her tattered cotton blouse and soiled sateen skirt, until the water was up to her shoulders. The horses, having satisfied their thirst, nuzzled the water with pendulous lips, and snorted, and began looking around for some grass.

"Say," Gypsy said then, struck by a sobering thought, "you didn't by any chance find *that* cache, too?"

"No. But I couldn't have used it even if I had. I was fasting."

Gypsy stood up, flexed his stiff shoulders, and looked with distaste at the last bite of jerky in his hand.

"Well, I ain't never done no deliberate fasting, but I know how you must've felt. I'm so hungry right now my stomach thinks my throat's been cut." He ate the last of the jerky and screwed the lid onto his dripping canteen. "With any luck we'll be there by day after tomorrow. Get some hot food. Get a good night's sleep, too, maybe."

He hung the canteen over his saddle horn and swung into the saddle. Rachel started coming out of the water.

"Stay and bathe if you want to," he told them. "I'll go on and make camp." And in a tone that signaled a change from idle conversation to important information, he said, "Just around the next bend in the creek yonder there's a draw, on the right side. Follow it to its head. That's where I'll make camp."

As Gypsy rode away, White Wolf led Big Red to a nearby patch of green bluestem grass and put a hobble on his front legs. He removed the bridle and turned the stallion loose to graze.

Rachel was the first to take off all her clothes, and White Wolf eagerly followed her lead. He dropped his begrimed buckskins on the creek bank and went naked into the water. Rachel washed the clothes in the creek, spread them over buffalo currant bushes, then went back into the creek.

They swam, splashed each other with water, and embraced, and kissed. Then they swam across the creek to the west bank, where there grew a stand of persimmon trees interlaced with tangled wild grapevines. They found a bower among the trees and vines that concealed them from the world.

An old wrangler from Fort Sill called Coot was searching for some runaway army horses when he came across the fresh hoofprints left by White Wolf's and Gypsy's horses. He followed the tracks down to Beaver Creek, where he saw Rachel and White Wolf cavorting together in the water. At first he thought it was just some Indian and his squaw having a bath, but when he sneaked closer and saw that Rachel was a white woman, he guessed who they were.

For the last three or four weeks nearly every newspaper in Oklahoma Territory had been carrying the story, in pictures and front-page headlines, about the murder of one of the Territory's most important men and the abduction of his wife by a renegade redskin.

This much was understood by Coot, the wrangler from Fort Sill, but what he didn't understand was what he saw with his own eyes: the two of them hugging and kissing and going off naked into the bushes. If she was a prisoner, she certainly seemed to be a very happy and willing one. There was more going on here than had been reported in the newspapers.

And Coot found a corollary mystery in the horses. He had been tracking two horses. Here was one, a bay, hobbled, feeding near the creek, but where was the other one? And when they came out of the water and got dressed and rode away, riding double on the bay, Coot guessed that there was a second rider around somewhere.

In the interest of collecting some reward money, Coot made a fast ride back to Fort Sill, where he went into the U.S. deputy marshal's office and checked the bulletin board. There he found a brand-new WANTED poster with the Indian's picture on it. The message on the poster announced that Corby White was wanted for murder and abduction, and a thousand-dollar reward would be paid for information leading to his capture, dead or alive. There was a warning that the fugitive should be considered armed and dangerous.

"That's him," Coot said.

A bulletin went out over the telegraph to all the law enforcement offices in the area to be on the lookout for the renegade and his white woman captive, Mrs. Shelby Hornbeck.

"Only she didn't look too much like a captive to me," said Coot to Clovis Pinkard, the deputy U.S. marshal stationed at Fort Sill. When pressed on his meaning, Coot allowed as how the two of them were carrying on mighty friendly, swimming naked together, and kissing, and suchlike.

A reporter from the *Oklahoma City Daily Democrat* was at Fort Sill at the time. After hearing Coot's story, he immediately wired a dispatch to his newspaper, saying that the renegade Cheyenne killer and Mrs. Shelby Hornbeck—"reportedly a kidnap victim"—had been spotted about twenty miles from Fort Sill. This news was sufficiently sensational to make headlines in most of the newspapers in Oklahoma, but the real sensation of the story lay in the hint that according to the man who spotted the fugitive, the kidnap victim might not be an entirely unwilling one.

The word reached U.S. Marshal Silas Renfro in the cattlemen's town of Woodward, near Fort Supply, where he and his posse had been waiting for just such a break. They had lost the fugitives' trail in the Little Sahara and hadn't been able to find it again. On receiving word that Corby White had been spotted, the marshal loaded his posse onto a train—the horses in livestock cars, the men on flatcars—and headed for Fort Sill.

Among the posse were Sheriff Alva Harriman and Deputy Dexter Bingham, both of whom had been sworn in as deputy U.S. marshals in order to legitimize their presence in the posse. Both were in the small group of posse leaders who, after detraining at Fort Sill, met in the office of Deputy U.S. Marshal Clovis Pinkard. Coot showed them on a wall map where he had spotted the redskin and the woman captive.

"But like I said to Deputy Pinkard here," Coot said to Marshal Renfro, "I'm considerable suspicious that the woman ain't being held agin her will. The way they was carrying on? Kissing, and hugging, and going off in the bushes together, naked as the day they was born? Didn't seem to me—"

Dexter snapped, "Whatever my sister's doing, she's being forced to do."

Coot tipped his head to Dexter. "If you say so."

"There's two more posses on the way," Deputy Pinkard said to fill the strained silence. Tapping his finger on the map, he continued. "One's coming from Duncan. About twenty men. They headed southwest, trying to get ahead of 'em. Another's forming in Wichita Falls, led by Texas Ranger Cole Tucker. They're gonna move up here, where Beaver Creek empties into the Red. They'll make sure they don't cross the river into Texas. We got 'em boxed."

"Looks like," said Marshal Renfro, idly fingering his long drooping frontiersman's mustache, which was completely gray, a whitish gray that matched the ice gray of his eyes. "Well, then, let's go get 'em."

CHAPTER FIFTY-THREE

ON THE MORNING OF THE FIFTH DAY, JUST BEFORE WHITE Wolf was due to relieve him as lookout, Gypsy, from his vantage point on a rocky ridge, saw through his binoculars a small thin cloud of dust rising in the distance. When White Wolf came to relieve him, Gypsy handed him the binoculars and pointed toward the dust.

"Posse?" White Wolf asked, studying the dust through the binoculars.

"Either that, or a bunch of Indians, or maybe a troop of cavalry out of Fort Sill. Whoever it is, though, they're coming this way and moving at a pretty good clip. Fresh horses, likely."

"Wouldn't be Renfro's posse then," White Wolf said. "By now their horses'd be as jaded as ours."

"Maybe," Gypsy said, taking the binoculars back. "But if we was spotted along the way, it might be a new posse." He swept other areas of the northern horizon with the binoculars. "And if that's the case, there'll be other posses showing up pretty soon, getting in on the chase."

"There." White Wolf pointed to a place on the eastern horizon where another thin cloud of dust had begun to rise from a depression in the land maybe ten miles distant.

Gypsy trained the binoculars on the dust. This time he could see the men and horses as they rode up out of the depression and onto the skyline. They were too far away to identify, but they didn't seem to be soldiers or Indians.

"Looks like another posse, all right. Big one. By God, *navestax*, they must want you pretty bad. Or by now they might know I'm riding with you. Well, I reckon we gonna have to make a run for it."

No longer concerned about being seen, they now kept their

horses to the open roads and trails as they rode in a long-striding lope, following Beaver Creek in a southeasterly direction. At one point they walked their horses in the creek for perhaps a quarter of a mile, then came out of the water on some rocks and turned away from Beaver Creek, headed in a southwesterly direction, toward the Red River's Horseshoe Bend.

When they crossed over Kiowa Ridge, they stopped behind some boulders to give the horses a rest. Gypsy scanned the country behind them with his binoculars. He watched Marshal Renfro's posse come together with the posse from Duncan. Combined, the two groups formed a posse of sixty or sixty-five men. But it was the five or six Arapaho tracker scouts that worried Gypsy.

"Damned good, those trackers," he muttered with grudging tribute when he saw them find the horseshoe marks on the rocks that Gypsy and White Wolf's horses had made when they came out of Beaver Creek. "And here they come," he added with a weary sigh. He glanced back at their two lathered and fatigued horses, appraising their condition. Big Red, having carried a double load, seemed to be in slightly worse shape than the sorrel, but neither of them seemed to have enough strength left to outrun the posse's fresh horses for another ten miles, which was about how far it was to the Red River—not that they had much hope of escaping, even if they did reach the Red River. But if they could get to the supplies and food Gypsy had cached in the Cave of the Ancient Ones, they could at least make a stand, maybe buy some time.

"Well, we better get going," Gypsy said to White Wolf and Rachel, but he raised the binoculars for one more look at the oncoming posse, and what he saw brought grim satisfaction to his voice when he said, "Well, well, what d'you know about that! I do believe that's Sheriff Harriman with 'em. And, bless my soul, is that Deputy Dexter Bingham riding next to him?" To Rachel: "What kind of horse is Dexter riding these days?"

Rachel had to think for a moment. "He's got two or three, I think, but most of the time he rides a piebald."

And still in that tone of grim satisfaction, Gypsy said, "Looks like it might be him all right." He returned to his horse and replaced the binoculars in their case. "The river's about an hour away, and they're about twenty minutes behind. To beat 'em, we'll have to ride flat-out all the way. Think your horse can do it?"

"He'll give it everything he's got," White Wolf said, patting Big Red's fatigue-trembling shoulder.

They began the long run off Kiowa Ridge down into the Red River basin, following an old Indian trail, with Gypsy in the lead on the sorrel and Big Red close behind. White Wolf was leaning forward to lower wind resistance, and Rachel, with her arms around his waist, hung on tightly as they plunged along the twisting trail, through gullies and ravines and across pastures, the horses' hooves clattering on rocks and thundering on turf.

Once they came around a corner and almost collided with a Mexican on a burro coming from the opposite direction. Had the Mexican been riding a horse, Gypsy would have stopped and taken it, but a burro would do them no good, so they rode on, leaving the startled Mexican in their dust.

The Mexican had hardly recovered from the start of the near collision when he began to hear the thundering hoofbeats of many, many horses galloping toward him. This time he rode the burro off the trail and was going to hide in a blackjack thicket, but the posse came over a rise and caught him in the open.

Marshal Renfro raised his hand and brought the posse to a lumbering, milling halt. He had one of the Arapaho trackers fetch the Mexican. He asked the Mexican if he had seen two riders pass this way.

"Sí, sí, señor," the Mexican said, and took off his sombrero out of respect for the many badges he saw. "Dos caballos. Tres jinetes."

At first Marshal Renfro thought the Mexican was merely confused. "Three riders? Two horses and three riders?" He held up his fingers so the Mexican would be sure of the numbers.

"Sí, sí." The Mexican held up his fingers to show that he, too, could count. "Two horses, three riders."

"I told you there was two horses," Coot said.

When Marshal Renfro asked for a description of the riders, the Mexican said he didn't get a good look at them, but the one riding single on a blaze-faced sorrel was un negro.

Marshal Renfro's eyes narrowed menacingly, warning the Mexican that he had better not be mistaken. "A nigger?"

"Un negro, sí."

"And the other two? An Indian and a white woman? Riding double on a bay?"

About who was riding the bay, the Mexican wasn't so sure. The one riding double on the bay was possibly a white woman, *sí,* but he could be sure only of the face of the man whose horse had almost run over him, and that was the face of a black man, with a beard, *absolutamente.*

Renfro shifted around in his saddle, giving this some thought; then his eyes drifted dreamily toward the south, as if trying to envision the pursued riders, and murmured, "I wonder . . ."

When the posse was within two miles of catching up with them, and coming on fast, Gypsy reined the sorrel to a stop and spun around to wait for Big Red. They were about a mile from the Red River now, on the last wooded rise leading down to the river's escarpment. Big Red had begun to fall farther and farther behind, and it had become obvious that something would have to be done, and Gypsy had been looking forward to doing it, and this looked like a good place to do it.

"You two go on. I'm going to slow 'em down some." He dismounted and reached for his buffalo rifle.

White Wolf seemed reluctant to leave. "If there's going to be fighting . . ."

"Ain't gonna be no fighting," he said as he pulled the long rifle and its aiming stick from the scabbard. "You go on. Head for the cave. I'll be along directly."

They rode on.

From a saddlebag Gypsy took a buckskin bag filled with cartridges and then jerked the binoculars from their case. After a few words of praise and comfort to the groaning horse, he hurried to a likely place above a limestone outcropping. The spot overlooked a wide expanse of prairie grassland, across which the posse would have to come, and here they came. They were about a mile and a half away when they first came into view around a heavily wooded spur of Kiowa Ridge.

He pushed the aiming stick into the ground, rested the long barrel of the buffalo rifle in the fork of the stick, and, lying prone on the green grass and dead leaves, propped up on his elbows, waited, watching through the binoculars as the posse approached.

Which would it be, Sheriff Harriman or Dexter? He would get only one good shot, so he had to choose which one of the two was going to die. The only reason Dexter had lived this long was his relationship to Maxwell, and once again that consideration influenced Gypsy to let him live, at least for a little while longer.

Laying the binoculars aside, he wet the end of one forefinger in his mouth, held it up to check the direction and velocity of the breeze, set the sights on the buffalo rifle for four thousand yards, took aim at Sheriff Harriman, and waited—waited for that optimal moment. Adjusted for windage, the rifle was aimed at the center of Sheriff Harriman's chest when Gypsy took a deep breath, held it, and gently squeezed the trigger.

Sheriff Harriman, riding abreast of Marshal Renfro in the front rank of the posse, toppled backward out of the saddle before they even heard the shot. The bullet entered his chest and exited from his back, bringing with it a spray of blood and blown-to-bits flesh.

As panic and confusion gripped the front ranks of the posse, Marshal Renfro shouted, "Cover! Take cover!"

The men scattered in all directions, looking for a rock or a bush to hide behind. Renfro, having instinctively made mental notes of the terrain as he rode along, wheeled his horse and galloped toward the head of a ravine about a hundred yards behind and to the west of the open area where they had been caught. Most of the men in the posse followed him at breakneck speed and were so bunched up that Gypsy needed only to fire into the bunch to bring down two horses and one man before they reached the cover of the ravine.

Once in defilade behind the wall of the ravine, the posse turned into a milling mass. Renfro was out of the saddle at the moment his horse came to a sliding halt in the ravine. He grabbed a pair of binoculars from his saddlebag and scrambled up the south wall of the ravine. The ambusher's rifle had stopped firing before he reached the top, so there was no smoke or muzzle-flash to reveal the ambusher's position, but from a quick scan of the landscape with the binoculars Renfro picked a limestone outcropping on a wooded rise about three quarters of a mile away as the most likely place from which the firing had come.

Some of his men—Deputies Clovis Pinkard and Dexter Bingham among them—snatched their rifles from their saddle scabbards and scrambled up the bank of the ravine after Marshal Renfro, to poke their heads above the edge of the embankment, talking, panting, cursing.

"See anything?" Deputy Pinkard asked.

Dexter was almost babbling. "That was a"—trying to get Renfro's attention, trying to make him understand—"a buffalo rifle. And that Mexican—he said a nigger. Riding with them. Don't you know who it must be?"

Ignoring him, Renfro said to Pinkard, "No, I can't see 'em, but I'm pretty sure it came from around that outcropping yonder."

"Why, that must be nearly a mile away," Deputy Pinkard said. "Dexter must be right then, it'd have to be—"

"Gypsy Smith!" Dexter cried. He was experiencing the numbed shock of seeing Sheriff Harriman killed, with the realization that *he* might have been the one who got the bullet. He had been riding directly alongside Sheriff Harriman, so Gypsy could just as easily have killed him as the sheriff. "That Mexican said a nigger was riding with 'em. Don't you see, Marshal? It has to be Gypsy Smith."

In a slightly condescending voice Renfro drawled, "You're right, Deputy, you're most likely right. Ain't another nigger in Oklahoma can shoot like that. Maybe not any white men, either, far's that goes." Lowering the binoculars, he said to Deputy Pinkard, "Clovis, take five of our best men and a couple of scouts. Ride down the ravine till you get out of range of that damned buffalo gun, and then swing around and see if you can come up behind that outcropping. My guess is, he'll be long gone by the time you get there, but if there's any shooting, we'll come running. If it's clear, give us a wave with your hat. And Clovis," he added over his shoulder after Deputy Pinkard had reached the bottom of the ravine, "don't take no chances. Don't even think about trying to capture him. If you get within rifle range, kill the sonofabitch."

* * *

Gypsy had fired only five times. The last four had been wild shots, but the field vacated by the posse was strewn with the carnage of two men dead and one wounded, one horse dead, another wounded. He could have killed any number of horses whose riders had dismounted and taken cover behind the nearest rocks and bushes, leaving their horses exposed. But he figured the five shots were sufficient for his purpose. That would hold them for a while. He shoved another cartridge into the chamber of the Grim Reaper, then grabbed the aiming stick and the binoculars and, keeping low to the ground, jogged back to his horse.

White Wolf and Rachel intersected with the Red River about a mile below Medicine Bluff. While they were riding west along the river's northern escarpment, looking for a trail that would lead them down the escarpment to the river below, White Wolf's attention was caught by a thin dust cloud boiling up from the river's floodplain about two miles to the south. Then he saw the riders, coming fast across the floodplain, about thirty or forty of them, widely scattered.

"Another posse," he said. "And they've spotted us."

An instantaneous calculation made him doubt that they could get to the cave before the posse got to them, but that was their only hope, so when they came to a ravine that cut through the escarpment and led down to the river, White Wolf sent Big Red plunging and skidding down the steep trail along the sides of the ravine. More than once Rachel was almost thrown from the horse, but she hung on to White Wolf with all her strength, and he stayed firmly in the saddle as Big Red jolted and stumbled in the rocks and shale along the steep trail.

When they came out of the ravine onto the riverbank, the front-runners of the posse coming in from Texas were within half a mile of them, and the cave was still about a quarter of a mile away. The river—broad and shallow, made up of many braided streams meandering through the sandhills and willow thickets—lay between them, but the possemen were coming at full gallop, churning through the streams, coming over and around the sandhills, through the thickets, fanning out all along the southern side of the river to block White Wolf if he should try to cross into Texas. And the front-runners were soon within easy rifle range, though they didn't fire at White Wolf for fear of hitting Rachel.

With his rib cage heaving and his legs wobbling, Big Red lumbered along the sandy bank of the river. His breath came in deep rasping groans, and from his wide-flaring nostrils came trickles of frothy blood. It appeared that he might collapse at any moment, but he went on, all the way to Medicine Bluff.

White Wolf pulled Big Red to a stop near the foot of the scree leading up to the mouth of the cave. In actions that flowed together in one uninterrupted movement, he lifted his leg over the saddle horn and slid to the ground and reached up and helped Rachel off the horse and jerked the saddlebags off.

"Up there! The cave! Take these, run for it." He flung the saddlebags to her.

She caught them and whirled to scamper up the scree.

He jerked the 30.06 rifle from its scabbard, then reached under the horse, unfastened the cinch, and pulled the saddle off. As he unbuckled the bridle and flung it away, he said, "Go on, Big Red, you're free. Go on!" He slapped him on his lathered shoulder.

But the sound of the slap was almost simultaneous with the *splat-thunk* sound made by a bullet hitting Big Red from the other side.

The three front-runners in the Texas posse were closing fast across the river bottom. And now that Rachel was halfway to the cave and out of the line of fire, they had begun firing on the run as soon as they were within range. The shots were wildly inaccurate, so it was only chance that one struck Big Red in the chest directly on the other side from where White Wolf crouched. Had the horse not been there, White Wolf himself would have taken the bullet.

Big Red jerked, screamed, and staggered sideways toward White Wolf. When he tottered and began to fall, White Wolf jumped backward to keep the horse from falling on him.

"Goddamn you," he said to the oncoming riders. Dropping to one knee behind the dying horse, he brought the rifle to bear.

Seeing the rifle, the posse's front-runner—the one who had shot Big Red—tried to veer away, knowing how much more accurate the rifle would be than his pistol. But the first shot from White Wolf's rifle hit him in the throat and knocked him out of the saddle.

The other front-runners wheeled their horses and dashed for cover, but now those who were coming up from behind had begun firing with rifles. The bullets struck all around White Wolf, ricocheting off the rocks, kicking up little spurts of sand around Big Red's twitching body. White Wolf began scrambling up the scree toward the cave, where Rachel, having reached the mouth of the cave, had turned to wait.

"Go on!" he yelled. "Get inside!"

But they weren't shooting at her, and she couldn't bring herself to run into the cave while the bullets were ricocheting off the rocks all around him. She expected to see him hit at any second as he scrambled up the scree, but he got within a few feet of the cave entrance before his right leg was knocked from under him. He fell sprawling amid the rocks, and when he tried to get up and go on, he couldn't move his leg. Beneath the buckskin pants blood streamed down his leg and into his boot, and the leg was useless.

When she saw him fall, Rachel dropped the saddlebags and started down the incline toward him, but he shouted, "Go back! Go back!" and she stopped.

Using his hand to pull his leg around, he leaned back against the rocks, facing outward, and brought his rifle to his shoulder. He fired at the advancing possemen, who were within a hundred yards of him now. Their shots were wild because they were firing on the run, but White Wolf rested his elbow on a rock, cradled the rifle in his hand, and fired very accurately. He knocked a man out of the saddle with the first shot, and once again the riders scattered for cover. And as they were retreating or veering away, two more of them toppled from their saddles without White Wolf's firing another shot.

The shots came from somewhere above him. Someone was on the top of Medicine Bluff, firing down on the posse with the big *crack-boom* sounds of a buffalo rifle. The possemen were thrown into panic by the deadly accuracy and range of the terrible-sounding gun.

After blowing the first two men out of their saddles, Gypsy, lying prone on the rim of Medicine Bluff, caused further chaos among the widely scattered posse by bringing down a running horse at a distance of over half a mile, just to show them he could do it. And those who took refuge in willow and tamarisk thickets or patches of shrubbery were soon sent scattering for more substantial cover because the buffalo rifle from atop Medicine Bluff kept up a steady *crack-boom, crack-boom,* sending its huge bullets ripping through the foliage like scythes.

With the posse routed and pinned down by the buffalo rifle, White Wolf dragged himself the rest of the way up the scree to the safety of the cave. He moved by placing the rifle in front of him and then using both hands and his one good leg to shove and pull himself up the rocky incline, until Rachel, defying his order to get back, scrambled down the incline to help him. She took the rifle in one hand, grabbed the back of his buckskin shirt, and helped tug him struggling up the rocks.

By the time they gained the mouth of the cave, some of the possemen had begun popping up from behind sandhills or boulders to take shots at Gypsy on top of the bluff, but they were too quick to be accurate, and their shots were usually answered by a *crack-boom* that sent sprays of sand or rock fragments over their heads.

White Wolf crawled on his hands and one knee into the cave. Rachel snatched up the saddlebags, and as soon as they were safely behind the boulders that formed the lip of the cave, White Wolf wrenched around so that he could sit with his back resting against the boulders.

Rachel fell on her knees beside him. Dropping the rifle and saddlebags, she made useless motions with her hands, as if her hands wanted to do something but her mind couldn't tell them what to do.

"Cut the pant leg," White Wolf said, handing her his knife.

Rachel slit the blood-soaked leg of his buckskin pants to above his knee, exposing the wound in the calf of his leg just above the top of his boot. From the torn flesh of the exit wound a steady stream of blood flowed. Wincing with the stabs of increasing pain, White Wolf unbuckled his belt, stripped it of the hunting knife and his medicine bundle. Rachel used the belt as a tourniquet just below the knee.

Then they heard Gypsy's voice shouting down to them from the top of the bluff. "Hey, down there! Hey, *navestax*! Can you hear me?"

White Wolf leaned his head back to yell upward and outward, "I hear you." His voice reverberated eerily through the cave.

"I'm nearly out of ammo, my horse is shot, and Renfro's got me cut off," Gypsy shouted. "I'm coming down. Can you keep those bastards below dodging for a little while?"

White Wolf, using his hands to tug his paralyzed leg up under him, got into a kneeling position behind the boulders. "Rifle! Hand me the rifle."

Rachel gave him the rifle and, while he fired, resumed her efforts to strap the belt around his leg tightly enough to stop the blood flow.

The boulders made a perfect parapet, behind which he was protected and over and through which he had a wide field of vision. He fired as fast as he could bolt the rounds into the rifle and take aim at one of the many possemen who popped up above sandhills or boulders to take potshots at Gypsy as he climbed down the bluff. The chance of White Wolf's hitting one of the possemen wasn't good, but the bullets whanging off rocks and thudding into sand were sufficient to keep them from staying exposed long enough to take accurate aim at Gypsy.

Gypsy, carrying the buffalo rifle, leaped into the cave and hunkered down behind the parapet of boulders. A few bullets followed him into the cave, to ricochet with banshee shrieks off the walls, but the only injuries Gypsy suffered while climbing down the bluff were scratches and abrasions from bushes and rocks, not bullets. "If that's the best those buggers can shoot, we got nothing to worry about." Then, seeing White Wolf's leg, he said, "Ah. I see you wasn't so lucky. How bad is it? Let's have a look."

"The bleeding's just about stopped," Rachel said.

Gypsy leaned his rifle against a boulder and helped White Wolf turn around and ease down the boulder to a sitting position, then move the leg around so that it stretched straight out in front of him. White Wolf grimaced a few times, and his face was beaded with sweat, but he made no sound.

Kneeling beside him and inspecting the wound, Gypsy said, " 'Scuse me for asking, Miss Rachel, but do you happen to be wearing a petticoat?"

She shook her head.

"Makes good bandages," he explained.

Rachel threw off the wolfskin that she had been wearing like a shawl. "Here." She unbuttoned her tattered and torn cotton blouse. "Use this."

"Good. Keep out the dirt and flies. I'll get some medicine, and some sticks for a splint, keep it from wobbling around, case it's broke."

Leaving his rifle leaning against a boulder, Gypsy, in a shuffling crouch, darted into the cave's interior. There was still enough late-afternoon sunlight angling into the mouth of the cave to illuminate the recess, though the shadows had become so dark on the western wall that Gypsy had to look around for a moment before he found the pile of rocks and slabs of selenite under which he had left his cache. He wrestled away a few big stones and then pulled from among the pile of rocks a rawhide Indian parfleche similar to the one he had hidden at the trapper's cabin in the Glass Mountains. He opened the parfleche and dumped out its contents, among which were canisters and cans of food and boxes of ammunition and a coffeepot. There were also a few medical supplies, including a bottle of merbromin.

He packed his coat pockets with medicine and cartridges for the buffalo gun, then used his knife to cut strips of rawhide from the flap of the parfleche. Next he grabbed the coffeepot and filled it at the small sump of water in the corner at the rear wall of the cave, then went to the cache of firewood piled near the front of the cave and picked out a few of the straightest sticks.

When he returned to White Wolf and Rachel, he first peeked over the parapet to make sure nobody was trying to sneak up on them, then said to White Wolf, "The boot's gotta come off, *navestax.*"

He looked at White Wolf for agreement, which he received in the form of a teeth-clenched nod. Then he and Rachel set about cutting and tugging the boot off the leg, after which Gypsy examined the leg and pronounced it fractured but not shattered. He and Rachel washed the wound, bathed it in merbromin, and bandaged it with strips torn from her blouse. Next they used the sticks and the rawhide strips to make a splint.

A few grunts and strangled cries escaped White Wolf's throat as Gypsy was making the splint, and beads of sweat trickled down his face, but he got through the ordeal without losing consciousness.

As Gypsy was finishing the splint, they began to hear the slight subterranean rumble of hoofbeats coming from overhead and then the faraway sounds of men's voices.

"Renfro and his boys," Gypsy said. He glanced over the parapet to see the possemen on the river bottom below waving from behind their sandhills to the men on top of Medicine Bluff. "Well, that must make about eighty to a hundred of 'em altogether. What d'you think about them odds, *navestax*?"

"What can we do?" White Wolf asked.

"Do?" He washed the blood from his hands by pouring the last of the water from the coffeepot over them. "Well, the first thing we do is get you farther into the cave, and make us a cooking fire, and have us a hot meal. What d'you fancy? Pork 'n' beans? Canned stew? Hell, I think I even got some hard-tack. With all that, and hot coffee, too, we'll be living in the lap of luxury."

"For how long?"

Gypsy tipped his head speculatively and said in a more somber voice, "For as long as we got—a week, maybe. Maybe longer. As long as the food lasts, anyway. We ain't in much danger of getting shot by them. Hell, two of us could hold off an army from up here." He paused for a thoughtful moment and then added as a rueful afterthought, "Unless, of course, the army had a cannon. . . ."

CHAPTER FIFTY-FOUR

COLE TUCKER, THE TEXAS RANGER IN CHARGE OF THE TEXAS posse, was at first inclined to put some of the blame for his losses on Renfro himself when they joined forces on the river bottom.

"In your bulletins you said we was after some Indian renegade and a white woman captive. You didn't say nothing about
them being teamed up with the most notorious nigger gunman
in Oklahoma. And him with a goddamned buffalo rifle! Why
didn't you tell us? We rode right into it."

"We did, too," Renfro said impatiently, looking down on the
ranger, a short man.

Ranger Tucker had taken Renfro aside from the main body
of the combined posses for a conference of leaders. Lower-
echelon possemen—chief deputies, lieutenants, and runners,
along with a few newspaper reporters—hovered in the vicinity
of the two legendary lawmen.

"As for letting you know," Renfro added, taking offense at
the Texas Ranger's complaining tone, "we didn't know he was
with 'em till a little while ago." And to show his disdain for
the ranger's excitability, he calmly rolled a cigarette.

Having failed to gain the moral high ground with that thrust,
Ranger Tucker said, "Well, what about that woman? Your bulletin said she was kidnapped. You sure 'bout that?"

Renfro raised his knee to tighten his pants across his buttocks, struck a match on the seat of his pants, and lit his
cigarette. "Well, I wouldn't bet on it," he said.

"Looks like she was helping him. 'Cept for fear of hitting
her, we could've got that damned redskin easy. Then it turns
out she's trying as hard as he is to get away. She even helped
him into the cave after he was hit."

"That don't mean she wasn't kidnapped," Dexter protested.
He was among the men who hovered around Renfro. "Whatever she's doing, he's making her do it."

"He's hit?" Renfro asked.

Ranger Tucker gave Dexter a supercilious look before he
turned back to Renfro. "In the leg. One of my best men got
him. Jim Blaine. Dead now. That damned buffalo rifle tore a
hole in him as big as a baseball. God, I wish I could get my
hands on that nigger."

"You and about a thousand other men," Renfro said. "What
about that cave? Any other way out of it?"

"No, it ends, oh, fifty-sixty yards back from the entrance.
Used to be a limestone cavern, probably went for miles, but a
cave-in blocked it off. No way to get past it."

"You sure?"

"Should be. I hunted Indian artifacts in there."

Renfro nodded and turned to Deputy Pinkard. "Put a cordon of men around that cave before it gets dark, so they can't slip out tonight. Rotate 'em every four hours, make sure they stay alert. Better give 'em a password, keep 'em from shooting each other in the dark." Then, without missing a beat, he turned to another of his nearby deputies, a clerk-runner, and said, "Harry, I want you to ride to the nearest telegraph office—over at Waurika Station, that'd be—and send some telegrams. Where's your pad?"

The clerk-runner hurried to his horse to fetch a writing tablet from his saddlebag, and Renfro turned back to Ranger Tucker. "We're gonna have to get provisions for a day or two for all these men. You got somebody who can handle that?"

"Who pays?"

"The taxpayer—who else?"

"I mean, budget. Our budget's—"

"I know what you mean." The clerk-runner returned with a stubby pencil poised over a writing pad. "Harry here is my requisitions clerk. Work it out with him," Renfro said, and to Harry, "Work with the rangers on getting enough supplies in here for a day or two, but before you do anything else, I want you to send some telegrams." Dropping the cigarette butt and grinding it out under his boot, he went on, "The first one goes to School Superintendent John Maxwell at Agency. Tell him we got his daughter and her kidnapper trapped down here. Tell him he might want to come on down here, case his daughter refuses to come out. He might could talk her into surrendering."

"What're you saying, Marshal?" asked the *Harper's Weekly* reporter. "Are you saying Mrs. Hornbeck is—"

Renfro pushed the reporter aside. "Then send one to the commanding officer at Fort Sill. Tell him we got Gypsy Smith and that renegade redskin Corby White trapped in Medicine Bluff Cave. Tell him I'd be obliged if he'd send me down a cannon quick as he can."

CHAPTER FIFTY-FIVE

IT WAS A LITTLE BEFORE FIVE OF THE FOLLOWING AFTERNOON when Maxwell reached the river. He had hitched a ride in a buckboard bringing supplies from Waurika Station to the possemen. By then a throng of excited and even festive people had gathered behind a long sandy ridge that protected them against rifle fire from the cave. The ridge had been formed by wind- and waterborne sand collecting around piles of boulders that had been deposited on the plain by some ancient flood. Willow bushes and tufts of grass had taken root in the sand, and here and there the boulders protruded through the sand, offering the possemen both protection and good firing positions.

But there was no shooting going on when Maxwell arrived. Marshal Renfro had ordered the men to hold their fire until they were certain that Mrs. Hornbeck wasn't being held against her will. In the meantime, the hungry possemen had built small cooking fires, and whiskey bottles were being passed around, and the encampment had begun to take on the look of a holiday outing. Most were possemen, some were Klansmen, some were people from nearby towns who had come out to see the show. There must have been about two hundred men and a few women already gathered at the site, with more arriving every hour.

Indeed, just as Maxwell's buckboard was approaching the area from the east, another group of riders could be seen coming in from the west, riding across the floodplain in a steady trot, a column of men in dark blue uniforms, riding two abreast, pennants and guidons flying. Following them came a horse-drawn cannon, and bringing up the rear was a canvas-covered supply wagon. A cheer went up from a few of the lawmen and spectators when they first saw the column of troopers approaching, but the cheers died quickly when one of them with a pair of binoculars said, "Jaysus Chee-rist! They sent them nigger troops."

The buckboard in which Maxwell was riding stopped near the western end of the sandhill ridge, where Marshal Renfro and the other leaders of the combined posses, Dexter among them, had formed a sort of command post.

Dexter went out to meet Maxwell and said by way of a greeting, "We's beginning to wonder if you'd get here in time."

"How's Rachel?" Maxwell said.

"Far's we know, she's all right. That teacher's pet of yours got shot in the leg, looks like, but they're still up there in the cave, all three of 'em."

"Mr. Maxwell," Renfro said, breaking off a discussion he had been having with one of his Arapaho scouts, "glad you could make it." He glanced toward the approaching column of soldiers. "Here comes the cannon. Looks like you got here just in the nick of time."

He motioned Maxwell to a lookout point at a nearby crevice in the sandhill, from where, through the branches of some scrub willows, they could see the opening of the cave in Medicine Bluff.

"That's where they're holed up, and there's no way out. The only thing they can do is surrender or die. Now, they tell me you're close to that renegade redskin. Think you can talk him into surrendering? Or at least letting your daughter go?"

"I can try."

"Well, I'll give you till we get the cannon set up, and if they choose not to surrender, they can just kiss tomorrow good-bye."

Nettled by Renfro's cold-bloodedness, Maxwell said, "Even if my daughter's still there?"

Renfro gave him a stern look. "Mr. Maxwell, we got evidence that your daughter's not being held against her will. Maybe she began as a kidnap victim—*maybe*—but now she's acting more like an accomplice. Yesterday one of our men crawled down from the top of the bluff and got close enough to talk to 'em, told 'em to let the girl come out, but she refused. Do I need to repeat that? *Refused.*"

The vehemence with which Dexter came to Rachel's defense was surprising. "It was Gypsy Smith who said she refused. Nobody heard *her* say it, did they? And even if she did, how do we know she didn't have a gun to her head?"

Renfro gave Dexter a sidelong look of annoyance and continued to address Maxwell as if it had been he who protested Rachel's innocence. "And we have witnesses who say that they're mighty lovey-dovey, her and that redskin. Even so, we're willing to hold our fire till you've had a chance to talk to her, see if you can get her to come out."

The approaching column of Buffalo Soldiers was drawing near the encampment. At its head rode Captain Beauregard Pierce.

"Wait," Renfro said to Maxwell, and turned to Deputy Pinkard. "Pass the word to the men. I don't want nobody making trouble with these nigger soldiers. Anybody does, they'll answer to me."

Pinkard hurried away. Renfro, with Ranger Cole Tucker and a few other posse leaders collecting around him, turned to face Captain Pierce, who sat easy and tall on a big dun gelding, dressed in his gold-braided uniform and yellow bandanna. When he signaled with a raised hand, his first sergeant called, "Colummmmm, halt!" And as the column came to a well-disciplined stop, the captain, accompanied only by his first sergeant and his orderly, approached Renfro and the others.

"Marshal Renfro," Captain Pierce said as a greeting.

Renfro nodded. "Captain. We didn't expect a cavalry outfit. I asked the colonel only for an artillery piece."

"What do we need with all these soldiers?" Ranger Tucker complained.

Captain Pierce didn't dismount. Speaking from the lofty height of his horse, he said, "I wouldn't know about that. I just follow orders. We brought the cannon, and we can do the job." He raised up in his stirrups to peer over the top of the sandhill toward Medicine Bluff. "That's the cave?"

"That's it."

"And there's been a de facto truce in effect since yesterday?"

"If it wasn't, you'd be dead by now. I bet Gypsy Smith's got that big old buffalo rifle aimed at you right this second." His tone was one of a good-natured Kentuckian teasing one of his darkies. "But I guess you got nothing to fear, you and him being friends, I hear."

From the height of his saddle Captain Pierce looked loftily down on Renfro. "Gypsy Smith and I know each other. We are not friends. But you needn't have any doubts. Even if we were, that wouldn't keep me from doing my duty." He turned to his first sergeant. "Bring up the gun, Sergeant. Bivouac the men, post guards, keep 'em segregated."

The sergeant wheeled his horse and sprinted back toward the column of Buffalo Soldiers. Captain Pierce dismounted, handed the reins to his orderly, and said, "Very well, then, Marshal, if you'll brief me on the situation . . ."

Maxwell stood idly by while Renfro briefed Captain Pierce on how matters stood at the moment. While Maxwell was waiting, three newspaper reporters accosted him. One of them was the *Harper's Weekly* writer, who introduced himself and asked, "Would you mind answering a few questions about your daughter and that Indian?"

"Yes, I would mind," Maxwell said bluntly.

"But, sir," said the reporter from the *Oklahoma City Daily Democrat*, "our readers are very interested in what's going on here. Can't you tell us anything?"

Even a photographer had arrived on the scene. With his huge camera and wagon filled with glass plates and paraphernalia, he planned to take pictures of the dead outlaws after they had been killed, and he wanted to know if Maxwell would consent to be photographed as the father of the kidnap victim.

Maxwell was about to tell them to go to hell but was saved from the necessity by, of all people, Dexter, who used his authority as a deputy to shoo the reporters and the photographer away and keep them at a distance. It was one of the few times in his life that Maxwell found himself the beneficiary of an unsolicited favor from Dexter, for which he was both puzzled and grateful. And he became even more puzzled when Dexter took him aside and said in an undertone, "Listen, tell Rachel that everything's going to be all right as long as she keeps her mouth shut about what really happened at Kingstree that night. Understand? She don't have to worry none about going to prison if she does what I tell her."

"What d'you mean? What did happen that night at Kingstree?"

"Never mind. You just tell her—"

He was interrupted by Renfro, who called to Maxwell and identified him to Captain Pierce as the father of Rachel Hornbeck.

"He's gonna see if he can talk 'em into surrendering. How long'll it take you to get the cannon set up?"

Captain Pierce glanced to the place about fifty feet away where the cannon had been wheeled behind the sandhill. The four-mule team was being unhitched by the teamsters, and the gunnery sergeant was directing about a dozen soldiers in positioning the cannon behind a copse of scrub willows.

"Fifteen minutes."

Turning back to Maxwell, Renfro said, "All right, I'll give you thirty minutes to see what you can do."

"Thirty minutes?" Maxwell asked scornfully. "Hell, I can hardly walk over there and back in that time. I want at least an hour."

Renfro glanced at the angle of the sun in the western sky. "All right. But no more. We have to get this over with while there's still light. I don't want to have to spend another night here. And don't go in the cave," he added as an afterthought. "You understand? Talk to them from outside the cave." In response to Maxwell's look of inquiry, he explained, "We can't run the risk of you being taken hostage." And in response to Maxwell's look of disdain: "Well, if that redskin really took your daughter hostage, why wouldn't he take you, too? Tell me that." When Maxwell made no answer, he added in a slyly triumphant voice, "Or is it that you don't think she's really a hostage?" After a pause, in which he got nothing but another disdainful look from Maxwell: "Besides, Gypsy Smith's in there with 'em, and who knows what that crazy nigger might do? It ain't as if he's got anything to lose."

At the use of the word *nigger*, Captain Pierce, without another word, turned and left the gathering, striding toward his cannon emplacement, followed by his orderly leading their horses.

"You don't have to worry about his taking me hostage either, Marshal," Maxwell said. "Gypsy Smith's a friend of mine."

The marshal nodded with a sort of bitter satisfaction, as if he should have known as much. "In any case, I don't want you going inside that cave, you understand? We can't afford for you to be mistaken about the goodness of your 'friends.' "

"Look, Marshal, are we going to stand around here and talk till the sun goes down?"

Renfro pulled a watch from his serge trousers and tapped it with a forefinger. "Five-fifteen. You got an hour."

"Looks like your father's coming," Gypsy called over his shoulder.

Rachel was at the campsite with White Wolf behind an outcropping in the middle of the cave. In a crouching posture she dashed from the campsite to the parapet. She was wearing Gypsy's coat. The thin cotton camisole hadn't been adequate to keep her warm during the night in the cave's dank chill, and Gypsy had insisted that she take his coat, which hung on her like a blanket.

"It is!" she cried, peeping over the parapet at the man wading across the braided shallow streams on the wide sandy river bottom. "It's Daddy!"

She dashed back to where White Wolf sat against the wall behind a formation that served as a protective barrier against any bullets fired into the cave. The formation had also served as a screen to prevent anyone on the outside from seeing the glow of last night's cooking fire. White Wolf's splinted leg was stretched out in front of him, resting on the pelt of the white wolf. He leaned forward and crossed his arms over his left knee and cradled his head on his arms. When Rachel came to tell him that Maxwell was coming, White Wolf's face, flushed with fever, pinched with pain and sleeplessness, registered no reaction.

"I never thought I'd see him again." She dropped to her knees beside him and took his hands in hers. "Is it getting worse?"

Forcing an apologetic grin, he said, "I have to pee. Ask Gypsy to come back."

Rachel returned to the front of the cave and told Gypsy. He leaned the rifle against the rocks, went to where White Wolf sat, and helped him to stand on his one leg. He supported him like a crutch as they hobbled back into the darker recesses of the cave to the nook in the back wall that they used as a privy. Even at the expense of acute pain, White Wolf tried to mini-

mize the humiliation of his helplessness by hobbling to the la-
trine area, rather than urinating in a can and having someone
empty it.

"Listen," he grunted as they hobbled along, "Mr. Maxwell's
gonna try to get us to surrender. Help him convince Rachel to
go, will you? No need for her to die here with us."

"You're sure that's what's gonna happen, are you? That
we're not gonna get out of here alive?" Gypsy's voice was one
of forced bantering, an instinctive attempt to keep their spirits
up. "You don't believe in miracles?"

"Like what?" White Wolf leaned against the damp rock
wall, balancing on his one good leg, unlacing the fly of his
buckskin pants.

Gypsy gave the question a moment's thought. "Who
knows?" Gazing at the ancient picture carvings on the wall of
the cave, he said, "You might pray to those Indian gods of
yours for a little miracle. Barring that, though, I 'spect you're
right, *navestax*. This's where me and you come to the end of
the trail."

CHAPTER FJFTY-SJX

MAXWELL WADED ACROSS THE LAST CHANNEL OF THE RIVER
and stopped at the base of the bluff for a moment to look at
the bloating and fly-swarmed carcass of Big Red on the riverbank. Then, with his boots squishing water, he climbed the
scree toward the cave. He could see possemen standing on top
of the bluff and crouching behind almost every man-size boulder along the way up the side of the bluff.

"Hello, the cave!" he called when he was near the opening.
"I'm coming in."

When he dropped down behind the parapet of boulders, he
found himself facing Rachel. They gazed at each other for a

moment in silence, she fearfully scrutinizing his face for
signs of anger and accusations, he grimly scrutinizing her
for signs of who she had become. In her crude moccasins and
ragged sateen skirt, in the voluminous and ill-fitting frock
coat, with her ash-soiled face and uncombed hair, she looked
like an adult image of the ragamuffin she had been as a child.

He opened his arms to her, and she, suddenly released from
her fear of his anger and accusations, flung herself into his embrace.

"Daddy!" She pressed her face against his chest, clinging to
him like a child. "Oh, Daddy, I'm so glad to see you. I'm so
glad you came."

He held her close, resisting his inclination to say, as he
would have said to her as a child, "Shh, it's all right. Everything's going to be all right." Because he knew now that things
would never be all right again. So he just held her in silence,
brushing his hand over her tangled hair, patting her shoulders.

"Come," she said then, pulling back and trying to smile.
"Come see Corby. Only he's not Corby anymore, he's White
Wolf now, since his vision quest. That's what he'll want you to
call him."

"I know." And when he turned to see Corby—White Wolf—
supported by Gypsy Smith, hobbling toward him, he went to
him and said, "Here, lean on me."

White Wolf put his free arm across Maxwell's shoulders,
and with Gypsy on one side and Maxwell on the other, they
helped White Wolf to the rock ledge at the campsite, where he
could lean back against the cave wall and lift his wounded leg
up and rest it on a boulder in a horizontal position.

As Maxwell and White Wolf shook hands, White Wolf said,
"Good to see you again, *nihoe*," using the Cheyenne word for
"my father" that conveyed affection and respect without real
kinship, in the same way that he would have addressed venerable elders of the tribe as "grandfather." "I wish it could've
been under better circumstances."

"I, too, *naha,* I too," Maxwell said, using the Cheyenne
word for "my son" in the same way that White Wolf had used
nihoe. He turned to shake hands with Gypsy. "Well, Gypsy, it's
been a long time."

"Ain't it, though? Over four years. I hear you married Miss Eula, and that she's pretty as a picture these days."

"How is Eula?" Rachel asked.

"Just fine. She sends her love to all of you. Told me to tell you that she's saying special prayers for you." He included the three of them in a glance as his face sobered. "But I don't know if prayers are going to be enough to . . . Listen to me, all of you. We haven't got much time. They just brought a cannon in from Fort Sill. You saw it? Well, they've told me to tell you that you're going to have to surrender or you're going to die. They told me to tell you that the choice is yours. And you've only got a few minutes to make up your minds."

"Choice!" Gypsy snorted. "For me that's no choice at all. The only choice for me is to die here by cannon today or by a hangman's noose tomorrow. And I'm sure's hell not gonna give them Klansmen the satisfaction of seeing me swing from a rope. Now, having said that, so you'll know what you can tell Renfro for me, I'll excuse myself and get back to lookout duty, let you talk to these two alone."

He went back to the parapet. Maxwell sighed and sat down wearily on the ledge beside White Wolf. Rachel came around White Wolf's splinted and swollen leg, dropped to her knees and sat back on her heels, looking up at White Wolf and her father.

"And you?" he asked White Wolf. "Can I convince you to give yourself up? You don't have a chance, you know, if you stay here. If you give yourself up . . ."

"They'll hang me. You know it, and I know it. And you know, too, that a Human Being who dies by hanging can never enter the Spirit Land."

"Maybe they won't. Maybe . . . in court . . . maybe we could make a case."

"No. I killed those two deputies in Hornbeck's barn, and I've killed a couple more since then, and since they think I killed Hornbeck, too, I don't stand a chance, and you know it."

With a flicker of desperate hope in her eyes, Rachel blurted, "I could tell them the truth, that I killed Shelby and that it was an accident."

"You?" Maxwell said. "*You* killed—"

"I didn't mean to," she said.

"It wouldn't matter," White Wolf said. "They'd just send

you to prison and hang me anyway." And because he saw that
Maxwell was still disposed to resist that conclusion, he called
on Gypsy. "What d'you say, Gypsy? Am I right?"

For a moment Gypsy seemed hesitant to get involved in the
discussion but then said, "Well, *navestax*, I know you wouldn't
want me to tell you a lie at a time like this, no matter how
comforting, so I have to tell you the truth: they'd hang you all
right. The law, or the Klan, one—whichever got to you first."
He gave Maxwell an apologetic look, tipping his head as if to
say, "That's the truth of it," then turned back to his vigil.

As if that matter were settled, White Wolf took Rachel's
hand. "But you—you must go."

"No!" She shook her head. "I'm staying with you."

Maxwell, astonished by the finality of Rachel's declaration,
took off his spectacles and rubbed the blur of tears from his
eyes. When he put the spectacles back on, he took a deep
breath of determination. "Now, listen to me, Rachel. Corby's
right, there's no reason for you to die. As far as the officials
know, Corby killed Shelby, and as long as Dexter sticks to his
story that you were kidnapped, they'll never know any different. So you won't even have to go to prison if that's what
you're afraid of. There'll be some scandal about all this, sure,
all right, but it won't be anything you can't live down. Rachel,
you're young. You've got a long life ahead of you. Don't
throw it away."

She lowered her head. "If he dies, I wouldn't want to live."

After a moment of silence White Wolf picked up the coffeepot and slowly poured the water over the splinted and bandaged wound on his leg. "Helps keep it cool," he explained to
Maxwell, and handed the pot to Rachel. "Get me some more,
would you?"

Rachel took the pot and darted toward the sump hole in the
back of the cave. White Wolf turned to Maxwell and said in a
voice barely above a whisper, "Give me a minute or two with
her, and then . . . when I tell you, take her away. By force, if
you have to."

Maxwell placed a hand on White Wolf's forearm, pressed it
gratefully, and said with a look of relief, "Bless you for that,
Corby. You're the only one who can convince her to go. As for
you, is there no way I can convince you?"

"No. And I'd be grateful if you didn't mention it again. I'd be grateful, too, if you'd stop calling me Corby. My name's White Wolf, and it's what you must call me in the time we have left, so there won't be any confusion about who I am when I get to the Spirit Land. White Wolf is the name the spirits will know me by. I spent just about all my life being confused about who I was. I wouldn't want it to be that way throughout eternity."

As Rachel was returning with the water, Gypsy, taking advantage of the break in conversation, announced from the parapet that a band of Indians was approaching.

"Comanches," he said. "Looks like a pretty big party."

He didn't seem to attach much importance to the news, but Maxwell, using the announcement as an excuse to leave Rachel and White Wolf alone for a minute, actually felt a sort of desperate outlaw hope as he hurried to the parapet to get a look at the Indians. They were coming in from the west, riding at a canter along the floodplain, headed directly toward the place where the Buffalo Soldiers had set up their cannon, and there didn't seem to be any women or children with them.

Maxwell said hopefully, "Maybe they're coming to rescue you?"

"And get slaughtered themselves? Naw, the Indians don't have no fight left in 'em. I 'spect they just coming to give me and White Wolf a good send-off."

White Wolf, hearing Gypsy's assessment of the situation and accepting it without a doubt, took the pot of water from Rachel and set it aside and took both her hands in his.

"Come here," he said. "Sit. I want to talk to you."

She took a seat beside him on the ledge. "I know what you're going to say, and I don't want to hear it." She looked down at their clasped hands, refusing to look at him or hear him.

"But you have to, Rachel, for my sake as well as your own." With his left hand under her chin, he lifted her face, forcing her to look at him. "Listen to me, Rachel. Do you *want* to die?"

"No!" she blurted. "Of course not! But I don't want you to die, either, and if you do, I—"

"But I have no choice. You do."

"But ... how? How can I? You said ... we said we were

a part of each other. We said we'd always been part of each other and always would be. So how can I live, and you not?"

"That's why I want you to live, Rachel. You understand? So that a part of me'll go on living. As long as you live, as long as you love me, the part of me that's within you will go on living. Don't you see?"

She was crying now. "But I *can't*! I can't just leave you here to die. How can I?" She seemed on the verge of losing control, of becoming crazed by the agony, regret, loyalty, love, despair, by a wish to go on living and yet a wish not to go on living if she had to live without him.

"Yes, you can. You can do it for me. Go on now. Say goodbye and go."

She threw her arms around his neck. "I can't! I can't!" Crying and clinging to him desperately, she kissed his forehead, his eyes, his cheeks.

"Yes, you can. You can do it for me. Please, Rachel. Do it for me. Live for me."

He signaled to Maxwell, who left the parapet and came to put his hands on Rachel's shoulders. He was prepared to pull her away by whatever force was necessary, but to his surprise he found that she didn't resist. There was something like resignation in the way she released White Wolf, something like a recognition of finality in the way she stifled her crying, in the way she took his hand and kissed the back of it as she said, "I love you," and then pressed the back of his hand to her cheek. "I've always loved you. I always will."

"And I've loved you all the days of my life," he said.

Sensing that Rachel was about to break down again, Maxwell pulled her gently to her feet.

"Come on, now, Rachel. We haven't got much time."

She allowed herself to be turned away. Limply she followed the guidance of Maxwell's hands, as if she wanted to bear no responsibility for her movement. She kept looking back over her shoulder until they reached the parapet, where, catching a glimpse of the world outside the cave, she suddenly buried her face in her hands as if refusing to see it.

Maxwell signaled Gypsy to hold Rachel if it became necessary, then turned and strode back to White Wolf, who was struggling to stand. Using both his hands, he lowered his splinted leg to the floor, grimacing with pain, and used his rifle—butt end down—as a crutch to push himself into a standing position, tottering on one leg.

"Well, then," Maxwell said, and reached out to put his arms around White Wolf's shoulders. "Good-bye, *naha*." Gingerly, so as not to unbalance him, Maxwell embraced White Wolf, and White Wolf returned the embrace with one arm.

"Good-bye, *nihoe*, and *haho naheto*. You've been a good friend to me all my life. For that, *haho naheto*."

Maxwell spoke the traditional Cheyenne good-bye to one who is about to die and travel the Hanging Road—what white men called the Milky Way—to the Spirit Land: "*Nimeaseoxzheme*—May your journey be a good one." And then, as if he could no longer trust himself to keep his composure, he turned and strode back to the parapet. There he briskly shook hands with Gypsy. "Good-bye, Gypsy, and—and *nimeaseoxzheme*."

"Thank you, John Maxwell, and you, too, when your time comes."

Rachel was still standing with her face buried in her hands, refusing to see the world, her shoulders shaking with stifled sobs.

"And good-bye to you, Miss Rachel," Gypsy said, touching the brim of his hat. "You take good care of yourself, now, y'hear?"

Without looking, she stretched out her hand to him. When he took it, she jerked his hand to her tear-wet face and pressed the back of it against her cheek for a moment, and kissed it, and said, "Good-bye, Gypsy. I'll never forget you."

Seeing that she was on the verge of losing control, Maxwell took her arm and gently nudged her forward. "Come on now. We're out of time."

CHILDREN OF THE DUST

CHAPTER FIFTY-SEVEN

IT WAS CHIEF QUANAH PARKER HIMSELF, FLANKED BY THREE Rains and a half dozen other Comanche headmen, who rode up to the leaders to protest against the firing of a cannon into a place that was considered sacred ground to all Indians. But not only were their protests summarily dismissed by Renfro and Captain Pierce, Texas Ranger Cole Tucker actually threatened to arrest them for being off their reservation.

"When you're on this side of the river," he informed them, "you're on Texas soil, in violation of the law and subject to arrest."

Chief Quanah and Three Rains acted as if they couldn't understand a word of English. To Captain Pierce they spoke Comanche: "Medicine Bluff is sacred burial grounds for our ancestors, the Ancient Ones. Would you desecrate it with your wagon gun?"

"Look, Captain," Ranger Tucker said to Captain Pierce, "it's the army's job to keep these Comanches on their reservation, ain't it? Well, do your duty, and send 'em back across the river."

Renfro said, "Don't get your bowels in an uproar. We came here to get those two killers in the cave, not to get in a fight with a bunch of redskins. But he's right, you know," he said to Captain Pierce, swallowing his pride and trying to sound like a reasonable man addressing a peer. "You should order them back to the reservation. There's enough tension around here as it is, without them."

But Captain Pierce, enjoying his authority, ignored the white lawman. Speaking to the chief in Comanche, he said, "If the fugitives in the cave do not surrender, I will have the wagon gun fire into the cave. Those are my orders. If you wish to protest this action, you must see Colonel Medford at Fort Sill."

The Comanches had known all along how futile their protests would be, but they informed Captain Pierce that they should at least be allowed to stay and do a medicine dance for the benefit of their two friends who were trapped in the cave.

"We will return to the reservation after we have done the medicine dance and the wagon gun has sent our friends to the Spirit Land."

Knowing that it would be less trouble to let them stay than to force them to go, Captain Pierce said, "Very well. But you must do your dance away from the white men, and you must remain peaceful, and you must return to the reservation as soon as this is over. Do I have your pledge?"

Chief Quanah Parker gave his pledge, then rode away with his people to set up an encampment on the river bottom west of the sandhills, out of the line of fire but very much in the open. Unlike the white men and the Buffalo Soldiers, they had no fear that Gypsy and White Wolf would fire on them.

"You told them they could *stay*?" Ranger Tucker said. "Well, if that don't beat all! For your information, *Captain*"— sneering the title—"some of my Texans are old Comanche hunters, and if—"

"Take it easy," Renfro said. He was in complete agreement with Tucker, but there was already too much wrangling and tension among the various groups congregated at the scene. If the leaders themselves had a falling-out, the whole scene would soon collapse into chaos. Captain Pierce, after all, uppity nigger though he was, was still in charge of the cannon.

"Here they are," called one of the men on the ridge of the sandhill, announcing the arrival of Maxwell and Rachel.

Having made their way across the river bottom, they came through the willow-grown crevice in the sandhill, Maxwell with his arm around Rachel's shoulders, guiding her along as though she were blind. As soon as they were safely behind the sandhill, a swarm of reporters surrounded them, ogling, questioning, pleading. Pushing to get close to Rachel, they said, "Did they let you go? What happened? Were you a captive, Mrs. Hornbeck? Why did they let you go? How have you been treated? Did you—? Have you—?" And the photographer was saying, "Please, Mrs. Hornbeck, would you . . . ?"

It was Dexter who once again took the situation in hand. "Get away from her. Can't you see she's in no condition to talk? Step aside." He took Rachel's arm and, with Maxwell supporting her on the other side, guided her toward Marshal Renfro.

"She's in no condition to talk right now," Dexter said to Renfro, and to judge from her looks, he was right. Dressed in the oversize man's coat, the ragged and soiled sateen skirt, the crude moccasins, with her soiled and grief-stricken face, her eyes red and swollen from crying, her hair disheveled, she was obviously in no condition to be interrogated; but Renfro gave her an icy look and asked, "You all right, Mrs. Hornbeck?"

Rachel said nothing. She seemed to be in a state of shock that rendered her speechless and unreachable.

"She's all right," Dexter said. "She just needs to rest for a little while, give her a chance to compose herself, away from these reporters. Ain't that right, Rachel?"

She didn't appear to have heard.

Renfro started to say something else to her, but Captain Pierce interjected, "The supply wagon. Take her there if you like. The guard'll make sure nobody bothers her."

Dexter seemed nonplussed for a moment. To accept a good turn from a black man, even if he was wearing the uniform of a cavalry officer, was something that required a momentary adjustment of his bias; then he said, "Yeah. Sure. The supply wagon."

Captain Pierce's speaking out of turn caused Renfro to grind his teeth with resentment and contempt, but he got on with the business at hand by saying to Maxwell, "Well? What's the report from the cave? They're not going to surrender?"

While Maxwell gave his report, Dexter hurried Rachel to the canvas-covered army supply wagon that stood a few paces behind and beyond the cannon emplacement. The team had been unhitched, and two Negro soldiers with carbines stood guard over the wagon.

In the distance a drum had started. The Comanches had begun their medicine dance for White Wolf and Gypsy.

Dexter helped Rachel gently into the wagon. Beneath its canvas cover the wagon was piled with crates of field rations and a storage case filled with cannon balls. Rachel sat on one of the field ration crates. Dexter sat on another, facing her.

"You all right?" he asked.

She looked at him for a moment with vacant eyes, as if she didn't recognize him, and said, "Why're you doing this? Why're you being so nice to me?"

In a whispery voice he said, "I'm gonna be nice to you from now on, Rachel. And you're gonna be real nice to me. We're gonna be nice to each other from now on."

But she wasn't gulled. "What d'you want? Why'd you lie to them about who killed Shelby?"

"Lie? Lie? Listen, I'm gonna tell you exactly what happened that night in the barn, and it's exactly what you have to tell Marshal Renfro and anybody else who asks you about it. You hear? If you want to save your neck, listen to me, and get it straight."

"Why? What do you care?"

"Why, can't you figure it out? You're a very rich widow. If they knew you killed him, his will would be invalidated, you'd get nothing. As his innocent widow you get everything."

She gave him a look of smoldering hatred. "Damn you. Damn you to hell. I should've let him kill you."

Stung by her ingratitude, he snapped, "Yeah? Yeah? Well, you didn't, sister dear, and now you'd better start being nice to me 'cause I'm the only thing standing between you and a hangman's noose." Then he tried a more reasonable tone. "Now, dammit, Rachel, don't be a damned fool all your life. Listen to me, and we'll be rich."

Inside the cave Gypsy was crouched down behind the parapet of boulders. White Wolf had resumed his seat on the ledge a few yards in from the cave entrance. He had struggled to a standing position as Maxwell and Rachel were leaving, thinking he would move to the parapet beside Gypsy in order to get off a few last shots at the besiegers before he died, but found that the pain in his leg increased to the point of almost causing him to lose consciousness, so he had to sit back down on the ledge and lift his injured leg back to the horizontal. He then began to prepare himself for the end.

From his saddlebags he took the small hollowed-out elk horn containers of paints and proceeded—slowly, ritualistically—to paint designs on his face: two streaks of red across his forehead, black circles around his eyes, a streak of yellow down the length of his nose, one cheek painted black with white dots, the other cheek painted white with one large yellow dot.

"Going out in style, are you, *navestax*?" Gypsy asked, though he knew it was more than just a matter of style. The tradition of the Plains Indians called for a warrior's face to be painted before burial, so that when he reached the Spirit Land, the ones who had gone before would know that he had died as a warrior.

When he had finished with the paints, White Wolf secured the wolfskin to his back like a cape and pulled the wolf's head over his own like a hood. Now he was ready to sing his death song. But first he said, "Gypsy?" When Gypsy looked at him, he continued in a voice that was abashed with the inadequacy of words, "I'm sorry that you're here on account of me. If you hadn't come to warn us, you could've got away. For that, *haho naheto*"—as if it meant more to say thanks in Cheyenne.

Gypsy shrugged. "Maybe. Maybe not. Don't much matter anyway. If they didn't get me today, they'd get me tomorrow." Then he grunted with a sort of bitter amusement. "You know the only thing I regret? The only thing I regret is I won't be taking Dexter with me. Complete the list. Yes, sir, if I could just get a shot at Dexter, I'd die a happy man." He raised up above the boulders to see what was happening on the river bottom. "Well, like the gambling men say, you can't win 'em all."

But he hadn't given up hope. He could have killed three or four more men by now but had refrained from firing in hopes that Dexter might be lulled into a sense of safety sufficient for him to show himself. But now that they had the cannon ready to fire, it was apparent that he wasn't going to get his chance at Dexter, so he decided to take whom he could. The soldiers on the cannon were operating behind a camouflage curtain of willows, so he couldn't get clear shots at them. Besides, they were just poor damned colored soldiers who were here only because they were ordered to be.

"And the worst thing about it all," he said as he scanned the ridge for a target, "it's gonna be colored men who kill me."

"They're Buffalo Soldiers?" White Wolf asked.

"Yep. And if I ain't mistaken, their commander is none other than my old pal Captain Beauregard Pierce himself." He snorted. "He's gonna kill a black man on orders from a white

man so he'll be a credit to his race. Aha," he said as he
brought the buffalo gun to bear on the head of a man—a white
man, probably drunk, certainly careless—who kept inching his
head up above the ridge like a curious and stupid ground squirrel gingerly poking his head up out of a hole to see where the
hawk is. "Come on," he coaxed, getting the man carefully in
the sights. "That's it. Just a little more. Thaaaat's nice." He
took a deep breath, held it, and squeezed the trigger.

Crack-boom! roared the rifle, and before the man on the
river bottom even heard the sound, his head disintegrated.

When Maxwell told Renfro and Captain Pierce that Corby
and Gypsy weren't going to surrender, Marshal Renfro said,
"Well, Captain? You ready to fire?"

"Anytime," Captain Pierce said. "Get your men off the
bluff."

To a nearby deputy Renfro said, "Send word over to the
men in the cordon. Tell 'em to get off the bluff. We're going
to fire the cannon. And you men up there," he shouted to the
men hunkered down behind the ridge of the sandhill, "put a
few rounds into the cave. Keep 'em pinned down while our
men on the bluff pull back."

It was then that the *crack-boom* sound of the buffalo rifle
echoed across the floodplain, and one of the drunks on the
ridge—a member of the Texas posse—had his head blown off.
So it was with renewed fury and vengeance that the possemen
on the ridge began firing into the cave. They were joined by
the Klansmen and many of the spectators, who, drunk and
whooping it up, scrambled and stumbled up the ridge to get off
a few shots just for the fun of it.

"Keep down, you stupid bastards!" Tucker shouted, racing
toward the place where the man had been shot. "And be careful, goddammit, don't hit our own men. Jesus Christ!"

Satisfied that Dexter would look after Rachel, Maxwell lingered among the leaders, hoping—praying—that something
might happen that would allow him to influence events and
somehow stop the killing.

Within the supply wagon Rachel clamped her hands over
her ears, trying to shut out the multitudinous sounds of a bi-
zarre celebration: the crackling rifle fire, shouts and laughter
and curses of drunken men; the distant sounds of the Coman-

ches chanting and dancing to throbbing drums. But then came the voice of one of the men at the cannon, saying in response to a command, "Lock and load."

Then the voice of the gunnery sergeant, shouting to be heard above the din: "Fire!" And suddenly the air was rent with a sound like that of a thunderclap.

Gypsy hunkered down to reload and let the wild fusillade expend itself. Then he edged up to get in position for another shot, and that's when he saw the puff of smoke from the cannon. A second later he heard the explosion and then heard the long and growing-louder screeching sound of the oncoming projectile.

"Here it comes!" He dropped down behind the boulders.

The projectile hit the face of the bluff about twenty yards to the east of and ten yards below the mouth of the cave. The earth shook, a geyser of rocks and dirt spurted from the face of the bluff, and rubble cascaded down to the river below.

Inside the cave, the walls and ceiling shook and rumbled. Slabs of selenite fell crashing from the ceiling, rocks were dislodged from the walls, dust spewed through newly opened cracks in the alabaster.

"Getting zeroed in," Gypsy said. "Next one'll probably be a bracketing shot on the other side. It'll be the third or fourth one that gets us."

He got up, leaving his rifle leaning against the boulders. He picked up his hat, slapped it against his leg, then put it on and adjusted it squarely on his head as he walked back to White Wolf.

"Well, *navestax,* if you don't mind me leaving you here, I think I'll go out fighting."

White Wolf nodded. "I'd join you if I could."

Gypsy held out his hand. "It's been good knowing you, White Wolf."

"You, too, Gypsy. *Nimeaseoxzheme*—May your journey be a good one." They shook hands. "Who knows? Maybe we'll meet on the Hanging Road and make the journey to the Spirit Land together."

"Maybe so. If you Indians are right, maybe we will. If the Christians are right, though, I 'spect I'll see you in hell."

Then they heard the second *boom!* of the cannon. They

froze for the few seconds that it took the projectile, with its screechy, whistling sound growing ever louder and more ominous, to hurtle toward them. This time the projectile struck on the west side of the cave about ten yards from, and level with, the opening. Again the earth shook, and again a great cascade of rocks and dirt and boulders rumbled down from the bluff, bouncing and crashing in the scree. Some of the debris tumbled all the way to the river, partially covering Big Red's carcass on the riverbank.

Inside the cave an enormous section of the ceiling came crashing down with a deafening roar. Walls shifted, rocks and pebbles rained down, and a choking dust billowed up from the debris.

The concussion from the blast and the falling ceiling knocked Gypsy down, but neither he nor White Wolf was hurt. Gypsy got up and brushed himself off.

"Well, they're almost on target now, looks like. The third one'll likely be it. I better get out there while I can." As he made his way through the fallen rocks toward the opening, he pulled the .44 Colt from the right holster and flipped the chamber out to be sure that it was fully loaded.

At the parapet he turned once more to look at White Wolf. "What's that the Cheyenne warriors used to say when they were going into battle? *'Hoka hey,* it's a good day to die'?"

And without waiting for an answer, he touched the muzzle of the .44 to the brim of his hat as a parting salute; then, pulling the .44 from his left holster, so that he had a gun in each hand, he leaped up onto the boulders of the parapet.

He stood on the boulders for a moment in full view of all the men on the river bottom, his arms raised high into the air, and then he yelled at the top of his voice, "*Hoka hey,* you sonsabitches! It's a good day to die!"

CHAPTER FIFTY-EIGHT

DEXTER PULLED RACHEL'S HANDS AWAY FROM HER EARS. "Listen, now. We got to get our stories straight before Renfro questions you."

But he might as well have been talking to an unconscious person. The blast from the cannon had reduced her to an almost comatose state of shock. And though she seemed not to be hearing him, Dexter kept saying, "You didn't kill Shelby, you hear? Corby did. You went into the house and got the gun because you were—listen to me, now—you were trying to protect Shelby, and Corby took the gun away from you and shot—"

When the cannon fired the second time, something snapped in Rachel. "Stop it!" she yelled, and scrambled out of the wagon. "Stop it! Stop it!"

Dexter couldn't hold her. She jumped down from the wagon. The group of leaders gathered near the cannon were startled to see her dashing toward the cannon, and the four black soldiers who were operating the gun were even more startled to find themselves suddenly assaulted by a deranged white woman.

Rachel pummeled them with her fists, crying, "Stop it! Stop it, damn you, stop it!" They could ward off her blows easily enough, but they didn't dare grab her, she being a white woman, so she pummeled them unimpeded, saying, "Stop it, damn you! Stop it!"

Maxwell left the group of leaders and rushed to Rachel, but it was Dexter who grabbed her. He had leaped out of the wagon, stumbled, and rushed to grab Rachel's flailing arms from behind just as Renfro and Captain Pierce recovered sufficiently from their surprise to respond.

"What the hell is this?" Renfro demanded.

Maxwell said, "Rachel! Rachel!" but she was struggling so fiercely against Dexter's hold that he couldn't get her attention.

"Get her back to the wagon," Renfro said to Dexter with chilly contempt. "If you can't control her, handcuff her to the wagon wheel."

"Let her go," Maxwell said to Dexter. "I'll do it."

Dexter ignored him. Angrily he pulled Rachel back toward the supply wagon, holding her arms pinned behind her back. She had ceased yelling now and had almost ceased struggling by the time they reached the wagon, but Dexter, not willing to take any more chances, pulled a pair of handcuffs from his belt. Maxwell grabbed his arm.

"Leave her alone. I'll take care of her. Leave her alone."

Dexter shoved Maxwell away. He began to manhandle Rachel again, and so disdainful was he of Maxwell that he was taken completely by surprise when Maxwell, recovering from the shove, jerked Dexter around and brought a fist up into his solar plexus with all his strength. Dexter clutched his abdomen, groaning and gasping for air.

"Leave her alone, I said."

Dexter stepped back out of Maxwell's reach, staring at him with eyes widened not only by surprise but by fear and respect, too.

"Rachel?" Maxwell put his arms around her. He had expected her to throw herself into his arms and cry, as she might have ended a temper tantrum of old, but while she allowed him to go through the motions of comforting her, she was not softened or touched by his concern. On the contrary, there was a look in her eyes of a trapped animal that would bite the hand that tried to free it from the trap. "Rachel, there's nothing you can do."

Then his attention was diverted by a sudden stir of excitement and surprise that occurred simultaneously among all the men scattered along the river bottom.

"It's Gypsy Smith," someone shouted. "He's come out."

And for the moment that Gypsy stood on the lip of the cave, in full view of everyone, his arms raised, an expectant hush fell over the gathered throng. All rifles were being trained on him, but for a moment they all held their fire, transfixed. Even the Comanches doing their medicine dance fell into a baffled silence. Like the white men and the Buffalo Soldiers, they could hardly believe that Gypsy Smith had raised his arms in surrender. Then they heard, faintly from across the distance, the Indian battle cry that Gypsy hurled at his enemies.

"*Hoka hey,* you sonsabitches! It's a good day to die!"

Gypsy fired two shots from his .44 Colts before the hundred or more rifles opened up on him. He could hardly expect to hit anyone at such a distance with the pistols, but it was enough for him that he could go out fighting. To make it harder for them to hit him, he leaped down from the lip of the cave and dashed, crouching, firing, ducking, along the eastern face of the bluff, while a fusillade of rifle bullets, like grapeshot fired from a cannon, tore into him and the earth all around him.

In rapid succession he was hit in the thigh, the left shoulder, the hand. One bullet knocked his hat off. He dropped the .44 from his wounded left hand, but, struggling to remain standing, he fired the last four bullets from the gun in his right hand, and as he fell, he picked up the dropped gun. Then he was hit one, two, three more times, and after each hit he fired a round from the .44, but then he took a bullet in the head that slammed him back against the bluff so forcefully that he rebounded and pitched forward to fall, tumbling and sliding and bouncing, down the scree.

His body came to a stop in the scree about one third of the way down the bluff. A small slide of shale and pebbles followed him down and partially covered his body. He came to rest facedown, his right hand under his body, his broken left arm and broken right leg askew, his body bleeding from many bullet wounds.

Many of the riflemen kept firing, and though most of them missed, Gypsy's body was hit at least a dozen more times after he was dead.

"Hold your fire!" Renfro shouted, and the rapidity of the firing quickly diminished, leaving only an occasional shot from some drunk who wanted to be able to say that he had shot Gypsy Smith.

"Well," Renfro said in a coldly gloating voice to no one in particular, "that's that. Maybe we should have a moment of silence for the passing of the great Gypsy Smith." But there was real admiration, however grudging, in his voice when he added, "No matter what the color of his skin, gunfighters don't come any better than he was." He began rolling a cigarette, and to Dexter, who had joined the group to witness Gypsy's death, he said slyly, "Well, Deputy Bingham, I reckon you'll be able to sleep lots better at night now, won't you?"

Dexter didn't answer, but he did look very relieved.

After Renfro put the pucker string between his teeth and pulled the tobacco sack closed, he said, "Well, Captain?" He glanced at the angle of the sun on the western horizon as he licked the tobacco paper. "Sun'll be down in a little while," he added, as if Captain Pierce, being a Negro, might not see the significance of that fact. "What d'you say we get the rest of this over with and go home?"

Captain Pierce had been on the point of ordering his gun crew to fire the third round from the cannon, but Marshal Renfro's patronizing suggestion caused him to delay the firing for a moment, just to remind the marshal who was boss of the big gun.

While they waited, they began to hear a sound, a very peculiar sound. It was coming from the cave, the sound of someone singing. Ordinarily they wouldn't have been able to hear singing from such a distance, but the cave seemed to act as a sort of gigantic megaphone, amplifying the sounds with its echoes, with the overlapping echoes giving the sound a tremulo effect. But the eeriest thing about the singing was its subterranean tone. Coming from within the cave, it sounded as if the singing were coming from the earth itself.

"What the hell is that?" someone asked.

"Singing!" someone exclaimed incredulously. "That bastard's *singing*."

"His death song," Captain Pierce explained, as if singing were a perfectly natural thing for a man to do before dying.

A hush began slowly to settle upon all the men at the scene, and especially the Comanches were quiet. They had stopped drumming, dancing, and singing when Gypsy came out to die, and they had yelled encouragement to him as he fired his last shots, but now they fell into a sort of reverent silence as they stood and listened to the eerily amplified sounds of the death song.

"Well?" Renfro said to Captain Pierce.

Glad to have another excuse to delay the firing of the cannon and thereby annoy Marshal Renfro, Captain Pierce said, "We'll give him time to sing his death song."

"How long? Once a damned Indian gets started singing, he's likely to go on forever."

"We'll give him a minute or two. That doesn't seem unreasonable to you, does it, Marshal?"

Renfro grumbled into silence, and they listened, and some listened intently, though few of them understood the words of the song. Among those gathered near the cannon, only Maxwell could understand some of the words. Most were too blurred by distance and by the tremulo effect of overlapping echoes; but Maxwell could at least understand a few of them, and the obvious effort he was making to translate them prompted Rachel to ask, "What's he singing?" They stood near the wagon, he with his arm around her shoulders. "Tell me what he's singing."

Cocking his ear toward the cave, he shook his head. "I don't know. I can only make out a few of the words."

"What? Tell me."

Straining to sort out the blurred words, he said, "It's just a—a simple chant. He's says . . . he's singing of . . . not just his own death song, but, as best I can make out, for the Ancient Ones. For all Indians. *Human Beings.* Something, something, I can't . . ."

> . . . buffalo dies,
> the eagle dies,
> the wolf dies
> but the earth goes on—abides—
>
> > abides forever.
>
> Now . . . die . . . my spirit will
> travel the Hanging Road
> to the Spirit Land.
> I will ride my red stallion
> on the Hanging Road.
> His spirit . . . take me there,
> To the Spirit Land,
> where dwells all the Human Beings
> who . . . gone before . . .
> and they will greet me as a warrior
> who died in battle.

Some of the men in the area began talking again, and a few fired their rifles into the cave, and the sounds caused the song to become blurred until all that could be heard were infrequent and undecipherable fragments.

Throughout the chant Renfro kept glancing at Captain Pierce, who ignored him until Renfro said, "The sun's about to go down."

Captain Pierce looked westward, as if to confirm that fact for himself, and said, "So it is, so it is," and so impressed was he by the startling beauty of the evening sky that he let his gaze linger on it for a moment. The bloodred sun was still above the horizon, and above the sun, in varied hues of scarlet and pink and salmon-yellow, clouds of many shapes and sizes made prisms of the sun's rays.

The captain continued to contemplate the beauty of the sundown until the death song ended. Then he turned and nodded sharply to his gunnery sergeant, who whirled on the gun crew, raised his right hand as if he held a baton, and then brought it down.

"Fire!"

For the third time the thunderclap roar of the cannon momentarily deafened the bystanders. Everyone stood motionless for the three seconds it took for the screaming projectile to reach the bluff and hurtle directly into the mouth of the cave. And because of the cave's amplifying acoustics, the sound of the explosion was hurled back across the river as an earth-shattering roar.

The whole of Medicine Bluff shook and trembled, and the roar continued long after the explosion was spent, becoming the roar of a landslide, the roar of a mountain collapsing in upon itself. A huge portion of the earth on top of Medicine Bluff—the portion that formed the roof of the cave—suddenly collapsed, pulling trees and bushes and boulders into the roaring maw, leaving a dust-billowing chasm on the top of the bluff, a chasm that was the approximate size and shape of the cave into which it had collapsed.

Tons of debris hurtled down the face of the bluff in a landslide, covering what had once been the mouth of the cave. It poured down the scree to cover completely the body of the bay stallion on the riverbank and continued its dusty torrent down into the river.

The Cave of the Ancient Ones had ceased to exist.

CHAPTER FIFTY-NINE

POSSEMEN, KLANSMEN, SPECTATORS, REPORTERS, AND INDIANS began streaming across the river to get a closer look at the damage done to Medicine Bluff by the cannon. Marshal Renfro dispatched a group of deputies to recover Gypsy Smith's body.

The white men crossed the river with a festive air, celebrating their triumphant participation in a historical event. The Comanches crossed the river to see the destruction wrought by the wagon gun and to mourn not just the passing of their friends White Wolf and Gypsy Smith but the last vestiges of the Ancient Ones.

None of the Buffalo Soldiers crossed the river. Although proud to have once more done his duty, Captain Pierce saw no cause for celebration, so he had his troops prepare for the march back to Fort Sill.

Nor did Marshal Renfro cross the river. He stayed behind to question Rachel, and Dexter stayed behind in hopes of being able to guide Rachel through the interrogation, though Renfro's questions seemed more in the nature of a formality than a serious effort to elicit the truth.

"Just a few confusing points to clear up" was how he put it, and added, "If you don't feel up to it now, we can, of course, postpone it till we get back to Guthrie."

"What d'you want to know?" Dexter asked, hovering at Rachel's side, protective, with a lawyerlike alertness.

Ignoring Dexter, Renfro said to Rachel, "I want to know about Mr. Hornbeck—how he was shot and under what circumstances."

"I told you," Dexter said. "The Indian took the pistol away from Rachel and killed Mr. Hornbeck with it."

"After he'd killed the two bodyguards with Hornbeck's shotgun," Renfro prompted with a look of puckish cynicism.

"That's right," Dexter said. "She had gone into the house to get the pistol because the Indian was holding all of us at gunpoint with the shotgun."

"Deputy, haven't you got something to do? Why don't you go help bring Smith's body back?"

"I didn't mean to interfere, but she's obviously in no condition yet to answer questions, and as long as I know the answers . . ."

It was true that Rachel seemed incapable of responding to any question that required thought. Still in a stupor of shock and despair, she stared with unfocused eyes at something unseen by anyone else, and though her face registered Renfro's questions, she made no effort to respond until he, in a tone of almost sarcastic accommodation, sighed and said, "Well, how about a simple yes or no to a couple of questions." After a slight pause he added, "Is it true what Deputy Bingham says? Is that what really happened the night your husband was killed?"

To Dexter's surprise and great relief, Rachel finally broke the surface of her stupor by saying in a very small voice, "Yes."

"Ah, I see," said Renfro. "Now we're getting somewhere. So after he—the redskin, this Corby White—after he killed your husband and the two bodyguards, he dragged you off with him, kicking and screaming?" And after a short pause, in which Rachel seemed to have nodded, Renfro continued, "And when did you stop kicking and screaming?" But when it became apparent that he wasn't going to get an answer, he said, "Let me put it this way. You were spotted by two different men on two different occasions, once by a trapper in the Glass Mountains and once by an old wrangler who saw you and the redskin swimming together in Beaver Creek. Both men said you and him was . . . well, as one of 'em put it, 'lovey-dovey.' "

As if offended, Dexter said, "She did what she had to do to stay alive, Marshal. Ain't that true, Rachel?" His voice was one of tender solicitude, and he hurried on without waiting for a response. "And if you have any idea of prosecuting her for anything that happened during the time she was held captive

. . . well, Marshal, you know yourself how quick a jury would acquit her."

Renfro pursed his lips beneath his drooping mustache for a moment, pondering some grave decision, and then, in a voice that was not only polite but downright conciliatory, he said, "Why, I never had no idea of doing anything like that, Mrs. Hornbeck. Just doing my job is all. Trying to get everything straight, so I can file my report and put the case behind us."

He made it sound as if he had never so much as entertained a suspicion about her, but the truth was obvious: with Dexter's having exonerated her of any blame in the killing of Shelby Hornbeck, there was no chance of proving otherwise, not as long as they both stuck to the same story, so there would be no profit in pursuing the matter. After all, if Renfro couldn't prove that she was at least an accomplice in her husband's murder, then she was, as of that moment, the inheritor of the bulk of the Hornbeck estate, which made her one of the wealthiest women in Oklahoma, and it would be very injudicious to make an enemy of her.

So he said, "Well, then, I reckon that about clears it up. Sorry to've troubled you." Then his tone passed from being conciliatory to being almost obsequious as he said to Maxwell, "I'll see that you and Mrs. Hornbeck get a buckboard to the nearest train station. I imagine you'll want to be getting back home as soon as possible."

"Thank you," Maxwell said with more politeness than sincerity, "but we've accepted an offer from Captain Pierce to ride in the supply wagon to Comanche Station. We'll catch a train from there."

A group of festive riders caused a commotion when they returned from across the river with Gypsy Smith's body. Limp and bloody and bullet-riddled, the body lay facedown across the haunches of Deputy Pinkard's horse.

The photographer signaled for the riders to bring the body to where he had set up his huge hooded camera near his wagon. "Hurry," he called, "while there's still some light left."

The riders were eager to have photographs commemorating such a historic event, so they took Gypsy's body to the photographer's wagon. At the suggestion of the photographer they stripped the body of the bullet-torn shirt, so that the photograph would show not only the many bullet holes in Gypsy's torso but also the KKK scars that were carved into his chest. Then, using the tailgate from the wagon as a slab on which to strap Gypsy's body, they leaned the body upright against the wagon.

"Pardon me," Renfro said, glancing toward the activity. "I better go get my picture took. Ain't every day a man can get his picture took with the likes of Gypsy Smith."

"What's going to happen to his body?" Maxwell asked.

"Oh, we'll take it back to Guthrie, show it off a little, then turn it over to the coroner."

"If nobody claims it, I'd like to know, so I can. I wouldn't want him to be buried in a pauper's grave somewhere."

"Oh, I'm sure them niggers over in Freedom'll claim it. I'm sure they'll give him a real hero's burial." He touched the brim of his hat to Rachel, who still had not so much as looked at him, and gave Dexter a comradely wink as he turned and walked away.

Dexter's sigh was that of a man who had just survived a close call. Relieved and vaguely condescending, he said to Rachel, "All right. You done all right." He started to say something else but seemed to forget what it was and followed Renfro to the photographer's wagon.

"Hurry, now," the photographer said to those who wanted to have their pictures taken with Gypsy's body, "while there's still a little light left." He was charging twenty dollars apiece for the pictures, and there seemed to be no end of men who wanted them.

Dexter and Marshal Renfro had one taken together, standing on opposite sides of the body, posing with rifles cradled in their arms like big-game hunters displaying a prize trophy.

It was almost dark by the time the mules were hitched to the supply wagon and Rachel and Maxwell climbed inside for the bumpy ride over rutted wagon trails to Comanche Station. Maxwell used his coat to make a padded seat on one of the supply crates and sat close enough to put his arm around Rachel's shoulders if she should need comfort or support. But for a long while they rode without touching and in a strained silence, a silence heavy with things waiting to be said, and finally Rachel, wiping her tears with the handkerchief Maxwell had given her, asked him, "Do you blame me?"

"Blame you? For what?"

"For lying. For agreeing with Dexter's lies, anyway. For playing the innocent victim."

"Nobody could blame you, my dear, for saving yourself."

"But I didn't do it for myself," she protested.

Maxwell puzzled over that remark for a moment, but before he could ask for an explanation, she said, "Do you think White Wolf would?"

"Blame you?" After a moment's speculative silence he said, "I suppose you did exactly what he would've wanted you to do, expected you to do."

"I didn't do it for myself, though," she said again.

"What do you mean? If not for yourself . . . ?"

"For the child," she said. "I did it for the child."

"The child?" he asked, but it was not really a question, because he knew the answer.